SHARON

The
Violin
Maker's
Daughter

bookouture

Published by Bookouture in 2019

An imprint of StoryFire Ltd.

Carmelite House
50 Victoria Embankment
London EC4Y 0DZ

www.bookouture.com

ISBN: 978-1-78681-979-6
eBook ISBN: 978-1-78681-978-9

Part One

1943 Colmar

Chapter One

'How can I fit my whole life into a suitcase?' Sarah's voice cracks; it is almost a wail. The tears she holds back sting her eyes and she closes them, tightly, to gather strength, and then opens them again and glares at her father, fierce and firm. 'I can't leave you, Papa.'

The other girls have gone to bed; she is alone with her parents in the small upstairs room they call the parlour, long and narrow, as is the house itself. Her mother, sitting next to her on the stiff-backed sofa, places a comforting hand on Sarah's knee, and it is enough. Sarah throws her arms around her mother, and Leah holds the sobbing girl, pats her back, croons comforting words.

'I won't leave you! I can't!

'It's all right, darling. It's just a precaution. We will all be together again – soon.'

'We should stick together now! Leave all together. We are a family.'

Now Josef himself speaks. He has finished adjusting the strings of the violin he holds and puts it carefully aside, laying it lovingly in its case on the dining table.

'You must go, Sarah. We will follow when we can, in time. It is the only way.'

But his voice cracks too. He tries his best to hide it; he has to be brave, strong, for Sarah, for Leah. Only he knows that deep inside he is crumbling into pieces.

He closes the case, stands up, puts it away. He never brings work upstairs; he leaves his tools and instruments downstairs in his workroom – but this half-violin belongs to Sofie, his youngest. They keep their own instruments up here, in the parlour. A violin for each girl, five in all since Sofie has started to learn, his own precious violin, a cello for Leah. A string sextet, and Sofie. But they hardly ever play together now. Too loud; too dangerous. Who would ever have thought that a family playing music together of an evening could be dangerous? Surely it's the most innocuous, the most pleasing of occupations? Surely even Germans should understand that?

But these are not ordinary Germans. Not real Germans. Since they marched into Colmar in 1940, Josef and his family have very quickly grasped the fact that, now, everything is different. Every little thing, down to the language they speak and the names they bear. They are lucky: their surname is Mayer, a quintessentially German name, and Josef, too, is German as well as Jewish. Sarah did not need to change her name: it is, fortunately, French, Jewish and German. But Amélie, Thérèse, Manon and Sofie: they were forced to change.

Now the four youngest girls are, officially, Amelia, Tanja, Inge and Sigrid. Josef still calls them all by their real names, deliberately. Leah rebukes him whenever he does; she uses the new German names. Always.

'We might as well get used to it,' she says, again and again. 'For the duration. Just in case.'

'Just in case of what, exactly?' Josef always replies. 'Do you think a gang of Boche are going to break down our door and ask the girls at gunpoint what their names are? What language they speak?'

The cheek of it, he'd raged at first. A person's name is surely the most personal part of him or herself; how dare they take that away! But of late he has been forced to mitigate his rhetoric, and never speak of it outside the four walls of his home. For now, he knows – they all know – they could lose far more than their names. Losing your name is almost a joke, these days, when the secret grapevine brings news of what else Jews in Germany are losing.

Here in Alsace they had all cushioned themselves in a pad of complacence, at first. Hitler might have annexed their province, so that it was now Germany instead of France. But it had been German before, and then French, and then German again and then French again, like the baton in a relay race. Who cared, as long as life went on as ever? Now, German has been made the official language instead of French. Josef speaks both fluently, as does his wife; and the girls, who cannot remember the last time Germany was in charge, had, like all other Alsace children, simply had to learn and get used to the new language, the new words for everything. As children do, they learned swiftly. Now they are all fully bilingual.

The street name has been changed, of course, the old sign torn down and a new one nailed on: now it is *Gerechtigkeitsgasse*, Justice Lane, instead of the much more fitting *rue des Géraniums*. Their own little house, just one in the row of lopsided timber-framed traditional Alsace buildings lining the lane, is one of many whose windows in summer carry boxes of geraniums flaring out and over, spilling down in cascades of brilliant red blossoms lovingly tended by Leah. Other wives place flowerpots overflowing with flowers in front of their homes, around their doorsteps, fixed to the walls. In these days of swastika banners and posters all over the town this backstreet has somehow escaped the regulation defacement; the Nazis haven't found it – not yet – and flowers still reign supreme.

One of the first things the Nazis did after marching in on 1 November 1940 was to deport all the Jews. They were packed onto trains and transported down to Vichy to await an uncertain fate. At least, people said, at least not to Germany. They had been allowed to take one suitcase of personal items and 100 francs each.

But Josef Mayer refused to go, taking refuge in his very German-sounding name and the fact that he was not a practising Jew, never attended the synagogue, hobnobbed with very few Jewish people and was, basically, simply a violin-maker of Colmar, happy to make violins, maintain his home, pay his bills, love his wife and raise his daughters. What more could a man want, and why should the Nazis notice him, and care? He scoffed when his friends advised him to leave. He refused to run away. Where would he go to? His life was here. His workshop, filled with the most exquisite instruments, each one unique, handmade, irreplaceable.

It was true that even in the years before the war demand for expertly made instruments had declined drastically, but they managed. His reputation was good, and reached right up to Strasbourg in the north and Freiburg in the east, in Germany. There was no way he could start again from scratch in a faraway country, no way he could take all his precision tools with him and no way he would leave it all behind.

And so he had simply gathered his family more tightly than ever around him, advised them to keep a bland presence in the town, stay at home as much as possible, keep their heads down, and life would continue as ever. They weren't really Jews. What was a Jew anyway, but a human, like everyone else? He simply couldn't believe that life would get worse in Colmar, worse than swastika banners and posters and Boche everywhere and everything in German. He had changed his own sign in his shop window, from Violin-maker Mayer to *Geigenbauer* Mayer. Surely that was compliance enough?

They, the Germans, couldn't demand more.

Chapter Two

But they did. A year later everything had changed. The reports coming out of Germany – they made his blood run cold. That *Reichskristallnacht* – could it be true, that the Nazis had rampaged through the towns and smashed in the windows of Jewish businesses? That Jews were being forced to wear yellow stars, driven from their homes, carted away, to who knows where? It was too far-fetched. Josef refused to believe it at first. He thought that caution and silence would protect them, as well as the innocuous name Mayer.

'Keep your heads down. Don't discuss politics, not with anyone. Fade into the background,' he told them all, and that had worked, for a while. Officially, now, Colmar was *Judenrein*, free of Jews. Nobody knew.

But then…

Early one recent morning Josef woke to the sound of smashing glass, followed by footsteps running away. Hastening down to the street, he cried out: '*Merde!*'

Glass shards and splinters all over the cobbles before the shop, a huge hole in the shop window, the rest of the glass splintered and cracked. His own soul splintered at the sight. And he knew at once: the respite was over, they were no longer safe.

Leah appeared at his side.

'*Josef, j'ai peur!*' she whispered. And he too, for the first time since the war had started, knew fear: real fear, for his family, for their lives.

What were the most precious violins worth in comparison? Nothing at all. His instruments, his livelihood, they were all nothing. The fear was a visceral, living thing, coiled through his being like a venomous snake poisoning him from within. It was over, this silenced life they'd been living.

Who had done it? They would never know. Who knew they were Jewish? Who would harbour such hatred? A few close friends knew, but he couldn't imagine any of them doing this. But people are only human; they talk, they gossip, and sometimes an ill-advised word or two could spread in the wrong direction. It didn't matter, their time was up.

He and Sarah cleaned up as best they could. A few neighbours came out to help: Yves Girard, his friend the cobbler from two doors down, and the haberdasher and his wife, the Petits. They all whispered among themselves, expressing shock and disbelief and hatred of the Nazis, of what had become of their charming town. Other neighbours, those who didn't come out, watched from behind twitching curtains. Had they approved of the attack? Had they known? Had one of them, perhaps…? The sense of trust and bonhomie that had made this little cobbled lane with its picturesque timber-framed houses and flower-boxes a haven in the Nazi stronghold that Colmar had become had been shattered along with that glass.

'I warned you,' Yves told Josef. Yves was his closest friend, a widower in his seventies, who Sarah and her sisters all called 'Uncle'; he had fought in and survived the last war. And yes, Yves had told him to get out right from the start, to go with the other Jews. But now it wasn't a smug 'I told you so'. Now, while brushing up the last tiny splinters from between the cobbles, Yves said, 'I can help. We'll talk tonight.'

That night Yves had come round with a bottle of Riesling, given to him by 'a friend', and while emptying the bottle – which was necessary after the morning's shock – Yves told him how, exactly, he could help.

'You must go,' he said, 'you must all go, one by one. But first, tell me – you once spoke of a brother in America, do you think he would help? Take you in if you came to him?'

Josef nodded. 'He would, Karl would help. But how can I go? There are seven of us, five of them children! How could we ever escape?'

'There is a way – I have friends who can help. There is a woman near Ribeauvillé who hides Jews. She knows the right people. They are taken over the Vosges Mountains and into the Zone Interdite and then from safe house to safe house through France to Spain or Switzerland to safety. You must go as soon as possible. This is only the beginning. Trust me. I'll send Jacques to you.'

A few days later, Jacques came with more information and advice. Jacques, it turned out, was a Resistance leader from further north, doing what he could to defy and defeat the Nazis. He spoke little of himself, but later, Yves told Josef more.

Like all men of Alsace under the age of thirty-five, Jacques had been conscripted into the German forces, the Wehrmacht. He would have been forced to fight for the Third Reich, and against France. There was no right of refusal; men who refused were sent to camps and even, perhaps, executed. If they ran away, their families were persecuted. Jacques was an exception because his father was one of the best and most prominent winemakers of the region, and good wine was Alsace's treasure, the very reason why France and Germany had played tug-o-war with the province throughout history.

Jacques had not minced his words. 'You all have to go, but you can't go together. It has to be carefully planned. Give me two weeks, then you must send your eldest daughter – the seventeen-year-old. What is her name?'

'She is Sarah.'

'Sarah must go first. Then two more, the next two daughters. How old are they?'

'Thérèse is fourteen. Amélie is twelve.'

'They must go as soon as possible after Sarah. Sarah must go first, with an escort. I already know of a possibility. Then we will find someone for the next two girls.'

'Can't all three go together?'

'No. Again, a group of four is almost impossible. Too much responsibility for the escort, who will also be a Jew needing to flee; her safety is also at stake.'

'How can I send young girls out into the world? They are still children, they must stay with their parents!'

'There is not space in safe houses for a family of seven. It is just too dangerous and too difficult. Yes, your daughters are young but we will provide reliable escorts for them, women of middle age, like mothers. The youngest girls, how old are they?'

'Manon is seven, Sofie is only five.'

'These two youngest can go with you and your wife. You must understand, it is very difficult to arrange for a whole family to escape. Difficult and dangerous. We will do it, but we must reduce the family as far as possible.'

'How can I send young girls away? My daughters? How can I send them on a perilous journey without us? They have always been so protected, so safe…'

'You cannot protect them, and they are no longer safe. Not one of you is safe. The longer you stay here, the more dangerous it will become. You should have left in the early days.'

'I know that now.'

'Very well. Now I must go. Prepare Sarah, and I will come back and take her away.'

'You will take her yourself?'

Jacques shrugs. 'I will do my best to come myself. I cannot promise.'

'I can't send my daughter away with perfect strangers! She would be terrified, so would we! You understand, she has lived a very protected life. She is very close to us and hardly ever leaves the house.'

'I don't expect you to give your daughter into the hands of a stranger – I will arrange it. If I cannot come myself, I will send someone you can trust absolutely. More I cannot promise.'

'But where will she go? How…?'

So many questions, so many uncertainties. Danger everywhere – how could he do it?

'She will be taken first to the safe house in Ribeauvillé. The woman there is very brave and good. I will escort her myself, if possible. If I send someone, they will have a password.'

He thinks for a while, and then says, 'The password is this: you will say to them, *how was the wine harvest this year?* And they will reply: *not as good as 1917. That was the best year.* Remember those words and don't forget to ask.'

They discuss more details, of the route Sarah will be taken over the Vosges Mountains into the neighbouring province of Lorraine. Jacques reassures Josef that it is safe; he himself has done this before, many times, escorted fugitives over the mountains, into Lorraine.

'There, they are helped to Metz, where they'll meet more helpers, and then from safe house to safe house to the South of France. Some fugitives traverse the Pyrenees into Spain and then perhaps to the Americas; a few make it into Switzerland. Yes, there is danger but it is minimal compared to the far greater danger of staying in Colmar.

'And once you have all escaped, you can meet again and build a new life together.'

Jacques speaks calmly and reassuringly. Meanwhile, Josef battles his fears. This is the only way forward. He knows it in his head. And yet his heart cannot accept it. Josef shakes his head.

'I cannot do it. Cannot send my Sarah away, my Amélie, my Thérèse. My daughters are my life!'

After all they have spoken of, after all Jacques' calm reassurance, he cannot do it.

And so, the next day, another visitor knocks on his door with the three prearranged knocks, and when he calls out from the window above, *who is it?*, an impatient voice: 'The wine harvest was good this year, Monsieur Mayer, and now would you please let me in.'

The voice sounds female and when he descends in the dim light of the stairwell at the back of the house to open the door, he sees that he has not misheard: the visitor is a woman. Middle-aged, she wears a long black skirt, a black blouse and a black hat, but her face is pale and drawn, her hair pulled back in a bun at the nape of her neck. She holds out a hand to him. He shakes it.

'Margaux Gauthier. You are Sarah's papa. I believe Jacques has told you a little of me. You have certainly drunk my wine.'

She is the woman from Ribeauvillé, the woman Jacques has spoken to. She is different from Jacques. She does not speak calmly, reassuringly; she does not try to convince. She speaks dramatically.

'Monsieur Mayer,' she says. 'Imagine you are in a three-storey house. There is a fire downstairs, the whole ground floor is in flames. You and your family are trapped on the top floor. You cannot go down the stairs. Smoke is creeping under the doors; you are already breathing it in. Your children are crying. Your wife is terrified. You go to the window, open it, and down there, in the street, you can see the dark shadows of your friends, your neighbours. They are holding out a sheet; it is a safety net, firm and solid, held tightly by them all. They are calling to you to jump. What do you do: do you wait for the fire to engulf you, do you jump yourself, or do you push your first child out?'

There is very little Josef can say, after that. He agrees to send Sarah, and the other girls, as soon as it is possible.

'Thank you,' he tells Margaux. 'You are a stranger to me, and yet you risk everything to help me. I cannot thank you enough.'

He is almost in tears, but Margaux's answer is unsentimental.

'I do it for Alsace, for liberty. We must free our home from this pestilence. If all goes well, one day you can all return. This is what I hope and pray for: that Alsace may live again, as France, and free.'

Chapter Three

The two weeks between the shattering of the window and the planned departure of Sarah have been fraught not only with fear and danger but with heartbreak and gloom.

Josef and Leah understand with their heads that they must flee, and that Sarah, as the eldest, must flee first. That they must send her off into the wide world, a world of peril; that they will not know for months, perhaps years, how she has fared. They grasp it with their reason, with common sense. But hearts are sometimes strangers to common sense, and their hearts will never grasp it, never agree. Their hearts cling to her more than ever, refuse to let her go just as she refuses to go; at the same time persuading her that she *must* go. How can they do it, all of them? How can they push her out into the terrible unknown, how can *she* leave *them* to what is, perhaps, an even more terrible unknown? How can any of them survive that rift, the tearing apart of an entity so closely welded together it is, really, just a single entity, that whole and wholesome thing, an intact family?

She is their firstborn, the child that changed them – as firstborn children always do – from unformed post-adolescents with hopes and dreams and all the world open before them into mature adults with responsibilities, cares, an unbreakable bond not only to a scrap of wailing humanity but to a place and a home and money and work and food.

They discovered for themselves the terrible thing that all new parents realise for the first time: that there is something, someone, in their lives more precious than they are to themselves and to each other; something, someone, the loss of whom would destroy them, shatter them – just as that glass pane has been shattered. Irreparable. Letting her go is like pitching a diamond into a river, trusting it will be carried to safety, to be picked up downriver by someone trustworthy and handed back to them intact. Impossible to conceive of, yet they must do it. That night Jacques convinced them, over that bottle of Riesling, with some help from Margaux. Jacques, so young himself, yet so experienced, so passionate, so credible. He had talked into the night and somehow calmed their fears, led them to trust and to find the strength within their hearts to do the impossible. To cast that diamond. They must do it.

But it is not just the spectre of personal loss and fear for Sarah that has churned up their lives in those two weeks. Something else happened, something that terrified Josef and Leah to the core. It happened just a week ago.

Josef and Sarah were both in the shop, working quietly together on the only commission they'd had all year. It was for the eldest daughter of a well-situated burgher and businessman of Strasbourg who had done well, thrived, even, since the Nazis had taken over. Such people were the only ones who could afford to give their children something as precious as a violin. They were known as *collaborateurs*, and reviled by the Alsatian citizens loyal to France. This man's daughter had shown such musical talent as a child she must now have an exquisite adult instrument, handmade especially for her. It pained Josef to take a commission from such a person, but really, what choice did he have? He had to maintain his family, and work was scarce, and besides, could anyone afford to refuse to work for the Nazis and their helpers?

And it wasn't the violin's fault that it was going to a *collaborateur*; it would still receive the luthier's full attention, and the same love would be poured into the making of it as were it a violin destined for the greatest maestro on earth. Josef had been taught this by his own father: even the most mundane job, do it with love. That is the secret to a good and happy life. His father had learned it from his own father, the last of the male Goldberg line of expert luthiers. Now, even the Mayer line was dying out, as far as males were concerned, which was why Sarah, and not a non-existent son, was his apprentice.

Sarah has been following him into his shop since she was a girl of five, watching him work, peppering him with questions. She has listened to the voices of violins from their very beginnings, when they were just crude blocks of wood, right up to the moment when she can hold a finished instrument in her hand and draw a bow across its strings and hear its final voice. She has grown up with violin voices. But most of all, she knows how to give a violin its voice, its best voice.

No son could have been a better apprentice. It is as if Sarah's fingers, Sarah's very heart and soul, have inherited the collective wisdom of all her luthier ancestors, concentrated and intensified, Goldberg-Mayer-Plus-X. She possesses a sensitivity he has rarely seen among his colleagues, and certainly surpassing his own. She is more than a craftsman; she is an artist.

Josef has always known that creativity requires the ultimate humility; that arrogance and bluster have no place in creating a true work of art, that the *I* must disappear to allow the juice of genius to flow. But Sarah does it better.

On that particular afternoon, they were working together, as usual, in the narrow room behind the ground-floor shopfront, Josef's workroom. The walls were hung from floor to ceiling with the tools and paraphernalia of his trade: planes of different sizes, purfling tools, saddles and nuts, bridges; ribs and templates, loops and tailguts and, of course, the precious wood, pre-cut into blocks, spruce from the Vosges forests.

Sarah had been given the *collaborateur*'s daughter's violin; she called it the Adrienne, for that was the girl's name. The Adrienne was to be the first violin Sarah had made completely on her own, from start to finish, without even a word of advice from her father. And she had promised herself it would be as good as any violin made by any seasoned violin-maker in Alsace, in France, in Germany; she would give it her all, because it was her first, and because it was going to a girl, like her; a musician who, she hoped, would treasure it for ever, just as she treasured her own violin. She had chosen the wood for it, holding the initial rectangular blocks next to her ear, tapping them with her finger to hear their inner voice; she could now recognise at once the potential of each block.

Having chosen the best Tonewood wedges, centrejointed and flattened, she'd used the finished rib assembly placed on the flattened side to draw the final shape of the violin. Sawed to outline, she'd carved the long arch then the cross arching, then using thumb planes shaving and smoothing, switching to toothed blade thumb plane to smooth yet finer again, finally finishing with thin scraper steel to create the finish.

With the mould removed from the rib assembly, she'd glued on the back and then the belly to make the corpus of the violin.

Once the corpus of the violin was made came the most exciting part: to knock with her knuckles and listen to the resonance of the corpus imagining how the finished violin will sound. This was specialist work, the crux of a luthier's skill, but from the beginning Sarah had an instinct for it: a sure planing hand, a finely tuned ear.

Now, she balanced the violin's back plate on her thumb. It hovered there, perfectly straight, perfectly poised. Satisfied, she viewed the Chladni patterns made by tea leaves: she sprinkled the leaves into the slight curvature of the back plate, adjusted the frequency of the plates beneath the violin, watched the tea leaves jiggle and dance and finally settle themselves into a particular pattern, then read that pattern to decide that at last, she'd got it right: the violin had found its true voice. But this time the tea leaves gave a completely unexpected jolt as the door to the shop flew open and banged against the wall, and two soldiers crashed through it and into the tiny room, their jackboots crunching on the wood shavings and sawdust that littered the floor, to stand there glowering, arms akimbo.

Both soldiers were tall, Aryan to the tips of their long bony fingers and the icy blue of their eyes and the straw-yellow bits of hair beneath their black-visored caps, the only apparent difference between them being their age and the numbers and types of insignia on their lapels. One was definitely in his fifties, the other a young lad of hardly more than twenty. The older one spoke, the young one kept silent. Josef thought of them as father and son.

'Herr Mayer,' said the father, 'we have reason to believe that you are Jews. That you are a Jewish family that has somehow evaded the compulsory evacuation that took place two years ago. Is this true?'

'Of course not!' Josef summoned all his bravado. Yes, perhaps it was cowardly to deny his heritage, but his family was at stake – their safety, their lives. He would deny till the end of his days and not feel a twinge of guilt.

The father produced a page of paper, and read from it. 'Josef Mayer, Leah Mayer. Five daughters: Sarah, Amelia, Inge, Tanja and Sigrid.'

'Why… why do you think we are Jews?' Josef tried not to stutter, and was only mildly successful. His voice was too weak; with a deep breath, he summoned some splinters of courage and confidence.

'We have German names! I am a Mayer – what could be more German than that? I have followed the legal measures demanded by the new regime and changed any French first names in my family to German, Christian ones. We follow the rules.'

'Nevertheless, we have been informed that you are secret Jews, therefore of impure genealogy. You must provide within the next seven days a certificate of Aryan ancestry, an *Abstammungsurkunde*. We need papers for yourself and your parents and your grandparents. You must bring it to the civilian registry, to the *Einwohnerbürgeramt*, within those seven days. Once you have provided the paperwork for you and your wife, you shall be removed from the list.'

'What list?'

'It is none of your business. Just be assured that you are on a list of people who are still polluting our society. You shall be counted as guilty until you have proven your innocence. Good day, Herr Mayer.'

And just like that, they were gone, father and son both, clicking the heels of their black boots as shiny as black ice and just as treacherous. Gone from the shop, but not from their lives. Josef knew his days were numbered. The respite was over.

Chapter Four

After that encounter there were no more excuses; no more delays could be countenanced. Even Josef knew now, without a doubt: Sarah had to go, and they had to prepare for their own departure. There were several problems, the biggest being time; time and papers.

The papers. How could they get an *Abstammungsurkunde* of Aryan descent for himself, his parents and grandparents, when Josef was Jewish, through and through? And in seven days? If he could not produce them, he had no doubt as to the consequences: they would all be deported into Germany's darkest depths. Everyone had heard of the German camps: labour camps from which no one ever returned. Jews and other undesirables who entered those camps disappeared; they would not be heard from again until the end of the war. Nobody knew what went on within those camps, but rumours were rife and hair-raising, and nobody doubted that the camps were the equivalent of hell on earth, from which there was no return, black holes into which one simply disappeared, sank into the darkness.

Josef's friend and neighbour Yves had, in the final days, been their constant guest every evening, advising them, calming them, consoling them.

'It is fairly easy to get papers,' he had said. 'There's a good forger in Colmar. He can do anything and make it look real. But he would need some more information. Your name, your parents' names and so on. But it will take time. And I myself am curious: how did you come by such a German name as Mayer?'

Josef shrugged. 'It's a long story, a *Geigenbauer* story. You probably will not have heard of Goldberg-Mayer violins. They were famous in the last century; beautifully-made violins of exquisite voice. Goldberg and Mayer – both came from Bubenreuth, a small Bavarian town, which is the capital of the violin-making trade in Germany. Both were excellent at their art, and in competition, but then one German Herr Mayer married a Jewish Miss Goldberg and the two companies merged, becoming better than ever. But Jewishness is passed on through the female line, and she was the last remaining Goldberg. Since she was female and the trade is passed from father to son, there were no more violin-making Goldbergs. So, Herr Mayer dropped the Goldberg name from the company and the violins became simply Mayers. At that stage, perhaps, the family could have been Aryanised. But the Mayer children – three boys, my grandfather and his brothers – married Jewish women and so we stayed Jewish, but with a German surname. Considering the anti-Semitism that was already creeping around in Bubenreuth and the whole of Bavaria, it was a good decision to keep the Mayer name, but in another way, I think it was a wrong decision: Mayer is too ordinary a name for such extraordinary instruments! Goldberg-Mayer sounds much better.'

'But how did you end up in Colmar?'

'One of the Mayer brothers married a lady from Strasbourg, daughter of a violin-maker. He was able to take over his father-in-law's trade there. From Strasbourg it was only a short hop to Colmar, and that was through my wife Leah, who is not Jewish. Her father is a Colmar joiner and owned this building, which he gave to her when she married me. He is a good man. See this beautiful table?' He fondly fingered the surface of the table at which they sat. A fabulous table, of solid oak, with beautifully rounded and carved legs, ending in feet like lions' paws.

'He made it himself and gave it to us on the birth of our first child, Sarah's birth. He made it big enough for a large family, and indeed, now we are seven, it is very useful!'

Josef reached out to fondle the cresting rail of the chair on which Yves sat.

'The chairs too are beautiful, all made by him, by hand. Yves, it is terrible! What will I do with all my possessions, the instruments, the tools, the furniture, when we all leave? What will become of the house?'

'I would advise you to do this: since Leah is not Jewish, and the house was gifted by her father, an Aryan, put it entirely in her name. That way it will be safe until you return. The instruments: well, they are easy to hide. How many are there?'

'One cello, a viola and five violins, a few child-sized. The cello, the viola and Sarah's violin and mine are extremely valuable. I also have one very exquisite violin I made for a Strasbourg customer who never paid and never collected it. Business has been terrible these last few years. People used to come from Strasbourg and even Freiburg to buy my violins – that is no more. No one has the money for a custom-made instrument and no one has the money even to buy a violin and play music or give their children music lessons. Music itself has become a luxury. I could never have supported my family through violin-making these last few years – it is my father-in-law who gave me work. What can I do, Yves? How will we survive if we flee? How—'

'You cannot worry about these things, you must take one day at a time. Now, you should start hiding your instruments. I will take one violin and hide it in my attic. I know people who will take the other instruments; trustworthy people. The cello will be a bit difficult, but that too we can hide and it will await your return.'

'But, Josef, the paperwork is far more urgent. You must write down everything you have told me, all the names, going back as far as you can: where they were all born and where they were documented. You know the Germans love documentation! I will need all that to get the forgeries done. Tomorrow, you must go to the register office and beg for more time: a month. Tell them a week is too short because you need to have documents sent from Bubenreuth and it will take time. You may even have to go there yourself. Since you are claiming Aryan descent, they will grant you that time. It is enough.'

And so they sat together and planned together, planned for a future that was in reality a black hole. This was war. People died and disappeared and nobody could guarantee a happy outcome. But Yves fired Josef and Leah with hope.

'Righteousness will prevail,' he said. 'Righteousness and goodness will prevail in the end. We must keep our hope and our trust and our courage.'

But that was all he had to offer Josef, who now stands at the edge of a precipice, his precious daughter before him, and it is he who must give her that final push, hoping at the bottom of the cliff are friends – strangers, really – ready to catch her, just as Margaux promised. It is the most terrible thing he has ever had to do.

Yves comes one night with a pair of boots.

'These are good, strong mountain boots for Sarah. They are good German-made boots that will last a lifetime. A man from Freiburg brought them to me for re-soling a few years ago – they belonged to his wife, he said. They used to go wandering in the Vosges. Then he never returned to pick them up. I wrote him a letter reminding him of the boots. He wrote back to say that his wife had passed away and he did not want them – I should keep them and sell them as he had no use for them. But I never sold them. They are expensive, even second-hand, and nobody in Colmar could pay for them. So here they are. They are quite special. They might be a bit big, but with a thick pair of socks…'

They fit her perfectly.

Chapter Five

And now it really is over, the respite. Their last night together, and Sarah's suitcase still stands empty on her bed, in the tiny room in the eaves she shares with Amélie and Thérèse. She has simply refused to pack. She can't, she says. She can't choose what to take and what not. She can't leave her violin behind; though the violin is already gone, has been gone for a week now, stored in some old cupboard in Yves' attic.

What if, when they come for her, she refuses to go? She has a stubborn streak, and it has revealed itself most potently in the last week, when they told her.

She has to go. All alone, with some stranger, into the night, into the country, into the mountains, into France; and then somehow, to America, to some uncle she's never laid eyes on in her life and doesn't care about, in a place called Connecticut that she can't even pronounce. But her parents have forced her to learn the address by heart. Just in case.

'In case of what?'

'In case you lose… you know. Lose your things. Your papers, your address book with telephone numbers and things.'

Everyone is so vague. Nobody knows anything. All they will say is that she has to go, tonight; that someone will come for her, a stranger, a man, or perhaps a woman.

The worst thing is at the dinner table, at the table that isn't even theirs. They have exchanged their beautiful oak table with the curved legs and wonderfully patterned surface revealing the artwork that was in the wood itself for some cheap four-legged thing that looks like an old door nailed to leftover blocks from the sawmill; the real table is being kept for when they return. Which they will, one day, for sure, her parents say. They must flee now, but they'll all come back.

'When?' That's Sofie, the youngest, just five and full of questions.

'We don't know, darling. Now, finish your soup like a good girl.'

'It's not soup, it's just cabbage water.'

'Sofie! How dare you! Do you know how hard Maman and Papa work to feed us, how hard it is even to get a few vegetables? That's what war's like! And we're in a war! In the middle.' This from Thérèse, who is fourteen and knows a lot about everything. Thérèse is always reading; if she can't find a good story to read, she reads old newspapers, history books, books about the discovery of Incas in Peru – anything the library can produce. She reads books in French and German. She is forced to read German, these days, for all the French books in the library have been thrown out and replaced with German books, just as all their French teachers have been sent to Germany to be retrained and in the meantime replaced with German teachers who make them learn a horrible spidery script and only speak, write and think in German. Thérèse, as the best-educated of them all, also knows the most and they all listen when she speaks.

'I don't care about the silly war,' says Sofie.

'Well, you have to care because we're in it and all of France is full of German soldiers and the Germans are evil and wicked.'

'Really? All of them?'

'Yes. All of them. They are born wicked and they go about killing people and raping women and—'

'What's raping?'

'Finish your soup and stop chattering, children, and Sofie, Thérèse is correct: it might be only cabbage soup but it's better than nothing and that's the choice at the moment, cabbage soup or nothing.'

'I wonder what nothing tastes like.'

'Not good at all,' says Manon, who is seven. 'Nothing tastes like nothing. You just get hungrier and hungrier and then you starve and then you're dead.'

'Don't talk like that! It's scary! Everything is so scary and now poor Sarah has to go off and we don't even know when we'll see her again!'

'Why does she have to go? Why can't we all go or all stay?'

'Because this is war, *ma petite*, and the Nazis are here, now, in Colmar and they want us to leave.' This from Josef, who thinks it is time for his youngest daughter to finally face reality. She simply hasn't adjusted well to the restrictions, to the secrecy, to the fear that now lurks in the shadows of their once so-safe home.

'But what if we don't want to go? Why should we do what they say, why should what they want win?'

'Because they are Germans and Alsace is now part of Germany. Germany is evil: Germans are evil, and there's a man in Germany called Adolf Hitler who is the most evil of them all and he wants us to be gone. He hates us and wants to chase us out.' This, once again, from Thérèse. 'And if we don't go, he'll probably kill us.'

'Thérèse! Don't say that!'

'But it's true. Isn't it, Papa? He wants to kill all the Jews.'

'Not kill, *chérie*, that's going too far. He doesn't want to kill us, but he sends Jews away.' He turned to Sofie. 'Thérèse is right: there's a bad man in Germany, like a king. You know how kings can rule countries and what they say goes? Well, he's like that and he just doesn't like us Jews.'

'Why not? What have we done to him?'

Josef shrugs. They'd had this conversation again and again and still she doesn't understand. It's difficult, if not impossible, to make a child who has only ever known love and kindness understand the concept of hatred and cruelty.

'We've done nothing wrong. He just doesn't like us, that's all.'

'He's so stupid! Why is a stupid person a king?'

'It seems the German people wanted him to be king.'

'But why? Are they bad too?'

'I don't think they're all bad, *chérie*. But maybe they thought he is good for them and their country and they just follow what he says.'

'But why do they follow a bad man?'

'Maybe they don't know just how bad he is.'

'Papa, stop lying to her! Of course they know! They know very well and they approve of it and follow his orders. Look at *Reichskristallnacht*. It wasn't Hitler who went about smashing in glass windows, it was ordinary Germans. Just like they did to us. I hate the Germans! I hate Hitler! All Germans are wicked!'

With that, Thérèse leaps from her chair and flees the room. They hear her footsteps pounding up the stairs to the attic, to the little room she shares with her elder sisters.

'Are you lying to me, Papa? It's wrong to lie.'

Sofie looks at her father with such huge innocent eyes that his own eyes swim with tears. He wipes them on his sleeve, gathers his inner reins and says, as firmly as he can, 'I'm not lying, my dear, I'm just trying to explain to you as best I can. I don't understand it myself. No decent human being can understand such behaviour. That's why I like to believe that most Germans just don't realise how bad this man is and what evil he is capable of.'

'Like chasing us from our home?'

'Exactly. I like to believe in the best of people, that all humans are inherently good—'

'What does *inherently* mean?'

'It means that goodness is what we really are, at the core of our soul, but it can be covered up so that we don't see it.'

'So even that bad man, that bad king, would have goodness inside him?'

Josef is stumped. If he says yes it would be a lie, because, from what he knows, there is not even a minute grain of goodness in Hitler. But if he says no, he'd be contradicting his own words.

'Well, I read somewhere that he likes dogs,' says Manon. 'And you like dogs too, Sofie, and you said once that people who like dogs are good people.'

'Not him though. Definitely not him.'

Manon holds up two fingers, with a little piece of potato between them. She presses her fingers together, flattening the potato.

'This is what he wants to do to us. Just tell her the truth.'

Leah gasps in horror and Josef flings Manon a look that says, quite clearly, *that's enough.*

Sarah has said not a word throughout the conversation. It is as if she isn't there. Only her parents notice, throwing her an anxious glance every now and then. They alone know what she is going through, because they are going through it themselves. Sarah's last night; the agony is unbearable, but bear it they must.

'I think I'll go and pack now,' she says, and stands up. 'I'll just say goodbye. Please, don't make a fuss. I'll see Thérèse upstairs…'

She moves from sister to sister, hugging each one and saying goodbye. Manon will not let go of her.

'Don't go, please don't go,' she whispers.

'I have to. You'll come too, soon, and we'll meet in France or America or somewhere. I'm sure of it.'

Manon holds her all the more tightly and heaves with one last sob, then lets her go. She moves around the table to Amélie and then to Sofie.

'Goodbye, favourite little sister. Be good to Mama and Papa and eat up your cabbage soup! I'll see you soon.'

Sofie, who can't grasp that her beloved big sister will be gone for a long, long time, kisses her on both cheeks and smiles up at her, the bravest of them all.

'Bye-bye, Sarah, and have a good journey! I'll see you soon when I come with Mama and Papa.'

They hold each other, far enough away that they can look into each other's eyes – a rare moment of stillness for little Sofie, a bundle of energy who can't keep still or silent for even two seconds. But her eyes now suddenly pool with tears; she jumps from her chair and flings herself at her big sister, clinging with all her might, sobbing as if her heart would break, gasping out words, one by one, between the sobs.

'Don't go, Sarah! Please don't go! I love you so much! I'm afraid I won't see you again.'

Sarah holds her close, lets her cry, comforting her only with hands that roam up and down the little back, sometimes massaging the head of dark unruly curls. And when at last the child is still, all cried out, she helps her back into her chair, peels away the clinging arms, dries her eyes with the napkin their mother hands her and whispers,

'We are all sad that I have to go, *mon petit choux*, but we'll meet again sometime, somewhere. I promise.'

She stands up straight, gulps, waves at her other sisters, whose faces are all wet with tears, and at her parents, whom she'll see again, later that night, when the girls have gone to bed. Then she slips out of the door, struggling with all her might to hold back her own tears.

Thérèse, at fourteen the closest to her in age but perhaps the most sensitive of all the sisters, is asleep already in the tiny attic bedroom they share, her body rising and falling peacefully and rhythmically beneath the blanket. Sarah has not said goodbye to her, but maybe it is better this way; she cannot face an emotional scene. She kisses the warm cheek, sticky with dried tears, and whispers her goodbyes.

It is only when she is down on the floor, in the narrow space between their beds, kneeling before the empty suitcase on the floor, that she remembers an admonishment her mother once gave her:

'Never make a promise you can't guarantee you'll keep.'

Chapter Six

But Sarah cannot pack. Kneeling at the empty suitcase, she finally breaks down herself. She has put off packing all day long, all week long; her mother has urged her again and again to just do it, to get it behind her, but she has left it to the last, to this final night, and now she still can't do it. She springs to her feet and rushes from her room, pounds down the attic stairs back to the first floor. They have cleared the table by now and Amélie is standing at the sink washing the dishes; Mama is putting away the rest of the scraps of food they need for the next day, Papa is wiping down the table and Manon has taken Sofie up to bed. Sarah bursts through the door.

'I can't do it!' she cries. 'I can't leave you!'

'Amélie, leave the washing-up, I'll do it later. Go up to your sisters, make sure they're in bed, read a story to Sofie.'

It is Mama's brisk, no-nonsense side coming to the fore. Soon the kitchen is empty of all the girls except Sarah. The three of them move to the front part of the parlour, near the windows overlooking the street, and take their seats, Sarah next to her mother, Josef on the straight-backed chair opposite them.

'How can I fit my whole life into a small suitcase? How can you send me away? This is my home, Mama, Papa. I can't go!'

'But you must, my darling. There is no other way.'

'But I am so afraid! I have nothing to hold onto, I am all alone!'

They have no answer. They sit in silence, holding hands, giving each other what little strength they have, but it is truly little, and faltering, and diminishing all the time as unbidden thoughts creep upon them from dark corners, thoughts of an uncertain future in a war that threatens to last for ever.

At last Leah says, hesitantly, slowly, fearing her husband's reaction, 'Perhaps we can pray? That helps sometimes.'

Josef curses. 'Pray? What good will that do? Do you think praying will stop the war, stop that devil Hitler?'

'No. But it might give us strength.'

'One of your Christian prayers, I assume? You forget we are Jewish? That you, too, are Jewish, now?'

Leah has, indeed, been raised a Christian, and converted when she married Josef, but only in name. Josef is an agnostic; they do not observe any Jewish traditions. They do not pray.

'No, Josef. Of course not, not a Christian prayer, and I don't know any Jewish prayers. But I know some psalms. They're Jewish, aren't they? David was a Jew, wasn't he? The psalms are Old Testament. I was taught some of the psalms and the twenty-third just popped into my head: "The Lord is my shepherd".'

'Isn't that the one about being led through green pastures beside still waters? That psalm is a mockery of what we are going through.'

'But there's one line, that's the line that occurred to me. And I thought, maybe it's appropriate, maybe it will help.'

Her voice, though still hesitant – she knows Josef's stance on religion, that it's all balderdash – is somehow confident, more so with every word she speaks; a confidence that rises up from inside her. It is all they have left; they have to do it, there is nothing else.

'Let us join hands, then. I will say it. Just that one line, I promise, Josef. Nothing about green pastures and still waters.'

Reluctantly, Josef shrugs. He does not move, so Leah places his right hand in Sarah's left, takes his left in her right and Sarah's right in her left.

'Shall we close our eyes?'

Josef snorts, but complies, as does Sarah. They sit there for a few moments, silent, eyes closed, holding hands, breathing. Then Leah speaks, quietly, her voice strong and yet cracking just a little. 'Yea, though I walk through the valley of the shadow of death, I will fear no evil, for thou art with me, thy rod and thy staff to comfort me; thou preparest a table before me in the presence of my enemies.'

She does not speak the following words of the psalm; how can she speak, now, of cups running over and goodness and mercy? But that rod and that staff – they are comforting words. They help. Already she feels stronger, comforted. So she repeats the verse, again and again.

'*Yea, though I walk through the valley of the shadow of death, I will fear no evil, for thou art with me, thy rod and thy staff to comfort me.*'

And a strange thing happens. To all of them, but perhaps most potently to Sarah. She feels that rod, that staff; they are right here, within her, and gradually, as she repeats the words, her fear melts, a sense of trust and strength enters her being. It is as if she has an internal staff, something strong and stable yet unearthly, right there in her heart; something to cling to now and in all the days ahead.

Eventually, Leah stops repeating the verse and they sit in silence in the dark, their breath the only movement in the room. Finally, Sarah lets go of her parents' hands and stands up, brushing down her skirt.

'I will go and pack now,' she whispers.

Leah also stands up. 'I will help you.'

Chapter Seven

As arranged, someone comes to collect Sarah at midnight, knocking on the back door three times, and then once more after a short pause. The back door of the house opens onto a large courtyard shared by most of the other houses on that side of *Gerechtigkeitsgasse*; it is a fairly secluded area that vehicles cannot enter, where neighbours sometimes gather to share gossip out of the view of other neighbours, or even to visit each other semi-secretly. The ground is cobbled and on the other side are a large barn and the backs of a different row of houses.

Josef opens the back door a crack, just wide enough for the visitor to slip through, a figure all in black.

'How was the wine harvest this year?' he says.

The answer comes immediately: 'Not as good as 1917. That was the best year.'

And again, the voice is female; and again, it is Margaux Gauthier. He lets her in.

'She is waiting, all packed.'

'*Très bien*. Then let her come. Say your goodbyes quickly, we must hurry a little.'

Sarah is already halfway down the stairs, followed by Leah. They have wept enough, held each other enough for the night.

Margaux frowns when she sees the suitcase. 'That is unsuitable,' she says. 'You are not going on holiday to the Riviera, you know. How will you carry that thing over the mountains? One change of clothes is all you need. Never mind, bring it along. I will find something for you. Do not be afraid, it is going to be all right. Do you have your papers?'

She holds out her hand as Sarah nods. Jacques had decided she could travel under her own name, keep her original papers; after all, she is, officially now since the annexation, a German and she'll be safest with genuine German papers, and travel will be easier. But she needed a cover story, which they have worked out together: she is Sarah Mayer, an Alsatian German, on her way to Metz, the capital of Lorraine; she is going to live with an uncle and work in his grocery shop. When she leaves Metz, she'll be on her way towards Paris, to stay with an uncle to work in his grocery shop there. After Paris, she'll be on her way to Poitiers to stay with an uncle and work in his grocery shop.

Margaux checks her papers and nods. '*D'accord*. Let's go. Don't look so worried, I will keep you safe.' She hands back the papers and Sarah tucks them in the little leather bag over her shoulder.

I must be brave, she says to herself. *Margaux will keep me safe.*

But is that also just another empty promise? Sarah says nothing. One last quick embrace and she is out the back door, following Margaux into the night, into the courtyard, down the narrow back lanes of Colmar.

The van looks black in the shadow of the beech tree under which it is parked, but as they draw nearer, Sarah sees that it is actually dark red. On the side it bears an elegantly cursive sign, in white letters: *Laroche-Gauthier. Vins de Qualité*, with a stylised drawing of a vine leaf. Sarah is familiar with the brand: Uncle Yves often brought round a bottle from this very same vineyard. The familiarity of it all helps her to feel confident.

'I'm sorry, I can't let you sit in the cabin,' says Margaux, 'you must hide in the back. I'm afraid hiding is going to be your destiny for a while.' She opens one of the double doors at the back of the van, and Sarah climbs in. Margaux shines a torch into the interior of the van, lighting up a sort of channel between several wooden crates, all bearing the Laroche-Gauthier signature in green paint, all full of bottles. There is a piquant smell, of fermentation and old wine and something indefinable, something old and musty, somehow pleasant, familiar. 'Go to the back,' Margaux says, her voice low, urgent, 'make yourself comfortable. There is a little space there for you. If you hear German voices, if the yellow, the Boche, stops us, you must hide as best you can. Don't worry about it, I will deal with it – I know what they like. Still, you must stay quiet if they open the back. They won't see you hidden behind the crates and I doubt they will search. *D'accord?*' Sarah nods, and makes her way, bent double, along the channel of crates.

Just before Margaux switches off the torch and closes the door and the light goes out, Sarah sees the crates on the right are full of empty bottles, whereas the bottles in the left crates are full. She huddles in the small space cleared for her at the front, a blanket and a cushion laid down for her to sit on. She does so, and a few moments later the van moves off. From now on she has a new status. No longer Sarah Mayer, the luthier's daughter, now she is only a fugitive, without status, on the run from an evil so great that even to bring her mind close to imagining it is beyond her.

They have not driven for more than twenty minutes when Sarah hears urgent voices shouting outside and the van comes to a halt. The thrum of the motor falls suddenly silent. Her heart pounds like a jackhammer; this must be one of the controls Margaux has warned her about. There is a gap between the cabin and the back of the van and she can hear clearly what is going on up front: the window being wound down, the sharp barks of the Germans, Margaux's quiet, almost friendly replies.

'Papers!'

The flap and crackle of paper, then silence for a while as, most probably, Margaux's papers are inspected.

'What are you doing driving at this time of night?'

'Ah, *mein Herr*, you must be new around here otherwise you would know me and recognise my van. Have you not yet heard of Laroche-Gauthier wines? Superb wines, loved by your comrades-in-arms! I have just delivered a few crates to the German officers billeted in Villa Schönblick. I deliver them regularly and I am well known.'

'Who delivers wine past midnight?'

A feminine chuckle, then Margaux's cajoling voice, at first almost coy in tone, becoming more confident with every word.

'Who would blame me if I take the opportunity to visit a little friend in Colmar before returning home? Surely we must take our pleasures while we can? And I am sure you, too, enjoy a fine wine with friends now and again? Have you ever tried this excellent Pinot Gris? It is truly outstanding, one of my best. I would be happy to let you sample some – yes, go ahead, keep the bottle with my compliments. And if you like it – well, come into my little shop on the Wilhelm-Strauss-Gasse and say that "Margaux and fine wine go together like milk and honey" and they will give you a special price with my compliments… Yes, keep the whole bottle; it is yours! I enjoy spreading good cheer. Is that all, *mein Herr*? Thank you. May you enjoy the wine, but I would advise you not to drink while on duty, keep it for when you are with your sweetheart, she will love you all the more for it. Thank you… *auf Wiedersehen*!'

The motor springs into life and the van drives off.

It takes Sarah's heartbeat at least ten minutes to return to normal.

They drive for almost an hour in all; by that time Sarah has given in to her exhaustion and has spread the blanket in the small space between the crates and lain down and tried to sleep, but she can't. Her mind clings to memories: familiar faces, her mother's voice, her father's hands, her sisters' laughter. That last heartbreaking cry from Sofie: *I love you, Sarah*! And in the opaque blackness of the van's interior, she weeps again, silently, sometimes, and then in racking sobs. And then she hears her mother's words: *thy rod and thy staff to comfort me.* And somehow she is comforted.

But all journeys come to an end. She has at last drifted off into a kind of dazed oblivion when Margaux's voice and the van light, both together, wake her. She rubs her eyes and pulls up her knees and sits up.

'We made it! We are home, without incident! You are now safe! You can come out.'

Safe, for the time being, Sarah thinks. For this is just the first night of an endless row of nights followed by days. She creeps to the van's door and Margaux holds out a hand and helps her out. She yawns and stretches and looks around. Above them looms the dark hulk of a huge building; to the left are more, smaller buildings, barns, perhaps; outbuildings, stalls, stables, farm buildings. She takes a step forward but stumbles, and Margaux catches her, helps her find her footing, then reaches into the van for the suitcase.

'Come, let's go inside.' Margaux holds her hand, leading her to the end of the building and a door, a back door in two halves, like a stable door. She removes a huge black key from the waistband of her skirt, sticks it in the keyhole, turns it. The top half of the door opens; she reaches inside and opens the bottom half as well.

'So,' she says now, 'Welcome to Château Gauthier! You are very welcome, Sarah, and we will help to make you feel comfortable. For now.'

Chapter Eight

'Would you like to eat?' asks Margaux and Sarah shakes her head. 'Just water,' she says, and Margaux fills a glass for her. She gulps it down. Then Margaux fills another glass, hands it to her. 'You can take it down with you.'

Down where, exactly?

'Come,' she says.

They leave the house and Margaux leads her over to one of those farm outbuildings she'd seen in the moon's glow, long low hulks, seemingly without windows. She'd thought they were stalls, but they aren't. That pungent smell again, of fermentation and mustiness. Margaux switches on a light and a dusty bulb overhead throws a dim light into the space and Sarah sees the vats: a row of huge barrels, as high almost as the ceiling, on their sides in rows against both walls. Each barrel has a sign on it: *Gewürtztraminer 1942*, *Pinot Gris 1942* and so on.

'Last year's wines,' explains Margaux, and leads her past the barrels into another room, a long room where the smell is far less dominant. Here, there are crates, just like the ones in the van last night, stacked in their hundreds against the walls, some on wooden pallets. Margaux glances at her as if to say, *are you with me?*, and leads her to the far end of the room. There, the crates are stacked on a kind of trolley on wheels, with a handle; Margaux pulls at the handle and the trolley moves forward, and there, behind it, is a small wooden door in the brick wall. Margaux fumbles on a small ledge above the door, produces a long black key, inserts it into the keyhole and opens the door. That is where the blackness first hits Sarah, a blackness so thick she can almost touch it; but Margaux switches on a torch and a funnel of light opens up and she takes her hand and walks forward, the light plucking a pathway through the impenetrable blackness. A slight sound that Sarah can't identify fills the room. A cobweb brushes against her face and she lets out a little scream of fright.

'Shhh!' admonishes Margaux. 'Rebecca's asleep in here.'

Who's Rebecca? Sarah wants to ask, and wishes she'd asked more questions in the kitchen, accepted the offer of food, relaxed and found out a bit more about what is happening, what is going to happen. But she'd been, is still, so very exhausted, and Margaux had seemed disinclined to talk so Sarah had simply followed.

The torch's circle of light swerves to the left and Sarah's question is partly answered; a woman, wrapped in a flimsy blanket, the back of her head revealing a mane of dark dishevelled hair, sleeps on the ground, on a mattress. A faint but rhythmic rasp comes and goes in time to the rise and fall of the sleeping form, the gentle ebb and flow of breath.

Margaux leads her further on, and then shines the torch on another mattress: an empty one, with a pillow and folded blanket at one end.

'You must sleep,' she says. 'You must sleep here. I will get you in the morning.'

Sarah clambers out of sleep, stretching one limb at a time. She rubs her eyes, but when she opens them, there is still blackness all around her, pitch blackness, and a smell, that musty acrid pungent smell that reminds her of something. And then the day before, the night before, drops into her mind with full force and she sits up, remembering.

The blackness is so very thick. Is there a light switch anywhere? No. Margaux had given her a torch last night, and she fumbles for it on the floor beside the mattress. What time is it? No watch, no clock. How long has she been sleeping? Surely it must be morning, but the room is as black as ever, except for the small funnel of light provided by the torch. Sarah slowly lets the light wander through the darkness, and then gets to her feet to inspect more. She needs to pee, quite badly. Margaux had encouraged her to do so before coming here last night, but she'd been too nervous, too anxious, to attend to her body's needs. Where could she pee? The need is desperate, now, getting more desperate by the minute. She shines the torch along the floor. Margaux surely couldn't have kept two women in this room all night without facilities? She takes a step, and her shoeless foot hits against metal; shining the torch down, she sees it is a bucket, empty. Next to it, a heap of old newspapers. Relief floods through her: a toilet, surely? She pulls up her skirt, pulls down her drawers, squats over the bucket. The rattle of pee hitting the metal is intensely comforting, but even more so the sense of release as her bladder empties. The sense of relaxation, of being able to breathe again, her most urgent need satisfied.

That done, other needs rush in to bother her. Where is Margaux? What time is it? How long has she slept? That other woman, that Rebecca…

She slips on her boots, ties the laces and steps tentatively forward, lighting her way across the dusty floor, to the place where Rebecca sleeps. The mattress is empty, the blanket tidily folded at its foot. So, Rebecca has gone; it *is* morning, perhaps even late morning. Sarah feels as if she's slept an aeon, but it must have been only a few hours. Then again, she'd slept so deeply, so soundly, it could even be past midday. Her body feels tight, wound up, filled with unreleased energy, the vigour of youth restrained, swaddled.

What now? Margaux had said she'd come and get her, but she hasn't; or if she has, she has left her to sleep.

Where is the door? Would it be open? She shines her torch once more around and following its beam, finds the door. She tries to open it, but can't: it is locked. She is locked in here, in this dense blackness, virtually a prisoner, Margaux's prisoner! Panic rises up in her – the darkness! Shining the light up to the roof, she sees vast nets of cobwebs covering the ceiling. Everything is black: the walls, the floor, the very air. Shining the torch along the far wall, she sees another door, a narrow one. She walks over to it, tries it. It opens. Led by the light, she steps over the threshold, and then lets out a gasp of astonishment as she moves the light slowly around the scene before her. She is in a room like a library, with rows of shelves before her. But the shelves are filled not with books but with bottles. Bottles filled with wine. Dusty old bottles that look as if they haven't been touched in centuries. Sarah knows nothing about wine; her parents have only allowed her an occasional sip, but she does know, vaguely, that old wine is good wine, and valuable. A sense of awe fills her; of being in a house of treasure, the treasure being not sparkling jewels and nuggets of gold, but these ancient bottles. And she chuckles, immediately guessing the reason for this treasure trove so deeply hidden away. Margaux had given a hint the night before: 'The yellow love good wine,' she'd said. 'It's the reason they love Alsace and want to keep it intact.'

This is almost certainly her best wine, hidden away, concealed from the hated Boche. Clever woman.

She steps back into the first room, the black prison; she is thirsty now, and remembers the glass of water she brought down last night. She returns to her mattress and drinks it.

There's always the wine, she thinks to herself, *at least I won't die of thirst!* and chuckles at the thought. The ability to chuckle, to see a humorous side to her plight – it surprises her. She searches her mind for fear, for the misery of her situation, but there is none – it seems that night has cleansed her of the fog of despair. Margaux will come, sooner or later. It is just a matter of waiting, of curbing her impatience. Now, the worst thing is this blackness. *Come! Come and get me! I am awake and waiting!* She wills it with all her might; and Margaux must have picked up the silent message because not five seconds later a scraping sound comes from the door as the key turns, and a welcome voice calls:

'Sarah? Are you awake? It's time to get up! Breakfast is waiting – you must be starving!'

Chapter Nine

Margaux first takes her upstairs to the big family bathroom, where she runs a warm bath for her. 'You'll feel better when you feel clean. Then come down to the kitchen and join us.'

Her voice is so warm, so welcoming. Another reason never to leave. Isn't it enough that she'd left Colmar, left the swastikas and the Nazi officers and the threat of arrest, had come to this charming place in the country, far away from it all? Looking out the bathroom window, she sees hills followed by more hills, rolling away to the horizon, covered in the orderly lines of grapevines. Not a swastika in sight. Just the green of the vines and the blue of the sky, and a golden sun that is almost overhead.

Now, in the kitchen, the sense of home and safety only intensifies. It is a kitchen with an atmosphere – the atmosphere of *home*. The kind of place where you settle in and never want to leave because it's safe and cosy and nothing bad can ever, ever happen there. And you don't want to remember that you are just passing through, that a world of danger is waiting for you out there... Three women greet her with smiling faces: Margaux, standing at the stove with a kettle in her hand, waving her in and gesturing for her to take a seat; an older woman, whom she instantly recognises as the mysterious Rebecca from last night because even now, tidied up and caught into a bun, that head of hair is more an unruly mane than a *coiffure*; and a girl of maybe her own age, beautiful, whose hair is long and golden and falls in loose curls over her shoulders, and whose eyes are a darker shade of that very gold. She sits in the sunshine streaming through the window and her hair seems to glow, like fire. Her smile seems lit from within.

'My daughter, Victoire,' says Margaux, indicating the girl, '…
and now you can finally meet Rebecca face to face!'

'*Bonjour!*' the two women chorus, and '*comment ça va? Tu as
bien dormis?*'

She nods, and tries to smile; it would surely be rude not to,
after such a warm welcome, but that very warmth, the whole sense
of *homeliness* that this place breathes into her, seems to throw up
more than ever the loneliness of her situation, makes her aware
that this is all temporary. That she is alone, a fugitive, and has lost
everything that is anything to her. She feels so frail, so fragile…

'Yes, I slept well, thank you,' she says, and takes a seat. Margaux
places a bowl of steaming gruel in front of her. It is grey, and doesn't
look very appetising, but her mother, too, has served her similar
dishes, similar meals of indeterminate and unappealing appearance,
and she knows there is no choice.

'It is sweet,' says Margaux. 'I keep bees, we have honey. The
grapes are not yet ripe, so no fruit, but it tastes better than it looks.'

She tries the gruel, and indeed it is delicious, with the sweetness
of honey. Her appetite returns and she eats hungrily while listening
to Margaux, who, in contrast to her reticence the night before, is
overflowing with words today.

'The first thing you need to know is that we are constantly on
the alert here. My old father lives in a hut at the entrance to the
estate and he keeps watch. If the yellow approach, he will alert
me through this thing' – she holds up something that looks like a
telephone, but isn't – 'and you and Rebecca must run out the back
to the cellars and hide.'

Rebecca reaches out and takes Sarah's left hand in hers.

'We are in this together, you and I!' she says. 'I am from Winzenheim. I was looking after my father until he died. We could
not flee with the transports in 1940 so we were hiding at a friend's
house. When Papa died, I knew I had to flee too. So it will be you
and me. Together.'

'When...?'

'In a day or two. As soon as Eric can make it.'

'Eric?'

'Eric is the young man who will lead you over the Vosges to France,' says Margaux. 'He will come when he can.'

'Oh – I thought Jacques...' Jacques had led them to believe that *he* would be the one guiding her over the mountains. He had said he knew them and the forests that covered them like the back of his hand. Boasted, even. Jacques' words had given them all the confidence necessary to make of Sarah a fugitive. He had sounded so confident, so strong – and now it was to be some Eric, some stranger?

'Jacques is a busy man,' says Victoire, noting her disappointment. 'He has much to do, organising the Resistance in Alsace. He cannot escort you – but Eric has done the trip many times. He will be your guide. You can trust him.'

She nods; what choice does she have, now?

Rebecca, meanwhile, has asked Margaux a question and now the two women, engaged in their own little conversation, stand up and leave the kitchen, and Victoire and Sarah are alone. They chat together for a few minutes but then it bursts from Sarah:

'I hate this war!'

'Me, too!'

'At least you can stay here in safety, and don't have to flee!'

'I know I am lucky. But, Sarah, I think it will be all right. You will find a place of safety and when this is all over, you can come back and we will play music together and be friends.'

'I wish. I wish so much. I miss my parents and my sisters so much...'

And yet, she realises now, she has not thought of them once since getting off her mattress an hour or two ago. Meeting people, talking, eating, thinking about the days ahead – all of that has driven the past from her mind. Perhaps that's the secret, she thinks. Stay in the present, cast your mind forward, gather strength for what is to come instead of wallowing in the past, in sorrow and doubts and fears. Her mother's parting words come back to her with vivid intensity: *thy rod and thy staff...* She actually whispers the words aloud.

'What did you say? You look far away.'

'Sorry – it's nothing. I was just remembering something. My family...'

'Tell me about them!' So Sarah does, and when she's finished, Victoire speaks of her own family.

'There are four of us – two brothers and one sister. My older brother, Leon, was conscripted into the Wehrmacht. My other brother was forced to join the Hitler Youth and was taken away to Karlsruhe. My sister is the eldest, but unfortunately Mama has disowned her. It's very sad.'

'Why? What has she done?'

'She fell in love with a Nazi officer and married him and moved to Strasbourg. Mama told her if she married him, she was no longer a part of this family and she still married him, so...'

Victoire waves her hands as if to say, *c'est la vie.*

'That must be awful for all of you. I couldn't imagine...' Sarah shudders.

'I know, it's terrible. How can you love a German after they have done such terrible things to our country? How can you fall in love with evil? I myself do not want to speak to Marie-Claire again, it disgusts me so much, but imagine how poor Maman must feel.'

'So now you are the only child left at home.'

'Yes. I am staying and I will be there for her. She works so hard and it is difficult for her. On the one hand, she tries to appease the Boche by bribing them with wine so that they are lenient towards her. On the other hand, she helps where she can. She helps the Resistance and she helps your people.'

They gaze at each other at the words *your people*, words that spoken by anyone else might have been divisive, setting her apart, in a category that makes her different, apart; but spoken by Victoire, with such warmth and sadness, the words actually draw them closer together. Sarah reaches out both hands in gratitude and Victoire takes them and they sit together for a while in silence, hands joined, and a sense of comradeship, of *we're in this together*, settles between them.

'Thank you,' says Sarah after a while. 'You and your mother are very brave to risk so much for us.' She leans forward and hugs Victoire.

'Well, I try to learn from her, from her courage and caring. She shows me how to live by her example.'

'How often do you…'

She leaves the sentence unfinished, but Victoire knows what she means to ask.

'Not so often. You are the third group we are sending across this year. Last year, it was four. It is a long route to go by foot, over the mountains, but Jacques knows it like the back of his hand and Eric, well, Eric has learned the way too and you will be safe with him. He is good.'

As she says these words she blushes, and Sarah immediately picks up on what is unsaid.

'You like Eric, a lot!' she says, and a smile plays on her lips.

'Yes, I do, I more than like him. He is handsome and clever and brave, and I think he also likes me a lot. I think I love him but what do I know of love? I hope that one day, when this is over…'

One day, when this is over. Words they all repeat again and again as if just by saying them, they can make it true. And everyone puts aside the fact that 'when it is all over' nobody knows what will be left, what pieces will remain to be picked up and pieced together. Who will be even alive, when it is all over.

Sarah sighs at the injustice of it all.

'I hate Hitler.'

'Yes. We all do. He has torn my family apart.'

'I was wondering – your father?'

'Papa? He is in Paris. He is from there, not from Alsace, and all French people who are not *alsacien* were forced to leave after the Germans marched in. I have not seen him since the war began – but he was not so close to us and I don't miss him at all, really. He was always in Paris or Strasbourg on business. He does not even know what Maman is doing, helping Jews to flee, and he would disapprove. He does not have her courage – he is basically a businessman and all he cares about is wine, the business of wine. But when the war is over, he will no doubt return.'

'Hitler has indeed torn you all apart.'

'But not as much as your family. Sarah, it breaks my heart to know of your plight. But always know that I'll be thinking of you when you leave, thinking of you, sending you strength, praying for you.'

'Thank you.'

Chapter Ten

Eric comes that evening. He is as Victoire had said: handsome; and it is apparent from the way he looks at her that he more than likes her a lot. Sarah sighs. She has had little exposure to young men up to now, as their life has of necessity been one of withdrawal and concealment.

Few friends came to visit them in the *Gerechtigkeitsgasse*, and similarly, they seldom paid visits. She has had no friends, male or female, since leaving school two years ago to start her apprenticeship with her father, squirrelled away in the luthier's shop and hidden from the world. Those schoolfriends she'd once had, none of them Jewish, all melted into obscurity. She'd had only her family; the only young people she'd known were her sisters.

But she'd read books; stories of love and romance had always drawn her in, a substitute for real life, perhaps. She had fallen in love vicariously a hundred times, knew what it felt like, lived through it with fictional heroines and could recognise it in others. Somewhere in her a spark had been lit and a little glow started, a longing to be looked at the way Eric looks at Victoire, to look back at someone with such depth of feeling. But a bleak future of hiding and fleeing and staying silent and boring and out of sight lies before her. Being a fugitive leaves no room at all for love, and it will perhaps be years before she'll have the freedom and the sense of safety to open herself to something so delicious. *When the war is over…*

'We must leave long before dawn,' says Eric over dinner, a *tarte flambée* concocted of the most unexpected mixture of ingredients: a potato base, cheese, eggs, cabbage and beetroot. Somehow, though, Margaux has managed to make even that delicious.

Once the dishes have been cleared away, Eric spreads a map out on the table and jabs at a spot near the top. 'This is the cabin we are heading for,' he says. 'We must get there before nightfall, so it will be hard going all day.' He looks at Rebecca.

'Do you think you can manage that? I mean, I don't mean to...'

'I know, I know, I am an old lady in your eyes and I will slow you down. But I am fit, very fit. Even when I was looking after my father, I worked in the garden behind our cottage. Do not worry about me, I will keep up with you.'

Eric smiles and nods. 'It will be hard, though, uphill all the way through the forest. Margaux, you have packed provisions?'

She nods. 'Yes. I have cheese aplenty, some good Munster. I have packed it in your backpack. Also, bread. It will be stale after a few days but...'

'No matter. Stale bread is also bread. When we get to the cabin we can light a fire and cook some potatoes maybe.'

'Jacques has stocked the cabins with provisions. It has a good store of potatoes, also a few canned vegetables and some apples, so you can even cook tonight. There is wood for the stove. Jacques has prepared it all.'

'Water?' asks Sarah.

'There is a stream running nearby. We will have as much water as we need. And the next day as well, when we proceed down the other side of the *massif*.'

He jabs the map a second time. 'This is where we are headed. The town of Clairmont, in Lorraine.'

Sarah asks: 'How far away is it exactly, this Clairmont? And where do we go to there? Who will we stay with?'

'There is a family, a woman, in Clairmont who will take you in,' says Eric. 'They always hide our Jews. But we always need to check with them first that there is room.'

Margaux looks from Sarah to Rebecca. 'You must understand where you are going and not just follow blindly. Just in case.'

Rebecca nods. 'How long will it take to get there? And where do we go from there?'

'We should be in Clairmont by the evening after tomorrow. After that, the family will arrange for you to go to Metz, which is here.' Eric jabs at the map again. Rebecca peers at the spot marked Metz.

'But... Metz is further north from Clairmont. I thought we were headed south, towards Spain?'

'You must go along the safest route, to homes that are safe and people who will protect you and send you on. There is a certain escape route you will take, and Metz happens to be on that route. I don't know how the route continues. Once you are there, you will be informed.'

'The important thing is your safety,' adds Victoire.

'There is never complete safety,' says Eric. 'You must be on your guard at all times. Watch your back constantly; trust no one except those we have approved. I don't want to scare you but it's best you know of the danger. Sarah's papers are German but it's not just about papers. If you are visibly nervous and the Gestapo suspicious, well, all it takes is one phone call to Colmar to expose you as a suspected Jew, but on the run. That is bad not only for you but your whole family. You are fugitives and you must never forget that. If you are caught, you will be sent to a labour camp...'

Sarah pales. She has known the journey is dangerous, but hearing it spelled out this way, by the very person who will be her guide part of the way, makes it all so much more real, and makes her all the more nervous. She glances at Victoire, who meets her eyes and places a hand over hers on the table.

'Eric will look after you,' she says, her voice firm and confident, but in her very next breath that same voice has changed to a plea.

'Eric – please – this time?'

'No, Victoire, not this time. Not with refugees. It is too dangerous. I will take you, one day, show you the route, so you can also be a guide in future. But not this time. We must do it alone, without refugees, so that in case anything happens it is just us, two people from Alsace. It is safer that way.'

'But you know very well that I am the best person to be a guide. You are a deserter – if they catch you, your life too is in danger!'

She turns to Sarah. 'Remember? All Alsace men between the ages of eighteen and thirty-five are conscripted into the Wehrmacht. It is terrible. That is why Jacques and also Eric and many others have formed a band of Resistance fighters in Alsace – all deserters. If they are caught, they will be executed.'

'I will not be caught and neither will Jacques.'

'Then why can't I come now?'

They argue along these lines for some time. Victoire had grumbled earlier that it was an ongoing conflict between the two. Sarah can well understand Victoire's need to participate, her bitterness at being left behind while Eric does the vital work of escorting refugees across the mountains. Victoire had told her how much she longed to do more, to be more active in the Resistance; how much she resented the protective attitudes of both Jacques and Eric. Yes, she is needed on the vineyard as well and enjoys helping her mother with the vines and the wines. But she longs for more adventure, for danger, even.

'I told you, Victoire. Next time, maybe, when I return from this trip. I am sure your maman agrees.'

They all look at Margaux, who shrugs, picks up the bottle of wine and refills all their glasses.

'I am glad that at least one of my children is not in the hands of the Boche,' she says. 'I am proud of Victoire and her desire to be of use. Yes, it is dangerous, but there is danger at this time whatever we do. Simply living is dangerous. This is war. We are at war with the yellow. But I appreciate that it is more dangerous for certain people.'

Here, she looks from Sarah to Rebecca. 'I wish you both a safe journey and a great escape to America. *Santé!*'

Eric pushes back his chair and stands up.

'So – that's it. Time to go to bed. We must make an early start tomorrow.'

That night, lying on their hard horsehair mattresses in the pitch darkness, Sarah and Rebecca talk until sleep overcomes them. Rebecca tells her own story:

'Like you, we were non-practising Jews and we did not register when we were told to at the start of the annexation. We thought we could get away with it: it was just my father and myself, on a quiet dairy farm down near Wintzenheim. We didn't think anyone knew we were Jews and anyway, we can outlast the Boche – they will lose this war as they did the last and we will one day be safe again.'

'Do you really think so?'

'I do. Good must always triumph over evil and there is no question who is the evil one here.'

'I hate the Germans! I hate them with every bone in my body!'

'All Germans are not the same,' says Rebecca mildly. 'You should hate the Nazis; they are the evil ones, the thugs. They are the ones who threatened my father and myself. They came one day saying we had been denounced as Jews and we had to produce papers proving our Aryan ancestry – our parents and grandparents had to be pure Aryan. We could not of course do that. Flight was the only solution.'

'Then where is your father?'

Rebecca's voice cracks. 'My father was a very old man. He was already ninety-one and very feeble. He told me to go on my own. But of course I would not leave him! I never would; he knew that. Then one morning I woke to find that he had slit his wrists with a razor. There was blood everywhere. I buried him that day and then I fled.'

Rebecca does not speak again. Sarah hears her give a muffled sob. And she remembers her own family and she, too, begins to cry.

'Are you all right, Sarah?' Rebecca's voice is cracked, but concerned.

'No, I'm not all right! How could I be? I've been abandoned by my parents, thrown out of my home!'

'No!' Rebecca's cry is sharp and authoritative. 'Don't say that, Sarah, don't even think that! Don't wallow in self-pity! Your parents made that decision because they love you and want to protect you.'

'I just don't understand. Why – why couldn't we stay together?'

There is a rustling sound as Rebecca stands up from her mattress. Seconds later, she is with Sarah, lying beside her, her arms around her.

'Tell me about your family,' Rebecca whispers. 'I want to know. We are going to be together a long time, we need to get acquainted, *n'est-ce pas?*'

And so for the second time that day, Sarah speaks of her family, and it brings her some slight comfort. She talks of her mother, the heart of the family, who cushions them all from hurt, encourages them, comforts them, gives them strength, nourishes them with more than food. Her father: taciturn, stubborn, gruff on the outside, soft as butter on the inside.

'Papa makes violins for a living, but he would rather play them,' says Sarah. 'He wanted to be a solo violinist, or at least play in an orchestra – but once I was born, he had to abandon that dream and settle down to provide for us. But I don't think he regrets it one bit. He's a family man; he adores us all.'

She speaks of her sisters: Thérèse, the firebrand, Amélie, the quiet dreamer, Manon, who is sensible and clever, and little Sofie, the girl who always talks back but whose heart is made of gold.

'I miss them all so much,' she says with a sigh, and nestles into the crook of Rebecca's arm. Rebecca hugs her tighter.

'With God's blessing, you will all be together again one day. But now, it's time to sleep. Tomorrow will be a long day.'

'Mmmm,' sighs Sarah, and with that she falls asleep, in Rebecca's arms.

Part Two

Vosges, Metz

Chapter Eleven

They all meet in the kitchen. Sarah wears the small canvas bag Margaux has given her over her shoulder; in it are her papers and one change of clothing. On her feet she wears the solid leather boots Uncle Yves has given her. An old woollen skirt and a cotton blouse, stockings and a cardigan; that is all. She envies Victoire the trousers she wears – how much more practical they would be, hiking up the mountain! But still, a skirt is less conspicuous. Trousers on a woman would only draw unwelcome attention. Not that there'll be anyone whose attention could be drawn, up there in the mountains…

Margaux insists that they eat a small breakfast of cheese and bread and drink some ersatz coffee. It is still dark outside, dawn a long way away. They speak in low voices. The atmosphere is tense, electric, so different from the relaxed bonhomie they'd enjoyed the night before. Eric is impatient, stuffing his mouth and downing his coffee in haste.

'Let's go now,' he says to the women, and Sarah swallows the unchewed food in her mouth and washes it down with coffee and turns to Margaux.

'Thank you so much, Margaux, it was so—'

Margaux kisses her on both cheeks and pushes her away.

'No long speeches. Go now.'

The van is waiting, Victoire behind the wheel. Once more, Sarah gets in the back, huddled into the space behind the crates, followed by Rebecca.

It is happening. As of now, she really is a fugitive, a refugee.

*

After about half an hour the van stops. The back doors open and Sarah jumps to the ground. The night is as dark as ever, but around them loom trees. They are in some kind of a copse; the road has been bumpy for the last ten minutes and Sarah can just make out that it is not tarmacked, just a dirt track that leads into the forest.

Victoire embraces her.

'*Bonne chance*,' she says. 'I wish you a safe journey. When the war is over you will be back, I know it.'

Sarah nods, holding back the tears. Since when did hope equal certain knowledge? Because all she has is that, hope. Hope is all anyone has in this damned war, even Victoire. She prefers truth to wishful thinking.

'I hope so,' she says, and the two embrace.

Victoire approaches Eric.

'Take care,' she says, 'I wish you'd let me come with you.'

'One day.' They embrace. Victoire watches as Eric wriggles into the backpack of provisions, and then she throws her arms around him once more.

'Take care. Take care, Eric. Take care of them and of yourself.'

Eric laughs and pushes her away.

'You women, always so sentimental and fearful! Of course I will take care of us all. Come on, ladies, *on y va.*'

He waves them onwards and marches off into the dark looming shadows at the edge of the thicket. Sarah glances once more at Victoire and marches off behind Eric, as does Rebecca. Just before they are swallowed by the trees Sarah turns to wave goodbye once more. Victoire still stands beside the van, watching, as if she cannot bear to tear herself away. As if she fears for them all. Even the little wave she gives is somehow tentative, tense, so different from the self-possessed, relaxed, laughing Victoire of yesterday. As if she holds some silent doubt within her. A premonition.

*

The light of Eric's torch cuts a funnel of light into the darkness. The trees are close, yet they seem to be following some kind of a path, and his strides are confident enough. Yet the very fact of being enclosed by trees, their trunks near enough to touch, imparts a sense of claustrophobia, exacerbated by the opaque darkness: oppressive, almost menacing.

Beneath their feet, the undergrowth crunches and cracks, breaching the cavernous silence. The forest floor is soft with a padding of rotting leaves and moss and twigs and composted earth, and the moist, not unpleasant smell of mingled bark and leaves and earth completes the sense of being slowly absorbed by an alien world, owned solely by powerful natural forces. Here, any autonomy she possesses as a human is annulled by the dark brooding stillness. Here, nature might be passive, but it is certainly not powerless.

They march on in silence, single file; the path, if it is even a path, tilts upwards, the incline steeper, it seems, by the minute.

When Eric speaks, it is like an alien's voice, incongruous with the forest's mood.

'Are you all right, ladies?' he calls. 'Let me know if my pace is too fast for you.'

Both the women call out that they are fine.

'Good,' he calls back. 'But if you want me to slow down, just give a shout.'

Chapter Twelve

On and on they trek, and night slowly melts into day, revealing the trunks of trees: spruce, pine, fir. Up above them, sunlight begins to filter through the needled branches, and glimpses of blue sky become visible between their spiky fingers. They are walking along what seems like a path, although so narrow it is hardly discernible, but Eric steps confidently forward and the two women follow, Rebecca first and Sarah bringing up the rear.

The gap between Eric and Rebecca grows wider, and Sarah, too, feels her feet growing heavier and her breath shorter as they wind uphill, the way sometimes bending sharply to the left or right in wide zigzags. Up and up. Sarah has the vigour of youth but is not particularly fit. At home with Mama and Papa in more recent years there was not much scope for exercise: she climbed and descended stairs, up and down, many times a day, from her room in the attic to the coal cellar, and that was the limit of her daily exercise. She stayed home most of the time, only venturing out to run errands, buy groceries, deliver messages. In the home. At home.

It used to be different. She used to cycle to school or, on Sundays, ride out with her sisters to visit the picturesque district of Little Venice, to the riverside lanes and fishmongers' district and market gardens. That was in a time when one could still laugh, when life was a joy and offered a future. Those days were long past. The three bicycles had been stored in the cellar for some time, growing a coat of dust.

She wonders now about them: has Papa given them away yet? What about the violins, the tools? Have they yet been distributed among trustworthy friends, as Papa had decided? How is the family? Do they miss her, are they safe? When will she see them again?

Such worried thoughts chase each other through her mind as she tramps upwards, distracting her and even slowing her pace, as worries always do. Rebecca, too, has slowed down considerably and Eric is now quite a way ahead of them. He has allowed them to stop once, beside a small spring of fresh cool water, for a quick breakfast, then it was on again. No time to collect fresh energy.

Rebecca stumbles; Sarah manages to catch her before she falls to the ground, and helps her upright.

'Are you all right?'

'Yes, yes, I am. It was just a stone. But, you know…'

'Yes, I know.' She calls out: 'Eric! Eric, stop!'

Eric not only stops, he comes back and joins them.

'Are you all right? Am I walking too fast?'

'Yes, we're all right and yes, you are too fast. Neither of us are used to climbing mountains, you know!'

'I'm sorry, I should have realised and watched out for you.'

'It doesn't matter but the path is getting quite steep now and we're both out of breath. Can we pause for a while?'

'Yes, of course. A little further on there's a ruined wall and an open field. It's a good place for a rest. I was actually headed there but maybe I was rushing. Can you manage twenty more minutes? I'll go slowly.'

The women both agree and they continue on their way, slowly now, the pace almost leisurely. If all were normal, Sarah thinks, if this were peacetime and not a time of deadly peril, this would have been a wonderful day out for her whole family. Now, it is a flight. But at least for the time being a slow flight; she can breathe more easily with the slower pace.

They reach a walled-off field, the wall itself hardly worthy of the name, more a line of crumbling stones, a gap where once a gate had been. Was it used, once, for grazing cows? So high up, in the forest? They settle themselves on stable stone seats and Eric passes around clumps of cheese and bread, and a water bottle he'd refilled earlier at the spring. It is good to rest, good to chat, as if this is just some kind of day excursion in a normal life. As if there is no war outside. Just forest and mountain and hill and grass and sky. Yet there is an edge to the harmony, an edge of discord. Nature can be extremely deceptive, promising peace, a thing so fragile, so easily destroyed by some mad human with megalomaniacal ambitions. World domination, and expulsion of Jews. That's why they are here. How can you appreciate the beauty of nature when your life could end at any moment, should you fall into the hands of the wrong people?

Don't exaggerate, Sarah, she admonishes herself. *They don't want to kill you, just send you off to some labour camp. Nobody is after your life. It's just a case of making Alsace* Judenfrei, *free of Jews.*

Uncle Yves had thought differently. *Life and death*, he'd urged. *You have to go.* Papa had never quite believed him, but the threat of labour camp was enough to force him to act. Better to flee of one's own free will and find a way to America even if it meant splitting the family apart, into the unknown. But this place, this bucolic paradise, this field of untouched green grass, a lake shining in the distance, purple hills against the horizon, blue sky above, drifting cotton-wool clouds, gentle sunshine, made the whole project seem ridiculous. Unreal. *This* is real. War is manufactured, artificial, an aberration. *An evil.*

'Ready to move on?' Eric asks. 'I really want to reach the cabin before dusk, and it gets a bit steep.'

So, on they go, back into the forest, up and up and up, following a path only Eric can see, so hidden it is between trees that all look the same. Sometimes steeply up, sometimes gently, but always onwards, unrelentingly westwards, following the sun. Between the trees, a cool moistness merges with the woody-earthy scent, embraces them with something that feels like the very essence of the forest.

The day moves on, inclines towards its rest. Shadows grow longer, the light subtler. The path, as Eric has warned, steeper, craggier.

'Nearly there,' he says, his voice chirpy, encouraging.

They come to what seems like a flight of stone stairs built into a steep mountainside, man-made, just like the ruined wall, but more intact, more maintained. Beside it rushes a small stream.

'Jacques built this,' explains Eric, 'to get to the cabin more directly. It's a bit of a steep and narrow climb. Here, take my hand.'

He goes ahead, slightly sideways, extending a hand for Rebecca to grasp. She climbs slowly after him, picking her way up the narrow steps. Two steps. Three, four, five.

'Careful, these are a bit wet, and slippery,' Eric warns, and at that very moment Rebecca cries out as she slips and stumbles and finally falls against Sarah, who is right behind her on step one. Eric holds onto her hand but her weight pulls him, too, down, and the three of them land on the mossy cushion at the bottom of the crag. Eric immediately disentangles himself.

'Sorry, I should have warned you sooner. It's very slippery. Are you both all right? Rebecca?'

Rebecca, too, has immediately pulled herself off Sarah and into a sitting position, bent double, grasping her ankle, her face contorted in a grimace of pain.

'It's my ankle,' she says. 'I think it's…'

'Not broken?'

'I don't know. It's so painful…'

'It would be a disaster if it's broken,' says Eric, his voice darkly sombre.

'I know. Maybe it's just sprained. Let me try it out. Give me a hand up.'

Eric, on his feet now, bends over and holds out his hand and pulls her gently up. Sarah, immediately on her feet, puts her arms around the older woman's body to help steady her. Rebecca stands on her right foot and cautiously tries putting weight on the other. The grimace on her face tells the story.

'I don't know, I just don't know,' she says. 'It's so painful! I daren't put any weight on it, in case.'

'And you shouldn't. But still, we can't stay here.'

'But, how will I get up the steps? I can't!'

'There's a long way up, it takes about twenty minutes longer. The steps are just a short cut – I shouldn't have tried it. But if the two of us support you, maybe you can hobble along.'

'How far away is the cabin?'

'Taking the long way, maybe ninety minutes, walking normally.'

'So, the short way, up the steps, it's just about an hour away?'

'About that, yes, but longer since you won't be able to walk properly.'

'Maybe I can climb the steps on all fours, on hands and knees?'

'You want to try that?'

'Yes, yes, of course. It might even be easier than hopping along for half an hour longer.'

'Good – then let's do that. We're right here to help.'

And so, slowly and carefully, they climb the steps, Rebecca creeping slowly up one knee at a time, one step after the other. Fifteen steps, with helping hands and words of encouragement, and at last she is up, at the top. Here, fortunately, the forest is less dense than down below and the path wider. It is possible to progress three abreast, Eric and Sarah on either side of Rebecca, linked arms supporting her as she hops on one foot.

And then they are there. The cabin is hidden away in a coppice, a small stone edifice, its tiled roof covered in moss, the windows no more than gaping holes.

'Jacques found this years ago, as a ruin,' says Eric. 'Before the war. He was hardly out of his teens, but he loved camping out here. He repaired it himself and now it's become so useful for our runaways. We can stay here a day or two if need be. To see if your ankle improves.'

'And if not? If it's broken?'

'If it's broken – well, I really have no idea. None whatsoever. No doctors up here, and you can't get back down again, and even if you could, you can't go to hospital, for obvious reasons. I'd have to leave you both here and get help. We just have to hope and pray it will get better on its own, and we can continue the journey.'

'What about food?'

'There are provisions here. Potatoes, at least, and water. Some conserves. We can live on that for a while.'

'What about the people waiting for us?' Sarah asks.

'They'll just have to wait longer. Delays are part of this whole thing.'

Sarah's heart sinks. Even with the best outcome, it will be a few days waiting for Rebecca's ankle to improve: waiting is not something she looks forward to. Fleeing is bad enough, but to sit around, inactive, no progress forward, an unspecified delay – it only adds to the sense of menace, of being a target for undefined enemies.

Please, God, make it not so, she prays silently to the God she's never believed in, who never answers prayers, who's failed her, her family, all Jews, so appallingly over the years.

An hour later they have settled into the cabin and a fire flickers cheerily in the cast-iron stove, for it is chilly up here in the heights. Sitting around a wooden table on some rickety chairs that look only fit for firewood, they are enjoying a simple meal of potatoes boiled over a wood fire – Jacques has also left an ample supply of logs for the fire – and cheese, and even wine, when a knock comes at the door simultaneously as it opens slowly, and a cheery voice says, 'Don't worry, it's only me. I came up right behind you.'

And it is Victoire.

Chapter Thirteen

'Jacques came,' she says, 'an hour after you'd left. He sent me after you. He said you might have to abort the journey. There's danger. The Boche have set up camp not ten kilometres away from the route down to Clairmont – the place is crawling with them. I was right behind you. He said this cabin is probably safe but the onward journey isn't – so don't go, at least not yet. Come back home.'

Sarah frowns. 'But then how will we escape? And anyway, Rebecca can't go anywhere.'

Eric explains Rebecca's problem – that she can't walk, that they have planned to rest a few days in the cabin.

'Well, that's a good idea anyway,' says Victoire, 'rest a while and see what happens with the ankle.' She turns to Rebecca. 'I'm sorry – are you in great pain? Would you like me to have a look at it? I did a Red Cross course last year. I may be able to help. And you know there's a first-aid kit here, in the cabin. Eric, didn't you get it out?'

Eric is graceful enough to blush. 'I'd forgotten,' he says, 'and anyway, I wouldn't know…'

'I do,' says Victoire. 'Come, let's have a look at it. Move over to the cot – let me help you.'

Leaning on Victoire's shoulder, Rebecca hops over to one of the two cots pushed against the cabin wall. There had been two extra mattresses piled on one of the cots, which Eric has pulled to the floor for later use. Victoire helps Rebecca to lie down on one of the cots and takes the damaged ankle in her hands. She holds it gently, moves it carefully. 'Does this hurt?' she asks. 'And this?' In both cases, Rebecca flinches.

'You should not put any pressure on it at all,' says Victoire, 'in case it's broken. We need to get you down to Maman – she knows a doctor who won't report you to the Boche. You should ideally have it X-rayed, but I don't think it's possible without you going to the hospital. We'll have to wait and see.'

'I can't possibly hop down to the château,' says Rebecca.

'I know. I'll go down and get help. A couple of fellows with a stretcher should do it.'

'Can we trust them?'

'You can trust anyone Maman trusts. But for the moment, you cannot continue.'

'*Merde.*'

'Tell me more about this Boche camp,' says Eric, later. 'How does Jacques know? Why does he think we should abort?'

'One of his scouts spotted them and came to report. It's a small camp, apparently to the north of Clairmont, but in the mountains.'

'That doesn't sound too dangerous to me. North of Clairmont would be far enough from our path, which is hidden – why would they find it?'

'Jacques is cautious – he feels responsible.'

'He really said we have to abort?'

'Well, that's his suggestion. He says it's your choice if you want to take the risk or not. And if you do, he said to give you this.'

She pulls a pistol out of her backpack, hands it to Eric.

He takes it and turns it around in his hands.

'You know how to use it, don't you? It's Jacques' own gun…'

'I know. He showed it to us once, and told us how to use it. It's the only gun we have.'

'…given to him by a French soldier who defected from the Wehrmacht. It's very precious to Jacques. He said if you decide to continue to take it for protection.'

'He lent me his precious gun?'

'I think he knows you'll choose not to abort. Not trying to make the decision for you, but...'

Sarah asks: 'But if we abort the whole escape, how will we get away, and when?'

'You can stay at our house as long as it takes, and go with the next batch of fugitives.'

'But that might be weeks!' It is a wail.

'Aren't your sisters due to follow you soon? Then you could join their group. It's just one more, and Rebecca could be your escort.'

Sarah considers this possibility. It is certainly tempting. Wait for Amélie and Thérèse and the three of them continue together, with Rebecca. Till then, stay at Margaux's delightful home, with Victoire. Safe. And comfortable, in spite of sleeping locked in a blackened cellar. And Rebecca would be with them, a woman she has learned to like and respect; a mothering influence for the journey ahead.

On the other hand, the prospect of forced inactivity drives her to the edge of despair. Now she has started on the escape route a new kind of energy has taken hold of her; it's like a force rising up within her, transforming her, melting away her fears and her sorrows and her insecurities. The tears of last night have been swept away by this rising tide, all she feels now is audacity: a sense that she can do anything, face anything, overcome anything. It's a new Sarah, a welcome Sarah, a Sarah who must face challenges in order to grow yet more, become yet more, pushing her onwards. The need to keep still, stay in one place, has landed on this newfound sense of adventure like a bucket of cold water, yet not extinguished it. She quivers with the need to move forward, not back. Château Gauthier might beckon with a vision of cosy evenings around that kitchen table in the company of friends, being regaled by Margaux's stories, sipping wine, as safe as it is possible to be in Alsace, and, best of all, waiting for her beloved sisters. But her whole being rejects it.

She has an idea.

'But then there'd be four of us, with Rebecca, and we don't even know if the Boche will come further south and make it even more dangerous, trapping us in Alsace. No, I have a better idea. Let us split up.'

They all stare at her. 'Split up?' Victoire frowns. 'How?'

'Rebecca has to stay here anyway, indefinitely. Maybe for more than a few days. And now *you* have come, Victoire, you can stay with her, help her, if necessary; fetch assistance, like you said. So, she can wait for my sisters and escort them. But I could continue, with Eric. He has protection now, a gun! If the Boche are camped ten kilometres to the north, what are the odds that they will find us, if we take the path down to Clairmont? Didn't you say it is all forest on that side, like everywhere in the Vosges? What are the chances of running into them, really? Eric, what do you think?'

'I would indeed like to finish the job,' says Eric.

'No,' Rebecca cries out, 'what are you thinking? You are only seventeen, a minor! You cannot travel alone through France! That is why you have been allocated to me, because you need an escort.'

'I'm nearly eighteen, not a child any more – why can't I go by myself, if Eric explains the route to me?'

'Because the world is dangerous! You have no experience! And the route does not stop at Clairmont, that's just the beginning. You must go down to the South of France. You cannot do that on your own.'

'But how can I gain experience, if you do not let me even try? Surely it is in doing things alone that one learns!'

Rebecca shakes her head. 'Not under these circumstances. Sarah, you might think you're very old, but in my eyes you are still a child. I'm sorry, but it is so.'

'I don't know about that,' says Victoire. 'Yes, she is young, but she has good documentation and she will only be going from house to house and will be meeting people along the way who will help her. It's really just a series of train journeys, isn't it? What's so very dangerous?'

'I agree,' says Eric. 'The most dangerous part is getting to Clairmont, through the woods. Once there it's just trains and since she has the right papers…'

'It's much more important for the two younger girls to have you as an escort,' Victoire tells Rebecca. 'They are the ones who really need an older person.'

'I think Sarah is perfectly capable,' says Eric.

'Her father would never approve. It's not part of the plan…'

'You hurting your foot was also not part of the plan, Rebecca. Let me go on alone, please! It's my sisters who really need you.'

Rebecca keeps shaking her head, while Eric and Victoire look at each other, frowning.

'There is actually a problem finding an escort for the sisters,' says Victoire. 'We were just discussing that the other day, with Jacques.'

Sarah, Victoire and Eric look at each other, and then at Rebecca, who is still frowning.

'It's three against one, Rebecca!' says Sarah. 'That means I go. I can do it, I'm sure. I feel so strong, now!'

'Feeling strong is not—' Rebecca begins, but Eric interrupts, as if the subject is closed. Holding up a hand, he turns to Victoire.

'Did Jacques really say the forest is crawling with Boche, or was that your embellishment, Victoire? What did Jacques say, exactly?'

Victoire gives the embarrassed chuckle of one who has been caught out. 'You know me too well. I admit, I made that up – Jacques just said there's a camp and increased risk. That if you go, you should take a gun. And that it was your choice. Of course, he did not know about Rebecca's ankle.'

'Neither did you. Did you perhaps think we'd take you along for extra protection? Was that your little plan?'

Victoire blushes, again. 'All right, I admit it. I knew you wouldn't want to abort so I was hoping someone – you, Eric – would suggest I come with you after all.'

'You little minx!'

They look at each other, half-smiling. But then Eric is serious again.

'Well, that isn't possible now. You have to stay with Rebecca. So, if I were to proceed with Sarah, and a gun, there is increased risk, but not extreme danger?'

'He didn't seem to think the danger was extreme but he wanted you to know.'

'How did he hear about this camp anyway?'

'It was spotted by Resistance friends further north, on the Clairmont side. One of them sent a message to warn us. We know that there was some fierce fighting between the Boche and the French army that side in the last war, so they are very vigilant and try to keep us informed. So Jacques was just being protective.'

'Typical Jacques! He is often overcautious.'

'True. But still, I would not take the warning lightly. If you do come back we could all work together preparing the next evacuation and then I could be of help…'

'Which is what you would prefer, *n'est-ce pas?*'

'You know I am eager to work with you, Eric, to join the Resistance. And you are wrong to reject me just because I am a woman.'

'It's not because you are a woman. I know how capable you are. It's because I love you and want you safe. Always.'

'And I want you safe. But we have elected to do dangerous work and we should be allowed to do it, if that is our decision. We know the risks and have elected to take them anyway, to put ourselves in the service of freedom. You should not deny me that chance. It is not about me, it is about the freedom of our country.'

Sarah and Rebecca exchange knowing glances. This is the ongoing conflict between the two of them and the discussion might go on for hours, as it had last night. Rebecca speaks up.

'Well, I'm exhausted now and I want to sleep. Let us decide in the morning who stays and who goes. Can I sleep on this bed? May I have a blanket?'

Eric gets up and fetches some blankets from a heap in the corner of the cabin, covers Rebecca and hands the other one to Sarah, who has stood up to go to bed herself.

'*Bonne nuit*,' he says. 'We will decide everything tomorrow.'

Chapter Fourteen

Once again, Sarah flings her arms around Victoire.

'Goodbye,' she says. 'We will meet again. I am sure of it.'

'So am I,' Victoire whispers. *'Bonne chance.'*

Rebecca is still asleep; they did not wake her up. Sarah turns and trudges off behind Eric, filled to the brim with that new force that had manifested the day before: energy and buoyancy and a sense of purpose. There was simply no way she could have endured the long and indeterminate wait for a second attempt to cross the Vosges. She feels like a racehorse at the starting post, overeager to take off, and filled with a confidence she has never before known in the secluded life she once lived. It is a new, reborn Sarah, ready to face whatever perils life can throw at her.

There had been no question when they woke to face a fresh day, because the vigour in her blood was just as fresh and Eric, keen to finish his task, eager to continue as planned, presented no more objections. If Sarah felt capable of travelling on her own, then so be it. Now that Victoire had arrived to care for Rebecca there was no need to wait, Boche or no Boche. Jacques' gun, his most precious possession, had been only the very final and conclusive nudge forward. Now, they both turn to give a final wave and march into the forest.

Sarah realises that her body is not quite in tune with her mind; she might be eager to skip and fly down the mountainside, but every muscle in her legs aches from the unaccustomed exertions yesterday, protesting with every step she takes and forcing Eric, too, to slow down.

'I'm sorry,' she says, 'it's agony!'

'No matter,' he replies. 'It will be better in an hour or two.'

And it is. The path downhill is the reverse of the uphill one of yesterday, a wide zigzag through a dense pine forest to the valley below. After a while Sarah's thigh muscles loosen up, and comply with a faster pace, and they walk with a briskness that had not been possible the day before – and a new insouciance, despite Victoire's warning. The day is so fresh, so bright, the birds chattering in the trees imparting such a sense of carefree abandon, they cast caution to the wind and chat as they march.

And so it comes as a shock when two men in Wehrmacht uniforms leap into their path, one of them – the bigger, stronger, older one – barking, '*Halt! Stehen bleiben! Hände hoch!*' and holding a gun aimed at them, its barrel pointed at first Eric, then Sarah, and back again.

And in that moment every last morsel of Sarah's newfound courage flees her mind and heart and blood and sinks into the earth. It was all nothing but bravado. Instead, sheer terror possesses her now. With careless insouciance they have run directly into the arms of the Boche. And it is all her fault, for insisting that they carry on today, not wait a single moment longer. Her hands shoot up, as do Eric's, Jacques' gun now useless.

Two soldiers, an older one and a younger one (*Did they always come in such a constellation*, Sarah asks herself, remembering the two who had burst into her father's workshop – an age ago, it seems). In this case, the older one has a red face splotchy with burst blood vessels like a closet drunkard, his cheeks spongy with excess flesh, small glinting eyes buried in padding, loose jowls wobbling as he speaks. The young one is the opposite: everything about him seems trim and well-shaped, the contours of his face well balanced, the features harmoniously ordered. He stands tall and straight, yet there is something almost defensive about his posture; he lacks the bravado and brash aggressive attitude of the older one, standing back while the other gestures and gives orders.

'We'll take the prisoners to the camp and question them there,' says that older one. 'Here, hold my gun while I search them.'

He hands his gun to the younger one and frisks first Eric, removing the gun and the backpack, and then Sarah, his hands probing, lingering, pressing, poking where they should not, wandering leisurely over her body. She closes her eyes tightly, grits her teeth to stop herself from crying out, bracing inwardly against the violation, her entire body rigid with repulsion.

The other soldier stands aside silently, watching, his gun moving somewhat hesitantly between Eric, who stands aside, arms still raised above his head, and her. He is considerably younger, fresh-faced; hardly older than she herself, Sarah thinks, a teenager, though tall and sturdily built. She is surprised, that he, this young, most likely very green, man, a boy, really, is given the task of escorting Eric forward, a gun stuck in the middle of his back, while the older, more experienced one escorts *her*. It is simply – odd. Wrong. But she has a nasty suspicion…

Chapter Fifteen

They walk for less than five minutes, between the trees, following not a path but, it seems, a series of markings cut into the trees, indicating the way the soldiers had come. The Germans' camp, when they arrive – just a two-man tent in the tiniest of clearings – turns out to be perilously close to their own route. It must have been child's play, finding them: she and Eric had been talking so freely, so carelessly, completely abandoning the warnings of the night before. How *could* they have been so insouciant? Why is it that the care and suspicion a fugitive would normally adopt within a town or city dissolved the moment they thought themselves alone with nature; not alone, in their case, but together on the easy part of the journey, downhill, two young persons led astray by the spring in their steps? They had been warned by Jacques to take care, and had ignored that warning. The walls have ears – but so do the trees. Carelessness had been their downfall.

'*Papiere!* Your papers!' yells the older one as soon as they arrive at the camp. Tentatively, both lower their arms, produce the documents they hold close to their bodies, within their clothes: identity cards, ration cards.

'Sarah Mayer!' says the older German, eyeing her up and down leisurely again. His gaze lingers on her breasts. 'Pleased to meet you, Fräulein Mayer. I am Sergeant Kurt Krämer. My young friend here is *Obergefreiter* Ralf Sommer. So, Fräulein, explain to me: what are you doing, walking through the forest so early in the morning?'

His voice is slow, slimy, as languidly lustful as his eyes.

'I am on my way to Metz to stay with relatives,' she replies calmly.

'On foot? Why not take the train?'

'This is actually the quickest way for me,' she says. The story she has prepared with Rebecca and Margaux the day before slips from her lips as easily if she is simply recounting the facts of her life. 'I am an honest citizen of Alsace. I live on a farm near Riquewihr. My father is poor; we do not have a car, only a horse-drawn cart and a few bicycles. It would take too long to get to Colmar by cart or cycle and then there are quite a few connections before I would arrive in Metz. The trains are slow and unreliable. We decided to walk to Clairmont and then take the train from there to Metz. It is far simpler. My cousin here agreed to escort me as he knows the way over the mountains. You have no reason to detain us. We have done nothing wrong.'

'Perhaps you have done nothing wrong – but your "cousin"?' He says the word mockingly, scornfully. 'Why is he not in the Wehrmacht, a fit young man like him?'

He hands her papers back.

'Tie her up!' he yells to the soldier called Ralf Sommer, who obediently fetches a bundle of thin rope from the tent. 'Tightly!' He looks at Sarah again, appreciation oozing from his eyes, and lowers his voice: 'And then tie her to that tree. A pity we didn't bring handcuffs, but we were not expecting to make arrests, especially not of beautiful women wandering through the forests.'

Sommer approaches Sarah almost hesitantly and grasps her wrists. He wraps the cord around them, ties a knot, but loosely, and as he does so looks into her eyes as if trying to tell her something. His expression is apologetic, almost frantically contrite.

She meets his gaze boldly. 'How dare you!' say her eyes. He looks away and finishes the job, tying her to one of the more slender pine trees, but again, loosely. Absurdly, considering the circumstances, she notices his hands: they are long and slim, and though the skin is rough when he touches her hands, there is something almost delicate about that touch: the hands of a musician. The thought rises involuntarily in her mind but she pushes it away. The hands of a thug, more likely. They come in all shapes and sizes and, she reminds herself, all Germans are thugs.

Krämer, meanwhile, has grabbed Eric's papers. 'Keep your hands up!' he shouts while he inspects them. 'Don't try to run, we'll shoot!'

He frowns and looks up and now repeats his question, this time far more belligerently.

'It is as I thought. A man of Alsace, therefore a German, therefore by law obliged to be conscripted into our armed forces. What are you doing, traipsing around in the mountains with a pretty girl instead of fighting for the Führer? Are you a deserter?'

'No, of course not. I have a kidney disease, which means I am exempted from military service.'

'Where are your exemption papers?'

'I-I have lost them.'

'Well, I do not believe you, and I do not believe you are her cousin. I believe you and she are up to no good. I believe you fucked her last night and you are going to fuck her again.'

He pushes his face right up close to Eric's.

'But you are in for a treat, Mr Eric Bäcker. Today, you are in for a delicious pleasure, because instead of fucking her, you will watch me doing so, and then my colleague-in-arms, this fine young soldier here. We have not had a woman in months; in fact, I believe he never has – a nice little virgin, what fun for him! We are both so very hungry, but not for food. So, this is what we are going to do – Ralf, bring the rope – we are going to tie you up too, nicely and securely, and then my colleague and I are going to have a wonderful morning enjoying the pleasures of the flesh, and you are going to watch. After which we will escort you back to our troop. As for the girl, as she says, she has done no wrong, so we will not arrest her – after pleasuring us, she can continue on her way to Metz. But you, you deserter, you will reap your just punishment. Have you heard of the Natzweiler-Struthof camp, near Strasbourg? You must have. That is where deserters like you end up, and most probably executed for cowardice. The Führer hates cowards and men who shirk their duty. They must be eliminated from the Reich, along with filthy Jews. Ralf, why are you standing there with those ropes? Tie him up, like the girl, but tighter.'

'You bastard!' screams Eric, and kicks the soldier called Ralf as he attempts to wind the rope around his wrists. Sarah closes her eyes tightly, trying to hold in the tears. In her mind she yells at Eric: *Don't fight them, you'll only make it worse. Keep your head down, don't make a fuss!* It is the advice her father has repeated over the last few years, ever more urgently. *The more you resist them*, he'd said, *the nastier they get. Why end up dead just because your pride is hurt? Keep your head down and do as they say.*

'What did you call my colleague?' Krämer, who had been approaching Sarah, now swings around and strides over to Eric.

'I wasn't talking to him, I was talking to *you*, you filthy Nazi bastard!' yells Eric.

Krämer marches straight up to Eric and slaps him across the cheek.

Eric's reaction is immediate and instinctive. A ball of spit flies from his mouth and lands with a splat in the centre of Krämer's face.

Krämer's reaction is equally immediate and instinctive. He draws his gun, aims carefully and shoots Eric.

Sarah screams. She screams and screams and wriggles to free herself from her bonds but though they have been tied loosely, they still aren't loose enough.

'You bastard!' Now it is she who is screaming insults, not keeping her head down. 'You evil, nasty Germans! I hate you! I loathe you! Rot in hell, you pigs!'

Chapter Sixteen

Sarah screams so loudly and she writhes so much, struggling against the ropes that bind her, her eyes wild and unfocused, that it takes a whole minute before she realises she is not the only one screaming. Eric is also screaming; he is alive! He is screaming not in fury or fear but in agony, and at last Sarah comes to her senses, and now Krämer, whose back had been turned to her as he interrogated Eric, moves away, putting away his gun, and she sees that Eric is bent over almost double, as far as the rope that ties him to his tree will allow. One of his trouser legs is covered in blood, and blood is still flowing from a hidden wound in his thigh.

When she notices this, her cries became more urgent: 'Attend to him! He needs a doctor, you swine! Stop the bleeding, he'll bleed to death!'

But Sommer is already attending to Eric, untying the rope around his waist that tied him to the tree, and when Eric is free, Sommer places his arms around him and gently lowers him to the mossy ground.

'She's right, sir,' he says quietly to Krämer. 'We need to stop the bleeding. I'll get the first-aid kit.' He rises to his feet and hurries towards the tent, returning with a green metal box with a red cross in a white circle on the cover.

Krämer stands aside, laughing.

'You're going to waste your time with that deserter? Why bother? They'll execute him anyway. Let him bleed, save us all the trouble. Me, I've got more interesting things to attend to.'

He turns to Sarah, still writhing to free herself from her ropes, pulling her hands against the loops that enclose them, and walks across to her.

'Hello, sweetheart!' he says in a silly crooning voice, smacking his lips, running his hands through his hair as if to enhance his attractiveness. She looks up and puts as much loathing as she can into her glare.

'Get away! Don't come near me, you filthy evil piece of scum!'

But he only laughs, removes his jacket, flings it to the ground and begins to unbutton his belt.

'Ha! A woman with temperament! I like that, heightens the fun.'

He comes closer, within touching distance, almost. Her legs, which have not been tied, thrash furiously, kicking out at him, aiming at his groin, but missing as he sidesteps, chuckling at her helplessness.

'A little tiger cat! Just the way I like my women!'

With that, he suddenly flings his body at her, clamping her legs against the tree. His hands work at her skirt, ripping the waistband, and then pull at his own trousers, hauling them down over his buttocks.

'I love to fuck a little wildcat! Come, sweetheart, give me a kiss, or a bite, or a—'

He does not complete his sentence because a deafening crack splits the air and blood is spurting from a jagged hole in his head and she screams in horror as he slumps heavily against her and sinks to the ground, the jagged wound leaving a trail of blood and brain matter and other messy body parts down her body, her clothes. She yells and writhes in utmost disgust and loathing. She spits between her yells because her mouth had been open, screaming, and some of Krämer's blood has entered it, and she has to spit it out. Maybe she has even swallowed some; that thought makes her retch all the more.

Krämer's body lies sprawled at her feet, a mess of blood and brain and white tissue instead of what was once his head. Sommer stands above the body, a dazed expression on his face as if in shock, staring at the still-smoking pistol in his hand. She continues to scream and writhe, helpless against her bonds.

Sommer wakes from his reverie and springs towards her. A knife materialises out of nowhere and he begins slashing at the rope that binds her, cutting through it where it binds her wrists and her waist. She screams and writhes and pulls at her bloodied clothes and yet she can't just strip naked, not yet; but she has to get rid of them, and tears her blouse from her body, revealing her thin vest and brassière, those, too, soaked in blood.

'You can get them off, go and bathe,' he says, 'do you have clean clothes?' Shuddering with revulsion, whimpering with loathing, she points to her shoulder bag, lying on the ground where Krämer had thrown it earlier. He picks it up, walks to the tent and returns with a worn-down bar of soap and a limp, slightly threadbare green towel.

'I'm sorry, the towel isn't a clean one,' he apologises, and points to a clearing in the woods.

'There's a stream down that way,' he says. 'You can wash yourself. I'd show you but I have to…'

He gestures towards Eric. Somewhere beyond her abhorrence she understands: he has to attend to Eric, still moaning on the ground. 'It's just a few minutes away,' he says, placing the soap and the towel in her hands.

He bows his head, walks to Eric, kneels down beside him.

She lurches towards the path clutching the towel, still keening, half-retching with horror and nausea, Krämer's toxic blood searing her face and hands and clothes, everything it touches, an abomination.

She walks only five minutes, and there it is: a spring and a small pool that run away in a clear stream through the moss, downhill through the forest. It is the most inviting thing she's ever seen.

At last she is able to strip off the bloody clothes. She throws them away from her; she cannot bear to look at them. When she is naked, she is about to step into the pool but then has a sudden thought – what if Sommer has followed her, left Eric to bleed to death and is secretly watching? After all, he too is a German, capable of anything… But it is too late now and the only thing to do is step into the pool.

The water is freezing, yet it is the most delicious bath she's ever had. She grabs a handful of moss and rubs soap on it and scrubs her face, her arms, her breasts; she washes her hair and the rest of her body until every inch of her tingles. Again and again the horror of that head exploding appears in her mind's eye as in a vision. Though the water is ice-cold, she lies down on the pebbly bed of the stream and lets it wash over her, scrubs her body with handfuls of moss to get the German's blood out of her pores, out of her system. But it seeps into her nevertheless and venom continues to rise within her, anger, hatred, sheer disgust. What if that German had had his way? How could she have lived on? Loathing fills her, loathing without discrimination or thought: pure loathing. She will never be clean again, never free from contamination.

Then she remembers Eric. She had forgotten him completely in the horror of her own experience. She has to get back to him. Sommer is alone with him and goodness knows what he might do – he is a German, after all, and Eric is helpless, wounded. She hurries out of the water, picks up the towel – but no, she cannot use it, a German has used it before her. She pitches it away with the bloody clothes and scrambles in her shoulder bag for clean underwear and vest and blouse and skirt and quickly gets dressed.

Boots! They lie there where she'd torn them off, covered in blood and brain matter. She can't throw them away – she has no change of shoes. She has no choice but to clean them and put them on again. Grabbing a handful of leaves, she returns to the water and scrubs away the worst of the blood from the leather uppers, but she cannot wash away the stain that covers one boot, nor the sprinkles of blood on the other. She'll have to wear them, just like that, stained with a German's blood. Trying not to retch, she pulls them on, ties the laces and hurries back the way she came, back to the clearing.

Eric and the German are sitting together, Eric leaning against the tree, the German bandaging his thigh. Both look up as she approaches. She ignores the German and looks at Eric.

'How are you? Is it bad? Are you still bleeding?'

'I made a tourniquet,' says Sommer. 'The bleeding has stopped and it'll do for now. I put a fresh bandage on it. It's just a flesh wound, the bullet scraped the edge of his thigh. He is so thin, it did not lodge in his muscle. But he needs medical attention as soon as possible. A hospital, or at least a doctor. I disinfected it with iodine' – he holds up his yellow hands – 'and we only had one bandage. We must get him to someone who can change the bandage and check the wound.'

'A bit difficult, up here in the mountains,' Eric says. He's biting his lip against the pain.

'I know.' Sommer looks at Sarah. 'You'll have to go down to Clairmont and fetch a doctor. I can't be seen anywhere. After what I've done – killed my superior – I can't go anywhere. As of now I'm on the run from the Wehrmacht. As a deserter.'

'They'll shoot you,' says Eric. *Good. One less German*, Sarah thinks. Inside she is still trembling from her ordeal, still screaming with fear, an overpowering fear that knows only itself, blind to all reason. The Boche! They are a scourge and must be wiped out. If she knew how she would shoot this one herself, with that gun still lying on the ground.

'Trust no one,' Jacques had said, and so had Margaux, and she cannot trust this one. So she does not look at him, only at Eric. But Eric speaks for her.

'You're quite the hero,' he tells the German. 'I'm sorry that now you'll be in trouble.'

Sommer chuckles wryly.

'*Trouble* is an understatement. As you said, they'll shoot me. No escape from that.' He points his chin towards the lump of Krämer's body, now covered with a blanket, Sarah notices. She is glad – she could not bear to see that disgusting bloodied corpse again.

'Thank you,' says Eric. Sarah feels she should be the one saying it, but she cannot. She lowers her eyes so as not to meet his, and takes Eric's hand, but Eric is looking at Sommer and he hasn't finished speaking. 'They'll have to catch you first. Come with us. You saved Sarah, in spite of the problems it would cause you; you put your own life at risk. That's a huge thing. But you needn't have killed him. A bang on the head would have done as well, and saved you a lot of trouble.'

'Trust me, a bang on the head would have solved nothing, even if you'd managed to get away. He'd have alerted the troop by field telephone and they'd have swarmed over here. It would have made things worse for all of us. No, for me, it's better this way. It gives me time to escape. They won't notice anything for at least a week, when we don't return from our reconnaissance trip. I regret nothing.'

Sommer shrugs and continues. 'Killing Krämer was just the trigger for a move I had to make anyway. I've been thinking of deserting for weeks, months even. I've always known this war is evil, always wanted to flee. But at the moment you're the problem. You see why I can't be the one to fetch a doctor. But I can help you out of the mountains, if you can hobble down. I'll have to flee once we reach civilisation. I'm a fugitive from now on.'

Just like me, Sarah thinks. Eric says, 'I have a much better idea. I'll still have to hobble, but not so far. We'll go back to the cabin.'

Chapter Seventeen

Eric tells Sommer about the cabin. He does not ask what they are all doing in a cabin in the mountains, he simply nods and agrees that going there is the best plan.

'We must leave as soon as possible. I will pack a few things.'

Now Sarah speaks directly to Sommer for the first time.

'You can go your own way,' she says. She does not look at him and her voice is curt and sharp, not the voice of one who has been rescued from a terrible ordeal. It is the only way to hide her fear. She must get rid of this interloper, this German, this enemy.

'I will get him to the cabin on my own. We don't need your help any more. Eric, can you stand up? Here, take my hand.'

Eric protests, but still takes the hand she holds out to him, pulling. But it is not enough; his legs are awkwardly placed and he needs further support. Sommer also stretches out a hand and pulls, and Eric finally stands on two feet. Sommer is on his injured side, so Sarah shoves herself between them and lifts Eric's arm around her shoulders.

'Lean on me,' she says. 'Can you make it?'

But Eric pushes her away gently. 'Sorry, Sarah, you're far too short. I need someone taller to support me.'

'I don't think he should come to the cabin,' she says in French, gesturing at Sommer. 'After all, he's…'

'Sarah, don't be ridiculous. He's helping us. He saved you! Try to be a bit friendlier towards him. Now, let him help me – move away.'

With a shrug she steps aside and allows Sommer to take her place. The men are of almost the same height, though Eric is much thinner and less brawny. Eric slings his arm around Sommer's shoulders and with Sommer supporting him around his waist hobbles forward.

'See, that's much better,' he tells Sarah, who shakes her head and looks away. She notices the two guns lying on the grass, one just short of Krämer's hand and the other where Sommer had thrown it. She picks them up, puts one in her bag and keeps the other in her hand.

For protection, she says to herself. *You never know.* She is confused, despairing, frightened, helpless. She is in the hands of this German; she has no choice! Waves of terror rise within her, visions of Krämer's lusting face looming before her, then the blood, oh the blood! She cannot think straight, cannot reason; waves of terror flow through her. She must get rid of this German, but she cannot, they are dependent on him, now. Perhaps she will have to shoot him. She must get rid of him.

She glances at the prone blanket-covered body of Krämer and nods her chin at it.

'So, what will you do about that? Come back and bury it?'

'He doesn't deserve a burial. Let nature take care of it. Wild animals, maggots—I don't care. The man is a monster. The things he's done…' Sommer shudders. 'I'll just leave it. When they notice we haven't come back – in about a week or so – they'll come looking for him and find the tent and his remains. They can think what they like. Burying it won't make a difference.'

She shrugs and speaks no more. The body is the least of their problems: they are stuck with a German. Eric seems stable enough and the bleeding has stopped but he is in obvious agony, his repressed groans emerging as little grunts from between clenched teeth.

'We'll get you there, Eric. It's less than an hour. Thank goodness Victoire came to join us!'

He nods, hopping along beside Sommer while looking behind him to talk to her.

'At this rate it'll be two hours. But I'll manage. Are you all right, Sarah?'

She nods. But she is not all right. She is a raging storm of emotion. Fear and loathing and helplessness and utter confusion. She cannot show it, she must pretend.

'Then let's go.'

The men shamble off, trying to find their stride on the path. Sarah trails behind them, desperation rising and intensifying for reasons that were rather vague to begin with but are becoming increasingly defined as time moves on. The more his rescue of her drifts into the past, the more her innate terror of him for being German, the loathsome enemy, grows within her, a gnawing sense of threat. As if all the accumulated angst she has ever felt towards that enemy, harboured unspoken in her heart, all the unavenged atrocities ever committed by a German against her people, have finally found a target, a lightning rod; and fear has transformed into red-hot wrath. This one act of gallantry cannot erase the mountain of crimes gone unpurged by his people. Their guilt has become *his* guilt. He has not atoned by saving her from rape, nor by helping Eric.

Soon the two men, progressing slowly side by side, arms linked, are chatting like old friends. Sarah, walking behind them, listens against her will. It is a strange and jerky conversation: although Eric's father is Alsatian and bilingual, his mother was from Metz and francophone, and only French had been spoken at home. He has learned to listen and understand German but not to speak it. Ralf is the opposite: he can speak a childish and broken French with a bad accent, but cannot at all follow the spoken language so both of them mix up languages using whatever words they know and the other might understand.

'I forced into Wehrmacht,' Sommer says in his broken French. 'Want study medicine but not possible.'

'Just speak in German,' says Eric, 'I will try to understand.'

So Sommer tells his story, in German. Eric nods as if he understands, although Sarah doubts he always does, but she, close behind, follows perfectly. Sommer had been conscripted a year ago but has never seen active combat, and is glad of it.

'I was always against this terrible war,' he says. 'Against Hitler. My whole family, my close friends. But nobody can speak it out loud. You never know who might betray you to the SS. We keep our heads down because if not, they go after your family.'

'Where are you from?' Eric asks, in slow French.

'I grew up in Freiburg. My parents still live there and my brothers and sister. I never wanted to be a soldier, I wanted to study medicine. My father's a doctor. We only ever wanted a life of peace. But here I am. Instead of saving lives I've just killed my first man.'

'A monster, you said?'

'Yes. I loathed him. He had been on the Eastern Front. He was always boasting about the Jews he had killed; he laughed about it, proud of it! He disgusted me. A thousand times I have killed him in thought. He is a beast, not a man.'

'Well, good riddance! And you saved Sarah.'

'I'm sorry I tied you up,' says Sommer, looking behind him to address Sarah. 'I'm sorry for what he said to you.'

She simply shrugs, but Eric says, 'Not your fault. You're a soldier, you had to obey orders.'

'But believe me, I would never have done, never ever… *that*.'

Eric chuckles. 'Well, that's obvious. I suppose killing came easier.'

'Yes. I'm sorry your cousin had to hear that and endure that. I'm sorry…'

'Stop apologising for things that aren't your fault. You're a hero. And she's not my cousin, she's—'

Sarah coughs loudly.

'Please don't speak of me in the third person. I'm right behind you and can hear every word.'

She speaks sharply, and her words have the desired effect: the men stop talking.

They have been walking for half an hour when the path narrows and begins to rise rather more steeply.

'You know what?' says Sommer. 'We should have done this from the beginning...'

He bends over, grasps Eric behind the knees – though carefully avoiding the wounded and bandaged leg – lifts him off the ground as if he weighs nothing and slings him over his shoulder.

Eric yells at the initial pain, but wriggles a little and says, 'That's better now. If you can manage it'll be much quicker this way.'

'You're light as a feather. And I'm a trained soldier... *fit wie ein Turnshuh!* As fit as a gym shoe!'

Their pace is now double the speed. Sommer turns again to address Sarah:

'Are you all right, Fräulein Mayer, or am I too fast? Can you keep up?'

'Of course I can keep up!' says Sarah, but she says it in snappy French.

She has come to a decision: in order to demonstrate her pure disdain for all things German, she will speak to Sommer only in French from now on. It is a petty, maybe childish, obstinacy, a tiny and pointless rebellion that benefits no one, she recognises that. But it symbolises something important. It represents a tiny Resistance of her own in a world where all real Resistance seems futile. It pushes him away; it keeps a distance, and keep a distance she must. He might have saved her from rape but there is still the rape his people are committing against hers. The hatred Germans feel for Jews. And he is one of them. What if he finds out that she is Jewish? What if...?

There are still the terrible things he might do, on his own; things he might do to *her*. She must push him away, and French is a barrier. A weak barrier, to be sure, but what choice does she have? She is stuck with this stranger, this German. She must put up all the barriers she can to ensure she will not be engulfed by fear. For still it is there: the overwhelming fear that this man, this German, is just like all of them. Dangerous. Wicked.

Chapter Eighteen

It takes them longer to reach the cabin than it had coming down, but eventually they get there. They find Rebecca sitting outside on a bench, her face lifted to the sun. She starts when she sees them, and leaps to her feet, her face turning pale at the sight: a soldier, obviously German, carrying Eric over his shoulder, followed, quite a bit later, by a sullen-faced Sarah.

'What… what's going on?' she cries as the soldier sets Eric on his feet. She sees the bandage, a bloody spot in its centre, but mostly, she sees the Wehrmacht uniform, and instinctively, flinches away. Eric raises a calming hand as the soldier sets him on his feet.

'It's all right, Rebecca. He's a friend.'

At that Sarah snorts and stomps into the cabin, but immediately returns to stand in the doorway.

'Where's Victoire?' she asks.

'She went to fetch water – she's—'

At that moment Victoire bursts through the trees, and she too glares at the German. Sommer has the grace to blush. He simply stands there, beside Eric, arms hanging at his side, the same hangdog expression on his face as he'd exhibited earlier.

Eric limps over to him and places an arm around his shoulders and says, to reassure Rebecca, 'I said, he's a friend. A deserter from the Wehrmacht, a fugitive like you and Sarah. And he saved Sarah. If you'd stop glaring, I'll tell you what happened.'

'You're wounded!' cries Victoire, noticing for the first time Eric's bloodied leg; her eyes had been fixed on Sommer.

'That's part of the story.'

'Come inside, lie down, let me look at the wound.'

'There's no need, yet – he took care of it. The bandage will need changing at some point. It's a bullet wound, a flesh wound. Not too deep.'

'You should see a doctor.'

Eric shakes his head. 'All in good time. Just let me explain…'

They help him inside, lay him down on a cot. Sommer stands in the doorway, as if unsure as to his welcome.

'Come in, come in, Herr Sommer!' says Eric, gesturing for him to come nearer.

Hesitantly, he approaches, and takes the chair indicated by Eric. Sarah, who has been sitting at the table, jumps to her feet, as far away from Sommer as she can get, but too curious to actually leave, stands next to it as if ready to run, trembling.

'What's the matter, Sarah?' asks Victoire. She places an arm around the girl, who falls against her. Victoire gently helps her to sit down.

'She's had a terrible experience; she's in shock, I think. We were caught; she was almost raped and then… well, let me start from the beginning.'

Victoire and Rebecca nod, still frowning in suspicion, but when Eric tells of the attempted rape, and how Sommer killed her attacker, their faces soften. Victoire goes so far as to walk up to him and shake his hand, introducing herself. She turns back to Eric.

'So, it seems you were careless in the forest, chatting away?'

'She was so excited. She…' He shakes his head, knowing it was his responsibility to keep the silence in the forest, no matter what Sarah wanted.

Rebecca shakes her head too. 'I knew right from the start that it wasn't a good idea to send Sarah off with you. She should have waited. I should have trusted my instinct, insisted she wait.'

'It's too late for regrets now, Rebecca,' says Victoire. 'Or "I told you so's".' She turns again to Eric, while Rebecca, silenced again, shakes her head and mouths the words *young people…*

'Have you told him— does he know about...?' She indicates
Sarah and Rebecca by pointing at them with her chin.

Sarah lurches towards Victoire, grasps her arm, leans towards her.

'He knows nothing,' she whispers, 'and it needs to stay that
way. You never know with a German. I don't want him to know
I'm Jewish... those thugs.'

The four of them cluster together and whisper, so that Ralf
cannot hear.

'But he saved you, Sarah! He's surely on your side?'

'The point is he doesn't know I'm Jewish. Who knows if he'd
have done that if he'd known? Don't Germans hate Jews? They
thought I was German – just a girl from Alsace visiting her family.
Let's keep it that way.'

Eric, coming up beside them, hears those last words.

'Sarah, calm down. You're safe now. Suspicion is good and we
shouldn't trust everyone but you're wrong about this one, very
wrong. Even while he was treating my wound he was telling me
he'd take care of you, that he wanted to desert the Germans. I'm
a good judge of character. You have to be, doing what I do. This
one is all right.'

'I agree,' says Rebecca. 'I think he's trustworthy.'

'That's my feeling as well,' says Victoire. 'You know, I have an
idea...'

Rebecca nods and Eric grins.

'I think I know your idea,' he says, 'I've been thinking it over
all this time. But we'd better find out more about him.'

They all sit down, except Sarah, who moves to stand near the
door again, and Eric, who remains lying on the cot, propped up
on one elbow.

It is an interrogation, Rebecca, Victoire and Eric firing the
questions, which come short and sharp. The answers are just as
short and to the point.

'What's your name?'

'Ralf Sommer.'

'Where are you from?'

'Freiburg.'

'How old are you?'

'Eighteen.'

'How long have you been in the Wehrmacht?'

'One year now.'

'How do you feel about Jews?'

'They are people, like everyone else.'

'Do they have a right to a normal life, in Germany?'

'Of course.'

'How do you feel about Hitler's harassment of the Jews? The hatred, the persecution? What did you think of *Reichskristallnacht*?'

'It's all horrendous, evil. It makes me ashamed to be German.'

'If you met a Jew, what would you do?'

He shrugs. 'Nothing special. I have known Jews, had Jewish friends. Before… before—' He stops, and starts again. 'Now, I'd probably make a special effort to be kind, because I feel guilt at what my country has done and is doing. It is simply atrocious and makes me feel such guilt, as a German.'

He looks from one to the other as he speaks these words, his eyes pleading to be believed, candour shining in them.

The questioning relaxes. Sommer is allowed to explain: that he had been conscripted against his will; that he had wanted to stay in school, study medicine, become a doctor like his father, an orthopaedic surgeon. The war put an end to that plan. His mother is a history teacher; he comes from a family of so-called *Bildungsbürger*, cultured citizens; he likes reading, especially the classics and history. He loves music: Bach and Beethoven; he can play some piano. He likes some sports, especially tennis and swimming. His friends are just like him: anti-war, anti-Hitler, horrified by Nazi ideology, but unable to act against it.

'Why did you shoot Krämer?'

'Wasn't it obvious? He was about to do a terrible thing. How could I stand by and watch?'

'Didn't you realise that shooting him would force you to desert, put your own life at risk?'

He shrugs. 'I had no time to think or consider, it had to be done. I did not consider the consequences, and I do not regret shooting him. I would do it all again to save her. It's normal, surely – how could any decent man stand by and watch a thing like that?'

He nods towards Sarah, who still stands near the door, as if ready to flee.

'So, what are your plans now?'

'I will escape into France, go down to the south, stay hidden, try to make a life there until the war is over.'

'That could be a few years!'

'As long as it takes.'

'How will you be able to do that, as an escaped German soldier?'

He hesitates. 'I know it will be difficult. I will have to destroy my papers, take on a different name. It might be possible to get some new documents forged.'

'You had not thought of these difficulties before?'

'To tell you the truth, I've wanted to desert since long ago, and when I was posted here in Alsace, I thought an opportunity might present itself – I was lucky not to be sent to the Eastern Front, like most of my schoolfriends. I knew that it would be difficult to hide in France, that's why I never did it. And then – well, the situation forced my hand. Krämer was a pig and deserved to die. In fact, that's an insult to pigs, which are intelligent creatures.'

Eric, Victoire and Rebecca all chuckle at that.

'We really should tell him,' says Eric.

'No, don't!' cries Sarah. 'I don't trust him.'

'I do,' says Rebecca. 'I can sniff out bad people – they stink. It's an ability you get with age,' she added. She stands up and moves over to Sarah, pats her on the shoulder.

'You are right to be mistrustful – it will help protect you on the road. But you should not fear this one, he's one of the good ones. There are good Germans too, Sarah. You must learn discernment. Now, come and sit down with us and let's discuss it.'

'But…' she protests, panic rising within her.

Rebecca turns to Sommer, who is drinking from a glass of water Victoire has handed him.

'We are Jews,' she says. 'Sarah and I are Jewish. We are escaping from Alsace because we were too late for the initial evacuation and now there is danger for us there. Our people are being wiped out and we were forced to flee the Nazis, just as you are forced to flee. We are heading for the north of France and then we will head south and make our way to a friendly country. She to America. I hope to stay in Spain until I can find refuge somewhere else. But we are homeless, on the run.'

'Like me,' says Sommer.

Eric, Rebecca and Victoire again exchange a knowing look.

'Yes,' says Rebecca. 'It's a perfect solution.'

'What's a perfect solution?' asks Sarah. 'Why are you all looking at me like that? I don't understand.'

'Don't you see, Sarah?' says Victoire, placing a hand on her shoulder, 'This makes everything much easier for us all. You and our heroic new friend can travel together—'

'No!' she cries, but Victoire ignores her and carries on. 'He can be your escort – you *do* need one, you know, as today has proven – and it can't be Rebecca, who needs time to recover. So does Eric. This is what we will do: Herr Sommer here will go with Sarah to France and accompany her as far as possible. There are people there, people who will help him hide along the route, get new papers for him.'

'But I don't want to…'

Victoire continues despite her plea. 'Don't you see, Sarah? Rebecca and Eric can't go anywhere yet. We'll all three return to

Maman as soon as they are able. Rebecca will then stay with us at the château. In a week or two or three, she will be the escort for your two younger sisters. It's a perfect solution, as there has been difficulty in finding a suitable person – female, and mature enough to take care of young girls. Would you all be happy with that?'

There is a general nodding of heads. Sarah alone cries 'No!' again.

All heads turn towards her. 'Why not, Sarah?' asks Rebecca gently. Sarah speaks, in French, almost a whisper.

'Because he is a wicked German. Maman said they are all brutes!' She turns to Rebecca, desperation in her eyes, and whispers. 'Please don't make me go with him! I… I'm scared of him! After what happened… it was awful, terrible… they tried to… and then the blood, the blood all over me, and he's a German, and…'

She is trembling now. Rebecca takes her in her arms. '*Ma petite*, I do understand. It must have been a truly terrifying experience. But don't you see, he's the *good* one, he's the one who saved you.'

Sarah shakes her head. 'The blood, the blood… after the shot… it was all over me!'

Rebecca holds her tightly. 'Yes, there was blood, because that beast was shot in the head! The blood was a good thing, *chérie*! This man here is a hero. If it wasn't for him… well, much worse would have happened than a bit of blood! You can trust this one.'

'Do not trust anyone, Jacques said!'

'But do you trust me?'

Sarah pauses, thinks, reflects. But the answer is clear.

'Yes. Yes, I do trust you.'

'Then trust me on this. It's important. This is war, and in wartime we must learn to overcome our fears. We all have to. We must face death, and blood, and people being killed – people we love, even. There is a lot of blood spilled in war and we all have to be strong. War proves us, it is the ultimate test. We can no longer hide behind our fears and give in to our weaknesses, we must grow inner muscles. Otherwise our fears dominate us, and we remain weak and helpless, victims of circumstances. In war we are tested to the quick. You too. You must be brave, *ma petite*. You must face your fear, steady your heart and hold your head up, and walk straight through it, and that is how you overcome it. Don't you see? This is nothing compared to what others must face. It is weakness, to indulge your fears at this time. Do not be faint of heart, little one! If you trust me, then trust me in this: there are some good Germans, noble Germans, and this is one of them. I do not use the word "noble" lightly. But with some people, it is possible to tell. It is in the eyes. You can see the truth in the eyes. Look at his eyes, Sarah. Can't you tell?'

Sarah risks a glance at Sommer, locks eyes with him. She cannot hold his gaze, which is frank and so utterly guileless, pleading. She is forced to look away. Now *she* is the one who feels guilty, for calling him a filthy German. Rebecca continues:

'Victoire's idea is a good one, and would solve many problems. I would be happy to escort your sisters – I'm sure they are every bit as delightful as you are and I will treat them like my own daughters.'

Sarah gulps at the word 'delightful'. She knows she is anything but delightful; she is moody, and irritable, and miserable. Not to mention cowardly, at this moment. Surely Rebecca is being sarcastic? She catches the older woman's gaze, questioning it for mockery. But Rebecca's eyes are warm and sincere and she takes Sarah's hand and squeezes it, and Sarah knows she means it: she really does find her, Sarah, delightful. How can that be? She feels childish now, and resolves to be more watchful of her moods. If Rebecca can be strong, so can she.

Rebecca continues, speaking loudly now, and in German so that Sommer can follow: 'This will mean that we can leave soon, as soon as the girls can be brought to the château and as soon as my ankle is healed completely. As it is, I am still limping badly and my whole foot is swollen. And as for travelling with this young man, I think he has proven his gallantry and he will not take advantage of you. You will be safe with him. It is not safe for a young girl to travel alone through France. I know you were ready to do it but I never had a good feeling about letting you go; it was an emergency. Now, I am relieved. I have been given responsibility for you in place of your parents and this is my decision.'

It is a long speech, and throughout the listeners, all except Sarah, keep nodding. Sarah only looks at her feet. She is struggling, and not quite sure what exactly she is struggling with. Yet she can feel the wall of fear and rejection she has built within herself crumbling, dissolving in the wake of reason, in the memory of that candid gaze. For deep inside she knows that Rebecca is right. Sarah shrugs. '*D'accord*,' she says. 'I will go with him.'

Chapter Nineteen

It is already late in the day; they decide that Sarah and Sommer must leave early the next morning to make the most of the daylight. After a simple supper of boiled potatoes, cheese and wine, they discuss the final plans, all sitting around the table. Eric spreads out his map on the table once again and points out to Sommer and Sarah the route they are to take.

'It's not difficult from here on,' he says. 'Take the path we went yesterday – that's the hardest part as it's not easy to find. But once you meet the wider path down to Clairmont you can't really go wrong.'

He traces the way down with his finger. 'The path passes a couple of farms when you reach the bottom of the *massif*. The one you want has a ruined barn next to the path, you can't miss it. There's a stile you'll need to climb over and then walk over the field to the farmhouse. The people are called Delauney. They are expecting two women – you'll have to explain quickly why you're there, Ralf.'

During lunch they had all exchanged first names. Victoire had lifted a battered old suitcase from the top of the cupboard. Inside was a variety of old clothes, including a pair of limp cotton men's trousers, a shirt and a jacket. They fitted Sommer badly; the previous owner had been Jacques, who was a little shorter and much lankier, but they'd have to do, though it was all slightly too small, the shirt straining at the buttons, the waistband too tight to be fastened.

'As for your uniform,' Eric had said, 'I'll burn it, along with your army papers. As of now your old identity is no more. You'd better think of a new name and a cover story.'

Sommer chose the name of a cousin of his who had been killed on the Russian Front. 'Karl,' he said. 'Karl Vogel. As for my cover story…' He thought for a while. 'I think the story you gave is the best – I am Sarah's cousin. If you don't mind,' he said, looking at Sarah. 'We are both German-speaking Alsatians escaping the annexation by fleeing to relatives in the South of France. How is that?'

'Your French is too bad for you to be Alsatian,' said Eric. 'It's best to keep as much to the truth as possible. You're her cousin, yes, but you're from Freiburg, which is the truth. And yes, use my cover story: you are exempted from military service due to a medical issue. Kidney problems. I do have that, by the way. It's true.'

'Why didn't you have your exemption papers, then?'

Eric shrugged. 'Because I don't have any. Kidney problems weren't serious enough.'

'Well, it's a good story. So, as of now I am Karl to all of you.'

Now, Eric explains their further progress. 'You will use a password when Madame Delauney opens the door to you. You will ask if she has preserved plums. In French, of course. That will be your job, Sarah. "*Avez vous des pruneaux conservées?*" and she will reply, "No, but I have a nice plum liqueur. Would you like to try it?" and then she will invite you in. She knows the rest. She will provide you with room and board until it is time to move on. You will travel by train to Metz. In Metz there is someone who can provide you, Karl, with forged papers; they might be able to come up with a better cover story. Until then you have nothing to prove who you are. Sarah, your papers are in order; you will be travelling as yourself. Fortunately, you do not need new papers – they are not stamped *Jude*.'

'What if we are stopped on the way to Metz?'

'That is indeed a problem, at least for Ralf. Originally, Sarah and Rebecca were supposed to go by train but there will be controls on every train so you will have to find some other way of getting there, perhaps even on foot. That's the easiest way to avoid controls.'

'Remember what Jacques said: that there's a lot of Wehrmacht activity on that west side of the Vosges,' says Victoire. 'You need to be very careful.'

Ralf speaks up.

'Well, you've already met that activity. It was me and Krämer. Our unit is quite a way further north-west, and the heaviest controls are even further north, in line with Strasbourg. We were the only ones anywhere near Clairmont.'

Eric's eyes narrow; he looks at Victoire, who understands the question in his eyes and translates for him. Eric says, in French, and Victoire translates: 'You know that for sure? And do you know of other Wehrmacht army units around the area?'

'Yes, of course. I've only a very low rank but I do know some of our positions in Alsace and Lorraine. The reason we were in the mountains was actually to map out the region in preparation for the Allied invasion, in case the war moved to the Vosges, like the last time. That was how we found you. We are the only ones, and our main camp is twenty kilometres away from here. We are scouting mostly north from here, towards Strasbourg and the Ardennes.'

'Then you should absolutely establish contact with the Free French Intelligence cell in Metz once you are there. They would love to have such information.'

Ralf nods. 'I'll do that. But how do I find them? Where do we go in Metz? Where will we stay?'

'I don't know. Madame Delauney will instruct you further. The less everyone knows of the route, the better. It is always one step at a time, and few names are exchanged. Keep it simple, as simple as can be. *D'accord?* You understand?'

Sommer nods. But then he scratches his head as if puzzling over a problem, and fidgets and coughs in open embarrassment, so Eric prompts: 'What is it, Ralf?'

'There is one big problem and I don't know how to solve it. I have no money, nothing at all. Not one *Pfennig.*'

Eric chuckles and replies in French, which Victoire translates into German for Ralf's benefit.

'Money is always a problem. But we have a fund for refugees. Margaux contributes to it and so do some of her more well-to-do friends. The whole escape route is funded by some rich American Jews.'

'I have some money with me,' says Rebecca, 'and since I am not going now I can give it to Ralf...'

'...and Maman will pay you back from the fund. Yes, that is good. But, you know, sooner or later money always runs out and then you just have to be creative. Sarah, you have money?'

She nods. 'Papa sold a violin just before we left and he gave me some *Reichmarks*. I just don't know if I can change them in France.'

Again, she speaks in French. Rebecca addresses her sharply.

'Stop being so childish. Our guest does not understand French. It is very rude to keep changing back to French.'

'But Eric does not speak German, so—'

Eric interrupts her. 'I understand it quite well,' he says. 'Rebecca is right, you should stick to German and if there is anything I don't understand, I will just ask. *D'accord?* It's very rude to discuss your common plans in French.'

Sarah blushes and stammers: 'I was just asking you about changing my *Reichmarks*. I didn't think he needed to know.'

His voice is gentler when he replies.

'Yes, you can change them – as long as you can prove you are from Alsace. Which you can.'

Rebecca turns to Ralf and translates for him. He nods.

'Thank you,' he says, 'and thank you for the offer of help with money. I don't want to be a burden on Sarah and I'm sorry—'

Now it is Rebecca who interrupts.

'There's nothing to be sorry for and Sarah has every reason to be grateful to you. Have you even thanked him yet, Sarah?'

She shakes her head, blushes and says, eyes lowered, in a very small voice, and in German, to Ralf, 'Thank you for doing what you did.'

'Any decent man would have done the same,' he says, looking directly at her. She hesitates, battling herself, then at last raises her head to meet his eyes. 'I just happened to have a gun, and I have a very good aim. It was nothing.' She nods, and looks away again.

Eric says, in broken German, 'It was a very big thing. And you helped me as well, probably saved my life. Without you I would have bled to death.'

It is Ralf's turn to blush. 'Well, you know, I wanted to be a doctor before this war started so it was just good practice.'

Victoire chuckles. 'You kill one man and save another man's life, all in one day! That's war, I suppose.'

During this exchange Sarah steals a glance at Ralf. He looks a bit ridiculous in his civilian clothes: the cuffs on his shirt leave a gap of several centimetres to his wrist, and between the tops of his boots and the hem of his trousers there is another gap. The spruce-smart soldier has given way to an uncomfortable-looking boy growing too fast for his mother to keep up. He looks younger, inexperienced, awkward. Less *German*.

It is hard to fear someone this gawky, she admits to herself, and can't help turning away to hide a giggle. He has kept his soldier's boots – there are no shoes in the cabin to replace them with. She, too, has no choice but to wear her old blood-splattered boots; she has now thoroughly scrubbed at Krämer's bloodstains and put the boots out to dry in the sun, but the stains will never go away. Hopefully she will, one day soon, have the opportunity to purchase new and uncontaminated footwear.

By now it has grown dark, and quite cool. Eric lights a fire in the pot-bellied cast-iron stove, and soon the flames flickering behind the glass lend a cosy glow. Victoire lights a few candles, which she places strategically around the room. She then reaches up to the top of the cupboard and produces a guitar case.

'We might as well celebrate our last evening together,' she says, handing the instrument to Eric. 'Let's have some music.'

Eric turns out to be a skilled guitarist and has a good repertoire of Alsatian folk songs, mostly in dialect. Victoire has the voice of an angel, Sarah thinks; though she herself also sings well, it is her sister Amélie who is the best singer back home. These songs remind her starkly of her family and tears gather in her eyes. She wipes them away fiercely.

Ralf, not knowing the Alsatian songs, has not joined in. Now, Eric turns to him. 'What about you? Can you sing something for us?'

Ralf hesitates, and then nods. 'But I can't play the guitar.'

'No matter. Just sing, I'll improvise.'

And he does. He sings in German, the rather sentimental but beautiful and now, Sarah thinks, very appropriate folk song 'Kein Schöner Land'. He sings in a pure, resonant tenor, a voice redolent with feeling and with longing. It gives her goose bumps.

Kein schöner Land in dieser Zeit,
als hier das unsre weit und breit,
wo wir uns finden
wohl unter Linden
zur Abendzeit, Abendzeit.
Da haben wir so manche Stund'
gesessen wohl in froher Rund'
und taten singen;
die Lieder klingen
im Eichengrund.
Daß wir uns hier in diesem Tal
noch treffen so viel hundertmal,
Gott mag es schenken,
Gott mag es lenken,
er hat die Gnad'.

Nun, Brüder, eine gute Nacht,
der Herr im hohen Himmel wacht!
In seiner Güten
uns zu behüten
ist er bedacht.

By the time it is over everyone is in tears, including Sarah; a sense of healing, of peace, spreads through her. It is the last song of the night; it cannot be topped.

'I think,' says Eric, 'it's time for bed. You should start early tomorrow.'

'As usual,' says Sarah.

Rebecca takes Ralf quietly aside and asks him to come outside with her: she has something she wants to say. It is a bright moonlit night and above the clearing the moon seems to be sailing across the sky as wispy clouds float past and cast a pale ghostly veil over the navy blue of the sky. The trees surrounding the clearing poke their spiky fingers upwards and seem to be whispering to each other in twinkling silence. Rebecca leads Ralf over to a log that serves as a bench. She gestures for him to take a seat and she does the same.

'I said earlier that I trust you not to take advantage of the situation,' she begins, 'take advantage of *her*. But I have had some more thoughts on the subject, and some fears. I need to talk to you. And you need to listen.'

'I'm listening.'

'But you must listen not only with your ears, for this is vital. You must absorb what I say with your whole being. It is important. You are two young people travelling together and it is very likely that you will develop – feelings – when you spend so much time together. Sarah is young and fearful and lonely. She is also inexperienced in the ways of men, and susceptible to false notions of romance, at an age when mothers must draw clear lines for their daughters – but she has no mother to do so. Thus, it is you who must draw the line and stick to it and you must have the maturity and the strength to uphold that line.'

Ralf smiles and raises a hand as if to stop her. 'I know what you are hinting at, but I think you worry in vain. She does not even like me very much, much less does she have romantic feelings for me.'

Rebecca snorts. 'It appears you have no experience of young girls. Do you have sisters?'

'Yes, one. She is ten. I have two brothers, one younger than me, one older.'

'Then you will learn something about growing girls from Sarah. She has deep emotions bottled up inside her and even she does not understand what is going on. The thing is, Sarah has been protected all her life, but especially so in the last few years. She is fused with her family, and has been cruelly ripped away. There's a gaping vacuum in her life; I felt it after just one night with her. She talked for hours, emptying her heart, trying to bond with me, reaching out to me. This is a girl who wears her heart on her sleeve. She *feels* more than she thinks, and is unable to suppress her feelings. She has always known love, great love, but now love is the one thing that is missing. Add to that the fact she's an adolescent whose only experience of the opposite sex is from totally unrealistic romantic stories – well, you can imagine. Or maybe you can't, being young yourself.

'The thing is, I know girls of her age. I was a secondary school teacher. Girls of that age – well, they are just one huge ball of emotion, seeking an outlet. I used to think that because a girl is young her love is unreal. It's not true, it's real enough. But it's a love untainted by hurt, disappointment, mistrust, fear – it's a love that is ready to give its all to the beloved, and it is huge. Ready to throw itself at the beloved, to be consumed by the beloved, possessed by the beloved; self itself disappears in that love.

'Such love is dangerous even at the best of times, in times of peace, because something so all-consuming opens itself up to all-consuming pain, for a happy ending is rare at that age. And after every hurt, a scar is left behind, until we can no longer love for the soul is just one big scar. That is the danger of young love at the best of times. But how much more so at the worst of times, a time like this! In wartime, when we are all in danger, when the future is not only uncertain, but fraught with fear and the danger of death. And how much more so, in Sarah's situation: a baby bird pushed out of the nest too soon, with no coping experience. She trusts everyone.'

'She doesn't trust me!'

'That's part of it. You're German and her only attitude is to see everything black and white, good and evil, and Germans are by definition evil, to be feared and mistrusted. Only French people are good and trustworthy. What use is such an attitude, with no differentiation, even in the best of times?

'Now, she's on the run, fragile already due to the separation from home and parents and siblings, having to hide, to watch her back – and having to put her entire trust in the hands of a young, good-looking, strong, manly companion. Don't you see? It is almost inevitable – you will be the victim of a tornado, a tornado of love! And I fear for her, and for you. You cannot handle it, if it is allowed to develop.

'So, I want you to promise me, Ralf: you will do nothing to encourage her. You will do everything you can to keep that emotion at bay. Sarah must learn to rein it in. She must learn to act rationally, to be guided not by emotion but by good judgement. And you are the only one who can keep her grounded. And you must. No matter what, Ralf, you must! No matter what the temptation, for you too will be hungry for love. Now tell me one thing – do you have a sweetheart at home, waiting for you?'

'No.'

'Well, that's a pity. It would have helped. Because I wonder if you are up to the task. A pretty, innocent young girl, looking up to you, placing her heart, her life, in your hands – it will be hard for you to resist, but resist you must. Everything else is far too dangerous to even contemplate. You cannot allow emotion to enter into this thing; your journey with Sarah must be one of necessity, of obligation, and you must be the strong one, the adult, the one to determine the quality of your relationship. You must be chivalrous and kind to her, but distant; you must hold her at arm's length. Do you understand?

'It will be hard enough, this route down to the South of France; letting emotion or, worse yet, passion, run wild – it would increase the danger a hundredfold. You must keep a clear mind at all times, unblurred by emotion. Do you understand? Can you do it? Because if you cannot, we will abort this plan immediately. Sarah will have to wait till I am fully recovered. Her sisters will have to wait for us to find a suitable escort. We would all prefer her to travel with you, but only if you can promise these things. Can you? Because it will be hard.

'War is a time when we must listen to our heads more than our hearts. You must not allow any feeling that takes possession of you to determine your decisions. You must be alert at all times, knowing you are responsible for this girl. You must think like a father for her. You must realise the seriousness of your situation otherwise you will jeopardise her safety and yours. Do you understand?'

Ralf nods. 'Every word.'

'The way she has behaved towards you – well, as an older woman I know what is going on. She will lurch this way and then that. What started as rejection will likely turn into its very opposite – this is the way of young girls. They are all feeling and lack the wisdom of older women who know that *they* are the ones who must control the appetites of men. Therefore, you must be the one to be in control. I am *in loco parentis* and I entrust her to you. It is a question of complete trust in you. Which is why I want you to give me your promise. I want you to take my hands and say those words in all sincerity.'

She holds out her hands and Ralf takes them in his.

'I promise. I will not betray your trust.'

Rebecca looks at him in silence for a minute, holding his gaze. His face is bathed in a silvery light and his dark eyes reflect clearly the almost-full moon swelling in the sky behind her. Through their joined hands she pours her strength and her wisdom and her trust into him, until at last she is satisfied. Finally, she says, 'Very well. Tomorrow, your adventure begins. It is time to sleep. Goodnight, Ralf.'

'Goodnight, Rebecca.'

'There may come a time when you will regret this promise to me, because you will find it ties you down. But it is all for the best.'

'I know.'

'One day this horrible war will be over and that is the time to follow your heart. Not now.'

Chapter Twenty

They leave before dawn, Sarah leading the way, almost leaping down the path as if to distance herself from Ralf. But he keeps up; he's right behind her, his long legs loping easily along as if the pace means nothing to him. She is soon out of breath and slows to a more leisurely walking pace. It's then that he speaks for the first time. Directly, to her.

'Sarah,' he says, firmly, loud enough for her to hear. 'Sarah! Stop for a moment. May I call you that, or would you prefer Fräulein Mayer?'

The last words carry a hint of mockery.

'You can call me Sarah,' she says, in French. Immediately she blushes, remembering Eric's rebuke. Yes, this insistence on speaking French to Ralf, her private little rebellion, is childish, but it is hard to swallow her pride and pretend the air is clear between them. Because it isn't, and they both know it.

But only he acts upon it. Now close behind her, he reaches out and grasps her upper arm.

'Sarah, stop for a moment.'

'Don't touch me!' she cries. He withdraws his hand as if bitten, and once again she quickens her pace. This time he does not keep up. He stands still and calls again:

'Sarah, stop, please stop! Just for a moment.'

She does not stop. He calls out: 'I'm sorry, I apologise. I beg your forgiveness.'

That makes her indeed stop. She turns around.

'Sorry? For what? As Rebecca made quite clear yesterday, you have done nothing wrong. What do you want forgiveness for? You are still German – the enemy.'

She speaks slowly, in French, holding his gaze. Does he understand? She repeats: 'For what?'

They face each other over a distance of some five metres. The path here is narrow, hardly wider than a single person's width. Above, the blue of the sky is little more than a sun-drenched splattering between the pine needles. The reality of her situation suddenly dawns on her: here she is, quite alone with this man, a German, virtually a stranger she's known less than twenty-four hours. He is bigger, stronger, faster than her. She hates Germans, and fears them. They are violent brutes. He could do anything to her, and she'd be helpless. She ought to be terrified.

And yet she isn't. The only emotion she feels at the moment is a strange constriction in her head, a sort of peeved pressure she cannot shake off, even though she wants to. She feels wronged but can't put her finger on exactly *why*. Even the excuse that he is German doesn't ring true. He isn't a thug. He proved it yesterday and her own innate sense of justice tells her she is being unfair. Yet her peevishness continues, a crowd of bees buzzing in her head, and she cannot shake it off.

'For being German,' he says simply. 'I heard what you said yesterday. I know you hate us all. But, you see, I can't help where I was born and I can't help my parentage so all I can do is apologise. It's not something I can change.'

He pauses. 'But I would change it if I could. I am deeply ashamed of what my countrymen have done, are doing, to this continent, to your people. If there is some way I can make it good again, I will. I just want you to accept my apology and… and for us, perhaps, to be friends. We are going to be stuck together for a while. We should be of assistance to each other and not proceed as enemies. It's not good to start a journey with bad feelings. Please, forgive me.'

They stand facing each other in silence. It is up to her, now, to make the next move. She has to accept his apology, forgive him for a sin he has not committed, is not guilty of; for he cannot change the circumstances of his birth any more than she can change hers.

German. Jew. Two babies born a year apart, and neither of them have chosen the label they will carry all their lives.

Rebecca's words from yesterday come back to her in full force. Yes, she is being outrageous, unfair, childish. Now is the time to shake off that silliness, and that fear. To grow up. She sighs, her shoulders slump as she admits defeat. The outraged bees stop their buzzing. A burden falls from her heart.

She walks back up the path towards him, holding out her hand.

'You are right, Ralf. I am being unfair to you. You have been only good to us. I thank you once again, this time sincerely. It is I who must apologise, I have been terribly rude.'

She speaks, at last, in German. He takes her hand, and shakes it.

'As I said, I hope we can be friends,' he says. 'I would like it.'

She hesitates as the last veil of her pride slowly dissolves and, finally, vanishes.

'So would I.'

From then on, the going is easier, both physically and mentally. She feels light of foot and buoyant of mind. There is no need to rush; even at a leisurely pace they will make Clairmont in good time and will arrive long before dusk. At midday they stop in a sunny clearing and sit on the grass to eat the last of the cheese and stale bread Victoire has given them as victuals, and they chat amiably for almost an hour. It is almost as if there is no war raging; a bubble of peace and harmony with no danger to them or their loved ones, no need to fear, no need to worry about the uncharted future. Just sit here, enjoying the moment, the blue of the sky and the green of the grass and the cool brush of a mountain breeze on their faces and the pleasant splash of a nearby brook.

'"The Pastorale",' says Sarah, lying back on the grass and closing her eyes to the sun.

'What do you mean?'

'Beethoven's Sixth Symphony, "The Pastorale". This is exactly *that*. No war, no Hitler, just nature: peace, harmony, the way it's meant to be. If it could only be this, always, everywhere.' She hums a few bars of the melody.

He nods. 'Unfortunately, it's not. It's just a pleasant bubble. I'm sorry to say that soon it's going to burst.'

'You've already burst it. Let's move on,' she says, leaping to her feet.

Chapter Twenty-One

They reach the outskirts of Clairmont in the late afternoon: farmland, meadows, cattle, buildings that all look the same.

'How will we find this farm?' puzzles Sarah. She is slightly anxious; they are now entering civilisation, if it can be called that, for it is a civilisation dominated and determined by the Nazi regime. The idyll is over; now they are truly fugitives, and anyone could be an informer. From now on it is a game of cat and mouse.

'Eric said a dilapidated barn next to the path.'

'I don't see anything like that. No barn, dilapidated or not, at least not next to the path.'

'That just means we haven't arrived yet. It's probably nearer to the town.'

Fifteen minutes later they cross a bridge over a stream and turn a corner through a small copse and there, to the left, is the barn, unmistakable with its collapsed stone walls, gaping windows and doors. What was once a roof is now mostly a moss-covered pile of broken tiles piled up against the broken exterior wall, as if they had simply slid away from the still-standing but obviously disintegrating wooden framework that tops the edifice.

Cows graze in the meadow it flanks, separated from the path by a wall of thick stone. A wooden stile offers entry into the meadow. There they stop.

'You go first,' says Ralf, and waits while Sarah climbs over into the meadow before he does the same. Most of the grazing cows look up at the intruders; some begin to meander in their direction.

'Talk about not attracting attention,' says Sarah wryly. 'Those cows are practically shouting to the world that we're here.'

'At least they aren't Swiss cows,' says Ralf, 'with huge jangling bells around their necks.'

'At least we didn't have to cross the Alps. The Vosges are foothills in comparison. I suppose we just have to cross the meadow in open view of everyone.'

'There isn't anyone. I don't see a single person.'

Indeed, the farm seems deserted. The cows have come to a stop and stand watching, inquisitive. No human is to be seen. As they grow close to the cluster of buildings that make up the farm proper a dog begins to bark, and then a second joins in. Both dogs leap out from behind the buildings and rush towards them, barking.

'Eric never warned us about dogs!' Sarah stops in her tracks. She has no experience with dogs, or indeed with any animals. Their father had once brought the girls a kitten, years ago, but it turned out that Sophie was allergic to cat hair. Nobody on their street owns a dog; there simply isn't space in the narrow houses.

But Ralf, it seems, is the opposite. 'Don't worry,' he says, noticing her trepidation. He crouches down, facing the dogs, and opens his arms as if to welcome them, and indeed, as they approach, they both stop barking, slow down and approach him with interest, sniffing; and then their tails begin to wag, and as he fondles their heads they grow excited, leaping and giving playful yaps.

'How did you do that? You practically tamed them!'

'They didn't need taming; they aren't wild, they're just doing their job. I showed them that our intentions were good. Go on, pat them; they'll like it.'

The dogs are now sniffing Sarah, wagging their tails, obviously begging for her attention too, so she pats their heads tentatively.

'Is this how burglars operate? Make friends with the guard dogs?'

Ralf chuckles. 'I think dogs have a sixth sense. They can smell out the bad ones.'

They walk on, the dogs leaping around them with tongues hanging out as if escorting them home, into a large cobbled courtyard surrounded on three sides by buildings. Hens scratch and peck in the gaps between the cobbles. The only other life to be seen is a collection of hutches with rabbits in them in front of what looks like a stable. The farmhouse is a large two-storey building backing onto the courtyard. And the back door stands open.

'You go first,' says Ralf. Sarah walks past him and up the three steps to the door. She peers into a dark hall, simultaneously knocking on the opened door and calling out:

'*Madame*? Madame Delauney?'

Silence follows, and she whispers to Ralf: 'I feel like an intruder.'

'You're not. Call again, louder.'

She does so. 'Madame Delauney! *Vous êtes là*?'

And then, at last, there comes a thumping of doors and a voice calling out from above: '*Attends! Je viens!*'

Then there are footsteps on wooden stairs, and at last, bustling down the hallway, a firmly stout woman with grey hair, fixed with a chequered headscarf but with a few strands falling out in front of her ears.

'*Bonjour!*' she says as she approaches, frowning slightly, suspiciously. 'What do you want?'

'*Bonjour, madame*,' says Sarah. '*Avez vous des pruneaux conservées?*'

Immediately comes the reply: '*Non, mais j'ai un bon liqueur des pruneaux. Voulez-vous un peu?*' Immediately followed by a gush of swift French. 'Welcome, welcome! You must be Sarah – but I thought there were two women? Who is this you have brought along?'

She shakes Sarah's outstretched hand vigorously, then ushers them both into the dark hallway, opens a door and gestures for them to enter. They find themselves in a large farmhouse kitchen.

'*Madame*, there has been a change of plan. Rebecca could not come. This is Ralf…' Here, Ralf stretches out his hand and, with an almost imperceptible hesitation, she shakes it. '…he is German.' *Madame* gives a slight gasp but Sarah rushes to explain and pacify her.

'He too is a fugitive and is in grave trouble as he has deserted the Wehrmacht and if they catch him, they will execute him. I can vouch for him. He has proven himself worthy again and again. You know, some Germans are quite good!'

She and Ralf exchange a smile and a twinkling of eyes as she speaks the last words, and Madame Delauney seems to latch onto the spirit of mutual trust they share, and relaxes visibly.

'*Bon*. But you must be very hungry after traversing the mountains like that – you must have some of my stew; it's only rabbit, but it's good!'

'It smells delicious!'

'Then sit down – there, at the table. Or would you like to use the bathroom first, freshen up? It's in the hallway – turn right, the door on the left after the stairs. Run along now, and I will serve the stew.'

It is, Sarah feels, just like coming home. Once again.

Chapter Twenty-Two

After dinner Madame Delauney shows them to their room in the barn – a proper barn, intact, opposite the stable, now a cowshed where the cows are milked. 'I can't put you up in the house,' she apologises, 'though I have rooms to spare. We have been searched once or twice and they always start with the house, they just barge in. But I can warn you in the barn.'

She shows them an unobtrusive cord in the hallway, and tells them it is attached to a bell in the barn. 'If it rings, you must escape immediately. Through the field you came through, and towards the forest. That is the safest route.'

She leads them to the barn and gives them blankets to spread on the bales of hay which are their beds, and to cover with. 'Times are hard,' she says.

'We're grateful – don't apologise. We know the risk you are taking.'

'And you know why. I hate the Boche.' She gives Ralf a severe look at those words and he squirms visibly. Though she speaks French, her meaning is clear and she emphasises the word *Boche*.

Madame Delauney told them her story during supper. Her husband had died before the war; her two sons, barely in their twenties, had fought for France at the start of the war just after the invasion; both had been killed. Her daughter was married, and lived in the South of France; her husband had joined the Resistance and was doing some kind of dangerous work in Paris. It was her duty to somehow avenge her sons.

'It is very hard, here,' she says. 'The Boche have taken half of my cattle and most of the chickens and rabbits and all of my goats.

They took my entire potato crop, leaving only a sack or two for me. I get my revenge by helping the very people they hate the most. Most of the farmers around here are like that. They all hate the Boche and are friendly to the Resistance. But one must be careful, a few are traitors.'

She talks and talks as if to relieve herself of a burden, Sarah translating everything for Ralf, and then she stops abruptly, saying it is time for bed.

'Tomorrow, we will discuss your further journey,' she says. 'But for now, rest and gather your strength. It will not be easy. The dangerous part has just begun.'

Up in the loft of the barn she helps them to rearrange the bales of hay to make beds that do not look like beds, in case the Boche come and they have to flee; they cover them with the blankets provided.

'If you do flee, just hang the blankets over the railing. That won't look suspicious,' she says. '*Bonne nuit*. Sleep well.'

And then she is gone, and they are alone. A dim light burns in a single dusty bulb above their heads, and in the half-dark, Sarah and Ralf sit across from each other on their bales. Neither is particularly tired; it is early yet, just past eight.

'Well,' says Sarah, 'that's one day finished. Many more to go.'

'As *Madame* said, it's just the beginning and it will get dangerous.'

'You understood her?'

Even in the dimness she can see his blush.

'I understood the word "*dangereux*,"' he admits. 'And… I have a confession to make. I studied French at school. Four years.'

'Really! Then how come you don't understand it? Or were you just pretending the whole time, making fools of us all?'

'Bad teachers,' he replies. 'It was all theory, all written work, grammar rules and so on. They were all German teachers who couldn't speak it properly so we had hardly any oral French. So when you all speak it, and with your Alsatian dialect…' He shrugs. 'As they say in German: *ich verstehe nur noch Bahnhof*.'

She frowns. 'You only understand train station? I don't get it.'

He chuckles. 'A German idiom. It's when someone speaks a foreign language and only understands a single word. In this case, *Bahnhof*. So sometimes I understand *Boche* and sometimes I understand *dangereux*, but that's about it. I guess the rest.'

'Well,' says Sarah, 'it's about time you learned spoken French. And I will teach you. You will know more than *Boche* and *dangereux* in future.'

'I look forward to your lessons.'

'*Bonne nuit*, Ralf.'

'*Bonne nuit*, Sarah.'

She awakes to the crowing of a cock. Rubbing her eyes, she sits up, stretches and yawns, then begins to pull bits of hay from her hair and clothes. It is everywhere; the sheet with which she covered her bale has loosened during the night. She stands up and walks to the opening of the hayloft. The farm is coming to life. Somewhere a cow moos, and chickens are once again scratching in the cobbled yard. Madame Delauney emerges from the barn carrying two buckets, the two dogs at her heels. A restful, tranquil scene, repeated in farmyards all over the world; at every minute, every second, there are farms waking up for a new day of feeding animals and tending growing things to feed people. This is what sustains the world. It is hard to believe there are madmen more intent on destruction than on sustenance.

She walks back and looks down on the still-sleeping Ralf, and smiles to herself. He lies on his back. In repose, his face is almost angelic around the closed eyes, but the dark stubble around his jaw has grown again, lending him a rustic appearance well in keeping with the bales of hay piled behind him. His hair, dark against the dull yellow of the hay, is dishevelled and full of hay. He looks like a farm boy, not a runaway soldier. She bends down and touches his cheek.

'Ralf, wake up!'

Immediately he springs to attention, sitting straight up, on full alert, his hand groping as if searching for something. *A gun?*

'It's only me,' she says, and he relaxes visibly.

'It is quite simple,' Madame Delauney says to Ralf after breakfast. There had been eggs and cheese and bread, and ersatz coffee with milk and no sugar; they had eaten ravenously. She glances at Sarah to translate. 'You cannot travel by train without papers. Well, you can, but it is practically a death sentence.'

Sarah's eyes open wide.

'So then, what should he do?'

'He must walk the distance to Metz. *Pas de problem*, it is possible and has been done before. There is a way. But it will of course take much longer. So…' She looks from one to the other, 'you will take the train, Sarah, and Ralf will walk. I would not even recommend a bicycle, which I could lend you, because it would mean taking the roads and that is where you will meet the *Polizei*.'

'So, it is *Polizei*, and not *gendarmes*?'

'Yes – like Alsace, they are trying to Germanise us. Of course we are not having it, but it means they are trying to take over our language as well as our country. It is disgraceful, but never mind. Now let me go and find the other map, which will show the hiking routes.'

She walks away from the kitchen table, where a map of Lorraine is spread out. Over it, Sarah and Ralf look at each other.

'I don't want to go on alone!' says Sarah.

'I don't want you to go alone either – I promised Rebecca I'd look after you.'

'No, no, that's not it! I don't need you to look after me. It's you I don't want to abandon; it seems cowardly for me to take the easy way by train. We are in this together.'

'*Are* we?'

'You know we are.'

He chuckles. 'You have changed your views very quickly. Yesterday, you said the opposite, if I recall correctly.'

Sarah blushes and looks away.

'Don't remind me of that silliness! We should be supporting each other now, all the way. If it is dangerous for you by train, it is also dangerous by foot. I will go with you.'

'And what good will that do? If they arrest me for not having papers, they will also take you in for questioning.'

She shrugs. 'My papers are in order. I am a German girl from Alsace on her way to relatives in Metz.'

'But why would a German girl be travelling with a German boy who does not have identity papers and does not speak a word of French? They will know I am a deserter, Sarah. One telephone call to Colmar to check your identity would expose you and your family. No, you must take the train and I'll meet you in Metz. Wait for me there.'

Sarah has a spirited retort on her lips but before it can escape, Madame Delauney returns and spreads a different map out on top of the Lorraine one. It is a faded and tattered map, somewhat torn along its folds, and obviously has been put to much use.

'I will lend you this,' she says. 'Please make sure you leave it in Metz so it can be returned to me – it is the only one I have. Look, see these little red crosses? They indicate places where you can spend the night. It will take three days and three nights, if you walk briskly and nothing deters you.'

Sarah translates simultaneously – she is getting good at this skill.

'During the day you will walk across fields and along footpaths inaccessible to cars. The farmers who own these lands are all complicit in the arrangement but do not want to be directly involved so you should avoid speaking to anyone. They will just wave you on but that is good since you do not speak French. They will not be happy hearing you speak German.'

'What will we eat?' asks Sarah.

'Why do you say "we"? *You* are taking the train, *Mademoiselle*!'

She says the word *mademoiselle* in that brisk, authoritative, no-nonsense tone that adults use with insubordinate children. Sarah feels that familiar rise of hot mutiny – a melange of pride and determination. Her voice is shrill with rebellion.

'I'm going with him on foot, Madame Delauney. I've decided it, my mind is made up!'

'It's not for you to decide – you are just a girl with no experience at all. This is a war and you are not capable of making informed decisions. It is for me to decide. If everyone who came through my doors would tell me how to organise their further travels I would quickly shut my doors. You do not understand. This is not a joke and it's not a party. I forbid you to go on foot.'

Sarah does not translate this speech; it is too embarrassing, diminishing. Her inner rebellion falters, stumbles, protests:

'But… I…'

Madame Delauney has lost all her affability. Her eyes blaze.

'I don't care who you are and what your relationship is to this boy and if you want to go with him just so you can sleep with him at night! I don't care about all that. I don't care about what you want, I care about your safety and the safety of everyone else in this network whom you would be endangering. You must keep to the plan, my plan. There is nothing brave or noble about going with him on the long walk, it is just being a spoilt child. I don't care what you want. You are going by train and that is that! *Compris*?'

There is nothing to do but bow her head in acquiescence. 'Yes, I understand.'

'*Bon*. Anyway, to return to your question: I will pack some provisions for him, which will last the three days. Nothing much. There will be streams and rivers along the way for water. And…' She looks Ralf up and down. 'He will need other clothes. We will look in the cupboards; my Henri's things would fit him – they are about the same size.'

At those words Sarah's bad mood vanishes. She translates quickly for Ralf and says, 'Oh, yes, Ralf, do that! Those clothes you are wearing, they are not flattering at all!'

He pulls at the cuffs of his shirt, but when he replies his voice too is sharp and his words critical.

'We're not going to a fashion show, Sarah. Really, it doesn't matter. I'm grateful for the clothes I'm wearing and the only reason to change them is not for aesthetics but to avoid being conspicuous.' He looks at Madame Delauney, smiles and says, very slowly, in badly accented French:

'*Merci, Madame. Je suis très content avec les vêtements de votre fils.*'

'Oh, but you can speak French! How wonderful! Very good, very good! Now come upstairs with me and we will find Henri's things.'

She ushers him out of the kitchen. In the hallway she grabs his hand and pulls him up the stairs, chattering in full-speed French the whole time. Sarah follows, quietly, completely mortified. Ralf's French, it seems, is far better than she had assumed, or else has improved drastically from one day to the next.

Chapter Twenty-Three

'So, your train ticket…' Madame Delauney presses it into Sarah's hand. 'And stop looking so hangdog. He will join you in a few days.'

'He's not the reason—' she begins but Madame Delauney is already shaking her hand.

'*Au revoir*!' she says. 'And may you reach the end of your journey safely.'

'Thank you so m—' But Madame Delauney is gone, walking through the exit doors of the Clairmont station. Sarah is on her own, for the very first time in her life, and it is, admittedly, frightening.

Earlier that day they had sent Ralf on his way and it had taken all of Sarah's strength not to fling her arms around him and beg him not to go; to take her with him, or to come with her. But she knows by now that implorations are useless; nobody over the age of twenty takes her seriously. Ever. Her changing moods and fears and flights of fancy, apparently, are liabilities during wartime. This war is forcing her to grow up quickly. She is on her own, now: the next challenge.

The first control comes after only half an hour. A pair of *gendarmes* make their way down the carriage, examining tickets and ID cards and ration cards, asking questions, listening to answers. She watches them surreptitiously, feels her heart speed up the nearer they come, her breath shortening. She checks her papers a thousand times. She wishes she'd brought a book to read, some knitting, anything to distract her, to keep her from glancing up as the officers come ever nearer. Surely they will notice her nervousness, surely it will make them suspicious?

And then they are there, standing before her, demanding her papers, staring at her (suspiciously?), asking her questions – where is she going? Where has she come from? She answers them all correctly, as instructed by Madame Delauney, and though she is sure her voice is trembling, they do not seem to notice. They nod and move on. Sarah breathes again, puts away her papers.

There are two more controls; she passes both without incident, her confidence growing each time they politely thank her and move on. This is easy! Why has everyone made such a fuss? Wartime or not, her papers are in order and everyone has surely exaggerated the danger.

Yes, papers are everything. In wartime a person's life can depend on having the right papers. A human being reduced to a piece of paper.

This is the adult world she is supposed to join.

She misses Ralf. Dreadfully.

Arriving at Metz, she leaves the station and removes the scrap of paper with the address from her skirt pocket. Madame Delauney gave it to her this morning just before she left. 'Just ask directions,' she'd said. 'It's about twenty minutes to walk, not difficult to find.'

Slinging her canvas bag over her shoulder, she looks around for someone to ask – there. A taxi driver, looking her way.

'Rue Chevalier?' she says. 'How do I walk there?'

The taxi driver launches into a detailed description: left turn, right turn at the florist, right again at the statue, and so on. She nods as if she is following, but in the end simply walks the way he indicated; she'll ask again along the way.

Twenty minutes later, she arrives at the door of 62, rue Chevalier. It is painted a cracked and peeling blue; next to it an unlabelled doorbell invites her to press it. She does so and waits.

Finally, the door opens a crack. A male face, bearded, frowning, peers at her through the crack.

'Good day,' says Sarah. She has mentally rehearsed her new password and it comes easily from her lips: 'The wedding is to be held in two weeks' time.'

The reply is swift:

'The wedding has been cancelled, the bride has Spanish flu.'

The door opens wide and Sarah enters. The man eyes her up and down briefly. 'It is just you? We were told to expect two women. Where is the other?'

'She could not come. There has been a change of plan. I will explain to you, if you would let me—'

'Yes. Come along.' Brusquely, he turns on his heel and leads her along an unlit passage through to the back of the house. They pass a staircase leading up into dark upper rooms, and one leading down into even more darkness. He opens a door and she finds herself in a kitchen: a kitchen worlds away from the cosy homeliness of Madame Delauney's or the motherly warmth of Margaux's. This one is stark, utilitarian, and could be called sterile if it were not so very messy. There is a wooden table in its centre, on which stands a once-white coffee pot, its cracks blackened with dirt, and several mismatched and similarly cracked cups, some with saucers, some without. Between the cups lie crumbs and the endpiece of a loaf of bread and a breadknife. A sink at the back of the room is filled with similar cups. A pile of plates with dried-on food remains sits on the countertop beside the sink. The tap drips. An open pot with what looks like the remnants of cold boiled cabbage sits on the gas cooker, a dirty wooden ladle beside it.

Sitting around the table are four people. They are all, in her eyes, old; all surely over thirty. The only woman might even be nearing, or past, forty. They scowl at her, glaring through a fug of smoke. A single cigarette, from which white smoke curls, passes from one to the other.

'She came alone,' says the man who led her in. 'She says she can explain.'

'Well, then, explain! We prefer to be informed in advance if plans change,' says the woman. No smiles of welcome, nobody introduces themselves. They are a nameless crowd, staring at her as if she were an intruder, irritation in their eyes. No invitation to join them.

Sarah sets down her bag on the floor next to her; she wonders if she should sit down on the one vacant chair or remain standing to answer their questions, inquisition-style.

'How old are you, anyway?' says one of the men. They all have beards; she can hardly tell them apart. Their hair is, without exception, long, unkempt, in one case even matted. *This* is the Metz Resistance?

'May I sit down?' she asks, and without waiting for an answer sits herself on the vacant chair. 'I am seventeen,' she says. 'My companion was to be an older woman but she sprained her ankle while crossing the mountains and had to remain in Alsace.'

'We cannot be responsible for children,' says one of the beards. Now she looks at him properly. He actually looks quite young himself: no older, surely, than twenty-five? His is the longest beard; it is quite bushy. Some breadcrumbs are caught in it. Sarah feels like reaching out and picking out the crumbs, the way she picked hay from Ralf's hair earlier that day, both of them giggling at their mutual unkemptness. Hay had been everywhere; the finer, smaller stalks almost impossible to remove. But now, no one is giggling. She feels like a criminal, under investigation, instead of a fugitive in need of assistance.

'You are really Jewish? You don't look it.'

'What is a Jew supposed to look like? Yes, my hair is not dark and my skin is fair and my eyes are blue, but I am indeed Jewish. I take after my mother, who is quite fair. Many Jews are fair.'

'Maybe so, but we have to be careful.'

'May I at least learn your names?'

'Names are dangerous in this business,' says the woman. 'If we do tell you names, they are only code names in case you are caught and they interrogate you. In that case the less you know, the better. It is for your own safety.'

'And ours,' adds one of the men.

Very well, thinks Sarah, they can continue as nameless *beards*.

'So, you can call me Alpha,' says the woman. She points to the oldest beard. 'And he is Beta. That is all you need to know for the time being.'

Alpha and the beards have much more to say; they speak swiftly and carelessly, interrupting each other, a deluge of information and rebukes sweeping over Sarah.

'We have instructions for you. You must visit some people in Metz – they asked us to help. That's why we are putting you up, but you must understand: we have no time to babysit you. You must fend for yourself – we will provide a bed and food, but that's it. We are *Gaullistes*. We are doing important work for the Free French. Important and dangerous work. We cannot be looking after you as well.'

'Much as we abhor what Hitler is doing to the Jews, it is not our job to facilitate their escape. Other people are doing that. We are here only in a capacity of assistance. It is all we can do.'

'In fact, we are putting ourselves in ever more danger by harbouring Jews. If we are found out, well…'

'So, you must keep your head down and stay out of sight. You must not leave this building. Someone will come to discuss your further movements tonight. It is now complicated as they will probably have to find another escort for you as they have compunctions about young girls travelling alone.'

'There is indeed a certain danger. The Boche tend to behave in a peculiar way around women and someone as young as her would not know how to fend them off.'

'It's going to be a problem – they will probably expect us to keep her for even longer while they find a suitable chaperone.'

'What were they thinking, the cell in Alsace, to send her on her way alone? They should have kept her longer until that woman with the sprained ankle is capable of travel.'

'Ridiculous decision, to send her – do they think we are a childminding facility here?'

'Actually—' Sarah begins and then stops. Quite gradually the group has moved from talking *to* her to talking *about* her, as if she doesn't exist, as if she is just a problem to be dealt with, a burden to be carried. With this stand-offish welcome, how can she even begin to tell them about Ralf? If she is a burden and a problem, an endangerment to them, how much more will they object to Ralf, a defector from the Wehrmacht with no identity papers? Better not to tell them. Better to do as Papa always said: *keep your head down*. When Ralf turns up, it will be time enough to tell them. Or perhaps those other people, whoever they are, will be more understanding of their plight? Madame Delauney had said they would help him get papers, but certainly not *these* people.

'Actually, what?'

'Nothing. I was just thinking – why can't I stay with those other people, the ones who will come to help? I don't want to be a burden…'

'It can't be helped. You cannot stay there, that's just the way it is.'

'The fewer questions asked, the better. You will find out as you go along that in this situation it is better to know nothing, to just do as you are told.'

They all seem to talk at once, interrupting each other, talking over each other, discussing her; impatient, unwelcoming.

'I will send a message to let them know you have arrived – they will probably send a contact around later today.'

'I will show you to your quarters. You have a room down in the cellar. Come with me.'

One of the beards gets up and signals to her to follow. She gets up; at the door she turns to look from one of the remaining beards to the other and to Alpha, but nobody returns her little wave of goodbye. They haven't even offered her coffee – cold ersatz coffee, yes, but still, isn't it normal to offer new guests whatever one has? Isn't that just normal hospitality? But these, she realises, are not normal people. They are outcasts, living on the fringe, like her; she is not a guest but an encumbrance, even a liability, and nobody is interested in her feelings. The rules of normal society do not apply. Already they are discussing something else, something apparently too secret for her to hear. They do not even look at her as she leaves.

The beard leads her down the cellar steps, into the darkness. He flicks a switch at the bottom and a dusty naked bulb gives out a dubious half-light. They cross the cellar to one of two doors in the rear wall; he opens it and signals for her to enter. She finds herself in a tiny box room with a bunk along one side, a table and a chair. A small window, its width greater than its height, near the ceiling lets in some daylight, but still the room is filled with a dreary dimness and smells of mould. A dark patch on the ceiling confirms the latter.

'There is a toilet outside the door on the left. There will be a little food later this evening and then some breakfast in the morning. If you want books to pass the time you will find some in the sitting room upstairs. Make yourself at home,' says the beard, and those are the friendliest words spoken since she entered the house. He walks out, leaving her alone in the dimness, in the mould.

The cellar at Margaux's home was also dark and had its own distinctive smell – of fermentation, and old wine, musty, and slightly nauseating, but at least she had known there were people upstairs who cared, a warm kitchen, friends. Here, she is without friends or anyone who gives a damn. Hurt feelings bombard her – she feels cast aside, an unwelcome drain on the group's resources.

Nobody here cares, she thinks, but immediately pulls herself together. *Why should they? Stop being a baby. Stop wallowing in self-pity. Stop it at once!*

Yes, it is true what they had said: she is a child, and since leaving home that is how she's been treated, and she has, mostly, relished it. First, Margaux, then Rebecca, even Madame Delauney, have mothered her; even when Rebecca scolded her, it was with the tough love of a mother correcting a beloved child for its own good. Even the men: Jacques, Eric and Ralf all deferred to her, protected her, wrapped her in cotton wool. She has been pampered, and has learned to enjoy it, to take it for granted. Coming here is a plunge into cold water.

This, she realises now, is the stark reality of war. If you cannot help then at least keep your head down and your mouth shut. Nobody cares about your feelings; your hurt is immaterial, and it is best to rise above it. People are being hurt, out there, in far more serious ways. *Grow up, Sarah!* she scolds herself.

It is time to become an adult.

Chapter Twenty-Four

That night, though, huddled in the bottom bunk, covered in a scratchy blanket, Sarah weeps into the hard horsehair lump that serves as a pillow. She misses them all so much. Most of all, her family – what has become of them all, what will become of them all? Hopefully, Amélie and Thérèse will soon be able to leave, and Rebecca will be waiting for them at Margaux's. Then Papa and Mama, with Manon and Sofie. That is the part that worries her the most – four of them together, and Sofie only five! How will she make it over the Vosges? Will they, too, come to these inhospitable resisters? Where will they sleep, the four of them? When will they all be together again, all seven?

She misses the fine people of Alsace, the friends she has found and lost in such quick succession: Jacques, Victoire, Eric, Margaux, Rebecca.

She misses Ralf most of all, misses him desperately. Her companion on this odyssey into the void, the one fixed point on her journey. He has become an essential: without him at her side she feels empty, lonely. He is the staff of the wayfarer she has become.

Wait a minute. No, that cannot be. The word *staff* evokes a memory, and the memory evokes something else: words. And the words evoke a feeling: *Thy rod and thy staff to comfort me...*

She repeats them, again and again. *For thou art with me...* Again and again and again. The words themselves become rods and staffs; together they become an anchor, bringing peace. The gaping hole in her being is filled with a sense of restfulness; the stormy sea of thoughts in retreat. She holds onto her anchor. Holds it fast. And indeed, they bring comfort. She sinks into that comfort.

She sleeps, comforted.

*

She wakes to a loud knocking on her door. Someone calls her name. She sits up straight in bed, heart pounding violently, the fear that has etched itself into her being rising like hot lava from its hidden depths.

It is the enemy… *gendarmes* – Gestapo! They have come for her – but no, it cannot be. They would not call her name – would they even knock? – and they would not sound so… so actually friendly. None of the beards, and certainly not Alpha, would use that tone of voice, those words:

'Sar-ah! Can I come in? Are you awake?'

'Yes, yes – come in! I'm awake!' she calls back, and the door opens and a woman comes in, a woman maybe in her thirties, with a smiling face. A woman who, unlike the others in this house, does not transmit to her the knowledge that she is unwanted.

'*Bonjour! Je suis Mathilde*,' says the woman, approaching the bunk on whose edge Sarah now sits. 'Sorry to wake you. You slept well?'

'Yes, yes, I did – what's the time?'

'It's six in the morning. I thought I'd come before the town wakes up properly. There are a lot of things we have to talk about. First of all, I'd like to say welcome to Metz. I am a member of a group that works together for the safe passage of Jews throughout France. We call ourselves the Jewish-European Network, JEN. As the name implies, we are a network of people concerned about Jews escaping Germany and France and we have organised homes along the route to freedom where people like you can stay, where you will be welcomed and given room and board on your way down south. I have been told the lady who was supposed to come with you had a little accident?'

'Yes – she sprained her ankle coming over the Vosges and could not walk. At least, we think it was only sprained and not broken. So…'

'So, you came alone. That is not good, Sarah – you should have waited. It is not our policy to send young girls like you alone on this journey, especially attractive girls. The Boche can be quite pushy, and—'

But Sarah is holding up her hand, saying *stop*, and now interrupts.

'Please, I am not alone. There is someone coming with me but he does not have papers, so he is walking from Clairmont. I wanted to tell the people upstairs, but I thought it would anger them, so...'

'A man? Who is he? Another Jew from Alsace, I suppose?'

'No. Actually...' and here she hesitates. 'Actually, he is German.'

Mathilde's jaw drops in shock and she gasps, but before she can say anything Sarah launches into the story of how Ralf had rescued her from rape, how he had carried Eric through the forest, how he had defected from the Wehrmacht, so putting himself in enormous peril.

'So, that is how it is. He is now my escort. I will wait for him and we will move on together. But he does not have any papers. We were told he can get forged papers here in Metz.'

'Yes, that is true. We will arrange it. But, Sarah, travelling with a German, even a defector – it could be problematic. There are spies everywhere. People who seem friendly are sometimes the opposite. Are you sure he is to be trusted?'

She nods vigorously. 'Yes, I can vouch for him. I also did not trust him at first but... well, you will see when you meet him. He is one of the good ones.'

'Well, since he is on his way we just have to take your word for it. I suppose it is a solution – it would not have been easy finding an escort for you. But still...' She shakes her head. 'Travelling with a young man, of any nationality, during wartime – it is risky. Young men are supposed to be in the army, fighting stupid wars, dying needlessly. It is the way of the world, the way of men – they like to fight. So, we must take extra precautions to protect you, and him. But we will discuss that further, later. I will bring someone else to talk once he is here. And now, what about some breakfast?'

She lowers her voice. 'Don't tell the people upstairs – they are an intense lot, aren't they, wrapped up in their work? – I doubt they have thought to feed you properly. I have brought you some bread, and some cheese – eat it down here and then you can go up for that stuff they call coffee.'

She pulls a brown paper bag from out of her bag and hands it to Sarah. Sarah peers inside the bag; the delicious scent of freshly baked bread wafts into her nostrils. She did not eat last night – she was not invited and did not care to invite herself – and now, at the word 'breakfast', at the delicious scent emanating from the bag, she hears, feels, the growling of her stomach. Yet still she hesitates.

'Yes,' says Mathilde, 'it is all for you – you need not look at me like that. Tuck in!'

'Actually, what I need most of all now is… the toilet!'

She already used it twice yesterday: a long, extremely narrow room, the toilet at the far end; dark, windowless. The toilet itself is old and cracked and seatless, an emergency facility. A small pile of newspaper squares on the worn-out tiled floor serves as toilet paper. The bottom of the bowl is crusted brown, the water, too, a rusty brown. When she's finished she pulls the chain and more brown water swirls into the bowl. She returns to Mathilde.

'I was wondering why I have to stay here, stay in a safe house at all,' she says. 'Why can't I just stay in a hotel? My papers are in order, nobody will know I'm Jewish. Papa never registered us as Jewish in Colmar.'

'We have to be careful,' says Mathilde. 'Anyone on the road is suspicious. You as a young girl, travelling on your own, you are prey for German soldiers. It is fortunate that your papers don't have that incriminating stamp "*Jude*", but that doesn't mean we should throw caution to the wind. A slight suspicion, a phone call to check your identity, and *voilà*, it's all over, for you and your family. You must wait here for Ralf. Now stop talking and start eating. My father is a baker – it is all quite fresh, for once! And there is butter, from my uncle's farm.'

Sarah sighs with delight, removes the bread from the bag and bites into its sweet softness.

'Heaven!'

'Just eat, don't speak,' says Mathilde.

When she has finished eating Sarah wipes her mouth with the back of her hand.

'Pure heaven!' she says again. 'Thank you. Now I suppose I'd better go upstairs. I would so much like a bath, but I'm afraid to even ask for such a thing. They are so hostile.'

'Really? Hostile? I think you're wrong. They are a little distant but certainly not hostile.'

'They made it very clear to me that I'm not wanted here. That I'm just a burden, a silly child they had to put up with.'

'Oh, Sarah! Don't take it personally. They are *maquisards*; their primary purpose is to disrupt the Germans, not help Jews. They risk their lives every day for the freedom of France. I expect they thought you'd interrupt their important work, being a minor, and it annoyed them. Please don't be offended, that's so childish. Their bark is worse than their bite.'

'I just didn't feel welcome. They didn't even let me explain about Ralf, they just dismissed me as useless.'

Her voice is peevish. Mathilde shakes her head. When she speaks again her voice is stern and has lost its initial warmth.

'Now you really are being a silly child! You must get it out of your head that people must welcome you wherever you go. You are one of the lucky ones. There are Jews in Germany and Poland and even here in France who are being persecuted just for the fact of being Jewish. So, you did not get the warm welcome you expect. Well, what of it? You have left your family and have to be a woman now, not a girl to be mollycoddled. These people are doing wonderful work to put an end to this terrible war. They don't have time to hug you and you probably did distract them, appearing like this without an escort. Instead of sulking like a petulant child, why not think of ways to prove them wrong?'

Mathilde's words feel like a slap, but it is a good slap as it chases away the peevishness nagging at her since the cold reception last night. It reminds her of Maman and the life lessons she has drummed into her: *never let circumstances defeat you!* Maman always said. *Rise above them. Whatever situation you find yourself in, discover what you can do to improve it, even if it is only to change your attitude. Attitude is everything.*

'I suppose you are right, I am lucky.'

'Now, let's go upstairs together. You will behave like an adult, ask for the bathroom, get dressed for the day, and then you will ask what you can do to help. *D'accord?*'

'*D'accord.*'

The bathroom upstairs consists of a small room next to the kitchen containing a toilet, a sink and a bathtub on little curved legs whose cracked enamel is a veined spider's web. A brown smudge around the interior hints that it has not been cleaned recently. The faded linoleum on the floor is also cracked, peeling away in hard leathery slices. Dust gathers in the corners of the floor. Spiders' webs form thick black nets on the ceiling. *Maman would have a fit*, Sarah thinks. *Even if you are poor, you can be clean.*

Mathilde is waiting for her in the kitchen, chatting with one of the beards. They look up as she enters; the beard deigns to wish her good morning and ask if she slept well.

'Thank you, yes.'

'Sarah was telling me that she'd like to help out in any way she can,' says Mathilde. 'Isn't that right, Sarah?'

She nods. 'Yes. I thought I'd start out by washing the dirty dishes. And maybe help clean the house? I suppose you haven't time for all that?'

The beard's eyes light up.

'Really? You would do that? We are a bit of a lazy bunch—'

'—when it comes to domestic duties,' Mathilde breaks in. 'What does one expect? Sarah will sort you out, *n'est-ce pas?*'

'Yes. I can't just sit around all day, waiting for—' She stops abruptly and looks at Mathilde, who nods and raises a calming hand.

'It's all right. I have told him that your German defector friend is coming.'

'It will not be a problem per se,' says the beard. 'We have had such people join us before. And if he is a soldier, he can even help in many ways.'

Sarah walks over to the sink, removes the dirty crockery piled up in it, puts in the plug and turns the tap. Water runs out: cold brown water. She fills the kettle and steps over to the gas stove, inspects the dials, looks for matches. While doing so she explains: 'Back in Alsace we were discussing it. He has information about the locations of German army units and some of their plans – he is willing to share that with you.'

'Fantastic!' says the beard, standing up. He turns one of the dials on the stove; the gas begins to hiss. He puts a lit match to it and with a whoosh a ring of fire leaps into being. Sarah glances at him and smiles her thanks. She places the kettle on it. The beard says: 'We will introduce him to the Free French cell in Metz. But… you are sure he is trustworthy?'

'Absolutely. I saw with my own eyes how he shot his commanding officer. The brute was trying to rape me and Ralf didn't hesitate, he shot to kill. That alone is proof that he himself is in big trouble. He was forced to flee. If the Boche catch him, they will execute him.'

While she is speaking Alpha and Beta enter the kitchen, she in a threadbare nightgown, he in his underwear. Their faces shine, slimy with sleep. Alpha yawns.

'Good morning. But this place is a hive of activity this morning! Hello, Mathilde! And hello – what is your name again?'

'Sarah. Good morning, Alpha.' She holds up a glass jar with what looks like a piece of slimy soap nestling in even slimier water at the bottom. She pours some of the slime into the washing-up water and turns off the tap. Now she only has to wait for the hot water.

'My word, don't tell me you are washing the dishes! That would be a miracle! Nobody here does any work – they all expect me to do it because I am a woman, forgetting that I am the eldest and must be served by my minions!'

She laughs; the first time Sarah has seen any sign of mirth on her face. It changes everything. She smiles too.

'I'm happy to do it, Alpha.'

Alpha slaps the air. 'Oh, stop with that Alpha nonsense! I am Claudine. This fellow here is Armand, the ragamuffin over there with the greasy hair is Raoul. The others should be down soon. We have work to do today.'

'So do I,' says Sarah, casting her eyes around the filthy kitchen.

After a perfunctory breakfast – chunks of bread and cheese eaten mostly standing, cups of ersatz coffee hastily swallowed – the four *maquisards* leave the building for their day's work, whatever that is. Alpha and Beta have proper jobs, full- and part-time, while the others are up to clandestine work as resisters. Metz, they have told her, is a garrison town, its streets filled with uniformed soldiers; formerly French soldiers and now, since the start of the war, the Wehrmacht.

Sarah washes the dishes, dries them, finds the right shelves to store them. She empties the overflowing bin – a large receptacle for rubbish, itself almost full, stands outside the back door – replaces the lid on a jar of home-made strawberry jam and cleans up the remains of the jam on the ancient stone countertop. Wipes all the surfaces until not a crumb, not a stain remains. Behind a high door she finds a broom, a bucket and a mop; she sweeps and mops the floor. She stands back and regards her work: the kitchen can hardly sparkle, considering the ageing furniture and fixtures, but now at least it is clean and even, in a way, inviting. Sarah feels a deep sense of fulfilment; she's done something desperately necessary, improved a small corner of the world. It is good.

In that spirit she cleans the rest of the house: hallway, sitting room and bathroom downstairs, three incredibly messy bedrooms upstairs. The clothes strewn around the floors she leaves on the mattresses – there are no beds – in order to sweep and mop the wooden floors. Folding and putting them away, she thinks, would be too intrusive.

At midday she cooks herself a simple meal of boiled potatoes; there is nothing else in the house. Her work done, she feels restless. She longs to leave the house and explore the city; Metz, she knows, is a city of classical architecture, with a medieval French quarter, a Gothic cathedral and elegant German and Italian streets and squares. She has seen so little of the world beyond Colmar and, just once, Strasbourg. But Claudine has expressly forbidden her from leaving the house, instructions well in keeping with her father's injunction to *keep your head down*.

She dawdles through the rest of the day, reading first one book, then another from the stuffed shelf in the sitting room. In a corner of that room is a rather battered guitar. She picks it up, tunes it and tries picking out melodies, singing to them. But a guitar is not a violin and, highly dissatisfied with the sounds thus produced, she soon gives up.

At the heart of her boredom pulses a single thought: she misses Ralf. She misses him desperately. They are in this together, a team. It seems so unjust that no sooner had they adjusted to each other, they'd been forced to part. She prays for his safety and longs for his arrival. And as one day bleeds into the next, each one emptier than the one before it, most of the cleaning now accomplished and nothing more to do to help, that sense of missing him heightens. It is almost like missing a limb.

The *maquisards*, in the meantime, accept her presence and even welcome it: after all, she cooks and cleans for them and does not intrude in their seemingly chaotic lives. They usually meet, all together, once a day to discuss their work, and she is not welcome at such times. It was during just such an important meeting she had first arrived at the house, thus the initial antagonistic reception. Now, all is forgiven, and she enjoys the evenings spent all together in the sitting room, chatting about this and that, and even playing (bad) music on the guitar and singing (badly). To her, not being privy to the essential work they are engaged in, it is all thumb-twiddling exercises in discarding the days. Waiting for Ralf.

She has nightmares. Every night, the same. She may have managed to push the arrest in the woods and the attempted rape to the back of her mind during the day, but she cannot escape it during the night. Again and again, she relives the fear, the horror, the dread, the disgust. Again and again, she sees Krämer's lecherous face, even more grotesque in dreams than in real life, looming, pushing towards her, and then the deafening bang of the gunshot and the face exploding in slow motion before her terrified eyes; a volcano of blood and tissue erupting, spilling over her, washing down her body, and she tied and unable to escape it. In the nightmare she screams, writhes, vomits in disgust. And then, out of the horror, Ralf. Ralf's face, smiling at her, holding out a hand, leading her out of the mess, leading her away, down a mossy forest path, and as they walk the nastiness fades away, and then a cool shower falls and she is cleansed, and then there is only her and Ralf, and she is miraculously clean, and he folds her in her arms. Inevitably, she wakes, trembling, trembling in memory of the nightmare's gore, yet tingling with the delight of Ralf's closeness, his arms around her, holding her close. It's the same nightmare each night, with variations. Once Krämer's sausage fingers reach out to pull her clothes from her and Ralf slashes them off with a butcher's knife. Another time she sits screaming on the forest floor with Krämer's bloodied head on her lap, squirming, unable to throw it off, but Ralf appears and pulls her to her feet and the head rolls away and she is miraculously clean and running, running down a path with him. Always those elements: sheer revulsion, Ralf appearing out of nowhere, rescue. Always a fantastical reconstruction of what really happened.

Two days pass thus; daytime boredom, night-time phantoms. Three days. Four.

Ralf must appear any day now. She listens for his rap on the door, crabby with anticipation and nervous tension. The waiting only adds to her tension. She is jumpy with apprehension. Why hasn't he arrived yet? Has something happened? Has he been caught?

That last thought takes hold and develops into an active fear, and then, as the fourth day lengthens, into certainty. Yes. He has been caught, arrested, imprisoned, interrogated, tortured. Imagination runs wild – where have they taken him? What are they doing to him? She knows, by now, the SS methods of torture. The *maquisards* consider it entertainment to regale her with tales of capture and the subsequent interrogation methods. Fingernails pulled out. Electric nodes attached to the body – the most sensitive parts – and shocks sent through wires. Heads dunked in water, again and again, held down until the lungs almost burst for air. Wrists tied to ropes, bodies hung from ceilings. Or even the simple method of preventing sleep, preventing rest, forcing captives to stand, whipping them for leaning against walls and furniture, even when their knees bend and bow, forcing them back to a standing position.

'They always talk, in the end,' says Claudine. 'No human can withstand such torture. They talk. That is why it's best to know nothing. If you know nothing, you cannot talk. But still, they will torture you because they want to hear what they want to hear and even if you don't know it, well, they enjoy the torture. That is the way of the Boche.'

By the end of the fourth day Sarah is certain beyond a doubt that Ralf has fallen into the hands of the Boche. Madame Delauney had said three days. The three days are long past, and he is not here. That's why she doesn't bother to join the group for supper – a supper that she herself has cooked, a stew of leftover vegetable scraps and stale bread – but retires early to her subterranean room to mope and simmer in her fears. Moping is somehow comforting; she can bury her head in her pillow – not easy to bury one's head in hard horsehair, but it is the thing to do, a way to consolidate her grief in the time-honoured manner of inconsolable heroines – and weep, wallowing in the darkest thoughts and fears. No rod and staff this time, no comfort, just solid, unmitigated anguish, consuming every atom of her being.

Thus, she does not hear the knock on the front door even though it is just above her open half-window, and even when they call for her down the stairwell, their voices do not penetrate the closed door of her room. He has to knock on that door, loudly, shouting her name, before any sound at all penetrates her abject self-pity; and then she immediately panics, believing it is the Gestapo come for her because, of course, Ralf must have revealed all under torture, and it takes a few moments before rational thought returns. She realises it is a somehow familiar voice and it is calling in a pleading tone, in extremely non-Gestapo words: *Sarah, Sarah, it's me, Ralf!*

The door opens, at the very moment that she hurls herself with a shriek across the room to open it herself. It hits her in the face and she almost falls to the floor; but then his arms are around her, hauling her to her feet, and then *her* arms are flinging themselves around him of their own accord and her weeping in a single breath is no more that of the bereaved but of the exultant, bursting joy,

joy uncontainable; and she is sputtering his name and he laughing into her hair and massaging her head and saying her name over and over again.

And then he pushes her away. Suddenly sober. Holds her at arm's length, and he is no longer laughing. He's changed. His chin is covered with stubble, his hair is longer, uncombed, his clothes now limp and musty with old sweat, dishevelled. To her he is still beautiful, but there is that distant, guarded look in his eyes as he holds her by the shoulders, an arm's length away, slightly frowning, and so, so serious.

'Ralf, what's the matter?'

'Nothing… nothing much. It's just, just, we must talk. I have so much to tell you. Let's sit down, shall we? I want to hear your story and tell you mine.'

'Yes, but first, first, I just want to tell you how much I—'

'Yes, but, Sarah, you must stop crying now, there's nothing to cry about. I'm back. It was a long and difficult journey but here I am. Come, dry your tears and let's sit and talk.'

He reaches up to the threadbare towel hanging on a hook and dries her eyes and then leads her to the dishevelled bottom bunk that has been her wallowing hole and sits her down on the edge. Then he looks around, sees the rickety wooden chair and draws it up to face her. He takes her hands in his, a brotherly gesture, and the eyes that meet hers are kind rather than emotionally at bursting point, like hers. They are serious eyes; too serious for her liking. This is surely a time of great delight and deliverance, but he does not show it. It is so disappointing. It means that he has hardly missed her at all. Not to the extent that she has missed him.

His earnestness is contagious, or else the realisation that her overwhelming relief is not mutual has a sobering effect, such that she has to justify her euphoric reaction. It is a question of saving pride… She now has to explain that overreaction of hers, this foolish flinging of arms and juddering sobs of relief.

'I was convinced you had been captured. I thought you might be dead by now, that they had tortured you. It was such a relief, you know, to see you there. I had to...'

He squeezes her hands, which are still in his, and laughs.

'I'm not so easy to capture, you know! I've been trained in stealth – I'm a soldier. I did not see a single soul, except once a goatherd, from a distance. I waved at him and he waved back. Madame Delauney's map was good, very accurate. I think I made it in good time – we said about three days, and it's been just a little more than three days. A bit too early to worry, I think!'

She pulls one of her hands away to wipe away a tear that threatens to fall. 'I suppose my imagination is too active. I feared the worst.'

'Well, the worst did not happen and here I am, from over the fields, over stock and stone. Alive and unhurt, but a bit hungry. I finished my rations – is there any food in this house?'

She manages a laugh. 'Not much, and knowing that crowd upstairs they'll have finished the stew I made. Maybe we can open a tin of something? And there's strawberry jam. Lots of it, from Claudine's mother's farm.'

He makes a face. 'I don't think jam will fill me up.'

'Let's go upstairs and see. I suppose you met the others already.'

'Briefly. They shoved me downstairs quickly enough.'

'It's how they greet people – shove them away. But their bark is worse than their bite. Let's go up and see what we can find.'

Together, they go up to the kitchen, now empty as the *maquisards* have moved to the sitting room. Sarah opens cupboards and pulls out whatever she can find: a tin of peaches, an ancient packet of biscuits, a wedge of cheese. Items she herself has tidied away over the last few days. Practical tasks always help, she finds, pushing away her disappointment. Despite her fears for his safety, she has imagined again and again the moment of reunion with Ralf. The hug that would last for ever, only ending when it turned into a kiss. The murmurs and confessions of true love, the promises, the vows.

You have read too many romance novels, Sarah, she tells herself as, their simple supper over, they return downstairs and prepare for bed. *This is not the way in real life. Real adult women don't throw themselves at indifferent men the way you did. They have far more pride.*

And repeating that wisdom to herself, she eventually falls asleep. The horsehair pillow is anyway not very cuddleable. Tonight, there is no nightmare.

Chapter Twenty-Five

The following day Mathilde returns, this time with Henri. Henri is from the Free French cell in Metz and is bilingual in French and German; he is eager to speak to Ralf. Sarah is asked to leave the kitchen while they talk – again, the less she knows, the better, for her own safety. All she knows is that Ralf has military information invaluable to the Free French, and that in return, they will be supplying him with forged documents and a new name and identity.

When Henri leaves, she asks Ralf:

'How long will it be till you get your papers, so we can move on?'

'The forger has a lot of work. It will take some time, maybe two weeks. Henri said he will try to persuade him to get it done earlier because we must be on our way.'

She can tell he is hiding a wealth of information; he has entered a new life of secrets. It is not her place to ask. Just as it is not her place to hug him, hold his hand, lean against him when they sit together on the sitting-room carpet each evening with the others, singing and talking and drinking cheap wine.

Claudine and the beards all take to Ralf immediately, and he to them – but again, conversation is still difficult as nobody speaks German and Ralf's French is still not up to scratch. He cannot follow the rapid exchange, and they find it hard to speak slowly and clearly.

Sarah, as promised, gives him daily French lessons – what else is there to do? They read French books together, or rather, she reads to him and helps him understand spoken French. She helps him with his accent, which is stilted and German, correcting him when he confuses f's and v's. He is a quick learner, but still, one day stretches into the next as they wait, hidden, at home in their basement room, never leaving the house. Claudine goes to work each day and returns each evening; the beards sleep till late and leave the house at night, doing whatever clandestine things they have to do.

Then one night two of the beards stay away. Nobody speaks of them, or why they are gone, but Sarah can tell by the heightened excitement in the house that they are on some kind of a mission and that it is, perhaps, dangerous.

The two beards are gone for a second night, and a third. It is almost as if they have never lived there; no one speaks of them, no one seems to miss them. And yet a sense of tense expectation lurks, never fully revealing itself, but *there* all the same. Sarah can't put her finger on it, but she feels it.

'It might be better if the two of you move out,' Claudine says one day. 'It's safer.'

'Move out to where?'

'I'll talk to Mathilde. She needs to find a new place for you.'

'Something's going on,' Sarah says to Ralf later. 'I wish they'd tell us.'

'It's better to know nothing,' he says. 'But I agree we should move out.'

'Do you know what they're up to?'

He only shrugs. 'I don't want to – it's better not to know. Don't worry, I'll look after you.'

She wishes he'd do more than look after her. She longs not for his protection but his affection; his arms around her as on the day he'd arrived, his warmth, his loving gaze. It seems to her that since that first spontaneous hug he's pulled away, retreated into himself, placed a wall between them. At times he seems even cold, as if his mind is elsewhere.

A disturbing thought comes to her: perhaps he has a sweetheart back in Freiburg. Perhaps that is the problem. Perhaps he is already promised to *her*. Somebody more grown-up, more experienced than her. And especially, not a Jew. That is where he drifts off to when that faraway look comes into his eyes… He is thinking of her, of his arms around her, his lips on hers.

Sarah dreams and fears and invents scenarios, all in a vain attempt to understand, to explain away Ralf's indifference, to justify his coldness. But always, she returns to the same conclusion: he was forced to be with her. He'll do his duty as an escort, as he promised Rebecca, Victoire and Eric. He'll accompany her down to the South of France, make sure she is safe. But that is all. The notion that he could actually care for her, beyond his role as guide and bodyguard, is just a childish dream. And she's a romantic fool.

And then, one evening, there they are, the two absent beards, knocking on the back door, falling into the kitchen when Claudine opens it, laughing, drunk with elation.

'You got them!' Claudine's tone is triumphant.

'Indeed!' says one of the beards and slides his arms out from the straps of a huge rucksack. It slides to the floor.

'Oh my goodness!' Claudine pounces on it, eyes gleaming as she tears at the buckles, opening the upper flap. She pushes her hand down into the interior and withdraws it, triumphant. She holds up a dark green, egg-shaped object, grinning in delight.

'What is it?' asks Sarah, and everyone laughs. The beards shake their heads, not even deigning to reply. She feels foolish.

Ralf laughs too, but kindly, not at her ignorance but at her innocence. 'It is a hand grenade,' he says. 'A handy little bomb.'

'Twenty of them! We got them from the cell in Nancy, they're part of a British Special Operations consignment. The Nancy guys let us have a few. We can wreak havoc with these!'

A beard shoves his own hand deeper into the sack, gropes and pulls out a gun.

'And these!' he says triumphantly. 'Four Stens! And ammunition!'

He twirls it in his hand, grinning, aims it at the door. 'Let the Boche come! Now we're armed!'

He throws the gun at Raoul, who catches it and proceeds to fish out three more guns from the backpack. Hands reach for them; he hands them out like Christmas treats. Jubilation and excitement fill the room; laughter, back-slapping and pretend-shooting, everyone talking at once, like children with a box of new toys.

Claudine turns to Ralf, who is obviously struggling to follow, and then to Sarah. She explains to the two of them that one of their main problems, due to the particular geography of Lorraine in the annexed part of France, is the lack of weapons of any kind.

'Elsewhere in France, the Resistance network has connections to a British organisation that helps with weapons and strategy: the SOE. Not us, we are isolated. So this delivery, it is pure gold.'

One of the beards picks up the precious rucksack and places it in the cleaning cupboard. 'So – here it is safe.'

They retire to the sitting room, where the two beards tell anecdote after anecdote of the adventures they've shared over the last three days. Everyone laughs and tells their own stories. A bottle of cheap wine makes a sudden appearance and they pass it around, drinking straight from the bottle. One of the beards picks up the guitar, cheering and laughing, drunk with this new achievement. Finally, slightly tipsy, they all drift off to bed.

Sarah dreams that the Gestapo are at the door, banging on it, screaming *'Machen Sie auf!'* So real, so vivid – but then urgent arms are around her and she is being pulled from her bed and they are Ralf's arms – at last! – but it isn't a hug, he is dragging her to her feet, shaking her, saying, *Wake up, wake up, Sarah!* in a sort of half-whisper, half-shout, in her ear and the banging on the front door is louder than ever. It isn't a dream, it is real. And then she is fully awake and on her feet.

The room is dark; the blackout curtain over the window does its job. But Ralf has switched on a torch and she can see him hurriedly packing all their possessions into their bags. He shoves her own bag into her arms, then pulls a sheet from the bed and pushes it towards her, gesturing. She'd been sleeping in her underwear, as always, and leapt half-naked from the bed, with no thought of modesty. Now, she wraps herself in the sheet.

'What shall we do?'

'We have to hide,' he whispers. 'Come on! Hurry up, don't just stand there!'

'Hide? But where? There's nowhere *to* hide!'

There is a crash as the Germans break down the front door. The sound of boots in the hallway upstairs, shouting in German; bedlam upstairs.

So, this is it – caught out in a safe house that has never been really safe. There is nowhere to hide. They can't run upstairs – it is too late, and even if they make it to the kitchen, surely the back door is also covered? They are trapped, down here in the cellar. Upstairs, it sounds as if an entire army has invaded the house. It is only a matter of time before it comes swarming down the wooden cellar stairs, boots thumping. There is shouting and swearing from upstairs; it seems they have captured one or two of the beards. Claudine, yelling. Crashes, bangs, even a gunshot – but there is no time to think or be afraid because Ralf has grabbed her arm and is pulling and pushing her across the room to the toilet door. *The toilet! What a ridiculous hiding place. What is he thinking?*

He is pushing her into the toilet. Stupid! Once they invade the cellar, their room, the toilet will be the first door they open. *They. Them.* That dreaded *other*, the enemy; the beast on the periphery of their safe little bubble, never far away. Now it is here, that beast, and the only place they can hide is this: the toilet. What an anticlimax. It is so ridiculous she almost laughs, but Ralf grabs a hook on one of the toilet walls and turns it, and another space miraculously opens up before them and he shoves her in and encourages her to 'climb into the tub'.

And indeed: a hidden bathroom, one half of the room that originally also held the toilet. An old cracked bathtub stands against the far wall and into it she climbs while Ralf closes the hidden door behind them carefully. He slides a rusty bolt into the locked position. It would be useless should anyone suspect the presence of a door, but a locked door always feels safer than an unlocked one.

He crouches down on the floor; really, there is no space anywhere else, except in the tub, and she knows he wouldn't want to be there, so close to her.

He turns to look at her over the rim of the tub, eyes wide open yet calm and calming, finger on his lips telling her to *be quiet*, as if she needed such instruction. Beyond the door there are noises: the Germans are in their room already. She hears their booming voices: *someone was sleeping here… the mattress is still warm… They must have run upstairs when they heard us… What's that door?*

The door to the toilet opens; someone shouts, '*das Klo. Leer!*' The toilet, empty. Boots stomping away again, back up the stairs. But the pounding of her heart deafening, louder even than the boots. Thunderous. Crashing in her chest, which feels about to burst.

She manages a whisper.

'Have they gone?'

'Back upstairs. I think they're in the kitchen.'

Indeed: more crashing noises come from upstairs; it sounds as if the house is being wrecked. Shouting, screaming. A shot; another shot. More screams. The noises diminish. Then there is silence. But the silence is almost more menacing than the racket.

'Have they gone? What about the others? Have they taken them? Oh, Ralf! The grenades, they must have found them! Will they be all right?'

'Not a hope in hell,' he whispers. He is no more than a black shadow, but now that she's grown accustomed to the darkness, she can make out the paleness of his face, the whites of his eyes. His voice is grim, laced with despair.

'Can't you do something? Can't you save them?'

'I could try,' he says. 'I could try playing the hero. And get captured myself. Is that what you want me to do?'

'No! No, stay here! Please stay here.'

'I will. Sarah, there's nothing we can do, really nothing. They knew of the danger, always knew it. And now they have been caught. This is the reality of war. I am not a coward.'

'I know. I'm sorry, I didn't mean to imply—'

And then he does it. He puts his arms around her, pulls her close. So close, she can hear his heartbeat too, mingling with hers. Feel his breath.

'I know. But, Sarah, we must hide for a while. No need for us to be captured too. I will stay with you, you're not alone. All right?'

She snuggles her face into his chest.

'All right.'

'When all is clear, we will figure out our next move, where to go. For now, we will stay here. Are you comfortable?'

At that she gives a wry chuckle. 'If you can call crouching in this old rust-bucket, in the dark, comfort, I suppose so. Ralf… what will happen to the others?'

He shakes his head.

'Nothing good.'

'Will they be killed?'

'Probably.'

That's when she begins to weep. And that's when he takes her in his arms and lets her weep against him, into him. But not for long. A moment later, he pushes her away.

Chapter Twenty-Six

'Wait here.'

Ralf slips out of the bathroom, shutting the door carefully behind him. She hears nothing for a while but the pounding of her heart, and her own breath, audible, panicked, fast. Once, a faint creak from an upstairs floorboard. Then nothing again but her heart and her breath. She wishes there was light, but he has taken the torch, and the single bulb that serviced the bathroom is outside the dividing wall, in the toilet. Alone in the darkness, she finds it better to close her eyes; then at least the darkness is confined to her body and not the world. She does so, shuts them tight.

But closed eyes represent in particular two human activities: sleep, and prayer, and because sleep is impossible, prayer rises within her, the little personal prayer that has accompanied her since fleeing her home in Colmar: *for thou art with me, thy rod and thy staff to comfort me…*

Over and over again. Slowly, her heartbeat slows, as does her breath, and the silence is complete again but for the words repeating themselves inside her, over and over and over again. Until, at last, calmness reigns within her. It will be all right, the Gestapo have gone. They, at least, are safe. But the others: Claudine, and Raoul, and the beards… She squeezes her lids tightly together as the thought of what they might be enduring arises, and it is unbearable, and her heartbeat and her breath react and once again the panic takes hold. *Ralf! Where are you? Come back!*

He is gone for what seems like hours, but can in fact surely be no more than ten, fifteen minutes. She has no clock, nothing to measure time with except for the pounding of her heartbeat.

And then, at last: footsteps drawing near, a low warning cry, 'It's me, Sarah!'

A slight tap on the secret door, and it opens. Light enters the room and he is there in that light.

'They've gone,' he says. 'It's safe to come out, the house is empty.'

She steps out and into the room. The light is on and now she can see his face: it is pale and drawn, his eyes wild and filled with shock. In the time between leaving her up to his return he has aged, it seems, years. 'What is it?' she says. 'What is upstairs…?'

She moves towards the door, but he places a hand on her wrist: it is icy cold.

'No,' he says. 'Don't— don't go up there. Not yet. I need to warn you – tell you… It's— it's terrible.'

'What's up there? Tell me! What did you see?' She tries to pull herself away but he grips her tightly.

'Let me go!' she cries. 'I need to— oh!' She cries out in shock as, looking down, she sees that his sleeve is covered in blood.

'They wrecked the place. And— and Sarah, Raoul is dead. Shot dead. On the stairs. There's blood – I moved him.'

'Oh my goodness! And… the others?'

'Gone, of course. Like I said. Arrested. I'd guess that Raoul tried to resist. You heard the shots – I'm thinking he might have tried to shoot first, but they got him instead.'

Sarah stands with her hands pressed to her mouth, eyes wide open with the shock of it all.

'We have to go,' says Ralf suddenly. 'We can't stay here. They might return, search the house more carefully – we have to get out. Get dressed, quickly.'

She hastily pulls on a skirt, a jumper, boots. He is already in his trousers and a vest; he must have pulled them on before venturing upstairs. Now he, too, pulls off the bloodied shirt, puts on a clean one, a jumper, shoes.

'Come, follow me. Upstairs.'

*

He hasn't exaggerated: the house is a shambles. In the kitchen, any furniture not fixed to the walls lies on the floor, chairs broken, the table on its side. The kitchen cupboard doors open, what little food had been in them strewn across the floor. Potatoes, carrots, turnips, tins, broken glasses, plates, cutlery – all scattered across the room. It has been Sarah's instinct for years not to waste any food at all and even now, as she whimpers at the wreckage, she bends to gather potatoes, carrots. Ralf, too, is thinking of sustenance: he stands at the tap, filling his container with water. Sarah stands up suddenly, remembering Raoul. She grasps Ralf's arm, urgently.

'Raoul, where is he? Where's the body?'

'It was on the stairs. I dragged it upstairs, laid it on a bed.'

'I want to see it!'

It seems awful, to leave poor Raoul behind. She hadn't liked him very much but that is now irrelevant: he had been fighting for his country's freedom, fighting against the hated Nazis, and to leave him discarded on a bed – it somehow seems disrespectful. Surely they should say goodbye, whisper a prayer over his body?

But Ralf will have nothing of it.

'No. He died bravely, Sarah. Obviously he thought he could defend the house against the Gestapo and paid the price. There's nothing you can do for him now, we need to be on our way.'

The bottle is full; he tucks it in his bag. Sarah picks up a few more carrots. Potatoes are useless on the road, they cannot be eaten raw. She tucks the carrots in her pockets.

'Where will we go?'

'I don't know. I need to find a telephone. Come on!'

Cautiously, he opens the back door. He pokes his head out, looks around the back garden. There is no sign of life, of hidden soldiers. He steps out, raising a hand to tell her to wait. Guardedly, he takes a few steps forward—

'Pssssst!'

His head swivels left and right, trying to locate the source of the sound, the hissing that now comes again, and louder, and a voice, a loudly whispering voice:

'*Monsieur!*'

It comes from the left, the neighbour's house, from over a low hedge separating the two backyards. A head looms over the hedge: a woman's head. She breaks into a barrage of French that he cannot understand. He gestures accordingly, holds up a hand to say *wait* and turns to the kitchen door, where Sarah stands. He gestures for her to come; she approaches.

'They are gone,' says the neighbour. 'The Boche has gone. But you must hide. You can come to my house for a while. Do not worry, we are on your side.'

She points to a gate at the end of the pocket of land. They walk through that gate and onto the woman's property, cross her back garden, go in her back door. Sarah drops her bag to the floor and clasps the woman's two hands.

'*Madame!* We are so grateful, so thankful. It is terrible, what has happened.'

'We are neighbours. The walls are thin, the windows were open – we heard,' says the woman. 'I am Madame Brisson. I have always lived here, always been a good Frenchwoman, a patriot. The mother of Claudine, she was my best friend. Of course I will help her daughter's friends! Claudine is so brave, working for the freedom of France. Now I will make you some breakfast and then we will discuss what is to happen.'

She speaks rapidly, so Sarah translates for Ralf.

'What we mostly need,' he says, 'is a telephone. Is there a booth nearby?'

'There is one at the corner of the street,' says Madame Brisson. 'But we can't go out… Would you…?'

She understands. 'Give me the number, write down the message, and I will make a call for you. *Mademoiselle*, sit down at the table. I will be back and make coffee for you in a second.'

She and Ralf leave the kitchen. Sarah's knees give way then, weak with relief, and she plumps down into a chair. For the time being they are safe. Maybe. For a little pocket of time.

Today, though, the reality of war has burst into her awareness for the first time. Up to now, it has all been so far away. A nightmare, thus unreal. Being torn from her parents, her home. The forced flight, the first refuge at the vineyard, escaping over the Vosges… It has been more an involuntary bad dream, seemingly unconnected to the war – the war itself, the fighting, the death, the carnage, was all so far away, so theoretical, theatrical. A speech on the radio, hushed voices, warnings of terrible possibilities. Even the arrest in the forest had not seemed like an act of war, just another scene in a scary play. Even when Ralf tied her up, it had not been war. Even when Krämer tried to rape her – even *that* was not an act of war, but the act of a brute: individual, personal. Even when Ralf shot Krämer and the bloodied remains of his head had scraped down her body and she had screamed in utmost terror – even that had not been war.

But this, this morning's drama – *this* is war. War has broken in through the bubble of her denial. There is nowhere left to hide. It is upon her, and from now on every step she takes, she'll be deeper and deeper inside its terrible bowels.

'I've spoken to the forger,' says Mathilde. 'He'll have your documents ready by tomorrow at the latest. You must leave Metz right away, you cannot stay here. I'm sorry but it's too dangerous for all of us.'

'Here' is the back of a tailor's shop. Mathilde is looking, in the meantime, for a temporary home for the night. She had come immediately, picked them up from Madame Brisson's, taken them through the back gates and back roads, brought them here to her brother's shop in the poorer part of the city. If the worst comes to the worst, they can sleep on the shop floor. Nobody has beds to spare. 'Everyone is *très sympathique*,' she says. 'All of Metz would like to help, but nobody has room. When war broke out we all evacuated to the south, but we all came back, except the Jews, and immediately every spare house, every spare room, was requisitioned by Germans. Metz is now packed. It is *Judenrein*, as they say, free of Jews; but instead, packed with Germans. We preferred the Jews.'

It has been accepted with dismay that Claudine and her group are a lost cause, as is everyone captured by the Boche; in this case, red-handed. It goes without saying that they'll all be interrogated and eventually tortured until they gasp the truth and then they'll be killed.

'You cannot blame them for talking,' Mathilde says. 'All they want is to put an end to the pain: to die. They know that once they speak, death will come. That is why you must flee at once.'

'But will the Boche question them about us?' Sarah asks. 'Surely not? Surely they don't know about us?'

'That's what I've been asking myself.' Ralf shakes his head. 'What do you think, Mathilde?'

'We do not know,' she says. 'That's why you must flee. Mostly the Boche will want to know about the Resistance cell in Nancy, where they got the weapons and grenades from. That cell is supplied by the British SOE, and the Boche is desperate for names and addresses. They are not looking for a defecting Wehrmacht soldier and a Jewish girl from Colmar, and would not think to ask. But…' She shrugs. 'But our friends might offer that information, hoping to deflect other questions. Hoping to distract. You are of lesser importance to the Resistance than the Nancy network. They might very well sacrifice you voluntarily. I'm sorry, but that's the way it is. It would be the lesser betrayal, with less at stake for the Resistance. So, you have to go – Metz is too hot for you now.'

Metz might be hot but Sarah shivers, and not from cold. Ralf places an arm around her, squeezes her shoulder, but only for a second; he quickly drops it.

'Don't be afraid,' he says. 'I'll look after you.'

Then put your arm back, she cries, but only in thought. *Hold me close. I am afraid, terrified, and I'm all alone. Please.*

But he does not replace his arm. He does not draw her to himself in comfort. In fact, he moves away; he rises to his feet and goes to stand against the door.

It is true what they say, Sarah tells herself. *Germans are cold, even the friendly ones, even the ones who hate Hitler. They are cold and have no feelings. They cannot care, they cannot love. Ralf is no more than a beautiful statue. He is doing his duty looking after me but my feelings are wasted on him. I must stop loving him.*

I must!!! But – maybe I can't.

Chapter Twenty-Seven

Ralf's documents are indeed ready the next day. His cover story has been kept as close to the truth as possible, as has his disguise: once again, he is a soldier, clean-shaven, hair close-cut, smartly dressed, in uniform. A German soldier, back from leave, returning to his regiment in the South of France.

'Your name now is Karl Vogel, as you suggested,' Mathilde tells him. 'But we've made you three years older; you're now twenty-one. It's better for one of you to be of age. Anyway, you look older.'

He does? Sarah frowns at these words and takes a closer look. He looks entirely the part: a clean-cut soldier, tall and handsome in his uniform, the scraggly stubble covering his chin now gone. And yes – in the two weeks she has known him Ralf has aged. Gone is the almost fresh-faced young soldier unproven in actual battle, a teenager; replaced by a man. But what is it that has changed? His features are exactly the same: the almost classical well-proportioned facial structure, and of course the individual features, dark brown hair, hazel eyes, ears, all unchanged. He is as handsome as before, and yet... What has changed, she realises, is internal.

A new inner depth filters through every atom of his face, his body, his stature, his stance, lending him an elusive quality of maturity, a sense of sheer competence that comes not through any quantifiable outer change but in a confidence that seems to leak from within. Experience has forced maturity on him; he has grown from boy to man in the blink of an eye. It shines in his eyes; gone is the quivering shame of the soldier who, as he tied her wrists, looked at her, begging for forgiveness.

Here instead is a man who has forgiven himself, not by excusing his errors, but by growing beyond them, replacing them with responsibility and strength. He exudes trustworthiness. It should have been clear to her earlier, right from the start: this is a man in rapid evolution. Clear to her from the immediate trust he evokes in complete strangers, starting with Eric and ending with Mathilde. Rebecca, Victoire, Madame Delauney, even the *maquisards*, all seemed to trust Ralf at once, when they had hardly met him, even knowing of his German military past. There is a magnetism to him that seems to automatically evoke that sense: that this is a through-and-through *good* man.

She was the last to sense it; she has been too wrapped up in her own conflicting emotions – her initial animal fear, causing her to repulse and deny the magnetism that draws her to him – to notice the change in him. Something else is at work within her, a thing hard to name: is it infatuation, love, lust? No, not lust. She too is drawn to him, but the attraction is spiritual rather than physical, her neediness a craving for emotional comfort and reciprocation rather than a carnal itch.

It is as if her soul, abandoned by family and all she holds dear, reaches out to him, yearns for his acceptance, thirsts for his acknowledgment, hungers for his love – and yet is cruelly thrust aside by his indifference. It is strange that his trustworthiness is clothed in such frigidity. But perhaps coldness is part of his new maturity. Perhaps maturity excludes reciprocation; holds love, and the inevitable neediness that is love's partner – the need to be entirely *one* with the other – at bay. Whatever it is she is alone with it, and lonely. So terribly lonely… her longing ending in frayed emptiness. Whatever it is: even his papers, now, reflect that maturity.

'So, I've skipped three years of my life? Nice!' he says, taking his new identity card from Mathilde and inspecting it. It might be new, but it looks old, the photo slightly cracked, the card on which it is printed softened at the edges. Karl Vogel, twenty-one.

'I wish I could be made older!' grumbles Sarah. 'I hate being a minor, everyone treating me as a child.'

'Your time will come,' says Mathilde. 'You are living through history, and it is forcing you into maturity, just like Karl here. But he's been out in the world a lot longer than you have, that's all. One day you'll show your own mettle. In the meantime, being seventeen is your lot.'

'I'll be eighteen next week!' she replies. Had she been at home there'd have been a celebration. Mama would have miraculously baked a cake out of carrots and egg powder and cornmeal and, because it was baked with love, it would have been delicious, and there would have been hugs all round from her parents and her sisters, and songs and laughter – in spite of the war. Here, though, this would be a birthday to forget. On the run, travelling with the cold fish that is Ralf – no, *not* Ralf, Karl. She must remember to call him that.

Mathilde is giving them rapid-fire final instructions: 'You need to leave now. Right now. The next train to Paris… Don't stop there but find the quickest connection to Poitiers and take that. Paris is swarming with Gestapo. Poitiers is safer – it's where the citizens of Metz were evacuated to when the war started. You'll be able to merge into the society you'll find there.

'Be wary, trust nobody. Not all French people are against the Nazis. In Paris, there's the Carlingue; it's a new secret organisation of French collaborating with the Gestapo and they're even worse. Some are ex-crooks; totally ruthless, hand in hand with the Gestapo, but even nastier, and harder to spot as they're in plain clothes, watching for people to denounce. They can be everywhere. You need eyes in the back of your head.

'On the train, you should travel separately so that you will be controlled separately. It's better, safer. Even now, walk separately to the station, buy your tickets separately. Don't look so scared, Sarah, it could give you away. One phone call to Colmar can end it for you. Your papers are in order, and what's more, they are genuine. Remember that, and try to look confident, natural. I will accompany you to the station. It's better. Remember, you are travelling to Paris to stay with relatives and find work. You have the address, memorised it? Tell me.'

Sarah repeats the Paris address she has committed to memory. She will not actually be going to this house, it is just a safe address established for her by JEN, given to her by Mathilde. Ralf – no, Karl – has a different address. They will meet in Paris, at the Gare de l'Est, take the Metro to Gare Montparnasse, and then separate again for the onward journey to Poitiers. She squares her shoulders, straightens her back. This, at last, is growing up.

Ralf sits in the same carriage as her, but in a different compartment. Mathilde insisted that they not sit together, for safety.

'You never know who's watching,' she'd said. 'People might wonder why a German soldier is so friendly with a simple French girl; it would cause antagonism. They notice things like veiled glances, gestures, facial expressions. You never know who might want to be helpful to the Gestapo. You never know. Stay apart, until you get to Paris.'

'Try to sit near to an older woman,' she'd told Sarah. 'Chat with her, pretend you are with her. It will help. But still, there is no cause at all for you to worry. You do not have the incriminating stamp *Jew* on your papers. Nobody in France is looking for Sarah Mayer.'

'Unless Claudine and her friends betrayed me…?'

'Even if they eventually do, it won't be right away. It will take some time before the police are alerted to look for you and by that time you will be in Poitiers. But you should maybe have used a different name in that house.'

'A bit late to be telling me that now.'

'Never mind, just get to Poitiers.'

At the station, Mathilde stood back as Sarah bought her ticket, a through ticket to Poitiers. She has never bought a train ticket before; it is necessary for her to do these things alone, as an adult.

'Now, goodbye, *chérie*. And good luck.'

Mathilde kissed both her cheeks. Turned and walked away.

Now here she is, in the compartment. She has chosen a seat, as Mathilde advised, next to a middle-aged woman with a bundle on her lap. The woman's hair is quite grey, and the lines around her eyes seem to be from laughter rather than age; suppressed mirth, for when the woman turns to greet her, her smile is contradicted by great sadness in her eyes. She's a woman, Sarah thinks, who ought to be soft and round but instead is gaunt and bony. Only a generous bosom hints a more generous figure in more affluent times.

They fall into easy conversation. The sadness in the woman's eyes is explained by two sons lost in the early summer of 1940, when the Boche first invaded France. At first, she speaks guardedly, as does Sarah, each gauging the other's attitude to the invasion, eventually finding their way through to trust. Trust, Sarah has found, is an instinct, a gut feeling. One must learn to trust not only the other but oneself, one's own sense of the other's trustworthiness, all the time knowing, nonetheless, a truly gifted *collaborateur* will have mastered the art of evoking unearned trust.

It is not easy to lie to Madame Leroi. Maman has drummed into Sarah the importance of telling the truth and so to deliberately deceive an honest friend – it pricks her conscience. But it is the only safe way. She is Sarah from Colmar, on her way to join relatives in Paris, to look for a job. That's her story.

'What kind of job are you looking for?'

'Well…' She can't very well say 'making violins' but surely there are violin-makers in Paris? Why not? But Mathilde has advised against it. Better something unskilled, less specific, just in case.

'Anything, really,' she says. 'I am good at all domestic duties so I thought maybe a cleaner. Or…'

'Can you cut vegetables?'

'Yes, yes, of course! I used to help my mother in the kitchen.'

'Then I can introduce you to my brother-in-law. He has a small restaurant near Montparnasse. Nothing fancy, mind you, nothing gourmet, just basic lunch and dinner for people who work in offices nearby. Could you do that?'

'Yes, of course! But it is possible that my uncle has already found work for me, in a shop.'

'Well, I will give you the address. If nothing works out you can write me a letter and I will help. But as always, be careful what you write.'

The first control is on leaving Lorraine to enter the *Zone Interdite*. Here, they must leave the annexed zone claimed by Germany to enter the 'forbidden zone', a buffer between the annexation and occupied France. The train is held up for almost an hour. German officers in slate-green uniforms swarm the carriages, moving with excruciating slowness from passenger to passenger, scrutinising papers and faces, asking questions, probing, sometimes even searching. When they come to her, she gazes up anxiously, convinced guilt is written into her every feature. *Steady. Calm. Breathe.* But her hand trembles as she produces her ID and her heartbeat must be audible as it hammers away in her chest.

'From Metz to Paris, is it? And what is the purpose of your journey, Fräulein?'

'I— I'm going to visit… I mean to work…'

She stumbles over the words. She starts again, but Madame Leroi interrupts, in perfect German.

'My niece is coming with me to Paris to visit my sister's family,' she says clearly and firmly. 'She has been promised a job in the family restaurant in Montparnasse.'

The officer nods and hands back Sarah's documents.

'Very well. But she will have a hard time dealing with the public if she is so shy.'

Madame Leroi chuckles. 'Ah yes – our Sarah has been very protected, she's a little mouse still! But she will not be working front of house at first. Paris will toughen her up. Is that not true, *chérie*? In no time you'll be an elegant young Parisian lady who can hold her own.'

She slaps Sarah's knee and gives her a jovial wink. Sarah forces a smile and nods. The officer also nods, unsmiling, and moves on, up the carriage.

When the two officers are out of earshot Madame Leroi turns to Sarah and whispers fiercely: 'You must collect yourself and learn to lie better and more convincingly. I do not know your story, but I can tell you are in trouble. I don't want to know the details, but you must pull yourself together. You are a nervous wreck!'

Sarah nods; she knows it. Her hands are wet with sweat; she wipes them on her sleeves and thanks Madame Leroi profusely.

'I'm sorry,' she whispers. 'This is my first time on my own and just a few days ago I was in hiding and they came and arrested my friends and…' She has the urge to spill out her entire story from beginning to end.

Madame Leroi is one such friend, one of those solid older women who, since the start of this trip, has immediately noticed her plight, read her mind, embraced her spiritually if not physically, lent her their courage and their confidence. Margaux, Rebecca, Madame Delauney – even Mathilde; and now this stranger who has seen at a glance her insecurity and stepped up to help. Unlike Ralf, who pushes her away, who helps on a practical level but offers her no hand when it comes to freeing her from her fears.

'Your candour betrays you,' says Madame Leroi now. 'Your lies lurk openly in your eyes. I am sorry you felt you had to lie to me and I won't ask why – most people have secrets in this war. And I won't ask why someone as vulnerable as you travels alone. You will have your reasons. But you must practise your lies when you are alone: they are transparent.'

'I am from Colmar,' whispers Sarah. 'I am Jewish, and—'

'Shhh! What did I just tell you! I don't want to know! You cannot go around telling strangers things like that, no matter how much you trust them. It's dangerous.'

'I'm sorry, I—'

'And don't apologise! You really are a little girl and should not be travelling on your own. You have no idea.'

Sarah lowers her voice yet more.

'I am not alone. I am travelling with a young man, a soldier. He's a German deserter and he's…'

'A German soldier? A deserter? Really? Is *your* young man? Can you trust him? I hope you are not eloping or something like that? That would not be good.'

She shakes her head vigorously. 'No, no, nothing like that. He is only accompanying me because I am a minor. We were told it was better to travel separated.'

'Ah! You *were told*. It sounds as if you are in good hands so I will now mind my business and won't ask any more questions.'

At the next control, near Paris, Sarah answers for herself and neither trembles nor stutters. Madame Leroi approves. 'You are a fast learner!' she says. 'Soon lying will come to you as easily as breathing. In a sane world lying convincingly would not be an admirable feature. Unfortunately, the world we live in is insane and we must learn these sneaky skills for our own safety. But still, the job offer remains. Probably you have a different plan but one never knows, *n'est-ce pas*? Now, let me write down my sister's address in Paris, and my own.'

She fishes out a small notebook and a pencil from her handbag and writes in it. '*Bon*! Well, my dear, I am getting out at the next station, in the *banlieues* of Paris. We must part company. It was enjoyable meeting and talking with you and I wish you well on your adventures, you and the young man. Even if he is not *your* young man, as you claim. Not yet, I should say. I suspect one day he will be. That is the way of life. Anyway, *bonne chance!*'

And she is gone, leaving Sarah once more with that sense of an inner vacuum. But soon the train is rolling in towards Gare de l'Est. Passengers are standing up, fetching their luggage from the overhead racks, re-packing bags.

And suddenly Ralf is there, standing next to her in the corridor, smiling at her with that distant, uncommitted grin of his that promises friendship while warning that distance must be kept. She understands and plays along. It is one of the lies of war that Madame Leroi has complained about.

'Ready for the next lap of our adventure?' he says.

Oh, yes, an adventure. For him this is just an adventure. Another lie, more distortions, more pretending that the insane is sane. He is head and shoulders above it all, not caring for anything but getting through it all safely, keeping her safe in keeping with his duty and, that done, moving on.

One day he will deposit her in the last safe house and go on his way to his own safe refuge. He cares nothing for her; he is indifferent to her reaching out for him, her loneliness, her need for closeness. Well, she thinks, squaring her shoulders, it's only for the time being. Soon, Amélie and Thérèse will join her, and then Maman and Papa, Manon and Sofie. Then they'll be a complete family again, and she can forget that Ralf ever existed.

At Gare de l'Est she steps down onto the platform and looks around for Ralf. He is no longer behind her. He has exited the carriage by another door, obscured by other passengers spilling out from their compartments onto the train's aisle, pushing in between each other. Then she sees him, and he her. He pushes through the milling crowd to join her.

'We made it!' he exults. 'Paris, the City of Lights!'

'And of love,' she adds.

'Yes, yes, that too. Now we're here I have to figure out how to get us to the Metro and then across to Gare Montparnasse for our onward journey.'

'I wish we could stay,' she says, sighing. 'To be in Paris, only to rush off again – it seems like a waste.'

'Sarah, this is not a holiday. One day, when the war is over, you can return and see Paris. And so will I. But for now, this is the most dangerous city in France, so we must move on.'

'I know, I was just dreaming.'

'Shall we go to a café first, have something to eat? I had my sandwich at lunchtime but I'm hungry again.'

'Yes, let's do that.'

'Let me take your bag.'

He heaves her bag easily across his shoulder, and they move off, following the crowd to the exit. Almost at once she notices: the glares. People walking towards them scowl, some muttering words she cannot quite make out, charged with disapproval and reproach. Some simply swerve away, as if to make a wide berth around them. One person spits demonstratively at the ground. It becomes clear: being with a German soldier might protect her somewhat from the Gestapo, but it does not endear her to the French.

The unimaginatively named Café de la Gare is just outside the station. Inside, most of the small square tables are already occupied. Sarah spots an empty one in the corner, near a door under a sign saying *Toilettes*. She points to it and leads the way over. It is good to use her legs again, good to escape the claustrophobic confines of a moving train. She sits down, her back to the door.

'I'll get us something,' says Ralf. 'What about an omelette and a roll? That would keep us going for a while.'

'Yes, and coffee.'

'I'll see what I can do about the coffee. It won't be real.'

He walks over to the counter at the back of the café and speaks to a young waitress wearing a checked apron with matching headscarf. She hands him a card but then immediately turns away. He is trying to speak to her and she turns to him again, but scowls as she replies, and stiffly walks away.

Ralf returns, two cups of coffee in his hands. 'In future it's better if you do the ordering,' he says. 'This uniform doesn't do me any favours. And they don't have any eggs. I ordered—' He breaks off and starts again.

'Sarah, don't turn around! Some German officers just walked into the café. They seem to be looking for someone… looking around. Stay calm, don't worry. If they come to us, act naturally. Everything is in order.'

It is easy for him to say. For her, the panic just beneath the surface surges forth. It is always there, lurking, waiting for the slightest cue to leap into action, stifling every other thought, threatening that carefully tended sense of safety. You can repeat it a thousand times: *don't worry, stay calm, don't be afraid, everything's fine…* but repeating words, even believing them to be valid, knowing they are the logical, rational truth, doesn't make them *your* reality, doesn't magically transform them into their opposite. The fear, the worry, the anxiety is still there; a beast skulking in the shadows of the mind, waiting for the slightest prompt to leap forward, devour all the good and confident stances so carefully nurtured.

She reaches for her cup of ersatz coffee. Anything for a distraction: think of coffee instead of panic. But it doesn't work and her hand on the table begins to tremble. It is all she can do not to twist around to see, to know what they are doing; if they are coming her way.

Ralf places his hand on hers, a still and steady hand, so much larger than hers it covers the evidence of her fear.

'Steady on,' he says. 'Act naturally, stay calm.'

There it is again: all the platitudes. She wants to shout at him, to yell, to tell him to shut up; she is scared, terrified, and she can't stop the trembling no matter how hard she tries. His face is so infuriatingly calm, smiling even, acting the innocent citizen enjoying a cup of coffee. Or maybe he isn't even acting, maybe he *is* this calm, so without emotion, so without passion; so very *German*. And in that moment she hates him. She pulls her hand from under his.

'Stop it!' The words fly out too loud, louder than she wants, almost a cry; and because they are too loud, she turns to check if anyone else has heard, if she's drawn attention.

There they are: proper Gestapo this time, in black uniforms. The chill that envelops her is by now familiar. Every time danger lurks it falls over her like a net, draining the blood from her face. In the moment of her turning one of the officers looks her way and she catches his gaze and she feels her eyes open wide in terror, sees him frown and start to head their way. Guilt, she knows, is written in every single line of her face.

'Sarah, look at me!' Ralf's cry is urgent, stifled, but nevertheless effective. She turns back, away from the Gestapo, looks at him, meets his gaze. His own face is still a mask of calmness, but the smile is pasted on and does not reach his eyes. He is talking now, and that too is calm, offering her some inane chit-chat about French bread, German bread, the lack of flour, how each country deals with the rationing. Cool and calm, while all the time her own heart hammers away and her hands, both now out of sight on her lap, continue to tremble.

In between the chit-chat Ralf offers words of wisdom. 'Sarah, please don't do that again! Don't turn around, don't look. They aren't after us. We used to get croissants in Freiburg, before the war; so light and fluffy, but now without butter. Sarah, stay calm, breathe slowly! Germans prefer pretzels to croissants. What did you eat in Colmar, croissants or pretzels? Which do you prefer? They're not interested in us, they're talking to some Jews sitting near the kitchen door. Giving them a hard time… Try not to listen. Try to listen to me. Keep looking at me, don't turn around…'

But she can't help it. Again she turns – surely it is natural to turn and watch when you hear shouting, which is what the men in the black uniforms are now doing? So, she looks to see who they are shouting at. Jews, Ralf had said; how did he know that? She turns to look and knows immediately. Yes, those people are Jews.

She has seen it already many times since arriving in Paris: the yellow star, sewn to a person's sleeve. Mathilde had informed her that all Jews have been issued one and are required to wear it at all times. It has to be neatly sewn onto the sleeve, and when one changes one's clothing, it must be removed and sewn on again, neatly and carefully. These Jews are identifiable by the yellow stars they are wearing. The officers are shouting at them – a group of four – because one of them is wearing a star that is simply pinned on, not sewn. She stares, transfixed. The guilty party sits hunched at the table while both officers yell at him. A hand flies out, hitting him hard on the head. He topples from the chair, lands on the floor sprawled flat, his chair clattering behind him. One of his companions, a woman with her star firmly in place, leaps to her feet, shock written all over her face, but one of the others, a lanky dark man, grasps her arm and pulls her back down to her chair.

The officer kicks the figure cowering on the floor, yells at him to stand up. Slowly, he pulls himself to his feet. They march him out of the café, one on each side, both grasping an arm, almost lifting him. A slight, skinny figure between the two massively built officers.

The whole café now, not just Sarah, stares in stunned silence, watching the guilty man being frogmarched onto the street. The Jewish woman at his table weeps into her hands. Her companions lean towards her, seemingly speaking words of comfort.

Sarah now turns to Ralf: 'What will happen to him? What did he do wrong?'

'They'll arrest him, probably put him in jail for a few days, fine him. I don't know… I really don't know, Sarah.'

'You don't know and you don't care!'

'How can you say that?'

'Because look at you! Sitting there watching, telling me to be calm and not bothered, just because you are a German and you have the right papers, but you realise that I'm a Jew, and I should be wearing that star, and I wish I was because I'm a traitor to my people!'

'Sarah, don't! Keep your voice down, please! This isn't the time—'

'But when? When will be the time to talk about how we feel, about the fear and the guilt and the outrage? I left my family behind, everyone I love, and I don't know what will happen to them. I'm all alone and have nobody to talk to because nobody *cares*! Not you – you're one of them, unfeeling, uncaring! Just sitting there telling me to be calm and to pretend nothing is wrong when *everything* is wrong! And I'm not like you, not a bit – I have feelings and I *care*!'

'Sarah – no! Stop!'

But it's too late – Sarah has leapt to her feet and is already scurrying across the café to the Jewish group's table, picking up the fallen chair, sitting on it, leaning across the table, exclaiming to the remaining three people: 'I saw what happened and I am sorry! I too am Jewish and I wanted to…'

But the people at the table aren't listening. The moment the words 'I too am Jewish' burst from her lips all three stand up. The woman speaks sternly to her: 'If you are Jewish then go back to your table and shut your bloody mouth! We don't know you for your own safety. Take her away and make her shut up!'

This last to Ralf, who has followed Sarah; has now placed an arm around her waist and, nodding to the three strangers, has turned her around to lead her back to their table. The three Jews turn stiffly away and leave the café.

Back at their table, Ralf sits her down and his voice now is in no way calming or placating.

'Sarah, you cannot do that! You cannot give in to your outrage and let it take control. You cannot! You have no idea… you must control yourself better.'

'Like you, I suppose: a paragon of control, a man without a single real feeling, a walking statue! You cold, empty, stiff old *German!*'

She spits the words, especially the last, an insult to end all insults. She glares at him, every last frustration curling through her and escaping her lips in an outburst of unmitigated rage. She shoots up from her chair, throwing it over, grabs her bag from the floor and storms to the café door. Once outside she stops for a moment, looks both ways down the pavement, looking for the yellow-starred Jews who left just a minute ago. Spotting them several metres down the road, she starts after them. But strong arms encircle her, holding her back, turning her around; and there, looking down at her, his gaze fierce and passionate and pleading all at once, Ralf's face, closer than it has ever been.

'Sarah! Sarah, you can't do this! You can't imagine how dangerous it is. We can't— People are staring. I'm sorry but…'

And then his lips crush down on hers and he is kissing her, right there in the middle of the pavement. Pedestrians swerve to avoid them as they did at the station, but their glances this time show not just disapproval but open disgust, revulsion, even, and the insults they murmur as they pass are not just murmured but spat out: *putain*, she hears, whore, and *collaborateure! Traiteur!* One man spits, and the spittle lands not on the ground this time but on her headscarf. But Ralf ignores them all and continues to kiss her, softly but firmly and with feeling. Sarah's initial struggle softens and she goes limp in his arms and finally, at long last, surrenders to the kiss and all the longing, all the yearning, all the hunger. All the thirst, all the emptiness and loneliness and sheer *neediness* of the past few weeks wells up inside her in a single wave that empties into him and she feels, she knows, with every fibre of her being, that she is not rejected. All of her joins all of him and no words are necessary but only this, this kiss, everlasting and whole and trumping all the agony and all the anguish and all the angst that has gone before, wiping all agitation from the slate of her soul.

Finally, he draws away, still holding her almost limp form in his arms, and they stand in silence, looking at each other, not smiling, not speaking except with their eyes, and yet she knows. For eyes can speak a secret language and that language opens up to her right there and then. It needs no grammar, no vocabulary, no tedious study for it is immediate and pure, directly spoken without words. Then at last words come, whispered urgently, ardently:

'Don't say that,' he says. 'Don't even *think* that. I am not a statue, I am a man. And I love you. I think I have loved you from the moment we met. But it is forbidden and must end here and now. But remember, do not forget it. Now come with me. Take my hand and come with me.'

He lets go of her then but she is still so limp, he has to catch her before she sinks to the pavement and jolt her upright. She catches herself, straightens her knees and smiles because joy courses through her and all the inner fug and all the awful jumbled memories, images – Krämer's ugly face, the bloodied head, the gun aimed at her, the hiding in cellars, jackboots tramping above her, screams, shots, demolition, chaos, a dead bearded *maquisard* – have been cleansed; pure she feels, and free. His hand is outstretched. She takes it and walks beside him, and now and then they look at each other and smile, exchanging a secret message, saying all the things they have no words for.

But eventually the reality of a Paris pavement and a Paris crowd rips away at their bubble of elation, specifically at *his* elation for she, still enveloped in it, cannot, will not, let go of this newfound joy but simply follows his lead, lets him think for her, lead her through the unwelcome and unwanted reality.

'We need the Metro,' he says. It is the cool, calm Ralf of before. 'We need to get to Gare Montparnasse and find a train that will take us to the south. You need to ask directions of someone; they will not speak to a German soldier.'

Sarah, hearing his voice but not the words, just smiles at him and nods.

'Sarah! Didn't you hear what I said? Snap out of it!'

The urgency in his voice does indeed snap her out of it.

'What did you say?'

'You need to ask directions – we need to find the nearest Metro station and take the train to Gare Montparnasse. I will wait here. You go off and find someone to ask.'

Sarah takes a deep breath. She can no longer hide behind Ralf's leadership, she must do this on her own. She walks away from him, raises a hand at a passer-by, an older man in a grey coat too thick for the weather and a grey hat. The man stops, a question in his eyes.

'*Oui?*'

'*Pardonnez-moi, monsieur*... can you please help us? We need the Metro.'

The man launches into a swift and detailed description of the way to the next Metro station, which turns out to be actually quite simple: back the way they had come, to Gare de l'Est. The Metro is there. She thanks him and he raises his hat and walks away. She returns to Ralf, hooks her arm with his, stands on tiptoes to kiss him on the cheek. He pulls away.

'Sarah, don't! You know it only draws unwanted attention.'

'Then you should not have kissed me first!'

Her words are playful, teasing and completely inappropriate.

'You must stop this flirting, Sarah! We need to be serious now. We need to get to Poitiers by nightfall as there's a curfew there.'

She giggles, skipping to keep up with him. His legs are long and he strides quickly as if in a hurry to get away from that telltale kiss.

'It's all your fault! Don't blame me, you started it!'

'Well, what was I to do when you make such horrible accusations? When you say such horrible things about me? And when you run off down the street after strangers? I had to stop you somehow. You were behaving like a silly girl.'

'What was *I* to do? I felt rejected by you. You've rejected me all along and they were Jews, like me. I just wanted to be with people who would accept me. Not with some cold statue.'

He stops at that word, grasps her arms and swings her to face him. Again, she lets herself go limp. She looks at him, waiting for his words, which she knows will be another rebuke. She likes his rebukes – they confirm the truth she already knows. They destroy the statue Ralf, allowing the real Ralf to show his face.

'Don't call me that! Don't call me that, Sarah! If you knew… if you only knew… But you are so impulsive, so – so emotional – and it is just not appropriate. You must stop it. You don't seem to realise – we cannot. It's not… not…' He falters then and she finishes for him.

'Not appropriate? You said you loved me and love is always appropriate. Love is the one thing that will keep me alive. I need it like I need air – I was suffocating.'

'Yes, but—'

'But I have to grow up and stop acting like an infatuated teenager. I understand. Very well, Ralf—'

'Call me Karl.'

She shakes her head. 'I can't, I really can't. You are Ralf to me. I will just avoid your name altogether.'

'Sometimes I just want to shake you…'

'You will have no need to in future. From now on I am a very mature woman and I will do exactly as you say.'

'Except call me Karl?'

'Except that. But otherwise I promise to be sensible from now on.'

'Good – but then please stop joking about it. You could have got us both in big trouble, back there at the café.'

'It was very necessary – it forced your hand.'

'This is not the time or the place for this discussion. Now we need to find the Metro and get to Gare Montparnasse. Stop giggling!'

'I can't help it. I was so terrified and miserable and now I'm not, so I have to laugh.'

'We have to be serious.'

'I want you to laugh too! And I know you want to as well. See, your lips are twitching. Go ahead and laugh! Stop being such a serious, boring… German.'

'Don't call me that!'

'But you *are* that: serious and boring.'

'One of us has to have their head screwed on tightly. You are up in the clouds!'

'It's temporary. It's all your fault. If you hadn't—'

'If I hadn't, you'd have run down the street like a madwoman and flung yourself at those Jews and we would all perhaps now be in jail. Sarah, please! Be sensible.'

She places her hands over her face and swipes slowly down from forehead to chin. Her smile has turned into a scowl.

'Is that better?'

His lips twitch again, but he holds firm and says, 'Actually, yes. Much better.'

'I can't hold it for long, though. I want to laugh and sing and hear violins playing in the sky. In fact, I want to play those violins myself so you'd better lead the way into this serious, boring life you want for me. Look, there's the Metro sign!'

'Good! Let's go.'

He takes her hand and they descend the stairs into the darkness of the underground. For a small second she is reminded of other dark underground places: Margaux's wine cellar, the basement at the Resistance house, and she shudders as sombre memories try to push themselves into awareness, casting shadows over her newfound elation.

But no, not now. Too long she has wallowed in the swamp of despair. She will bask in this sunshine, this sense of complete fullness that fills her body and soul. Ralf has declared himself and that is all she needs. The immense love she holds within her, that has lurked, unheeded, unrecognised, beneath the gloomy surface of her fears, has been released, having found a refuge in him, and refuses to go back into hiding. Yes, she must find a way to reconcile love with the reality of this terrible time. But not now, not here. Now, she feels her hand in his and all she can do is rejoice.

At the entrance to the Metro station Ralf places an arm around her, draws her close, but before she has time to enjoy his closeness whispers urgently: 'Sarah, don't turn around! We're being followed, I think. There's a man who was in the café with us. He's still behind us. He could be Carlingue. Stay alert and do exactly as I say, all right?'

'Of course.'

There it is again, the insistent jackhammer of her heart. She itches to turn and look but resists, instead hurrying along beside Ralf, scurrying to keep up with his long strides. He has dropped his arm from her shoulders and instead holds her hand, leading the way through the crowds descending into the underground station, winding his way through and pulling her behind him. In a narrower passage they hurry single file, as if late for an appointment and rushing to catch a train. This gives him the chance to turn to look at her and throw his glance further back. An expletive leaves his lips; his eyes throw out a warning. Yes, they have a stalker.

All of a sudden Sarah has an idea. She stops suddenly, drops into a squat. 'What?' Ralf asks, but then he understands and his eyes light up in praise. He stands above her protectively as she first loosens the laces on one of her boots and then leisurely reties them. The Metro crowd flows past, a river of human bodies.

Ralf grins down at her. 'That was quick thinking! He couldn't stop without drawing attention to himself. He's gone past. He'll probably wait for us further on. We need to turn back, come on!'

She stands up now and returns his grin, pleased that her ploy has worked. He holds out his hand, she takes it and they set off again, but in the opposite direction, doubling back on their route, hurrying against the flow of humanity, bouncing against bodies now and then, but not caring; running, escaping and, finally, emerging back into the sunlight. They have thrown off their follower.

'That's why we have to keep our heads down,' says Ralf. 'You running off to join those Jews at their table was the opposite of that.'

'I'm sorry,' she says. 'I didn't think, I just…'

'You *felt*. I know, I understand. Sympathy, and solidarity. But it was the wrong thing to do. You must learn to *think* rather than feel. Now we have to disappear for a while.'

They spend the next hour wandering through side streets, this way and that, asking directions, until at last they find their way to another Metro station. This one they navigate with ease, and before long, they are at Gare Montparnasse.

Chapter Twenty-Eight

Sarah wants them to travel together this time. 'I don't see the point in sitting separately. Why? We can just say we are a brother and sister. Or cousins. Or…' she giggles, 'a married couple. Why not?'

'We have different names, so we are obviously not siblings. Same for being a married couple.'

'Why not cousins, then?'

'It's just a precaution, Sarah. In case they really are looking for us, for either of us. Look what happened at the café, what might have happened! And you have seen how much they hate me, because of my uniform. See, I'm a danger to you more than you're a danger to me. My story is solid, my papers are convincing, but… still. What if they have been alerted to look for me? A young German on the loose, a deserter? So that's why. If I'm arrested, I don't want you involved. This uniform was not the best disguise.'

'I hate being alone. I'll behave myself. I won't do anything silly again, I promise.'

'You're not alone. I won't be far away.'

'Yes, but—'

'Enough, Sarah! No more discussion. It's the last lap of our journey. In Poitiers it will all be over.'

'What do you mean? What's going to be over?'

'Our journey. Poitiers is the last stop – you will be taken care of there.'

'And you?'

'I don't know.'

'But you'll stay with me, won't you?'

'I said I don't know, Sarah! I really don't know.'

'But you said you loved me. You did. You do, don't you?'

He does not reply. She grabs his sleeve and stops him. They stand on the platform, facing each other, but his gaze is fixed on something vague, beyond her, not meeting her eyes.

'Ralf! You said you loved me… It's true, isn't it? Look at me and tell me it's true!'

His eyes meet hers, then, and at last he speaks.

'It's true, Sarah. But this is the bit you don't understand. I'm not supposed to. I can't. It's nothing we can count on in any way. You should not take it seriously… please don't. I'm sorry.'

'What do you mean?'

'Sarah, we have to catch the train. It's leaving in a few minutes and we have to find seats. We can't stand here talking. Come on!'

He removes her hand from his sleeve, gently, holds it in his and tugs at her for them to continue up along the long line of carriages. She comes, but reluctantly, still talking. Her voice, now, is smothered in tears.

'What do you mean, Ralf? Tell me!'

'Stop calling me Ralf – I'm supposed to be Karl! I'll tell you but not here, not now.'

'When, then? Where?'

'When we get to Poitiers we can have a nice long talk and discuss everything. You have to understand, Sarah – in wartime everything is different. Love is different. People can't live normal lives, everything is dangerous.'

'What do you mean, love is different? Love is just love! Either it's there or it's not.'

'Look, here's our train. Let's get in – you go first.'

He almost pushes her up the steps and into the carriage. Looking over her shoulder, she says, 'Stop treating me like a child, Ralf!'

'Then stop behaving like one! Try to grasp the seriousness of the situation. This isn't some romantic novel you're living in! We had one close shave today – have you forgotten already?'

They edge along the carriage corridor, peering into the compartments, looking for suitable places to sit. She, in fact, is looking for two seats together and so she moves on; there is so much to discuss, so much she doesn't understand. It all seems simple to her. Yes, they are both on the run. Yes, it is wartime. Yes, they have to be careful. But they love each other! People who love each other belong together, stick together through thick and thin – where is the question?

But then she remembers her own family. They love each other, belong together. Yet they have separated. She remembers the moist agony in her mother's eyes as they said goodbye, the telltale tear stain on her father's cheek and his trembling lips. They have pushed her away, out of her home, just as Ralf is pushing her away now. War destroys love, destroys families. It was the very first lesson of war she learned: war means separation.

All the lessons she has learned till now have been brutal: pushed from the tight protective cocoon of family out into a cold, uncaring world, hiding and skulking about and lying and pretending. Twice she has encountered death. The image of an exploding head, blood and brains and bits of bone flying, will haunt her for ever; and then Raoul, shot for trying to be a hero. But love is the cure; love is the only remedy, the only antidote. Now she has found love but he is saying it cannot be. She turns around to exclaim:

'I don't believe you, I don't accept what you say! I—'

But behind her is not Ralf but a stranger, a grey-haired man in a beret. Peering back, she sees that Ralf has already slipped into the nearest compartment and taken a seat, is settling into it, not thinking about her. It is the last empty seat in the compartment.

Sarah is left with no choice. She enters the next compartment and plumps herself down into the next vacant seat, beside a young woman with a baby on her lap.

*

By the time she climbs out of the train carriage at Poitiers she is fuming. It has been a tedious journey: small talk with the young mother next to her, smiling and cooing at the baby (she loves babies and would like one of her own but not now, not this one), enduring the occasional police controls. They had forgotten to buy food for the journey, but the girl has willingly shared hers, breaking off a knob from her baguette and a corner of cheese for Sarah. She takes it reluctantly; the girl insists. She has a flask, too, with some bitter coffee – it tastes terrible.

And beneath it all Sarah nourishes a little seed of hurt: pride and offence and abandonment all wrapped up in a kernel of resentment, festering in the dark so that, by the time they arrive at Poitiers, it has grown roots and shoots and even branches; love has vanished and in its place is this ugly little plant of umbrage. If it were at all possible she would now walk off and leave Ralf to his own devices, but they are unfortunately inter-reliant, like it or not. They both have the address they are to go to, but neither of them knows the way there, and they must find it together. And anyway, there he is, waiting for her on the platform as she emerges from the carriage. Smiling, as if nothing has happened between them. And maybe, for him, it is so.

It seems that he has forgotten their squabble. His demeanour is relaxed, relieved. They have made it! Another lap of their journey successfully attained. Yes, there was still a way to go but in Poitiers, they have been told, they can settle for a while. Poitiers is a receiving post for fugitives from the north – from all over Europe, in fact – and they can find some anonymity in its crowds. But best of all: here, Sarah will be reunited with her family. First, Thérèse and Amélie will come, and then Maman and Papa and the younger girls. From here they will move on to Spain and America. As for Ralf... She frowns: she must find out his plans.

But here, too, menace lurks. As they walk through the station to the exit, already she can see many individuals wearing the yellow star identifying them as Jews. It curdles her blood, brings up bile. She feels guilt; she too should be wearing a star, if only in solidarity! What is it about Jews that make them so reviled in their own countries? Why? Maybe here, in Poitiers, she will find answers.

In the meantime, though, her own personal quandary is more pressing. She is very cross with Ralf and it is necessary to let him know. Instead of arguing, though – arguing never seems to get her anywhere with him – she sulks as she walks beside him, not even listening as he talks.

'I'm sorry I didn't think of packing something to eat and drink for the journey. I should have thought of it. I suggest we look for a café and have a bite before moving on to look for the house. It's not a good idea to arrive hungry and wanting to be fed. You must be starving – I am.'

No response. He looks at her. She feels his gaze but looks stubbornly ahead.

'Sarah?'

Again, she does not answer, does not turn. She feels his grasp on her arm. She tries to shake it off, but it only tightens.

'Leave me alone!'

'My God, don't say you're still brooding over that stupid conversation we had in Paris!'

'Yes, and I suppose I'm stupid too!' Again, she tries to shake him off but he does not allow it. They stand facing each other and this time she looks up and her scowl is genuine.

'You are anything but stupid. I never once thought you were stupid. But you are moody and emotional and everything I say seems to trigger some new mood.'

'Well, I can't help it, can I?'

'Yes, you can. You can grow up. You can stop letting your moods take charge of you. I told you I'd stop treating you like a child when you stop behaving like one. There's a war on and people are being killed and all you can do is sulk and moan. My God, Rebecca warned me, but I didn't think—'

'Rebecca warned you? About what?'

'About teenage girls and their emotional needs. That you are inexperienced and naïve and needy. And all I'm saying is it has to stop. Right now, this minute! You can't indulge your moods at a time like this.'

'I suppose you're better than me at that.'

'You know what, Sarah? Yes, I *am* better than you at that. I don't give in to moods and emotions at a time when far more important things are going on in the world than what's in my own little head. Yes, I have feelings too, but there's a war on and that comes first and we both have to be responsible. Not just me, Sarah. I can't be responsible for both of us. You really, really need to snap out of it!'

They stand facing each other as he falls silent. His gaze speaks more eloquently than his words; it accuses and understands and forgives all at once. It pleads for peace. It insists on compliance. It is firm and confident even as it is gentle and empathetic. In it is everything she lacked herself: in it is backbone. Something in her snaps and she hangs her head.

'I'm sorry,' she says. 'I suppose I have been childish.'

'You have, but you can do better. I know it.'

They walk on.

'I don't know what's wrong with me,' she says. 'Why can't I be strong and steady like you?'

'Nothing's wrong with you, Sarah. It's the world that's all wrong and you haven't had time to adjust.'

'You think I can adjust? Grow up and be like you?'

'Of course you can!'

'You must hate me for being such a baby.'

He stops her, grabs both her arms.

'Hate you? Oh, Sarah, if only you knew! But now…'

He lets go and walks on.

Chapter Twenty-Nine

Poitiers is, if anything, busier even than Paris, at least around the station. People milling everywhere, coming and going, so many of them wearing that dreaded yellow star. Asking directions, they make their way slowly to the house they've been sent to, the home, they've been told, of a Jewish family originally from Metz who had settled here soon after the start of the war.

'They won't put you up for long, but they'll arrange other accommodation for you in Poitiers,' Claudine had said. 'You can wait there for the rest of your family.'

Weary, exhausted, tired of travelling, longing for a place of relative safety, they eventually reach the house. A kindly-faced middle-aged woman opens the door. Before long they are sitting in the cosy kitchen, cups of tea steaming on the table before them, a basket of bread and pastries inviting them to taste. Butter! And sugar!

'What luxury!' says Sarah, and her hostess beams.

'Yes, all these things are forbidden; bakers can only make bread and pastries for the Germans. But we get them on the black market. As well as soap.'

But the greatest luxury is Madame Hoffmann herself, a petite, blonde, pretty woman.

'Call me Régine,' she says, and the warmth in her eyes tells Sarah all she needs to know: that here again is one of those extraordinary women who simply by being who they are hold the chaotic world together, prevent it from splintering into a million pieces. The world might be going completely mad, hatred and discord might seem to rule. Healthy young men might pour out, one nation against another, to kill and to maim and destroy each other. Allied and

Luftwaffe fighter planes might shoot each other down, drop bombs, destroy cities, devastate the countryside. People might flee in all directions. Mayhem and destruction and annihilation might reign. But Régine and her sisters provide an invisible band of humanity and strength. They hold the very foundation of society in their hands, will piece it all together when the chaos is over, will one day restore sanity to the world. From the moment she steps over the threshold, sits down at the kitchen table, Sarah feels it seeping into her, the calmness and confidence that even Ralf cannot provide.

Régine had been prepared to receive two women, not one young woman and a young man and, furthermore, a young man who is German, in the uniform of a soldier. Yet she takes that information in her stride, hides her initial shock, listens to Ralf's story and declares him welcome in her home.

'It is better to be a deserter than to sacrifice one's life for a madman,' she says. 'You did the right thing.'

On inspecting Sarah's papers, she exclaims, 'But you are not identified as Jewish! You do not have the stamp! But that is wonderful! You do not have to wear the yellow star!'

Sarah nods, and explains: 'My family is not religious. We are secular Jews. My father does not even know the rabbi in Colmar. And we have a typical German name, so he did not register us as Jews when we were told to do so at the start of the annexation. He thought we could get away with it. But someone betrayed us and we had to make a run for it.'

'Ah yes, betrayal. It is a curse, a curse we must all be wary of. But for the time being you are safe in Poitiers and these papers make you even safer. No one need know. Originally, the plan was for refugees to cross the demarcation line into Vichy. We used to help with that; it's not far from Poitiers. But last year the Nazis invaded, took over the Free Zone as well, so that possibility has been taken away. So, you must wait a while until your family arrives. We will help. Now you must tell me a little about yourself so that

I can figure out the next step. It is best you find work to support yourself until your family joins you, if only for a few weeks. What work could you do?'

'My father is a violin-maker and I was his apprentice,' says Sarah. 'I would love to continue that work eventually.'

'I don't know if I can find work for you in that field. It is quite unusual and I doubt there is much demand for violins in wartime. Still, people will always crave music and perhaps there is an opening for you somewhere.' She turns to Ralf. 'And you?'

'I am a soldier; that is all,' he says. 'I was not able to finish school – I was conscripted. I had hoped to be a doctor like my father. The war put an end to that plan.'

'Well, who knows? Perhaps when all this is over, you can fulfil that desire. For the moment I will think about what you can do in Poitiers and where you can stay. Unfortunately, you cannot stay here longer than a night or two. But I will find a good place for both of you.'

'We would like to stay together. We—' Sarah begins, but Ralf throws her such a stern look, she stops mid-sentence. Her eyes meet his; hers say, 'I understand. It's not about me and what I want.' He nods slightly, and smiles. She smiles back. Régine shakes her head. 'Staying together is impossible. Jobs are scarce. But I will find you something.'

Régine settles them in, shows them the rooms where they will sleep and the bathroom where they can freshen up. Hot water and soap! It is a luxury, and Sarah takes her time washing herself over the sink, washing her hair, her feet, and then her clothes. Then it is Ralf's turn. When he emerges from the bathroom she hardly recognises him. The stubble that had grown overnight is gone. She puts up her hand to stroke his cheek.

'So smooth again!' she says. 'I like it.' She raises her face to nuzzle him, moves her lips towards his – but he turns his head away, steps back, laughs.

'No nonsense now!' he says. 'We have to talk, Sarah. There's something I need to tell you. Can we go out for a walk?'

She nods. 'Of course. But, Ralf, isn't it good to be here? To finally be settled somewhere, not on the run? At last I feel safe, not having to look over my shoulder all the time. I love Poitiers!'

'We are still not safe,' he replies sombrely. 'Not even in Poitiers. Don't let your guard down, Sarah. We both have a long way to go until we are truly safe. That won't happen until the war is over.'

'But at least we will be together – that is the important thing.'

He replies only, 'Are you ready? You have your bag?'

'I don't need that damned bag any more, thank goodness!'

'True. Just bring your papers.'

'You have money? We can go to a café, maybe.'

He pats his pockets. 'All set.'

They explore Poitiers for a while and finally find a suitable little café, the Café Bleu, in a quiet and picturesque part of the city. They select stale-looking pastries at the counter and order coffee, then choose a table on the pavement outside.

'It almost feels like Colmar in peacetime,' sighs Sarah. 'For the first time I can relax.'

'Well, don't relax too much. Like I said earlier, keep your guard up. Even here, danger is just around the corner.'

'But I don't feel it lurking, for a change, and that makes all the difference. I feel free!'

'You are not free, Sarah, not as long as this war is still raging.'

'I know, I know! I'm just saying the war seems so far away here. It's almost as if—'

'Sarah, I told you back at the house that there's something we must discuss. Something I need to tell you. The thing is, you cannot just blot out the war because you don't see or feel it. As we speak, people are being killed, persecuted, abused. The fight against the perpetrators must continue. It is my country that is responsible and I, as a citizen of that country, have to do something. I have to respond. Because that makes me responsible. I have to help put things right.'

'What do you mean, Ralf? What can you do? You're just a deserter, a soldier without a home and without even a name and a country because they'd kill you if they knew.'

'That's exactly it. I've cut my ties with Germany but I am still German at heart and I need to help right this great wrong my country has done. Sarah, I am joining the French Resistance.'

'What? No! You can't!'

'I can and I will. See, when I was in Metz I met people from the Free French, de Gaulle's unofficial army fighting the Germans. They accepted me as a volunteer. As a soldier I have skills they need and can put them to good use. They want me to work with the Poitiers *maquisards*. I have a phone number – I am to contact them and I will join up as soon as possible.'

'No, Ralf, no! Don't, please don't! What about *us*? I've only just found you, we've found each other – you said you loved me. You can't go off again! Don't leave me!'

Tears gather in her eyes. 'You said you loved me!'

He glances around, puts a finger on his lips to warn her, then reaches across the table, takes both her hands in his.

'And I do. Don't cry, Sarah. It's true. I love you so much, I— But that's exactly it. I love you, Sarah. I do. I've known it ever since – well, actually, ever since I was forced to tie you to that tree in the forest, but I didn't realise it then. But now – yes, I tried to suppress it, deny it, but I can't. But it's because I love you that I am doing this. Because I want us to be together in a free and safe world, a world at peace.'

A waitress brings their coffees, slams them on the table, glares from one to the other. '*Bon appetit!*' she says, but her tone is mocking. They do not look up, do not acknowledge her. They ignore the waitress and the coffee and the pastries. Their eyes lock; Sarah sniffs, swipes her tears away with the back of her hand.

'It's dangerous, Ralf. You could get killed! You saw what happened to those people in Metz – they're probably all dead by now!'

'Yes, there is some risk, I know that. Still, I must do it.'

'Why do men always have to fight? Why do they have to go around killing each other?'

He chuckles wryly. 'Believe me, it would not be my first choice of profession. I am not a natural soldier. I want to be a doctor, a surgeon – put bodies together, not tear them apart. But sometimes reality takes away our choices. And now my only choice is this: to defy and defeat Germany, my own country. I cannot be at peace with myself unless I do so.'

'But – what about *us*?' She stifles the impulse to howl in sheer agony.

'God willing, I will survive and when this is all over, then we can make plans. And anyway, Sarah, we could not be together now. If I were to flee with you to Spain my options would be to stay in hiding or surrender to the Allies; I'd be a prisoner of war until the fighting is over. No, Sarah. Neither of those options suit me. I need to fight this thing; I cannot put personal desires in front of the thing that needs to be done. If we – I – do not resist this evil thing, I will be part of the evil – I will be a coward, thinking only of myself.'

'And if Germany wins the war? What then?'

'I cannot even begin to believe that will happen. To allow such a thought is to already entertain defeat. I cannot do it.'

'But…'

'Sarah, you must find the courage within yourself, the courage to support me just by understanding why I have to do it. Just knowing I have your support would be such a source of strength for me. Remember, you are not alone. Think of the women we have already met along the way – women who have lost sons, husbands, brothers. How strong they are…'

She cries out then: 'How *can* you? How can you say such a thing? Giving me as models women who have lost their men! As if I too must prepare myself to lose you!'

'That's not what I meant. I meant to say we must both be strong. And sometimes being strong means standing up to what is right, even if it causes pain and sacrifice, even if it almost breaks one's heart.'

'Not almost. It *will* break my heart if you go off to join the Resistance.'

'It won't, you will see. I have to do it, Sarah. My mind is made up. I have known it since we were in Metz. I've been deliberating since then and the conviction now is firm. The idea is new to you, so you are upset, but one day you, too, will be convinced.'

'I was right when I called you a statue. You are the most heartless, unfeeling, uncaring… A stiff, cold German, just like all of them. I trusted you. I…'

But Ralf is not listening. He places his hands on his ears, closes his eyes – scrunches them together, in fact – and his face tenses as if he is battling with some internal enemy, fighting a mental war, stifling his sobs even as his body heaves.

Sarah reaches out, places a hand on his head. 'What's the matter, Ralf? Talk to me!'

But he can't hear because his ears are covered. She places her hands on his wrists, tries to pull his hands away. He relaxes, drops his hands into hers, opens his eyes at last, meets her gaze, his eyes moist with eloquence.

She cannot bear the feeling in them, the very antithesis of the stiff, cold German of her rebuke. Remorse hits her.

'I'm sorry, I should not have said that. I didn't know, I didn't think…'

He speaks at last, and his voice is firm:

'Well, that's exactly your problem, isn't it? You *never* think. You only *feel*, and all your feelings just swirl around yourself. I've told you again and again to grow up, but you never do. Yes, I do love you. I love you with all my heart, Sarah, but you drive me to distraction. Hopefully, in a few years when the war is over, and you have seen more suffering, you will understand – that you and your feelings are not the centre of the world!'

He rises to his feet. 'Come, let's go. This is all too much drama for my liking.' He marches to the door. Sarah grabs the two pastries, throws some money on the table and a look of apology at the waitress, then runs after him. She comes up behind him and grasps his arm.

'I'm sorry. I'm sorry, Ralf! I know I'm being silly. I can't help it – it just overtakes me... Sometimes it's all too much, this war and everything.'

He places an arm across her shoulders, draws her close as they walk on. They pass a small park, just a square of green between two parallel streets. They sit down on a bench beneath a spreading oak, his arm still around her shoulder, her head leaning against him.

'Then you must be strong, Sarah, as we all must be strong. If we do not resist, goodness will disappear from the world. It will be a world of hatred and evil. You don't want that, do you?'

'No, of course not. But you see – I didn't know, nobody ever told me, just how terrible it all is. My parents, they did their best and they thought it was right to shelter me and protect me and keep me at home and never tell me what a terrible thing war is. There was little of it in Colmar, just soldiers swarming everywhere, and all I had to do was hide.'

'There's more to war than hiding, Sarah. Everywhere, fine young men in the prime of life are killing each other for nothing. Jews – your people – are sent away in trains to who knows where, their lives stolen. Keeping your head down just isn't enough against a bully. This is why I have to go.'

'But it's so hard. I only just found you. I wish we could always be together, I wish we did not have to separate. I am afraid of losing you.'

'I too am afraid,' he admits. 'You are the best thing that has ever happened to me. But we must wait, and do the right thing, and pray.'

'Do you pray?'

'I pray all the time.'

'I used to pray but not any more. It doesn't change anything, does it? The war goes on, whether we pray or not.'

'But it brings calm to the mind, and strength.'

'Yours is a Christian prayer?'

'Yes. My family is Catholic.'

'My father does not believe in God. He says the war is proof that there is no God. My mother is different: she believes and she gave me a little prayer when I left home. It is from a psalm of David. It goes like this: *For thou art with me, thy rod and thy staff to comfort me.*'

Ralf continues:

'*Thou preparest a table before me in the presence of my enemies. My cup runneth over. Surely goodness and mercy shall follow me all the days of my life, and I shall dwell in the house of the Lord for ever.*'

'You know that psalm, even as a Christian?'

'Of course. It's beautiful.'

'But so untrue, isn't it? Really, it's laughable. Because the very opposite is happening.'

'But it does good to remember, to say the words. Somehow it lifts the spirit. Maybe that is why we pray: to lift the spirit and give it strength.'

'Even if nothing changes?'

'*Especially* if nothing changes. Because it's in times of danger and difficulty that we most need strength.'

'I feel that it is love that gives the most strength.'

'Indeed. And maybe that is what God is. The power of love, acting within our hearts, giving us the fuel to fight on, even against the odds.'

'I love you so much, Ralf. It is the only thing that gives me strength. I have lost my family, my home – but I have found you. But you are saying I must lose you, too.'

'But you will find your family again. And you will find me again, when the war is over.'

'But there is no certainty. I need certainty. I hate this war, I hate it so much!'

He strokes the hair from her forehead. In the darkness, her eyes burn bright, gazing into his as if she would melt into him.

'Everyone hates it. I hate what it is doing to us all. I could not bear for you to be hurt, Sarah. But I cannot protect you. I cannot even protect myself.'

'When will you have to leave?'

'I don't know. I will contact them very soon, I think. Even tomorrow. This might be our last night together.'

'For the time being. You must add *"for the time being"*.'

'For the time being.'

Chapter Thirty

It is night when they return to the safe house. Régine is not pleased that they have stayed out so late. 'I was worried you'd miss the curfew,' she says. 'It is important not to be conspicuous in any way. Well, we have had our dinner but I left something for you. It is not much, just some stew. Sit down, eat! You must be hungry.'

The stew is simple but delicious; they eat ravenously and then Sarah yawns. The luxury of having arrived at a real home, a real family, with a mother who cooks and cares, and a real bed with clean sheets waiting – it is overwhelming, and the accumulated exhaustion of the past days, the past weeks, descends on her like the rubble of a bombed-out house. Régine pats her on the back.

'I will show you to your beds – you both need sleep. You, Sarah, will sleep in my daughter Stéphanie's room, and Ralf, you will sleep with our foster-son, Pavel – but stay down here for a moment, I want a word with you. Come with me, Sarah.'

Sarah nods and lets herself be led upstairs. Régine shows her into the small room with the crisply made bed.

'My daughter is in an internment camp, under arrest,' says Régine. Sarah looks at her in shock, and sees for the first time the deep anguish in her eyes.

'I'm so sorry. What for?'

'It does not matter. For a small stupidity. That is why I exhort you to be always careful. But I wanted to ask you something: what is it between you and Karl?'

'Karl? Oh, yes, Karl! It is nothing and it is everything: we love each other.'

'It is wonderful to find love in such ugly times but also tragic. I wish you well – but I would advise you to be cautious. You are so young, Sarah – too young to know the consequences of love.'

'I may be young, but my love is strong and will stay strong, whatever the consequences.'

'Ah yes, one says that in the throes of a romantic dalliance – but all I am saying is, do not commit yourself to anything. In war, everything can change at the turn of a pin. I am a mother of many girls – I am only saying, be careful.'

Sarah gives a nod of finality. She is not in the mood for a lecture, no matter how well-meaning, no matter how many daughters have been raised. Régine takes the hint and disappears. Sarah undresses, climbs into bed, and is asleep a moment later.

She wakes late the next morning, washes and dresses hastily and descends to the kitchen. Régine is there cleaning up – the family, it seems, has already breakfasted and made off to their schools, their work, whatever it is they do all day. She had met a few members the day before – teenage girls, a young child, a relative whose parents had escaped the Nazis, the Polish boy Pavel, whose parents have been interned.

'Your friend has gone out to the post office to make a telephone call,' says Régine. 'Come, have some breakfast. And when you have finished, I will show you something interesting. Here...'

She pats a folded newspaper lying on the sideboard. Sarah slips into a chair at the table, reaches for a slice of bread. There is butter on the table, and jam. Régine pours her a cup of coffee. There's a knock on the door: it is Ralf, back from his telephone call. He greets her, bends to kiss her and sits down next to her.

'It's all arranged,' he says. 'I will be off today to meet someone – I won't be back for some time, Sarah.'

She had been about to take a bite of her bread; instead, she drops her hand and stares. 'Already? Today? But… but it's too soon! We only just got here!'

'I'm sorry, that's just the way it is. They have been expecting me – the people in Metz told them I'd be coming and they are eager for me to join.'

'And what about me? *Us?*'

'It will be all right,' says Ralf. 'You must be strong and it will be all right, you will see.'

'You could die,' says Sarah desperately. The night of the Gestapo raid in Metz is ever close; the stamping boots above, the screams, the shots.

'And so could you. Death is always a possibility, even when there is no war.'

She gulps. 'All right, I will try.'

Régine, who had left the kitchen through the back door into the small garden, returns.

'Ah, there you are, Karl! Have you made contact?'

'Yes, I—' he begins, but she raises a hand to stop him.

'Don't tell me the details. The less we know of each other's business, the better. All I need to know is when you will be leaving. Not that I want to throw you out, but you know how it is.'

She is brisk, no-nonsense, unsentimental, yet warm and caring all at once. This is a house, Sarah has learned, where people – refugees, Jews, anyone on the run – come and go and are cared for and sent on their way. Now, Régine turns to her.

'Finished eating? Good! Now let me show you this…'

She opens the newspaper, finds what she was looking for and passes it to Sarah. 'See? This would be perfect!'

It is an advertisement on the Employment page, circled in black. '*Live-in nanny wanted for four children aged 2 to 10. Experience and references necessary. Call…*' A telephone number follows.

'You must ring them right away. Jobs like this are snapped up quickly. They have a telephone, they are obviously wealthy.'

'But I have no experience, no references!'

'Didn't you help your mother run her household and family? Don't you have younger sisters? That's enough experience. As for references, I will give you one, a character reference. Anyone can see you are trustworthy and reliable. Go and call them now.'

Not an hour later, Sarah stands outside the grand black door of a mansion in the wealthiest part of Poitiers, willing herself to press the doorbell. It seems that her insides are made of soft pudding, nothing stable, nothing strong. Ralf has told her to be strong, but strength is not a quality that can be conjured up at one's bidding. She is quaking at the thought of her very first job interview.

But it has to be done, there's no way out. Régine accompanied her to the post office, stood behind her as she made the phone call. The steadying hand on her shoulder helped as Sarah spoke to a clipped curt female voice that told her to come for an interview immediately. It is far too short notice; she'd have preferred more time to gather her wits and prepare herself mentally but that, it seems, is not how things work. If she didn't go now then someone else would, and the job would be gone. It does seem perfect: accommodation and job rolled into one. More importantly, a job she can surely perform, not needing any particular expertise. And now she's on her own. There's nothing for it; it has to be done.

Part Three

Poitiers

Chapter Thirty-One

To Sarah, the house that might possibly be her new home is magnificent. From the outside, it is entirely inviting: roses in full bloom climb up the peach-coloured brick walls, and the path from the wrought-iron gate to the front steps is also lined with roses, nodding in the sunshine as if in welcome. She lifts the lion's-head knocker. It falls with a resonant thud.

The door opens.

She must be a maid, this tall, thin, middle-aged woman in a black dress and white apron. She can't be Madame Lemoins.

'*Bonjour*,' says Sarah. 'I am here to speak to Madame Lemoins, about the nanny position.'

'Yes, *Madame* is expecting you. Come in.'

The woman stands aside to allow Sarah to enter a house that is grander than anything she's ever seen before. It's bigger even than the Château Gauthier, which had been impressive enough, but whereas Château Gauthier had a cosy, somewhat shabby atmosphere as if it absorbed and assimilated the loves and the personalities of all the people welcomed into its walls, and had acquired thus a personality of its own, the Maison Beaulieu is all carefully cultured, forbidding elegance. The welcoming exterior, Sarah finds, is only a façade, entirely deceptive, for once inside the welcome ends abruptly.

The hall is bigger than the whole first floor of her home in Colmar, kitchen and sitting room together, and fitted with such heavy, dark wooden furniture as to create a sense of overbearing oppression. But the furniture is the least of it. The first thing that greets her as she steps into the hall is a floor-to-ceiling portrait of

Adolf Hitler. It comes as a shock to her entire system; she draws in a quick breath and stops and stares before following the maid to an ornately carved oak door that stands ajar. The maid knocks, but it's just a pre-emptive knock because an impatient voice calls out: 'Yes, yes, come in!'

The maid opens the door fully and stands back as Sarah enters, walking into a room as heavily furnished as the hall. A group of weighty sofas and armchairs, upholstered in dark green velvet, form three sides of a square around a fireplace. An ornately framed portrait of Hitler takes pride of place on the wall above the mantelpiece.

On one of the armchairs, facing the door, sits the owner of the voice she spoke to on the phone, a woman, perhaps in her early thirties, who stands up as Sarah approaches, and holds out her hand.

'My word, but you are very young,' she says as a greeting. 'I wasn't expecting— How old are you? You've brought references?'

'I'm eighteen, *Madame*, but I am very responsible. I have four younger sisters and I have been my mother's right hand in looking after them. The youngest is five.'

'So is my Collette. Well, tell me more about yourself. What brings you to Poitiers all the way from Colmar, all on your own? Why are you not with your family?'

Sarah has prepared an answer. Together with Régine, she has thought up a story to explain her presence here, her search for a position. 'Do not tell anyone you are Jewish,' Régine advised. 'Remember, the walls have ears. Do not trust anyone.'

The story they thought up, which Sarah now begins to repeat – it's of course a lie, and she has never lied in her life before, but since leaving her home everything has been a lie and now the words drop easily from her lips – is simple. 'Stick as close to the truth as possible,' Régine said, and so Sarah now explains that she came to continue her apprenticeship as a violin-maker. Her father's brother lives in Poitiers – or rather, he *lived* in Poitiers because, to her horror, on arrival she discovered that he is dead, and so is his whole family. His home, his workshop, the entire quarter where he lived, near the railway station, had been bombed and totally flattened during an Italian aerial raid, in which the station and the supply trains it serviced had been attacked and surrounding houses bombed out too.

'That happened at least a year ago… how did you not know?' Madame Lemoins' eyes narrow as if she is suspicious. There's such a severe look to her: lips so thin they are no more than two red lines in her face, eyes that seem to peer into Sarah's soul, gaunt cheeks. But everyone has gaunt cheeks these days, Sarah included, and it's not fair to judge a person on account of too-thin lips. Any judgement of the woman, the household, comes from those portraits of Hitler. Does she even want this job any more? Can she do it? Can she work here, in a family supporting the man who has destroyed her family, her homeland, her life? But she knows there is little choice; Régine has warned her that many ordinary citizens of Poitiers are resigned to the Nazi occupation and are now openly collaborating.

'One cannot really blame them,' she told her. 'They are really only trying to survive, like everyone else. Most of us would do it, if it came to the crunch and our families' safety were at stake.'

'Never!' Sarah had proudly declared. 'I would never collaborate with a Nazi!'

Régine had shrugged. 'You are young, wait till you have children of your own. There is nothing a mother would not do to protect her children. Nothing.'

And now she, Sarah, is here, with a mother of four children, an obvious collaborator, and asking for a job. How quickly words said in haste and in pride are put to the proof! Perhaps Madame Lemoins only has those portraits to protect her children. Anyway, she has not yet been offered the job, so the question of whether or not she can collaborate with a collaborator by working here is still moot.

'My apprenticeship was arranged long ago,' says Sarah. 'My father thought it good for me to have a different *Meister* than himself; the demand for violins in Colmar has diminished to almost nothing in the last few years and I could gain more experience, and possibly work, here. He and his brother exchanged letters before the war and everything was approved. Of course, he wrote again to let him know I was coming this summer but did not receive a reply. We put it down to the breakdown of postal communication because of the war. After all, Colmar is no longer part of France. It now has a German postal service. Letters take a long time or do not arrive at all.'

Madame Lemoins seems to accept the story. She sighs. 'Ah yes, the war, the war! Such a nuisance! It knocks everyone's lives out of kilter… We all wish for it to be over so we can continue as normal.'

She pauses. 'References?'

'This is a letter from a friend. It is a character reference. I'm afraid this is my first job, so I do not have references regarding the job itself.'

Madame Lemoins reads Régine's letter, which praises Sarah's character in the highest terms. She folds the letter, returns it to Sarah and shrugs. '*Très bien*. Now, please let me see your papers. In these trying days the right papers are important – one cannot after all engage just everyone. One has to know who it is who will be under one's roof.'

'Yes, of course.'

Sarah produces her identity card. Madame Lemoins places a pair of spectacles on her nose and peruses the document. She looks up in surprise.

'A German identification card? You are German, you speak the language?'

'Yes, of course. All Alsatians are now German, and most people speak two languages. So I speak fluent German, *Madame*. I am fully bilingual.'

Madame Lemoins' eyes light up.

'Ah, excellent! German language will of course be a requirement here in France in future. It is essential. The children naturally have classes at school but a native-language person at home, that would be the icing on the cake. One must keep in step with our new German government. It will be more and more important as time goes on.'

She is silent as she returns the papers, frowning. Then: 'You do not have a ration card?'

'Not yet. I will apply for one. The one I had in Colmar – well, it is not valid here.'

'No, of course not.'

She stares at Sarah for another full minute, looking her up and down as if she can see past her clothing and her skin and her tissues and organs right down to her soul. Perhaps she can, thinks Sarah, and says nothing, allows the perusal. Madame Lemoins speaks again.

'So, you know about violins? Can you play one?'

'Of course! All of us at home play string instruments and we also all learned to play the piano, and some of us play the flute as well.'

For the first time Madame Lemoins smiles. 'Really? Well I never! I have been so anxious to find a music instructor for the children. They used to have a Jewish piano teacher, but we had to dismiss her when— Well, you know. It's all very distressing. And I could not find a replacement. She was very good, a very nice lady, and the children loved her, but unfortunately— Well, never mind. So, do you think you could teach my children? Piano and violin? Music is so important; we must not forget culture even during a war. It keeps the spirits up, doesn't it? I used to play the piano as a child but I was never very good – I do want my children to learn.'

'Yes, of course I could teach them. Of course, I'm not a professional musician and I've never taught music before, but I do play well and I have a good ear. I'd love to.'

Madame Lemoins makes a gesture as if brushing back her hair with her hands – hair of which not a tendril is out of place, all swept back in a neat chignon, shiny as satin. When she speaks again, her voice is brisk, no-nonsense; a voice that says it's time to move on to other matters.

'Well, then, that's settled. There are a few more applicants for the job but frankly, the ones I've interviewed up to now have not been up to scratch. Rather common girls, I'm afraid. When can you start?'

'I'm ready whenever you are.'

'Today? Can you move in today?'

'Yes, yes, of course. But still…'

'Still what?'

'Can you tell me a little more about the job? The children? What will be my duties?'

She clucks impatiently. 'My children – they are just children. Julien is the eldest – he is eleven. Then comes Jacqueline, who is eight. And little Collette, who is five. And the baby who is two years old, Michel. The three eldest attend school during the day, so you will look after the little one in that time. He has a nursemaid for the time being, but we are looking for someone who is more than that – he is hardly a baby any more, though we still refer to him as one. When the older ones return from school you will supervise their schoolwork, prepare a snack and their supper, entertain them all and put them to bed. You will have a day off every two weeks, on Sundays. Room and board is of course free – that is, it is subtracted from your salary, which will be paid weekly. And you will speak to them exclusively in German, so that they can speak it like natives. Any other questions?'

'No – no, *Madame*, that is all, thank you.'

'I suppose you'd like to see your room? Madame Elise, my housekeeper, will show you where it is. It is small but quite cosy and you will have your own little washroom. You may take a bath in the children's bathroom once a week. There is running hot water. Where is your luggage?'

'It's at a friend's house – I will fetch it at once, if I may.'

'Yes, yes, do that. Well then, that's settled. Madame Elise will show you around and then you can fetch your luggage and move in. The nursemaid is out walking in the park with little Michel at the moment – when you return, you will meet him and take over.'

She pauses. 'Oh, and I should tell you that my parents also live in this house – they occupy an annexe next to the kitchen. They dine with the family – that is, with myself and my husband. The children dine separately, in the kitchen, and that is your domain. You will eat with them and teach them manners. My sister Monique also visits from time to time – she is a little older than you. And my brother, Gaston. She studies in Paris, he works there; he is an architect. This is our family home, where we all grew up, so they come to visit quite frequently, and you will eventually make their acquaintance. In fact, Monique is visiting at the moment and you will probably meet her this evening. So, now I must dismiss you – other duties await me.'

She rings a bell on a small table beside the armchair, and immediately the woman in the black dress and white apron – so not a maid, but Madame Elise, the housekeeper – slides into the room.

'Madame Elise, I have engaged this young lady, Mademoiselle Sarah Mayer, as our nanny. Please show her around the house, show her her room and the nursery. That will be all. Thank you, Mademoiselle Mayer. Actually, I shall call you Mademoiselle Sarah from now on, *d'accord*?'

'*D'accord.*'

Chapter Thirty-Two

'I got the job! She engaged me on the spot!'

'Really? My word! You must have made quite an impression. Well done!'

Régine is so delighted she gives Sarah a hug and not three but four kisses on her cheeks.

'Well, there were two things that impressed her the most and which gave me the edge. She wants me to teach her children music; but most important, I'm to teach them German and speak to them only in German.'

Régine frowns.

'Really? That's odd. What is this woman's name?'

'Lemoins. I wasn't told her first name.'

'Lemoins? Living in that posh area of town? It must be… Yes, I am sure it must be… Édifices Lemoins. Did she say what her husband does?'

'No. She hardly mentioned him at all.'

'And their company?'

'Not a word.'

'It must be. Édifices Lemoins, the biggest construction company in Poitiers. They are snapping up all the contracts from the Germans because right now nobody else is building. It is they who rebuilt the station after the bombing. Those people are profiteers – they have become incredibly rich since the Occupation. They are *collaborateurs*. They collaborate with the Germans because they believe that is the side their bread is buttered. They believe in the ultimate victory of Germany and that France will in fact become Germany. They are traitors to France.'

Sarah tells her now of the portraits of Hitler in the house.

'I did not let that discourage me,' she says. 'Because you said that people do what they have to do to protect their family. You think I should not have taken the job? That I am being a traitor? Or it is dangerous?'

'No, no, of course you should take it. Working for them does not make you a *collaborateur* as well, especially as the job you do is not for the company but just looking after the children. The children are innocent and it might even be good for them to have you there with them instead of some stiff-necked Germany admirer. I am sure that the Lemoins family are not themselves Nazis. Nevertheless, it is all the more important that you hide from them the fact that you are Jewish. She believed the story about your bombed-out uncle?'

'Yes, she believed everything. I had the feeling that as soon as she heard I was fluent in German, she really wanted me.'

Régine nods. 'Yes, it can't be that easy to find a German-speaking nanny in Poitiers. And of course if Germany wins the war, it would be important that her children know the language well. It would be a head start in the new France owned by Adolf Hitler. So, you are now in a viper's nest, Sarah. It is likely also that she entertains German officers in her home, sucking up to them. It's what these rich *collaborateurs* do. So just be careful. Do your job and keep your head down. In the meantime, Karl is waiting for you. He went out and came back to get his bag. He said you should meet him at the Café Bleu at midday to say goodbye.'

Sarah gives out a small cry of horror.

'Goodbye? Already?'

'Yes, my dear. What did you think? Just as you have had to find a new life and move on, so has he. He will tell you the details when you meet him – or more probably not. I also do not want to know any details. It is better that way. I suspect what he is up to, but I do not want to know. But you – if you want to meet him, you should hurry.'

'But *Madame* told me to just fetch my luggage and go back there. My job starts today, when the nursemaid returns from her walk with the baby. If I do not come…'

'You have her number. Give her a ring and tell her that you will come later, at one o'clock or even two. Trust me, she will not dismiss you. She needs you more than you need her. Let the nursemaid work a few hours longer – your Karl will be waiting.'

When Sarah has packed, she comes back downstairs and looks for Régine.

'There's one last thing…' She hesitates.

'Yes? What is it, my dear?'

'My family. I am so worried. I think about them all the time. It's more almost three weeks since I left home and my sisters must have left too by now. I am desperate for news. I was wondering if I could write a letter?'

'A letter to whom, my dear? You cannot write to your home address.'

'No, I was thinking I would write to…'

Régine holds up a hand. 'Stop! Tell me no more. If you have a safe address, do not tell me. You must post it yourself, I don't want to know.'

'*D'accord.*'

'As long as you don't use this address, or even the address of Madame Lemoins.'

Régine opens a drawer in the hallway and removes a pen, a pad of paper and an envelope. 'Here, you can use this. As a return address use Poste Restante, Main Post Office, Poitiers. You must take it to the post office and buy a stamp and post it. Then you must check every now and then for a reply.'

Sarah sits down at the kitchen table and considers. She must word the letter very carefully, in case it is opened and read by Nazis.

No names must be mentioned. Nothing is as innocent and clear as it used to be, not even writing a letter for news of your relatives. In the end, she writes:

Ma chère tante,

I am writing to tell you that the family here is all well and we are all thinking of you. Summer has come to an end and at last I am eighteen – we did not celebrate much, just a glass of wine, but it was poor-quality wine and it made me think of your wonderful *Gewürztraminer* – nothing can equal that! I do hope you are all well. Has my dear cousin completed her Red Cross course? Have you news of the boys? I know you are worried, as every mother with sons fighting for the *Vaterland* must be.

What about your two nieces, and my beloved auntie? I do hope they had an exciting and uplifting summer with you, and that Auntie recovered well from her fall. I hope the family in Strasbourg are also well. I miss you all so much.

Your loving niece,
S.

PS please write to me at the above Poste Restante address as we shall be moving house soon. Knowing how long post takes, especially between France and Germany, it's better not to take a chance!

She folds the letter, places it in the envelope provided by Régine, seals it, tucks it into her bag. She will buy a stamp as soon as she can. She stands up, picks up her bag and moves to the front hall. Régine comes clattering down the stairs.

'So, you have finished? *Bien*, now off you go, and *bonne chance*, my dear! Do come back and visit from time to time.'

There are tears in Sarah's eyes as she leaves this house. Another temporary home, another temporary mother, another place of warmth and family and goodwill – the last for a long time, no doubt. Sarah knows that the next house will not be a home, the women living there will not be mothers, the family there will not embrace her as one of their own. Quite the opposite. She has no idea when she will find a home again, and a family. But one day, God willing, when the war is over, she will find her own family, and she and Ralf will *make* a home.

She turns up at the Café Bleu on time, having informed Madame Lemoins from a phone booth that she can't start until two o'clock. Madame Lemoins sighs but, as Régine predicted, raises no objection. Ralf is waiting for her at the Café Bleu. Leaning against the wall is his bulging backpack. He is now wearing civilian clothes, given to him by Régine.

She places her bag, packed and also bulging, for Régine has given her, too, many items of clothing, dresses and skirts and blouses from her several daughters. 'They won't mind,' she'd said. 'We own a fabric shop, it is no problem. But those boots! I will see what I can find of my daughters'. Mind you, leather being so scarce these days, it is hard to find good-quality shoes and yours are at least of good quality. But that stain on the right boot – it is so ugly.'

'No, I will keep these boots,' Sarah said. 'They are of sentimental value, and as you said, of very good quality. I do not mind that they are ugly.'

Now, she slides into the chair next to Ralf, leans over to exchange kisses on cheeks. His smile is a mixture of joy at seeing her and sadness at knowing they have to part again so soon.

His eyes light up when she tells him she got the job. 'But that's marvellous! Congratulations! Tell me about it – but first, let me order.'

He signals to the waitress and when she comes to the table with her pad and pencil, he orders coffee. When she leaves Sarah tells him about that morning's interview. He chuckles when he hears the part about her teaching the children German.

'It's good to know that German is good for something, at least!'

'It's not so good, Ralf. It means they are *collaborateurs*, trying to suck up to the Nazi occupiers.' She relates to him her conversation with Régine.

'I don't like the idea of working for people like that. Especially since they don't know I am Jewish. She sacked her last nanny because she was Jewish.'

'She will never have to know. This actually sounds like a very good opportunity for you. And you must get days off, times off? We can meet when I'm here.'

She shakes her head. 'Not much. Every second Sunday. Otherwise I must look after the children all day. And I can't come at night because of the curfew.'

'Don't the children go to school?'

'Three of them do. The youngest is just a toddler.'

'Well, there you have it. You bring the toddler. They have a telephone, you say? Give me the number, and I will phone you at the house when I am in town and you can go for a walk with the baby and come here. She won't have to know.'

'I don't like all the subterfuge. And having a man ring me? She won't like that – she's quite strict.'

'Perhaps I'll let Régine know, and she can ring you.'

'I don't like bothering Régine again. She has done so much for us already. It might put her at risk.'

'I think if she doesn't want to do it, she'll tell us. She doesn't seem like the kind to do anything she thinks is out of order. We can only ask, and she can only say no. Don't worry about it, Sarah. We will work it out.'

'I do worry. But mostly, I worry about you. Where will you be? What are you doing? Is it dangerous?'

He strokes her hand. 'I can't tell you much because I don't know much, but even if I did know, I couldn't tell you. All I can say is that I will make sure to meet you as often as I can.'

Sarah has said many goodbyes since the day she left her home in Colmar. That was the worst goodbye. But this one, the goodbye from Ralf, comes close. She must battle the tears all the way to her new home, because it doesn't feel like going home at all, and she has said goodbye to the last anchor in her life.

She is now completely on her own.

Chapter Thirty-Three

'Mademoiselle! You are late!'

'I did ring to say I'd be coming a bit later...'

'We appreciate punctuality in this house.'

Sarah slips past Madame Elise, not looking at her, her bag over her shoulder. It is bulging more than ever, due to all the clothes Régine has given her. She does not reply to the reprimand but simply glances at the housekeeper as she passes by way of saying, 'If you have a complaint, take it to Madame Lemoins.'

She knows the way to her room; it is in the eaves. It is small and sparsely furnished, but perfectly adequate and in fact more spacious and of a higher standard than her old room in Colmar, which was also in the eaves and shared with two of her sisters. Here, she even has her own little washroom and lavatory – a luxury. In fact, this room is the most comfortable – and the bed the softest, as she now sits on it and feels the generous give of the mattress – of all the temporary homes she's known since Colmar; physically better than Margaux's cellar and Madame Delauney's hay loft and the mouldy basement in Metz and the rattling train and even the simple *chambre* offered by Régine. But the house itself? It is cold. Not in temperature, but in ambience; this is a house where she will have to carve out her own hospitality from the chilly mood that seems to hang in the air. A mood, she is certain, created by the mistress of the house, Madame Lemoins herself.

Never mind, she will do it. This is a wonderful opportunity to finally create a new background, a new habitat, a new identity, built from scratch from the rubble of her fugitive status. She places her bag on the little wooden table beside the dormer window – she will unpack it later. Time to relieve the nursemaid of her burden, the child called Michel, who, as of now, will be Sarah's responsibility. Time to meet the first of her four young charges.

The children's bedrooms are all on the floor beneath this, on one side of the landing. Their parents' suite – out of bounds for everyone except the cleaning staff, as Madame Elise informed her earlier in the day – is on the other side. There is a clear division of space. Each child has his or her own room, and there is also a common space for them all, the nursery. Here, in these five rooms, is Sarah's future workspace, her future world. Each room carries a wooden sign on the door with the relevant child's name painted in primary colours, as well as a little symbol of childhood: a teddy bear, a rocking horse, a doll, a fire engine. These splashes of colour are the only indication, up to now, that this is not a house filled with the grimmest and most humourless of humans. Someone, it seems, has exhibited a sense of playful creativity. Sarah wonders who it is who suggested or created these signs. She is sure it was not Madame Lemoins herself.

She knocks briefly on the door behind the Michel sign and enters without waiting for an answer, eager, now, to meet the little boy who will fill most of her days. She can well remember Sofie as a two-year-old: how curious, how full of adventure and lust for life is a child at that age, and how easy it is to be infected by their spirit! That sense that the world is a magical, wonderful place throbbing with delight, every moment an opportunity for exploration, every new-seen thing a chance to open one's eyes anew and truly experience life freshly minted from the hand of God...

Michel's room is easily four times the size of her own, but it is empty. He must be in the nursery. Sarah shuts the door and moves along to its sign-less door, and again she enters after a brief rap.

This time, success. She sees Michel immediately, sleeping in a cot.

The nursery is quite enormous, by her standards, and filled with playthings galore; a virtual paradise for children. There are boxes with cars and other vehicles, boxes with dolls of all shapes and sizes, and more dolls sitting on shelves. Boxes of stuffed and wooden animals. Board games in boxes, stacked on the shelves. Books, stacked upright or horizontal, fill another floor-to-ceiling bookshelf.

Boxes of building blocks. Boxes of wooden train carriages and engines. Boxes of toys so mysterious Sarah can only guess as to their function.

She absorbs all of this in one glance as she enters the room, as the things it is filled with suck attention from the sleeping child.

'Shhh!' says a disembodied voice, and for the first time Sarah notices the second occupant of the room. She is sitting on a couch against the only wall that is not shelved. Sitting, or rather half-lying, leaning against a pile of cushions, both legs stretched out along the seat of the sofa. 'He has only just fallen asleep. Don't wake him; he's very crotchety when he wakes up and he'll only start bawling.'

The girl lays down the magazine she has been reading, stands up and walks towards Sarah. Slightly older than Sarah, she is short and rather dumpy, with a pasty-white face and a bored expression. The eyes now meeting Sarah's are dull, expressionless. She holds out a hand.

'You must be the new nanny. I am Clara. That is Michel on the blanket. He has been a very naughty boy today, demanding this and that. I took him for a long walk and let him run in the park and thankfully, he is now exhausted. I have been waiting for you for over an hour. Why are you so late? Anyway, I'm supposed to tell you what to do. Usually he takes his afternoon nap in his bed, but he was overtired so I brought him here and let him play in the pen until he fell over from exhaustion. This child is tireless, as you will soon see! The best times are when he is asleep, like now. When he wakes up, he will bawl the house down again. You must take him down to the kitchen and feed him. I will go down with you now and show you the things you are to give him. He still drinks from a bottle – that is the easiest way to calm him, just push a bottle into his hands. Come, let us go down now. The other children will also soon be home – what time is it? Two o'clock? Well, Collette finishes school at two thirty and the other two at four. Collette waits for them. They come home starving and you must feed them a small snack and then let them go to their rooms and play. They are good at entertaining themselves, so there isn't really much work with them – they are used to it.

'The older ones have homework then and you must supervise. Julien is very studious, so you can leave him to himself and let him work. He needs no assistance – but you shall see yourself. Here we are. See, in the fridge there is milk and butter. Here is the bread box. You give them all a slice of bread with butter and jam.'

The girl talks and talks and it is not possible or necessary for Sarah to respond or to ask questions. She only nods and follows with her eyes as the girl shows her this and that in the kitchen, which is at least six times as large as her mother's back in Colmar, and equipped with every modern appliance an industrious maid or cook could desire.

Clara's instructions briskly delivered and Sarah now fully informed as to her duties, she is finally on her own. She makes her way back up to the nursery. She sits on the couch, picks up the fashion magazine the nursemaid has left, leafs through it and waits for Michel to wake up, or the other children to return home, whichever happens first.

Chapter Thirty-Four

What happens first is that Michel wakes up. He sits up in the middle of the cot and rubs his eyes. 'Clara? Clara!' he calls. Sarah puts down the magazine and walks over to the cot, smiling. She remembers she is to speak only German to the children and so, as she walks, she says in German, 'Hello, Michel! I am your new nanny, and I think we are going to be great friends. Why don't you—'

But Michel does not let her continue. He takes one look at her, swivels his head back and forth frantically as if looking for someone and lets out a terrified wail. Sarah stops speaking – she cannot be heard anyway – and concentrates on her smile, making sure it is kind and loving, her arms stretched out. But when she reaches for him, leaning over the rails of the cot, his screams become even more panicky; he leaps to his feet and retreats to the far side where she cannot reach him, batting with his arms. It could not be worse had she arrived with a sharp knife and murder in her eyes. She calls, in French, trying to drown out the screams: 'Michel, Michel, it is all right! I am your friend, do not be afraid!' It does not convince him; she tries to grab him, believing that crying children need to be held, but he battles her away and she cries out in pain as one of his nails scratches her cheek. She touches it; her fingers come away streaked with blood.

Hand on cheek, she walks around to the foot of the cot to get nearer to him, but he immediately scuttles to the other side and his screams become shrieks of pure terror. Sarah stops, completely helpless: she has never encountered such behaviour before. She has not much experience with screaming children; her little sister was a perfect angel. She decides to seek help – the housekeeper, Madame Elise, should be able to advise. It means she must leave the child alone, but he will be safe in his cot. She smiles through his screams and waves him goodbye as she moves to the door and out into the upstairs hallway. As soon as she is out of sight the screaming stops. She re-enters the room; the screaming starts again.

It is a crisis. She shuts the door again – the screaming stops – and runs downstairs, calling for Madame Elise. She finds her in the sitting room, dusting the bookshelves. Madame Elise's duties as housekeeper apparently also encompass those of a maid, Sarah has already noted.

'Madame Elise!' she cries. 'Please, I need help. Michel has woken up and he seems afraid of me. I don't know what to do. He is screaming and won't let me near him. I think it's because I am a stranger. Perhaps if you – because he knows you…'

Madame Elise stops dusting and glares at Sarah.

'I am a housekeeper, not a nursemaid!' she says sternly. 'That is your job. It is what you are paid to do. If you are not qualified, you should not have applied. Now please go and perform your duties and allow me to perform mine.' So saying, Madame Elise turns her face away and returns to her dusting.

Sarah stands in the doorway, confused and helpless. What is she to do? The child is obviously terrified of her. How does one calm a terrified child?

Food, she thinks, and makes her way to the kitchen, looks around. There is a bowl of apples on the central table. She picks up one, looks for a knife and cuts it into slices, finds a plate and lays them out, and leaves the kitchen to return upstairs. In the hallway she almost bumps into Madame Elise.

'Where are you going with that?'

'I'm taking it upstairs, for Michel. I thought it would help calm him.'

'Didn't Clara inform you? There is a strict rule in this house: there is to be no eating, no food, in the upstairs rooms. It is an absolute rule. You must bring him down for his afternoon snack.'

'But… if he won't—'

'It is your job, and your problem. You must solve it.'

She takes the plate from Sarah and walks resolutely away, towards the kitchen.

Sarah returns upstairs. All is quiet in the nursery. Perhaps the child is now more settled and will accept her. She opens the nursery door and enters. Michel is sitting quietly in the middle of the cot, sucking his thumb. As soon as he sees her, he breaks into the most terrified shrieks she has ever heard. She stands still for a moment, wondering what to do. Madame Elise is correct: this is her job, and her problem. She thinks. What solution is there to panic, to fear; what can she do to calm this poor, needlessly petrified child?

It comes to her immediately.

Music.

And so, ignoring the screams, she approaches the playpen and sits down outside it, and starts to sing. She sings a song that is the most calming one in the world, the song sung by all German mothers to put their babies to sleep because it is so soothing:

'*Guten Abend, Gute Nacht…*'

It is a lullaby, soft and gentle. She closes her eyes and simply sings, not worrying about the child and his screaming. She keeps her voice low and calm and sings, repeating the simple verse again and again. She knows Michel cannot understand the words, which is just as well as he is not supposed to be going to sleep now: he has just woken up and should stay awake. It is the melody, the voice, he must listen to. She sings it again and again.

By the time she starts the second round, his yells are much less convincing: he is listening.

By the third round, he has stopped screaming.

At the fourth round, his thumb is back in his mouth.

He is staring at her, eyes big and round. Sarah decides not to stare back. She shuts her eyes, pretends indifference; she only sings. In singing, she remembers her youngest sister, to whom she used to sing this very lullaby. She remembers her mother, who would sing them all to sleep with it – it might be German, but she thinks it is the most beautiful of all lullabies in all languages, a night-time staple in her childhood home. Remembering little Sofie, tears come to Sarah's eyes. She misses them all so much. All these comforting, reassuring rituals that her mother, both her parents, upheld; buttresses against the terrors of a war that, she now knows, was raging far away but slowly closing in on them, breaking into their little bubble of familial serenity.

She sings. Other songs, in French, songs from her own childhood, songs her mother sang to all of them. Lost now in her own little world, feeling her own family around her, her mother's love, she has completely forgotten Michel and his screaming. But all of a sudden she feels a light touch on her cheeks. She opens her eyes: it is Michel. He is standing right in front of her, has pushed his little hands through the bars of the cot, and is trying to stroke away the tears now seeping from her eyes.

'Do not cry, *Mademoiselle*!' he is murmuring, in French.

She smiles at him. 'Ah, little boy,' she says, also in French. 'If only you knew. You are so lucky to be small… But are you hungry?'

'*Oui*.' He stretches out his arms. She stands up now and lifts him up. She carries him downstairs, and all the way down he is chattering as if he has known her all his life.

They are sitting at the kitchen table and she is feeding him buttered bread and jam cut into sticks – which she tells him are cars and his mouth is a garage – when the door bursts open and three children tumble into the room, chattering, exclaiming, being as loud and chaotic as children are wont to be.

Sarah smiles and stands up. They all fall silent at once, staring.

'Hello,' she says, in French, 'you must be Julien, Jacqueline and Collette. I am your new nanny. I'm sure your mother told you—'

'I do not need a nanny!' cries Julien. He grabs an apple from the fruit bowl, drops his satchel to the floor and storms out the back door. Through the kitchen window Sarah can see him racing across the immaculate lawn into the rhododendron bushes at the back. Hidden behind the bushes there seems to be some kind of a wooden building. A garden hut, perhaps.

'He has no manners!' says Jacqueline. She approaches Sarah, her arm stretched out, offering a hand.

'*Bonjour, Mademoiselle.* My name is Jacqueline. Welcome to our family.'

Sarah solemnly shakes the offered hand, and then turns to the younger child.

'…and you are Collette. I am delighted to meet you. I think we shall have a lot of fun together.'

Collette does not smile, but only fixes her gaze solemnly on Sarah. It is a penetrating gaze, one that seems to see right down to the bottom of her soul. And maybe it does. Once more, Sarah is transported back to Colmar, to her own family. Sofie, too, who is around the same age as Collette, has just such an all-seeing gaze. It is disconcerting. She looks away.

'I suppose I'd better go and fetch Julien,' she says, moving towards the back door.

'Don't worry with him,' says Jacqueline. 'He is just having a sulk, he will return when he is ready. But we are hungry. Hello, Michel! That looks good. Can I have one?'

'This is a motor car,' says Michel, picking up one of his jammy sticks. 'It has to go into the garage.' He opens his mouth to demonstrate the garage and Jacqueline opens hers. Michel drives the car into it and Jacqueline closes the garage door and chews.

'It is a Mercedes-Benz!' says Michel. 'They are the best cars – they are German.'

Sarah finds his vocabulary astonishing for his age. He is not quite three; at that age Sofie could still hardly talk. But Maman always said that each child is different, unique, and each develops at their own rate; a mother is someone who can immediately and naturally assess each child's needs and supply them as well as she is able.

Now Collette speaks.

'Madame Elise says you are German too,' she says. 'And that we now have to speak German. Because France is now German.'

'Well then, let us do that,' says Sarah, in German, and all three stare at her as if she has spoken gibberish. She realises that teaching them another language is going to be a challenge. She repeats what she has said in French, while preparing slices of bread, butter and jam for them all to eat. Before long they are having a conversation in two languages, Sarah naming everything in German and the children, all three, repeating the words: '*Brot. Butter. Confitüre.*'

Her heart soars. Madame Lemoins might be something of a dragon, Madame Elise might be something of a cold fish, but she knows now that she will enjoy working with these three, and even with the fourth, the young man who has stormed into the garden. She goes out to search for him, to lure him back into the house.

She was right: behind the rhododendrons there is a wooden cabin with a small front porch on which a wicker table and chair wait invitingly for visitors. It is a storybook cottage with its own miniature rose garden, the rose trees in pots circling an area of grass. An overturned red tricycle and a small sandpit suggest that this is a play area for the children. Sarah steps across the porch and knocks on the green-painted door.

'Go away!' comes the cry from within.

'No!' Sarah cries back. 'I won't go until you come out and talk to me.'

'I don't want to talk to you, I don't need a nanny!'

'Well, I believe you,' says Sarah, 'but your maman thinks you do, and she has employed me, so she is the one you have to convince. Perhaps I can be just a nanny for the younger children, and you only have to tolerate me. Because they do need someone, they cannot stay alone.'

It's a long speech to give with a raised voice, and Sarah can't be sure he has listened or that he cares what she has said. He reminds her a little of her sister Thérèse, who also has an extremely exalted, and not very accurate, view of her own maturity, and who is just as determined to shake off adult intervention in her life. 'I can play it by myself!' Thérèse will insist when they are practising a new violin piece, and she will get it wrong time and time again; and she can hear it is wrong, but instead of letting others explain to her how to correct her mistakes, she will figure it out herself. And in the end, she gets it right. It's a long-winded and rather time-wasting way of exerting one's independence, but it's even more of a waste of time to argue with her: she will come around on her own. As will Julien, Sarah thinks.

When there is no response to her long speech Sarah tries again.

'You can help me with the children,' she says, deliberately omitting the word 'other'. 'Clearly, they look up to you as the eldest. I too was the eldest in my family and I was allowed to tell them what to do, just like my parents. I was like a third parent. You can be a second nanny. I would have definitely needed help today because Michel screamed his head off when he saw me. He was terrified of me! I didn't know what to do! He was screaming as if I wanted to kill him – I wish you'd been there.'

A pause, and then Julien's voice: 'So what did you do? He seemed quite happy just now.'

'I sang to him.'

'And that worked?'

'Yes, it worked. He liked it very much and then he came to me himself.'

Talking through a closed door with a raised voice is getting on her nerves. It's time to change tactic, establish authority with underhand tact.

'Well, then, Julien, just think about it. I have to go back to the kitchen to the children because you obviously don't need me here, and that's my job. So, goodbye. I just wanted to say hello. You can call me Sarah. I hope we can be friends.'

With that, she turns and walks away. Just a few seconds later, she hears footsteps bounding across the wooden porch and then Julien is beside her.

'Michel does scream a lot. He's almost three but he screams like a baby sometimes. Maman says he is a spoilt brat, but I think he just screams to get what he wants. If I were his parent, I would just let him scream and not give him what he wants. Clara used to give in to him immediately and that's why he does it. I think it's stupid. The only reason he was screaming is because he thought Clara would come running, but she didn't, did she?'

'No, she couldn't. She had left by then.'

'So, you see, I'm right. Because in the end all you did was sing and he stopped. And he didn't get Clara to come running.'

'Well, there, you see. Now I know a little more about how to deal with Michel. Thank you for telling me.'

'*De rien.* It was obvious. I told Clara again and again not to give in when he starts to scream, but she always did.'

'Well, I certainly won't give in – you can be sure of that.'

'I can tell you lots of things about Jacqueline and Collette as well.'

'I think we will make a very good team, Julien. But I'm sure you must be hungry – here we are, at the kitchen. You can help yourself.'

Chapter Thirty-Five

The rest of the afternoon runs smoothly. The three older children do their homework: Julien briskly and needing no advice, Jacqueline reluctantly, constantly gazing out of the window and needing to be brought to task, and Collette eagerly colouring in a picture she has brought.

It's only later, after they've all put away their school materials, that Sarah realises she'd been speaking to them all in French all afternoon. She groans inwardly – she'll have to correct that, *tout de suite*.

'Now!' she says, her voice filled with authority, 'let's play a game in German, all right?'

She says it in German. All three stare at her, faces blank. She repeats it in French, then in German. 'The game is called, *ich sehe was, was Du nicht siehst* – I see something you don't see. And then I will name the thing I see in German and whoever guesses it can name the next thing. If you don't know the word, you come and whisper to me and I will tell you, secretly.'

The children, even Julien, immediately fall into the spirit of the game, and before long, they have named half the items in the nursery. Michel, despite being the youngest, is one of the most eager players. Once again Sarah notes his astounding capacity for vocabulary; he only has to hear a word once to retain it, repeat it with perfect pronunciation.

They have moved on to actually describing things, their colours and sizes, with Sarah writing everything down on the blackboard, when the nursery door opens. So engrossed are they in the game that nobody notices the intruder until a new voice breaks into the round.

'Well, well, well… So, my little nieces and nephews are turning into nice little Germans, I see!'

Sarah swings around, startled, and then jumps to her feet to greet the woman who has silently approached from behind. A woman not much older than she herself, but there any similarities end. Just that one first glance, and Sarah, whose confidence and sense of authority in this house has been surging forward in leaps and bounds since meeting the children, feels herself plummeting to the ground. Not physically, of course. It's more an inner collapse; a mental deflation like the sudden and silent release of air from a balloon, a reduction of spirit to its most humble origins; a prostration.

And yet the newcomer has done nothing, said nothing beyond that first innocuous greeting – spoken in a friendly enough manner – to elicit such a reaction. Quite the opposite. She stands there smiling, laughing even, now, as Collette and Michel both spring to their feet and propel themselves at her, springing into her arms, crying out, '*Tante Monique, Tante Monique!*' and she, laughing, hugging, welcoming the children, lovingly lifting Michel onto her hip, bending over to kiss Collette on the cheeks, all the while looking up at Sarah with the most agreeable smile on her lips, the friendliest sparkle in her eyes.

'Hello!' she says now, replacing Michel on the floor. 'You must be the new nanny. I'm Monique, Monique Beaulieu. Céline's sister.'

Céline, Sarah figures now, must be Madame Lemoins' first name. Madame Lemoins, a woman whose formality and stiffness of bearing has actually seemed to eliminate any adjunct as familiar as a first name.

'Oh,' Sarah says now, 'yes, Madame Lemoins mentioned that you were staying here, um… you… you're from Paris…'

Monique laughs. 'Well, no. I'm not *from* Paris. I'm from Poitiers, right here, just like Céline. But I live in Paris. I suppose that makes me a Parisienne, at least temporarily.'

Yes. *Parisienne*, that's it. That's the X element, the imperceptible yet inexorable *quality of being*, that subtle magnetism exuded by Monique that has reduced Sarah almost to stuttering, made of her a wilted creeper in the blinking of an eye. It isn't just the clothes, the outer appearance: a pencil skirt at the height of chicness, scandalously just sweeping the knees; the silky golden smoothness of the silky, slender legs beneath the skirt (silk stockings! Where does she find silk stockings?), the elegant patent leather shoes, slim and sleek, in which those legs end; nor the delicate fabric of the pale blue blouse that encloses what is obviously a perfectly sculpted upper body; nor the immaculate porcelain skin, possibly without cosmetic aid except for the bright red slash of lipstick; nor the sleek black hair swinging around her shoulders like a single satin curtain; nor the frank grey eyes, beautifully framed by impossibly long lashes, that right now behold – yes, that's the right word; they do not see, those eyes, they *behold* – Sarah, assessing her as if for innate value. An innate value, Sarah feels, that is comparable to some knick-knack on an ageing spinster's mantelpiece against a priceless Ming-dynasty Chinese vase in an emperor's palace. Instinctively, she knows it is this that makes servants bow and scrape before their superiors. It's all she can do not to fall to her own knees. She would do so willingly, gladly, were this current French etiquette.

'So, you are teaching them German,' Monique says. 'Preparing them for the coming Era Germanica. Not a bad idea.'

Is she being sarcastic? Can she be serious? It's hard to tell, for her smile seems genuine and even reaches her eyes. Now, she's holding out her hand for a shake. 'And you?'

'Er…' Is she supposed to say something? What?

'Your name!'

'Oh – oh yes, of course! I'm sorry. I'm Sarah… Sarah Mayer.'

They shake hands. Monique's is strangely cold; her own embarrassingly clammy.

'A German name – Mayer! So then, are you German?'

'I suppose so. I'm from Alsace – Colmar. I have German papers.'

'Put like that, it sounds as if you are reluctantly German. Why is that? And why did you come here, to Poitiers? To us?'

Too many questions to be answered at once, and too complicated. Sarah settles on the last question.

'Your sister placed an advertisement in the newspaper and I answered it. She called me for an interview and accepted me.'

'On the spot, apparently! Last night she was complaining about all the telephone calls… all the applications. And already she has chosen. Why is that, do you think?'

'Well, I think it's because she wants the children to learn German.'

'Very sensible. A good choice, if that was the only reason. Is it? Did she not ask about your references, your experience with children, your pristine character? Does one leave one's children with any old German girl off the street? Is that the main qualification?'

It's like a second interview, an inquisition worse than the first, and Sarah feels uncontrolled panic rising. This woman, this Monique – is she suspicious? Is she about to call her bluff? Monique has now turned her perfect back, is walking towards the window, where she looks out across the back garden. Her back stern, unyielding.

'I— I…' Sarah stands there helplessly, not knowing how to respond, petrified with guilt.

And then, as suddenly as she had burst into the nursery, Monique swings around, and in one glance assesses Sarah's discomfiture, and in the next breath she is laughing, laughing so much she almost bends double, holding her sides, grasping her belly, her hands fluttering in the air until, at last, she steps forward and grasps both of Sarah's, raises them, squeezes them, pulls Sarah towards her.

'Oh, my dear! Your face! You should just see yourself – a terrified rabbit in headlights! I'm sorry, I'm so sorry. I am awful, aren't I? Having my fun with you like that! I really, truly, beg your forgiveness. It's a naughty habit of mine... You looked so nervous when you saw me, I thought I'd have some fun. I really am an old meany. People tell me that but I just can't help it. Just ignore it... I'm not really such a dragon! It's my sister you want to beware of, not me! Oh, and her in-laws! Nasty people! Me, I'm everyone's best friend. Truly. Best friend, best auntie. *N'est-ce pas, enfants?*'

The children up to now had watched the exchange with puzzled faces, putting it down most probably to one of those incomprehensible adult exchanges that make no sense. But at those last words, and the arms Monique now hold wide for them, they all – except Julien, who nevertheless stands there grinning – rush at her, laughing, throwing their arms around her, Michel hopping from foot to foot, begging to be picked up.

'*Zut alors*! You will make a mess of my clothes – you act as if you have not seen me for years, even though I told you bedtime stories for hours last night!' She kisses each one, then reaches out for Julien, draws him to her also and kisses him on both cheeks – an attention he receives obviously with delight and yet embarrassment – and then looks up, meets Sarah's eyes and speaks to her again.

'As you may have noticed, my sister has not much time for... well, never mind. But they have me, and now you. If I was a little intimidating at first, well, it was for this reason. I did not want her to choose the nanny only because she speaks German. But I am a good judge of character and I think with you, she has the complete package. Welcome to our home. Take good care of my nieces and nephews. Not only must you teach them German, you must teach them love, a far more complicated lesson. Now stop looking so terrified – I really don't bite, I'm not going to gobble you up for dinner. Speaking of which, it must be getting close to their suppertime. Maybe we should go down to the kitchen and there you can maybe find your voice at last and tell me a little about yourself – I didn't mean to alarm you and you must forgive me and show me your true mettle. I don't think you are truly a rabbit. If you have come all this way from Alsace, you certainly have spunk. Me, the only journeys I take are between Paris and Poitiers. Come on, children, we are all going down. Let's see what surprise Auntie has found for you to eat today.'

'A surprise! A surprise!' 'What is it? Chocolate?' 'Sweets?' 'A toy?' 'A puppy?' The children cry out in glee as they all walk downstairs – that is, the adults walk, the children tumble and clatter. Monique explains to Sarah that the food shortages in Poitiers really are a bother, but that she manages to find little treats that she brings home to share with the children.

'I have my sources. Today, we will have… well, let's see. It's the surprise.'

The 'surprise' is a bowl of oranges in the centre of the table. The children squeal with delight and pounce on them. There's another surprise: chicken stew. 'I know someone who knows someone who keeps chickens and who can cook them,' she says with a wink to Sarah. 'Just don't ask for the details. It's my secret. I can also bring sausages, cold meats – and good wine.'

Sarah is unfamiliar with the gas range, so Monique explains it to her, shows her how to light the oven so as to warm up the pie. 'Just be careful that the pilot light is burning,' she says, 'otherwise you might blow up the whole house and all of us.'

Sarah's eyes widen with shock, causing another explosion of giggles on Monique's part.

'I'm sorry, I'm sorry,' she says, 'I really have to stop scaring you. But you also have to stop being scared. In time you will get to know me and you won't take me so seriously. The thing about me is that you must take every word I say with a pinch of salt. That's what they say in England – it means, don't take me so seriously. You speak English?'

Sarah shakes her head. 'No. Only a word here and there.'

'Ah! That is where I have at least one advantage. Because I do speak English – at least, the English one learns at school. But now it seems it will be a useless language. German is the way to go, German all the way. You are fortunate. So, tell me more, about where you came from, what brought you here.'

The kitchen by now has filled with the mouthwatering aroma of chicken pie. Monique removes it from the oven and places it on the table as she speaks, and as she portions it out and passes the steaming plates around and the children tuck into the delicious meal she prises Sarah's story from her, bit by bit; the story she has so carefully prepared, the story of the bombed-out uncle. And as she tells her story Sarah realises how easily, now, how convincingly, lying comes to her lips…

But truth speaks louder than lies and the parts of the story that are true stand out, and they are the elements Monique grasps.

'A violin-maker! Now, that is an unusual and interesting trade! And much more original than mine, I have to say – I am going to be a boring old lawyer in international trade. But violins, music – that is culture! I have to say, Céline has found gold in you. So, my nieces and nephews will all play the violin? That is wonderful! I think Collette at least might have a musical streak – she loves to sing, don't you, Collette? And she has the voice of an angel, and can hold a tune better than any of us. I think you will enjoy teaching her. The others – not so much, I think.'

She looks from Julien to Jacqueline, who are both too busy eating to listen.

'I will do my best,' says Sarah.

'But then, they will have to have violins,' says Monique. 'Apart from an old upright piano in my parents' suite, there is not a single instrument in the house. Not even a flute or a tambourine. I wonder if Céline has thought of that? I will have to remind her. They cannot learn the violin without instruments. But Céline is notoriously tight-fisted… We will see.'

*

And see they do. Later, when Sarah is getting the children ready for bed – Monique having drifted off to her own room soon after supper – Madame Lemoins approaches her in the upstairs corridor.

'I have just had a talk with Monique,' she says, 'and she has reminded me that the children will need instruments. I insist on only the best for my children, and Paris is the only place to get the best of everything in France. So, on Monday you are to go to Paris with Monique, to the best violin shop in the city, and choose four violins.'

Sarah coughs. 'Actually,' she says, 'I think Michel is too young to learn. He should wait another year, at least.'

'No, no, you misunderstood,' says Madame Lemoins. 'The fourth violin, it is for *you*. You cannot teach them to play unless you are able to demonstrate, to play yourself, to show them how it is done. Each of you must have your own violin. Culture is important. I insist. Of course, your violin will really be mine – that is, when you leave my employment, it will stay in this house. But as long as you are here, it will be yours.'

'What? Really? I— I don't know what to say…'

'There is nothing to say. You will have Monday as a day off instead of the following Sunday – Clara or someone else can come in for that one day to look after the children – and Monique will help you find an appropriate violin shop. And you will choose the best. But now, when the children are in bed, you must come and fetch me. I like to give them a final tuck-in and a kiss, and sometimes I read them a story, if there is time. *D'accord?*'

'*D'accord, Madame.* And thank you.'

That night Sarah hardly sleeps a wink. It is all becoming too much for her – too much goodness, too much perfection, everything one could wish for now falling into her lap. This beautiful house, lively children to look after as her job, good food, safety, Monique – who for all her terrifying urbanity is positioning herself in Sarah's life as a friend – and now, the icing on the cake, a violin! Music!

It's all too good to be true. Maman always said one should beware of good times because there comes a point where you reach the summit and the slide downwards is much faster than the ascent. But it's not the inevitable downward slide that keeps Sarah awake: it's guilt, it's worry. Why should all these good things be happening to her? Where is Ralf? Is he in danger? Is he at risk? And what about her sisters? Why have they not arrived in Poitiers? But most of all, her parents, and her youngest sisters? What of them? They have always been at the back of her mind, a lurking anxiety, even though the thunderous drama of daily events has tried to drown out that whisper of worry. But now, in the soft cosiness of a warm bed, the whisper becomes the voice of guilt. Cushioned in the heart of this family, she longs for her own.

Chapter Thirty-Six

The shop is about three time the size of her father's, but otherwise exactly the same. The same instruments hanging on the walls, but more of them. Violins, violas, a cello… The same door to the back, leading to a workshop, exactly like her father's: the same tools, the same shelf full of wood blocks, the planes, the ribs, the templates, the fitting screws – all the same. The same smell, the same atmosphere. It's as if music, unplayed music, hangs in the air, silent but potent, and it is all she can do not to reach out for one of the violins and start to play. She remembers her father, and his love of music; the duets they'd sometimes play on completion of a new perfect instrument. A violent, angry love rises up in her and it takes all her strength not to give in to the tears that seem to have gathered, unsummoned, behind her eyes. She is at first speechless, and Monique does the talking for her.

'We need a child's violin and three for adults,' Monique says.

Monsieur Rousseau, the luthier, a small, wiry man with a pointed beard and thin moustache, smiles, and waves his arms around.

'As you can see, they are all here. Take your pick.'

Sarah at last finds her voice. 'First, the child's violin. I think a three-quarters one. No point getting a half-violin – Collette will soon outgrow it. What about that one?'

Monsieur Rousseau reaches up and removes a small violin from the wall.

'Made in Japan,' he says. 'I do not make children's instruments myself – it's not worth it.'

'Indeed. My father didn't either. The ones he had were factory made, in China.'

'Your father was a luthier? You speak in the past tense – is he…?'

It is all Sarah can do not to blurt out the truth. And she would, if Monique were not with her. So once again, she lies.

'My father is in Colmar and is retired. I, too, am a luthier and I learned from him. I am now giving violin lessons – there's no work available for me.'

Monsieur Rousseau nods. 'It's my problem too – business is bad. Who is going to bother to buy violins in wartime? Sadly, our profession has become a luxury. Yet, how can people live without music? Surely it will help keep us sane in these hard times?'

They launch into a technical conversation about acoustics. Monique is clearly bored.

'Well, aren't you going to choose your violins?' she interrupts.

'Oh – well, yes, of course. What do you recommend, Monsieur Rousseau?'

'We want the best!' Monique interjects. 'The price is irrelevant.'

Monsieur Rousseau strokes his moustache. 'I have one very special violin,' he says, and reaches up to unhook it.

'This one. I didn't make it myself – it's a long story, how it came into my hands. It is originally from Italy – here, try it.' He hands it to Sarah. She tunes it, tightens the bow he hands her, clamps it under her chin, strokes the strings with her bow – and oh, the pleasure that sweeps through her at the pure, sweet sound that emerges! There is nothing to equal that delight; it gives her goose bumps. She plays a few bars of 'Salut d'Amour'.

'Very beautiful,' says Monique, clapping, as she finishes. 'How much are you selling it for?'

Monsieur Rousseau names a price. Sarah's jaw drops. She was expecting a high price – she knows the value of a good violin – but this is beyond reason. She quickly hands the violin back to him.

'Thank you for letting me play this one, but it's not in our budget. It's not for professional use – we just need them for teaching purposes. Could you please show us some more?'

Monique starts to protest but Sarah, for once feeling that she is the authority, insists.

'Three adequate violins, please – we don't need your best.'

Sarah tries out various violins for the next half-hour and finally picks out three, for Jacqueline, Julien and herself.

'Excellent selection,' says Monsieur Rousseau. 'I will have them delivered by the end of this week. Write down your address here.'

He passes the order book across to Monique, who enters the Poitiers address. She fills out a cheque, signs it, rips it from her chequebook and passes it over. Everyone is delighted: Monsieur Rousseau has sold four violins in a single transaction; Sarah is still buzzing from the thrill of being, once again, in a luthier's shop, so similar to her father's, immersed in the smell, the sight, the sound, the very atmosphere of violins in a state of gestation.

'So, what now?' Monique interrupts her thoughts. 'You are in Paris. What shall we do?'

'Well, I have to return to Poitiers,' says Sarah. 'If you could direct me to the station, I will get on the next train.'

'What nonsense! Who knows when you will have another excuse to be in Paris! You must make the most of your time here. Where would you like to go, what would you like to see? And don't say the Eiffel Tower!'

'I can't stay, Monique. I am employed, and even being here is part of my job. I don't want to abuse your sister's generosity in allowing me this time off from the children.'

'*Zut*! She should be delighted she has you. She already has a nursemaid for the day. Didn't she say it was your day off? She doesn't need you. Don't you worry, I will deal with her. Let's go to my place first and I will make a few phone calls for your peace of mind. You can spend the night with me and take the first train to Poitiers tomorrow.'

Sarah cries out in protest. 'No, I can't possibly spend the night here! Please don't try to persuade—'

'Well, all right. Not the night. But the afternoon – surely you can spend the afternoon here? We can go shopping. You need some new outfits, I have only ever seen you in those outdated country clothes. Wouldn't you like a bit of Parisian chic? I didn't like to criticise before, it's not my place, but really, Sarah, you must pay more attention to your appearance now that you are working for the Lemoins-Beaulieu clan.'

'I can't! Monique, you perhaps don't realise it but I'm not wealthy and I can't afford—'

'It is my sister's job to ensure that you are appropriately clothed. She must give you a clothing allowance. She must see that she cannot allow you to run around looking like some farm girl – it reflects on her. I will arrange it all. She probably never even thought of such things when she engaged you – her mind is occupied with business. That's where I come in. I have already decided to take you under my wing and the first thing to be done is a complete makeover.'

'But I—'

'I won't hear a word of protest. There is no need to spend a fortune, which is the first objection she will make. I have an idea. As I said, we will first go to my apartment. I have some things I no longer wear; they might fit you. In fact, I'm sure they will. You will return from Paris tonight looking like a different person!'

She slings an arm through Sarah's elbow and leads her purposefully towards the Metro station.

Protest, Sarah realises, is futile, and anyway, only half-hearted. Who could resist such an invitation? She has never had the choice of wearing pretty clothes. Even as the eldest child, her mother has chosen practical, humdrum dresses and skirts, often home-made or altered from her own clothes. It goes without saying that Monique's left-overs will be, if not the height of fashion, then at least stylish.

Monique is the temptress, leading her down unexplored new avenues. From that first day in the nursery, Monique, through the simple but irresistible technique of assertive speech, has manipulated her into a position of meek acceptance that morphs unexpectedly into bravado. Monique speaks, others fall into step behind her, and in doing so become more like her. Resistance is futile. But, Sarah thinks, did she even *want* to resist? Every idea Monique has come up with till now has been good, positive, a step forward, a progression into a bigger, better, Sarah – the Sarah she wants to be. A Sarah, she finds herself thinking, more like Monique. Monique is an ideal she can aspire to. A star, a leading light. The fumbling, socially awkward, immature girl from a humble luthier's shop in Colmar has to go. A new Sarah must evolve, and fate has thrown Monique across her path. Monique will show her the way forward into the new, elusive Self waiting for her.

Can she ever arrive? Striding along the pavement next to Monique, listening to the encouraging lecture now being delivered, Sarah feels a surge of new confidence. As the residual violin-shop buzz grows fainter, so too does a new call grow within her. If Monique believes in her then everything is possible. She can reach for the stars, and one day arrive – yes, even in wartime. *Only believe*, she thinks, straightening her shoulders.

Once, she stumbles, not noticing a kerb. Monique laughs, and points downwards.

'Those boots are far too ugly for Paris!' she says. 'They must be consigned to the *poubelle*. How could you come to Paris wearing mountain boots? I have just the pair of court shoes for you – light and elegant. It's not easy to buy nice shoes these days so we make do with what we had before, and mine would be perfect. I think they'll fit.'

Sarah looks down at her boots, at the dark stain of Krämer's blood across the right one, the dark dots of splatter on the left. At first, she couldn't wait to get rid of these boots. She hated them. But now? She feels a strange reluctance. These boots carry memories. The blood on them, Krämer's blood, is somehow no longer revolting.

That blood was the result of Ralf shooting Krämer, saving her. It represents their first real interaction, and what a dramatic one! She has worn them constantly since then. They seem a symbol of their flight, of their relationship, beginning with terror and bloodshed, through companionship and shared adventure, their journey into love. They tug at her heart. And yet?

They have surely served their purpose. She is here, in Paris, with the most remarkable young woman she has ever met. A woman she longs to emulate.

One day, hopefully, the war will be over and Ralf will return. He will find her a new woman, a *real* woman: no longer the innocent girl he has to protect, but a woman of substance, confident and chic. A woman like Monique.

She laughs. 'Yes, you're right,' she says. 'I do need shoes.'

Chapter Thirty-Seven

'There!' says Monique, giving the neckline one last little tug, flicking a bit of invisible dust from Sarah's shoulder. 'You look spectacular. The blue is just the right shade – it matches the blue of your eyes – and the fit is perfect. I've had that dress a couple of years now, but that sort of thing never goes out of date. How do you like it?'

Sarah regards herself in the mirror. She hardly recognises the woman she sees there – is that really *her*? That's a lady, it can't be her! She feels a disconnect, as if she is somehow physically attached to the ancient, almost threadbare, skirt and blouse that now lie discarded on the carpet of Monique's apartment; the kind of clothes that are inconspicuous because every woman wears them, every *normal* woman in wartime; women without the means to wear the fashionable styles produced by the couture houses of Paris before the war, but which almost every woman secretly covets. Monique, apparently, has too many of them and is only too happy to pass her discarded ones on to Sarah.

'Um, isn't the hem a little too high?' says Sarah, turning around before the full-length mirror, twisting her neck to regard herself over her shoulder. The dress reveals the upper curve of her calf; it almost reaches her knee. It feels daring, provocative. Shyness struggles with audacity. Can she? Would she?

'No, it's perfect! You have lovely legs – why hide them?'

'I like it,' she replies, doubtfully, 'but surely it's too good for me, too formal? Where will I ever wear such a gorgeous dress?'

'Oh, there'll be opportunities enough,' says Monique. 'I'll take you places. And Céline sometimes entertains and you will be required to put in an appearance with the children. As for streetwear, here are a couple of skirts and pullovers I no longer wear.'

She stands before the open wardrobe pulling clothes off their hangers and flinging them to the floor. Sarah is horrified at such casual treatment of good-quality garments; she picks them up as quickly as Monique discards them, lays them almost tenderly on the bed.

'That should do it!' says Monique, once they have picked out several. She closes the wardrobe door. 'Simple clothes but good quality – basic and yet elegant. Good thing that we're almost the same size.'

'I really can't accept—'

'Of course you can, I insist. Let me just find a suitcase for you to pack them in.'

She leaves the room and returns with a leather suitcase; together they fold and pack the clothes. Monique says, '*Zut*! I almost forgot shoes – I think I have just the pair for you. Rather, two pairs: one for the street and one to go with the blue dress.' She opens a second cupboard and reveals shelf after shelf of shoes. 'They are all years old and unfortunately out of date – the shortage of leather is a disaster for us women. Who wants to wear wooden clogs, or cork soles? But look, I can spare these and these. Try them on… Come, sit on the bed…'

Finally, Sarah is fully outfitted with clothes, shoes, a hat, a coat ('soon it will start to get cooler, you'll need a jacket for the autumn and a warm coat for the winter'). Monique has no stockings to spare – silk stockings are precious and scarce, only obtainable through connections – but she provides Sarah with liquid stockings: make-up for the legs. She shows her how to apply it, and the *trompe l'oeil* seam down the back. Make-up, too, for her face: an old powder compact, a stump of lipstick, half of an eyebrow pencil, some rouge. She teaches her how to apply it all.

Hours pass thus, and it's time to go so that Sarah can catch the late afternoon train home. She is overwhelmed with gratitude; it has been a special day, almost like a new birth, what with buying the violins and, now, this suitcase filled with the ingredients that will create of her a whole new self. What pleasure it is, to discard her old things! Yet still… old habits die hard. There's still life in her cast-off skirt and blouse, and as for the boots…

'Can't we find a place to donate these to?' she asks as Monique dumps them in the rubbish bin at the side of the house.

'Really? You think someone would want these old rags?'

'Yes, definitely. We can't just throw them out.'

'Well, if you say so. I'll give them to the maid. Maybe she'll appreciate them.'

'Really?'

'Yes. Don't worry.'

But Sarah still hesitates. She looks almost longingly at the cast-offs. Actually, she herself could still wear them. Maman would be appalled; she had made the blouse herself, and had been so proud of that skirt, old as it was. And the boots…

Sarah bends down and picks up the boots.

'Actually, Monique, I think I'll keep these. They're good-quality Swiss boots. They might be a little stained but there's a lot of life in them still. Perhaps they can be dyed and then they'll be as good as new.'

Monique wrinkles her nose as if at a bad smell. 'Well, I suppose if you want to go climbing mountains…'

'You never know,' says Sarah. She lays the suitcase on the ground, opens it, tucks the boots in. There's still just enough room. The boots remind her of Ralf. Their first dramatic meeting. That first trek through the mountains.

She will keep them for ever.

Just as they are walking out of the garden gate, a young man smartly dressed in a dark suit approaches.

'Gaston!' cries Monique, and the two of them exchange cheek kisses. 'What good timing! Gaston, I'd like you to meet Sarah Mayer – she's the governess Maman has employed. Sarah, this is my brother Gaston.'

Sarah and Gaston shake hands. Gaston's eyes narrow; they wander up and down Sarah's body so that she cringes and wishes she'd kept her old dowdy clothes, had rejected Monique's offer of face powder and lipstick.

'*Très jolie!*' says Gaston. 'But I thought Maman had employed a nanny?'

'She did, but Sarah has been instantly promoted to governess. She's more than a nanny. She speaks German – she *is* German. She will teach the children German and violin. She's rather special, Gaston!'

'Well, I can see that,' he replies. 'Why are you rushing away? Where are you off to?'

'Back to Poitiers. I'm taking her to the station. But perhaps we can all meet up next Saturday, at home?'

'I'll be there. Very pleased to have met you, Mademoiselle Mayer. We shall certainly meet again.'

He gives a little bow, raising his hat slightly, and slips in through the garden gate.

Monique laughs in glee. 'Typical Gaston! You need to be a little alert in future, Sarah – he's the biggest flirt in town!'

She squeezes Sarah's hand, lowers her voice. 'For you, he would be a very good *partie*. And I know for a fact that he is looking for a suitable German wife. If you play your cards right...' She winks knowingly, grabs Sarah's arm, and they walk off towards the nearest Metro.

That night, back in her bed in Poitiers, Sarah cannot find sleep. Her mind is a bees' nest, a thousand thoughts buzzing as she reflects on all that has happened today. So much! So many delightful developments! Her future looks so bright, despite this damned war. How she hates the war… it spoils everything. She hugs her pillow, pretending it is Ralf. *Oh, Ralf!* She sighs. *If only you were with me…*

She needs to tell him everything. He is her everything, and he must share in her good fortune; he must know. She must tell him!

There is a pad of paper and a pen on her table. She gets up, fetches both, props her pillow against the bedstead, leans back against it, bites the end of her pen and starts to write. The words pour out, and onto the paper, words bursting from her without plan and without thought, leaping onto the page the moment she has thought them:

My dearest Ralf,

There is so much I need to tell you! I am bursting with news and not to have you here to share it with you is the hardest thing ever. Where are you? It breaks my heart to think that you are in some camp somewhere in the hills, sleeping maybe on the hard ground, a gun near your head because there is danger, danger everywhere, and you are in the midst of this awful war instead of here with me. I love you so much and I want you to know that I am thinking of you every minute of every day. I know I cannot post this letter and you will never read these words, but I need to write them down even if I have to destroy them tomorrow – because I, too, am at risk, though not nearly as much as you. Where do I even begin? It's true, Ralf: I am staying in a home of *collaborateurs*! I do feel guilty – on the other hand, it is a fine house and the children I have to look after, I love them all and after all, they are innocent. I have to teach them German and give them violin lessons – imagine! And today I was in Paris again, buying violins! I cannot believe that I will once again have music in my life – it will be such a comfort to me. But not as much comfort as you would be, my love! I miss you so much it's like a burning ache inside me. Nothing can compensate except to have you here with me again. I wish you could have seen me today!

I have a new friend, she is the sister of my employer and her name is Monique. She is *très chic* and she is trying to make me *chic* as well! She gave me some really nice clothes – she is very rich – and showed me how to make myself beautiful. Beautiful for you, though of course she does not know of your existence! I wish I could tell her. I want to shout it to the world that I love you, only you, and will love you for ever! I hate this war as much as I love you. I have written to find out news of my sisters and parents but I think it will be several weeks till I have a reply.

I have written to Margaux in Ribeauvillé because of course I cannot write home. If ever we are separated, my love, we can find each other through her. One hears such awful stories of people separated through the war and I am so afraid it will happen to us. I have this dream, my darling: that you will decide that I am more important to you than the Resistance. That you will come back to me, here in Poitiers, and declare that you only want to be with me, just as I only want to be with you.

Damn this war, let it go to hell! Let us escape together. We can run away from it all, right down to the very South of France, and then cross the Pyrenees into Spain. That is the plan for my family, but you, too, are my family now! You must come with us.

If not, if you cannot leave this doomed Resistance, which is fighting a losing battle – (that is the truth, my love! Everyone here believes Germany will win) – then I will wait here for you, in Poitiers even if my family turns up tomorrow. I will not flee, I will wait for you – wait forever for you. Why, why, why, my love? I am crying as I read this. I want you so badly, want to be in your arms, to see your face, hear your voice. It is almost a physical ache, this longing for you, this fear for you! Please, my darling, do not do anything risky. Keep yourself safe, for me. Better yet, leave this war behind and come with me!

Your loving
Sarah

PS We discarded all my old clothes – but at the last minute I kept my boots. I will need them for our flight over the mountains! And I have become a little sentimental about them, bloodstains and all. After all, they represent exactly our very first encounter. They represent your bravery. They represent our love.

Chapter Thirty-Eight

A week passes, a second week. Sarah has learned the routine of the house. Madame Elise is a silent ghost who moves around unobtrusively, keeping the house shining: polishing the brasswork and the silver, putting things away as she moves, keeping the fires alight. A maid comes every day at ten for more rigorous cleaning: the two bathrooms and the kitchen, dusting and window-polishing. Sarah has nothing to do with either, only nodding as she passes them on the stairs or hallways. There is no need to discuss anything with Madame Lemoins. She keeps to her domain: the children.

What worries her most is that still there is no news from home, no news from Ralf. Sarah deals with her worry, the nagging sense that she is now completely alone in the world, by plunging wholeheartedly into her work with the children. She has grown very fond of them all, even Julien, who at every opportunity tries to demonstrate how grown-up he is, how little he needs her, and yet surreptitiously doubles back the very next moment to ensure that he has her support, her agreement. He is good at German, bad at violin; in fact, Sarah plans to suggest to his mother that he learn piano instead. He is convinced that the violin is a screechy girl's instrument, a thing for wimps. He is willing to consider the cello as well, if he has to, but he'd rather not. He is brilliant at mathematics and quick with his German and very interested in history.

'So, this book says that Herr Hitler is going to introduce a thousand-year empire. Does it mean he thinks he will live a thousand years?'

'I doubt it, Julien! It means that his regime is the start of this empire.'

'But how can he know? It's such a long time! History changes so quickly.'

'Herr Hitler is a very confident man, Julien.'

'Well, I think he's an arrogant prick! I can't stand it when Maman makes us listen to his speeches.'

'Well, Julien, it's fine to think that, but you must never, ever, say it out loud when she has her visitors. Do you understand me?'

'Yes, of course! I'm not stupid. But I can't stand them either!'

Julien's German has improved so much that Madame Lemoins sometimes allows him to join them at dinner when she has invited her German officer friends: Nazis. When they come, the hallway is full of their slate-grey greatcoats, all with swastika bands sewn onto the arms, neatly hung on hangers, their visor caps arranged in a row on the sideboard. Sarah has never met them herself, but she hears their raucous laughter; it echoes up the stairwell. She shudders when she hears it, and hides away in the nursery so as not to run into a Nazi by accident.

Jacqueline is not at all academic, not at all musical. She is a dreamy child who prefers to draw and paint, and she produces vividly coloured pictures, which Sarah praises and hangs on the wall. She, too, has many questions regarding history.

'What is a Jew, Mademoiselle Sarah?'

'Jews are the people who practise the religion of Judaism. They trace their origins through the Hebrew people of Israel to Abraham.'

'But Jesus was King of the Jews, n'est-ce pas?'

'So they say.'

'But why, then, are the Jews so evil?'

'Who told you that they are evil, Jacqueline?'

'Maman, when she came last night to tell me my story. She had a storybook, a German storybook, and that's what it said.'

'Really? Did she leave the book with you?'

Jacqueline nods. 'Yes. She says I should read it on my own.'

'And the book says Jews are evil?'

'Yes. It says they are bad people.'

'Did you ask your mother why?'

'Yes, I did. She said it's because they killed Jesus. But Jesus was a Jew too, wasn't he? So, they can't all be evil?'

'Jacqueline, my opinion is that nobody is evil just because people who share their religion or nationality or culture did something bad. I believe that everyone is responsible for their own deeds and we should all try to be good. Isn't that what Jesus taught?'

'Yes, it is. He said we should be good and kind, Mademoiselle Sarah. Don't you think so too?'

'Yes, indeed!'

'Then why don't you come to church with us?'

Sarah hesitates. It is true that she does not accompany the children to church on Sundays; she has made the excuse that she is not Catholic, like them. But *Madame* asked if she attends the Protestant church instead. She has made an excuse twice now – it is a problem she will have to solve sooner or later.

'It is because I am not Catholic.'

'But you could become Catholic, couldn't you?'

'Yes, if I wanted to. But Jacqueline, these are difficult questions even for an adult. I will think about it and give you an answer soon, *d'accord?*'

'*D'accord.*'

Collette is the one to watch. Not only does she remind Sarah so much of her sister Sofie, she is extremely gifted at the violin, far ahead of her older siblings. Like Sofie, though, Collette is rebellious and oversensitive, quick to tantrums, obstinate and disobedient. And yet it is Collette who, once or twice, has come up to the top of the stairs in the middle of the night, slipped in through Sarah's door, tiptoed silently across the floor and crawled into Sarah's bed, demanding cuddles and lullabies, eventually falling asleep in her arms.

The baby, Michel, is like any other toddler: he needs watching every minute of the day. As Sarah observed that very first day, he is brilliant at languages. His French is as good as Sofie's and his German almost as good after only a few weeks. He retains new words immediately, uses them correctly, pronounces them perfectly.

Even-tempered, well-behaved, he has never cried in Sarah's care; his tantrums have vanished overnight. He does cry, however, at night, when his mother tries to leave after saying goodnight. He screams then, and clings to her, and Sarah must come and take over – comfort him, calm him, sing him to sleep.

She loves her job. She loves these children. She wishes they were hers. She writes it all in her letters, the letters she writes in the silent dark hours of the night:

> One day, my love, we too will have four children, won't we? Just like these: two girls, two boys. And we will live in a lovely house with a garden and a garden house, just like this, and we will be happy together. Let it be soon, my beloved. Where are you now? Why have I not heard from you? Are you safe? I pray that you are. That I will see you soon and then we can run away together. I will have to leave this place, these children, but if I can be with you, I don't care. We will escape to the south, over the Pyrenees, just as we escaped over the Vosges.
>
> Oh, my dear. I know these are just dreams but I am in such despair, and it is at night, when all is quiet, that I am besieged by the demons of fear, and the only way I can keep them at bay is through these happy dreams. I long for you, or for just a word from you! There are such beastly people here! My only friend is Monique; she is good to me. But her brother – oh la la!

Gaston Beaulieu has kept his word. He has met her again, in his sister's home. He came last weekend. She was coming down the stairs with Michel in her arms when the living room door opened and he and Madame Lemoins walked into the hall, talking. The moment Gaston saw her, he stopped talking abruptly. Looking up at her, he smiled, a silky, sickening smile that made her skin crawl.

'Ah! We meet again, *Mademoiselle*! I was hoping I'd see you! How are you? How are the violin lessons?'

He grabbed her free hand and kissed it. She pulled it away.

'Gaston, really!' Madame Lemoins exclaimed. 'This is my children's nanny. Please behave appropriately – I won't have any more hanky-panky in this house!'

Gaston threw back his head and roared.

'Hanky-panky? How crude, Céline! And according to Monique this is your children's governess, not their nanny! How rude of you to suggest she would stoop to anything as vulgar as *hanky-panky*!'

'Considering your behaviour with the nursemaid, and the maid last year… I really should only employ women over forty.'

'Oh look, you've made her blush. Never fear, Mademoiselle Sarah! I shall always be on my best behaviour in your company. I have been warned by Monique that you are in a class of your own.'

Sarah, her face burning, rushed past them both and into the kitchen. She didn't dare slam or even shut the door – Madame Lemoins was, after all, her employer – so she couldn't help but hear the rest of his words as he called after her: 'Wait, don't rush off… I am none other than your humble servant, totally in awe! Oh dear, she's gone. I scared her off.'

Now, just as she is taking the younger children to bed, she runs into him again, skulking in the corridors.

'I came to apologise,' he says. 'I was rather discourteous when we met last week. I'm truly sorry…'

He doesn't look sorry. His eyes hold a twinkle that is anything but repentant – more amused than anything else, as if he finds the whole episode entertaining.

'Be assured that I did not intend any offence and I apologise profusely for any taken. It was unintentional – my sister is right, there is a crude side to my character, which I am trying to curtail. Be assured that my intentions towards you, *Mademoiselle*, are all entirely honourable. I just can't help it when I see a pretty face. Can you forgive me?'

'Yes, of course. Now please let me pass by.'

But he stands in her way. She steps to the side; the pile of towels she is carrying slips to the floor. He bends to pick them up, as does she. The timing is bad; their foreheads collide. She stumbles.

'Oh, my goodness! I'm so sorry. Did that hurt? Let me see – I do have a hard nut for a head. I trust you are not bruised? Let me help you up…'

He holds out a hand to her. She refuses, pulling herself up instead by holding onto the banister, bending again to pick up the fallen towels. He reaches out, grabs her elbow, pulls at it.

'I'm perfectly fine, thank you!' she says, more insistent than before, but still polite. 'Now please let me pass – I'm running the baths and—'

But before she can continue he has grabbed her waist, pulled her to him, shoved his head into her face; she feels his lips on her cheek, probing…

She doesn't even think. It's not a conscious decision, it's not a decision at all: it's just an automatic reaction, pure and simple. Her free hand flies out, smacks him hard across the cheek, and then she flees, pushes past him into the bathroom and slams the door. She flicks the lock shut, leans against the door, panting, quivering with dismay. What has she done? Struck her employer's brother! It's surely a sackable offence. Where will she go? She will have to apologise… But no! She won't apologise.

A new stance is hardening within her, an assertion, a decree to herself: *It is not I who is to blame, and I refuse to apologise. In fact, I insist that he apologise! I will not budge from that demand. No – not even if she sacks me.*

She has grown up a decade in five short minutes.

Chapter Thirty-Nine

She wakes with a sense of trepidation. In fact, she has hardly slept at all. She has been expecting a rap on the door, Madame Lemoins standing in the open doorway, incandescent with rage; she will be expelled from her bed, her room, this house, her job, her life. This nest of safety she has built for herself. Where will she go? The fear wraps around her like a cocoon, and yet each time she emerges from its grip defiant, unapologetic, more outraged than even before. She was right, he was wrong. The slap was justified! She will not crawl at *Madame*'s feet, begging for forgiveness!

But *Madame* does not come to her door. The morning unfolds like every other: waking the children, shooing them into the bathroom, washing and dressing Michel, the stampede down to the kitchen, preparing their breakfasts. As ever, Madame and Monsieur Lemoins have already left the house: their day starts even earlier, and ends later, than the children's. Sarah has only ever met *Monsieur* a few times, never spoken more than a few words to him. He glides in and out of his own home, mostly unseen. At the weekends, he spends some time with the children before they are shooed back upstairs, or into the garden, or Sarah takes them all for a walk to the park. She is the centre of their lives, today as every day.

There is also no sign of Gaston Beaulieu. The only adult in the house beside herself is, as ever, Madame Elise. Sarah breathes again. She can't wait for tonight, to write it all down, to tell Ralf what has happened. Her daily letters to him have become something of a diary: with no one to talk to, no one to confide in, there is always this. Her notepad, her pen, the bottle of ink… her thoughts emptying themselves onto paper. She knows she should destroy each letter each day, but she cannot. She longs for the day when she can hand them all over to him.

But this day ends on a slightly different note. Madame Lemoins returns home early. Sarah looks up, startled, when the kitchen door opens and the mistress of the house walks in.

'Sarah!' says Madame Lemoins. Sarah is feeding Michel his supper – scrambled egg smeared on slices of grey bread – and is cutting a slice into small squares for tiny hands, her back to the door. She jumps at the voice; the knife clatters to the floor. She leaps to her feet, bends to pick it up, stutters a welcome, tries to hold back Michel, who, in excitement at seeing his mother, is standing up in his high chair and crying 'Maman! Maman!' – all this at once. The snake of fear once again winds itself around Sarah – this is it, then. Madame Lemoins has found a replacement for her. She will be thrown out into the street. Now. Tonight.

But when she looks up at Madame Lemoins, she is astonished to find that she is smiling – a rare occurrence. Her eyes are as hard as ever – they have never been anything but hard – and the smile does not reach beyond the upcurved lips, but it is a definite smile; and then the lips part and Madame Lemoins speaks, even while scooping Michel into her arms.

'Sarah, I came home early to speak to you. My brother left last night and I assure you he won't be allowed back into the house until he has apologised to you. He told me his version of last night's incident, but I know my brother – I know him well. I have always warned him to leave my female staff alone but… well, boys will be boys, won't they? Michel, be quiet please, I am talking to *Mademoiselle* – I am sure he gave you enough provocation and he earned that slap, and the red mark across his cheek! I have often felt like doing the same myself. Well, he will apologise in time but I wanted to do so on his behalf today – I wouldn't want you walking out on me. I regret the incident and I assure you it won't happen again – or if it does, you will always have my full support. Please accept my apology.'

Sarah is too flabbergasted for words. She nods, and smiles assurance, and stutters a reply.

'Of course, *Madame*, it is nothing. I will not leave, I am happy here.'

'I'm so glad!' says Madame Lemoins. 'And now, why don't you take the evening off? As I am home I might as well finish feeding Michel, and I will take the children to bed myself.'

Sarah is speechless; she can do no more than nod again, take Michel from Madame Lemoins and replace him in his chair, pat him on the head, smile and leave the kitchen.

> My darling! You would not believe what happened today! All is forgiven! Though of course there was nothing to forgive, as I did no wrong. But I have learned something new today. I am as valuable to *Madame* as she is to me…

Her writing is breathless as she relates the scene with Madame Lemoins. She ends the letter, as always, with a declaration of her love.

> This is really my home, my safe place. But, my darling, the moment you declare that you are ready, that we can flee together, be together, I am yours, and that is what we'll do. I still don't understand your decision, but I respect it and always will. But one day, I hope you will choose me. I love you.
>
> Sarah

The following Saturday, both Monique and Gaston come down from Paris. Sarah is summoned to the salon; she comes, Michel on her hip carrying a wooden gun, his favourite toy. She glances at Gaston, then looks away again. Monique steps forward, both hands held out, taking Michel from Sarah, passing him to his mother, then taking both of Sarah's hands in hers.

'Oh, my dear! I have been told of my brother's terrible behaviour, and I have brought him here so that he can deliver his public apology. Gaston! Here she is – tell her!'

Sarah feels her face grow hot. It must be red as a beetroot. Why such a fuss? It would have been enough, surely, for Gaston to write a short note of apology? Instead, this: forced to face him, forced to look into that too-handsome, too-slick face, endure that slimy grin of false contrition, suffer those shallow words of flowered apology.

'*Mademoiselle*, I beg of you, please accept my most abject apologies and humble regret concerning last Sunday's encounter. Yes, I overstepped the mark, I crossed a red line, and I should never have made an overture towards you. I am a dastardly fellow! But believe me, it was meant as a compliment. I was unable to withstand your—'

Monique brusquely cuts in.

'Oh, Gaston, stop it! You've said your lines, now go away. Hopefully, Sarah will find it in her heart to forgive and forget – you do have a gift for ruining everything, don't you?' Madame Lemoins says, her eyebrows raised in worry. 'Sarah? Is that all right? Can you accept his apology?'

Everyone is staring at her, standing around her in a half-circle; only Michel is behaving normally, now down on the carpet playing with the toy gun. What else is there to do but nod and say yes? She can't say what she really wants to say, which is that she'd only be happy with a guarantee that she would never again have to set eyes on this unctuous creep, whose good looks are of the skin-deep, oily variety. *Keep him away*, she wants to cry out, but it's his house, apparently; put into his name, as the only male child. He owns this house and the appartment in Paris, and it's only the beginning, Monique has told her. Édifices Lemoins has a glowing future. When Germany wins the war – as it is sure to – there will be much building and rebuilding to be done, and Gaston is out to get those contracts. Paris will become the seat of the business, with Poitiers only a branch.

'Gaston knows which side his bread is buttered on,' Monique has explained, laughing, 'as do we all.'

It is a blatant admission of collaboration with the Nazis, and Sarah, as much as she is grateful for the comfortable respite from war, knows she must, one day, escape this house. It is a vipers' nest. For the time being, though, she must think of it as home, watch her step and keep her head down. With a surge of guilt she remembers her makeshift diary, the collection of *verboten* letters, some short, some long, she has written to Ralf. Why does he not make contact? Surely he can't be *that* busy? What do Resistance fighters do all day, anyway? Does he still love her? Does he even think of her? She must see him soon, hand him the letters, or else destroy them.

And what of her sisters, her parents? Now six weeks have passed since she left home. Her sisters should have been here weeks ago. Her parents must have fled by now; they had been given a month to produce the necessary papers, a month to flee. Surely they could all be here any day now?

Sarah is living in a cloud of unknowing, and it is unbearable. Her only place of refuge is that writing pad, that pen, that ink. It is the place where she finds peace. But it is a fragile peace at best; threat lurks in the background, ever present. She hides the pad of letters under her mattress. There it is safe, for now. She knows she should destroy them but cannot bear to. They are her only refuge, a place of comfort.

Chapter Forty

And then a week that changes everything. Two telephone calls from Régine, from the post office. The first on Monday evening: a letter has arrived from Germany, addressed to Sarah. It has no return address. She must come to collect it. It is too late for that today; Sarah must wait another day, another night, another sleepless night spent in the agony of unknowing. What will the letter hold, good news or bad? Her sisters' – even her parents' – arrival in Poitiers, is long, long overdue, so the news must be bad. They were captured, transported on those dreaded trains into Germany, to those dreaded camps! She has heard the rumours herself, now, and they are not good. The people transported there – they are never heard from again, they disappear into the void. Are they alive or dead? Nobody knows, nobody will know until the end of this endless war. And it does seem endless. What if war is the new normality, for ever and ever? What if there is no future, ever, apart from war? Sarah cries and fidgets and twists and turns in bed; she writes to Ralf, but she is too nervous even for that activity and soon abandons it, her anguished thoughts too chaotic to be organised into sentences, pushed down an arm into a pen and onto paper.

The next morning, as soon as the older children are packed off to school, Sarah prepares Michel for outdoors – it is getting quite chilly now – fetches his pushchair and marches off with him to the designated meeting place, a small park halfway between the two houses. Régine is already there, waiting. She welcomes Sarah with a motherly hug, in which a few of Sarah's twitching barbs of torment are absorbed. She hands her the letter. It is a light envelope, the address written in a hand Sarah does not recognise:

it belongs to none of her sisters, nor to either of her parents. It must be bad news, then! She cannot bring herself to open it, for her hand is trembling and already tears are gathering in her eyes, tears of anticipation of devastating news.

'Don't cry, dear,' says Régine gently. 'Would you like me to open it for you, read it for you and tell you what it says?'

Sarah gulps and nods. Régine pushes a finger into the flap of the envelope and prises it open. She removes a single sheet of paper. Sarah glances at it and looks away, because her heart is throbbing so insistently she is almost paralysed with fear. She cannot bear even the sight of that slip of paper – paper, words, that will change everything. She wishes it had never come. So much better to live in the hope of good news than be forced to face bad news, the bad news that is about to break.

Régine is reading the letter, her face hidden by the sheet of paper. And then the paper drops, revealing her face – and heavens above, she is smiling! She is actually beaming. She reaches out with both hands to draw Sarah into a hug, and she says, her voice breaking with tears, 'Sarah, Sarah – don't cry! The news is good! Your sisters are safe! Here, read it yourself.'

She hands the letter to Sarah, whose hands are still trembling. Sarah's eyes, alive now with hope and relief, touch hers, and then drop to read the slightly coded words:

Dear Simone,

We were so happy to receive your letter and to know that you arrived safely at your uncle's place. I'm so sorry this has taken so long but we too had no news of my two cousins and had to wait. They had to change their plans slightly as circumstances have changed, but yesterday we received the news that they are in Switzerland. They travelled via Basle with their aunt and made it down to the south, the French part, and are now comfortable in a town called Sion.

They have asked me to pass their news and love on to you.

Unfortunately, there is no news of their parents and other sisters. I will let you know as soon as I do receive news. We are all well. Maman is as busy as ever. I have finished my Red Cross course and am thinking of becoming a fully fledged nurse. Eric too is well and fully recovered from his accident. We all send our love.

Yours sincerely,
Valérie

When Sarah looks up her eyes are shining, still moist with tears, but this time they are tears of joy, not despair. She flings her arms around Régine, who holds her and allows her to weep. The accumulated anguish of weeks empties itself into the older woman's ample bosom, is absorbed by her hands gently rubbing Sarah's back. How good it is, to be in a mother's arms again, to be enclosed in the unique warmth and comfort only a loved child can know! How good it is to be a loved child again, instead of a frazzled fugitive without a future, captured in a net of constant fear! What safety, what liberation!

Sarah has missed this so much, so very much. It's like coming out of a freezing-cold day into the cosy warmth of home and hearth, allowing the delicious warmth from the fireside to seep through one's being. She could stay here for ever. Go home with Régine, live with her. But no, it cannot be. Michel starts to wail, now, and Sarah is torn back into the present, into the demands of duty and an uncertain future and the frigid ambience of the Lemoins-Beaulieu residence.

'I must go,' she tells Régine, extricating herself from her arms.

'Yes. Do you want me to keep the letter for you? It's probably safer.'

Sarah hesitates. She would love to keep the letter, hide it under her mattress along with the letters to Ralf. It is her most precious possession, right now. But no. Régine is right, it is safer with her. The letters to Ralf are not safe either – she really should destroy them in a day or two because… well, just to be on the safe side. But nobody is going to search her room. And surely Ralf will turn up soon and she can give them to him and, once he has read them, he can destroy them. She has poured so much of herself into them, it would be a pity… But as for this letter, it's the content that is important, not the letter itself. She does not need to keep it.

A last hug for Régine and Sarah is on her way back home, this time with a spring in her step.

But only two days later, she receives another telephone call from Régine. This time, there is no night of anguish spent not knowing what news the next day will bring. This time, the news is immediately good – the best.

'Uncle Louis has found the book you are looking for,' she says. It is the code they have agreed upon to indicate that Ralf is in town and seeking a meeting with her, at their prearranged café.

'Wonderful!' says Sarah, and indeed, a sense of wonder has descended on her, enclosed her in folds of joy. 'When shall I pick it up?'

'Three,' says Régine.

'Thank you. I'll be there,' says Sarah.

She is almost trembling with excitement as she lifts the mattress, gathers the loose pages of her makeshift diary, shoves them into the waistband of her skirt. Michel has just woken up from his afternoon nap and is crotchety. Today she has no patience, does not gently coax him into his clothes but shoves his arms into his coat, laces up his boots, heaves him onto her hip and carries him downstairs. She is just about to exit the front hall when the outside door opens and Monsieur Beaulieu enters. This is only the third or fourth time she has ever seen him; he is the first out of the house in the morning and the last in, and apart from a brief *bonjour*, they have never spoken. He is a small man, but wiry and doubtless strong; compact muscle. He smiles at her, removes his hat, reaches out his arms to take Michel from her.

'Papa, Papa!' cries Michel, a wriggling mass of excitement. Monsieur Beaulieu looks over Michel's head to meet Sarah's eyes.

'*Bonjour, Mademoiselle,*' he says. His voice is calm, polite. 'You are going out for a walk?'

'Yes, *Monsieur*. We are going to the park.'

'Well, I would love to go with you. It's such a fine day, and I could do with some fresh air – but what to do? I came home early precisely because I have developed a fever and need to rest. *Tant pis*! Another time. I have heard good things about you, *Mademoiselle*, and hope you are happy in our household. Thank you for taking such good care of my children.'

He nods, hands Michel back to her. Sarah is out the door before he can change his mind, before he can delay her further. She grabs Michel's pushchair from the outside porch, deposits her charge – more crochety than ever at being so rudely snatched away from his father – and pushes him out the gate and onto the pavement. It's a half-hour walk to the café, but Sarah makes it in less than twenty minutes. She almost runs, as if getting there early will ensure that Ralf, too, gets there early. But it doesn't. She barges through the door of the café, looks around hopefully, but can tell at a glance that she has arrived before him. She orders coffee at the counter and a jam pastry for Michel, chooses a corner table where they can have a modicum of privacy. She can hardly breathe for excitement; her eyes are fixed on the door, her heartbeat races every time it opens, and Michel's constant demands make her more nervous than ever – what if Ralf walks in just as she is wiping the jam from Michel's face? Just as she is picking up the bottle he has thrown to the floor, precisely to gain her attention?

Small children seem to know exactly when their carers are distracted, their thoughts not circling around toddler needs, and Michel is no exception. He scrambles to get out of his pushchair, to sit on her lap; wants her to sing to him, tell him a story. He continues to wriggle there on her lap, pushes pudgy hands into her face; pulls at her cheeks, her hair... But at least the waiting for Ralf passes quicker. When she looks up at the clock over the kitchen door he's already fifteen minutes late and she starts to worry. Did she get the time right, the day? What if he doesn't come at all? Michel has felt something strange around her waist and is digging away at it, pulling her blouse out of her skirt.

'Michel, no, leave those papers alone, they are not for you...' He's clinging to the sheaf of letters, she's prising them from his fingers, and it's while she is scuffling with Michel that a voice breaks into the tussle.

'Hello, Sarah!'

And then Michel is forgotten. She springs to her feet and straps the child back in his chair, ignoring his wails, and flings her arms around Ralf. He is kissing her, his lips on her forehead, her cheeks, her lips, everywhere, and they are both laughing and crying and trying to speak and kiss all at once. The reunion is even more joyous than the one at Metz, at the Resistance house, because now, well, now they are welded together, have been reaching out for each other across the silence and the distance, across a chasm of empty weeks that could only be spanned by love.

At last they both sink into their chairs, still holding hands, still talking over each other.

'Tell me, tell me everything! Every moment!'

'I've been dying with worry – the silence almost killed me!'

'You first!'

'No, you!'

Sarah wins that argument. She taps the little heap of papers on the table.

'I've written it all down, Ralf. You can read it all here, afterwards – so you go first! Tell me everything! Is it very dangerous? Where have you been?'

He glances at the papers and frowns, then turns back to her.

'I can't tell you much, Sarah – it wouldn't be safe for either of us. I'm with a group of friends, in the country, not too far away. They are good friends, doing good work.'

'But what exactly do you do? Is it dangerous? I worry about you so much, all the time. It is agony, not having news of you.'

'And it is agony for me, being so far from you and not knowing if you are well.'

'I am the safe one, Ralf. I'm the lucky one. You need not worry about me – but I need to know, what do you do? I worry that you will get yourself killed and I will never know because nobody would think to tell me. What exactly do you do?'

'I'm sorry, I can't tell you, Sarah. Just very vaguely: I train the *maquisards* in explosives, and we go around blowing up Nazi things. That's really all I can tell you.'

'Oh, Ralf! Explosives! It sounds so dangerous.'

He laughs. 'It's not, if you know what you are doing. I've been well trained, in Germany. We are careful.'

'I don't want you doing that stuff, Ralf! Why can't we just flee together, be together? My sisters are in Switzerland. We could go there. Or else to Spain and America, as first planned – over the Pyrenees! Why do you have to live this dangerous life? Is our love not important to you?'

'How can you say that? It's the most important thing in my life! It's just that there are bigger things, Sarah, and defeating the Nazis is bigger, and we can. The tide is turning. It's not a given that they will win. Hitler's forces are being demolished on the Eastern Front. And I want to help defeat them, create a peaceful world for us all, so we can have a life where we do not have to live in hiding, do not have to flee. I wish you'd understand…'

She sighs. 'I do understand, a little. But I cannot bear the separation. I think of you all the time. I cannot bear that my life is so comfortable, so safe, and you are out there fighting. I wish I could fight at your side. Are there any women among you?'

'A few, yes.'

'So maybe I could join you? Fight side by side with you, help you blow things up!'

He chuckles. 'It would be marvellous to have you join us but then I would be the one to be constantly worrying about you. I don't want you to fight, Sarah. I want you in Poitiers, safe, waiting for me. Better yet, I think you should go to Switzerland, join your sisters, wait for me there.'

'No. I have to wait here, for my parents, and for you. Why is it that the women always have to wait at home and the men put their lives at risk?'

'Because you are precious to us. Because we need your strength – it is what sustains us, keeps us going; knowing that you are there, praying for us; that we have you to return to. You are the backbone of it all, of our lives. We need you.'

'It just isn't right.'

'It is. You are the ones who uphold sanity in this world. What we are doing, fighting, killing each other, blowing up things – that is madness. It is you women that hold everything together. But let's not talk about that, it's just the way it is. Now, it's your turn. Tell me, how is it?'

She taps the letters again. 'It's all here, written down. I write you letters, at night; it's how I maintain my sanity, Ralf. I tell you everything. You can read them. Go ahead – they are in order.'

She hands him the letters, and as he takes them he frowns once again.

'I don't think…' he starts to say, but then his eyes look down and he reads. He reads and reads, and now and again he glances up to meet her eyes but then reads on. He is halfway through reading when he puts them down and looks straight at her.

'Sarah, where do you keep these letters when you are not in your room?'

'Under the mattress.'

He sighs. 'Sarah, you must not, you cannot. Under the mattress is the first place anyone would look if they suspect you of anything.'

'But that's it, Ralf – they do not suspect me. I am safe there, I've won them all over. Have you reached the part yet where Gaston tried to molest me?'

He shakes his head. 'No, who is Gaston?'

She tells him. 'Read on, Ralf. You will see. They don't suspect anything. It's the safest place I could possibly be.'

He shakes his head, lowers his eyes and continues to read. When he has finished he places the sheaf of letters back on the table, lays his hand flat on them and looks into the distance, saying nothing.

'You see? They tried to appease me; they definitely don't suspect anything untoward. Monique is practically courting me, sucking up to me. It's all because I am German and they think Germany will win the war.'

'But it won't. They are wrong. You are living in a house of *collaborateurs*, Sarah – even your good friend Monique is one. You have no idea of the danger. I want you to stop writing to me at night. Promise me you won't.'

'Oh, you are such a fusspot! You worry too much.'

'No, I am serious. I want you to promise.'

She rolls her eyes. He does not understand; he does not understand how embedded she is in this household, how much they depend on her, how much they owe to her. But he is serious about this promise.

'Very well then. I won't write any more.'

'Say you promise! A promise is an important thing to keep, Sarah. I always keep mine. Even the very, very hard promises – I have kept them.'

'What's the hardest promise you have ever kept? To whom?'

He hesitates.

'Tell me!'

'Well, I made a promise to Rebecca. Before we set off for Metz.'

'Really? What did you promise her?'

'It concerned you, Sarah. She guessed that we would fall in love. She knew it, back then; she thought it was inevitable.'

Sarah laughs. 'Rebecca is a very wise woman. She knew me better than I knew myself – remember how she persuaded me to trust you?'

He laughs. 'I remember. That seems like a different age altogether!'

'She knew fear would turn to love. So, go on. What did you promise her?'

'I promised her that I would not take advantage of you.'

She frowns. 'What on earth does that mean?'

'It means that you were a young woman and I was a young man and we would be travelling together, living together, and I would be tempted. And I had to resist temptation, restrain my feelings. Not – not touch you.'

'But why not?'

Ralf blushed. 'Because, because—I don't know. Because we might go too far? And then life would get too complicated?'

'But how can it be wrong to love someone? And what do you mean by going too far? I want to love you completely! Isn't that what you want too?'

'Oh, Sarah! How could you not know, not guess? Yes! Yes, of course! But we must wait until it all is safe – after the war we will marry and it will be different. But now – we cannot allow ourselves to get distracted.'

He reaches out, strokes her hair, pushes a lock of it behind her ear. She leans her head to the side, trapping his hand.

'When we were travelling, Sarah, every minute of every day I longed to take you in my arms. I still do. But I kept my promise and it was a good thing. Rebecca was right, I had to keep my feelings to myself. It was a matter of safety, for us both.'

'So, when I thought you were a cold block of ice, it was actually the opposite?'

He nods. 'That's about it, yes.'

Tears gather in her eyes, run down over her cheeks.

'I— I'm so angry at Rebecca for telling you that and I love you so much for making that promise. I love you so much, Ralf. I will never love another man, that's my promise to you. But you must keep safe, stay alive, for me. That's a new promise you must make.'

'All I can promise, Sarah, is to do my best.'

'Not take any foolhardy risks?'

'I can promise that, yes.'

'Come back to me?'

'I will do my best to always come back to you.'

'I want you to promise, definitely, that you will come back.'

'I take a promise seriously, Sarah, and that is a promise that is out of my hands, out of my control. All I can promise is to do my best, my very best.'

She's crying openly now.

'It's not enough, Ralf. It's not enough. I need to *know!*'

'There are things we cannot know, all we can do is stay strong within. That's what we must promise each other.'

'I'll try, but I don't know if I can!'

'We will both try our best. That's all we can do – our best.'

On her way home something occurs to Sarah. She has not promised not to write her letters to Ralf. He doesn't understand: she needs to. It is vital to her very sanity, this outlet. She will continue to write him, but as a diary, not collecting the letters to give to him, but destroying them after a few days. That's a fair compromise. He will never know, and she can't break a promise she hasn't given.

Chapter Forty-One

Winter arrives and the war drags on. They are all so weary of it all. Sarah keeps to her decision: she writes her letters to Ralf, keeps them for a few days, then – regretfully – burns them in the fireplace. Writing to him provides a vital emotional outlet; it allows her to pour out all she feels, all the frustration, the loneliness, the love. But now she pretends that the paper on which she writes *is* Ralf; that she writes upon his heart, that he listens, that he is right here with her, sharing her life.

My darling,

Today Monique took me out to visit some friends of hers – someone's birthday party. I was finally able to wear the beautiful blue dress she gave me a few weeks ago, when I was in Paris. I wish you could have seen me! I felt so beautiful! I wish you would stop seeing me as a young girl you need to protect, Ralf. I am a woman now. If you could have seen me that evening, you'd know it. I know I'm still a bit shy – it was quite apparent at that party, everyone was so sophisticated! But I am learning more and more each day.

I'm learning, Ralf. I have joined the local library and borrowed books on history and read them. I read newspapers now, too, and listen to the radio. Of course, I realise that much of what they are saying is propaganda. It's hard to believe what you said, that the war has now turned and the Allies are winning. That there might very well be an invasion soon. Here, it does not feel at all like that. It's all Germany this, Germany that, and they are all convinced that Germany will win the war in the end. They truly believe that God is on Hitler's side and thus Germany is destined to win. Isn't that ridiculous? I personally don't think God takes sides, but if He does, He's on the side of goodness, and Hitler is not good, and so he cannot win.

Did you know there is a camp just outside Poitiers, for foreign Jews? Monique mentioned it casually the other day. I feel so guilty, being a Jew and yet being so safe here in this house. I feel I am betraying my own people. Is it right? Is it moral? Yes, Ralf, I am thinking about it a lot, educating myself. I was such a silly, naïve little girl when we left Alsace, wasn't I? Like a little bird shoved out of the nest, and so resentful that I was being forced to fly. I wanted to stay in the comfort of home and the people I loved. But then I met you and learned to love you, and you taught me to fly. And I am glad. Not glad of the circumstances, but glad that they brought us together. I can't imagine there's a better man in the whole world, or anyone I could love as much.

You know, on the one hand I wish the two of us could just run away and be together in a safe country. Switzerland, with my sisters, or even America. But you are right: that is the way of cowards, thinking only of themselves and their little lives. I am ashamed of my cowardice. And I want to be near you, wherever you are, even in danger.

I suppose it is because I love you so very much but as I said, I'm growing and I now agree with you, that there has to be something bigger than us, and that the culmination of love is when you can sacrifice it for the greater good. And I admire you so much, because that is exactly what you are doing. I used to resent your decision for choosing to fight the Nazis rather than escape with me. Now I am proud of you. I wish I was as courageous! I think of you and want you so much but at the same time I almost burst with pride at what you are doing for us all. I hate the Nazis!

There's something else I need to tell you. Monique is courting one of them! The other night I was coming downstairs after putting the children to bed to get some food for myself, and I saw it – as usual there were some officers in the dining room, singing at the tops of their voices; but then the door to the study opened and Monique came tumbling out, giggling, in the arms of one of the officers! Not even one of the good-looking ones – he's at least fifty, with a paunch and receding hairline – ugh! They didn't see me – too busy with each other – but they kissed and then Monique said goodbye and left, and the officer went back into the dining room. Wiping lipstick from his face! So now I know that you are right – they are all *collaborateurs*, even Monique, and I do feel uncomfortable.

But then she is so kind to me, like when she took me to this party, introduced me to her friends. They were all very kind to me. It is so confusing. I do think she is trying to make a better person of me, give me confidence, and that is happening, definitely. I realise what a sheltered life I lived in Colmar and that is changing – Monique is helping. I think one day I will talk to her about the German officer.

I want to be completely honest with you, hold nothing back, so please don't be offended or worried about what I am about to say now. The thing is, Monique thinks I need a boyfriend. Or even a lover! Imagine that. And

I can't tell her I don't need one, I have you. That's why she took me to this party – she wanted me to meet a few men there. She told them all that I was German. I didn't like that. Why should they know that? Why can't I be French? I wish she wouldn't – that she wouldn't introduce me as German, and wouldn't introduce me at all! Not to men, anyway. You need not be jealous because I am not the least interested in any one of them. I love you, only you, and I will never, ever love another.

I wish I knew what exactly you are doing, where exactly you are, so I can imagine you doing it. You said you blow things up and that is frightening. Please be careful, my love! I cannot bear to think of you in danger. The more I educate myself about this blasted war, the more I wish I was braver and could join you wherever you are, fight alongside you for justice and peace. I miss you so much and I miss my family. I have not had any news about my parents and my younger sisters. I hope and pray that they are safe. I wrote to Margaux again but have not had a reply. I have heard that there is a huge backlog of letters everywhere and half of them do not ever arrive. That is so disheartening.

I wish the winter was over, I wish for so much, but most of all I wish for you. To be in your arms once again, if only for a minute. I feel like the parched earth, longing for the rain that is your love. When can we meet again? Every time the telephone rings, I jump, thinking it is you. But I know the rules: you will only ever call me between 10 and 11, when Madame Elise is out doing the shopping. I know that; and it hardly ever rings at that time but I listen for your call constantly and cannot bear the silence.

Well, now it is past midnight and at last I am beginning to feel sleepy so I will put this away for now. I have a new hiding place, but I won't tell you where as you would disapprove of all hiding places, wouldn't you? Keep safe, my love. Keep well away from the things you explode. I feel so much better, now that I have written this; it is as if you were right here by my side, listening. That's how I know it is the right thing to do. Yet still I will be good and destroy it one day soon.

Time passes so very slowly. But one day we will be together. I know it.

Sarah

PS Did you hear the terrible story about Sophie Scholl? She was a German student who was distributing information against the Nazis – but they caught her, sentenced her to death and executed her by chopping off her head! I could not believe it and I am still reeling with the horror of it. It also emphasises my own cowardice. I feel unworthy of people like her – and of you. I think you would probably prefer someone as brave as her, instead of a silly little fledgling bird like me!

Sarah folds the two pages of paper and gets out of bed; she pads across the room to the bookshelf. She picks the biggest book – it is a biography of Johann Sebastian Bach, borrowed from the library – and sticks the folded paper between the pages. It is her new hiding place. In a day or two she will burn it, and any other letters that have accumulated. It is a compromise; she *needs* to write to Ralf. It is her lifeline.

Chapter Forty-Two

The winter drags past, and soon it is January 1944. The fifth year of war. Will it ever end? It seems not; it seems all of Sarah's memories are shrouded in the veils of war, that the happy times before have all been erased. There is only this: fear, and hiding, and the sense of a world incomplete, frayed, broken.

She has seen Ralf twice during this dreary winter, and each time left him not only with renewed strength to face the empty weeks ahead, but the knowledge that their love has deepened, expanded, become an independent force of its own. It fills every cell of her body, every atom of her mind. It is high and it is deep and it is broad, but most of all, and to her astonishment, it is fulfilling, an ocean from which she can drink at any time. She has only to turn to it, remember it, to be filled with gladness. The despair and desperation of the early weeks of separation have turned to this: the experience of a love so strong it is with her constantly, whether or not he is with her. It is her very being.

She tells him this, propped against the cushions, leaning against the bedstead; she lets him into her soul.

> I feel now, Ralf, that our souls are as one – there is no separation, even when we are apart. How can I describe it? It's as if we share common ground, made of pure spirit, which abides in both of us at all times, whether our bodies are together or not. Our separate souls are superimposed on that common ground, and so we are together at all times, and yet each can live a separate life but with access to that common ground, which is the

love that connects us. And there is joy in that common ground, and the knowledge that wherever we are, we are together. Isn't that the true meaning of love?

Of course I still worry about you and pray for your safety, and of course I want you near me. But whenever I falter, and stumble into the claws of despair, I remember that love and it snatches me back, and I am strong and upright again. It is marvellous, Ralf! I hope it is the same for you. Well, I am going to destroy this letter as always, so you will never read these words, but I'll tell you when next we meet.

Above all, I am so very proud of you. Fighting for the freedom of France! I can't help thinking that with people like you on the side of righteousness we have to win this war. That goodness and justice will prevail, because they are of the essence of God. When that happens, when we are together, we must sort out this thing about religion. The fact that you are Catholic and I am Jewish doesn't seem to matter at all; I feel there is really no difference, somehow, it is all one. It is a confidence that comes from deep within. We will sort it out; perhaps one of us will convert – I don't mind at all – or we will stay as we are.

Fight on, my darling; you are my soldier, my beloved, a warrior for all that is good and sane in a world consumed by evil and madness. I am living in a house committed to that darkness, yet it does not touch me. I know, I just know, that all will be well in the end. The Nazis will flounder. *Vive la France!*

She smiles to herself, slips the letter under the mattress for the time being. Tomorrow she will hide it properly. Now, she just wants to sink into the enfolding arms of sleep.

*

It has been a good day; the sun is out in full strength, not a cloud in the sky. In the park, the very first signs that winter is retreating, snowdrops pushing through their white heads, and the birds seem convinced that spring is on the way, though it's only February. Michel, too, has been sunny. They'd played ball for a while, and then they watched the ducks at the pond and then he sat on her lap on the park bench while she read him a story about five little ducks scrambling up a bank behind the mother duck, one after the other. On the way home they sang a song about a duck and she promised him more duck stories that night, and now she is peeling off his coat and thinking it really is too warm, today, for a winter coat and boots. She sees Monique's coat hanging in the *garderobe* – good! Monique is home from Paris. No doubt they'll have a good little chat over a glass of wine that evening, with Monique telling her stories of her life in Paris, the men she knows, trying to persuade her, Sarah, to flirt more, to be more encouraging to men.

'But you are so pretty, when you make the effort!' Monique always says. 'You could easily have men falling at your feet! What about…'

As usual, Sarah will laugh and deflect Monique's attempts at matchmaking. 'I am too young!' she always says, or 'I'm waiting for someone really special,' or 'When the war is over.'

Monique has confided in her about her own love life, about the German officer who courts her when she is in Poitiers. 'I am not serious about him,' she told Sarah, 'it's just a bit of fun. As a Frenchwoman, I need to keep the Germans on my side. We all do. Yes, it means a bit of play-acting, sucking up to them, licking their bloody jackboots – but they can be really brutal to people who show open dislike, so…'

She shrugged. 'In reality, I know who I really want, and he's not a German.'

Monique is the mistress of a married man, in Paris. 'He will never divorce her so I am hedging my bets until I can make a marriage of convenience at some point. Like my sister did.'

Sarah was astonished to hear about this 'marriage of convenience'. The Beaulieu family, it appears, were floundering financially at the start of the war. They had once been extremely rich, their fortunes built on a chain of successful food processing factories, and owned the house in which they all now lived, as well as the apartment in Paris where Monique and Gaston live. But after the Occupation Germany had stripped the factories of all able-bodied male workers and their fortunes had crashed. In rode Monsieur Lemoins on a white steed; he had, Monique explained, always been in love with the beautiful Céline Beaulieu, but she had always rejected him – until now. Hervé Lemoins might not be as handsome as some of her other suitors, but his family owned a thriving construction business, and construction is never out of place in a time of large-scale destruction.

'One has to consider the circumstances, and do what is best for oneself,' says Monique. This life wisdom is completely at odds with Sarah's own newly found insights, but she has learned to accept Monique just as she is, without moral judgement. Monique is Monique: the most wildly entertaining, sweetly charming, extravagantly generous woman Sarah has ever met.

Michel is hungry, so Sarah prepares a snack and a glass of milk for him before heaving him onto her hip to go up to her own room to change into her indoor clothes. Yes, she now has comfortable indoor clothes and more solid outdoor clothes, all thanks to Monique's generosity.

She opens the door to her room – and gasps in shock. Monique is there, sitting on the bed, reading her letter to Ralf. The one she wrote last night, and forgot to hide, slipping it instead under the mattress, as she used to do. The one with all the... Sarah rakes through her mind. What did she write last night? Anything suspicious, dangerous, incriminating? But her mind has gone blank. All she can remember is the great sense of love blanketing her as she fell asleep. It was a love letter, as always. But the details that might have slipped in between the inevitable declarations of love – she can't remember a single one.

'What— what are you doing here?' she stutters, and steps across the space to the bed and attempts to snatch the letter from Monique. Monique gives a wicked cackle and raises her hand out of Sarah's reach.

'*Oh, la la*!' she says, and her voice is mocking. 'Now all is revealed! Little Miss Innocent has a lover! Who would have guessed?'

'It's not... it's not what it looks like,' says Sarah, but her voice is weak and unconvincing because she herself knows that it is exactly what it looks like.

Monique, holding the letter above her head out of Sarah's grasp, gets up, walks to the door, shuts it.

'Tell me then, Sarah darling – what exactly *is* it?'

Something gathers in Sarah, something she's never known before. Outrage.

'Give that back to me! It's mine – it's private! How dare you!'

She sets Michel on the floor and tries again to grab the letter, but Monique only laughs and dances away.

'Temper, temper!' she mocks. 'Who would have thought the sweet little Sarah could turn into a virago!'

Sarah changes tack. 'Please, Monique, give it back.'

Monique immediately complies.

'*Bien*. Here it is. You can have it – I've read it anyway. Now, Sarah, why don't you and I just sit down and have a little chat?'

She sits herself down on the edge of the bed, grabs Sarah's wrist and pulls her down too. Her voice changes. No longer mocking, it's gentle, consoling, understanding. It's the Monique of old, the friend and *confidante*.

Sarah, struggling with tears, sniffs and folds the letter and pushes it into her neckline. She dabs at her eyes and looks up at Monique, as fiercely as she can.

'It wasn't for you to read. It's not fair!'

'Look, Sarah, I know. I know I shouldn't be poking around in your room, reading your private letters. I know it was wrong and I apologise. I'm sorry. Can you accept that apology, and listen to me for a moment?'

Sarah sniffs again. She wants to slap Monique, run away, anything but sit here with a Nazi sympathiser who knows all her deepest secrets. She says nothing.

'So, all right, I understand. You're upset, and rightly so. And you're scared and you feel guilty. After all, you sneaked into our home under false pretences. You're Jewish.'

Her voice hardens at that word and she glares at Sarah, who says nothing.

'Aren't you?' Monique prompts. 'Don't bother denying it. It was in the letter.'

Sarah nods.

'Do you realise the *trouble* you could have got us all into if it had come out? Do you know what the Nazis do to French people who harbour Jews?'

Do you know what the Nazis do to Jews? Sarah wants to retort, but says nothing. Neither does she nod.

'I mean, we have German officers going in and out of our house and you're a Jew. Without a yellow star armband. I can't even begin to think of the danger to my family.'

They stare at each other, unflinching.

'It seems you're not about to apologise,' says Monique. 'And worse yet, this lover of yours, this Ralf – he's in the Resistance, isn't he?'

Sarah only shrugs. There's no point denying or admitting it. Monique knows. She continues:

'So, the question is, do I hand you over to the Nazis? I could do that, you know. You *and* your Ralf. That is, you, and they'll get the secret of Ralf's identity out of you. They have their ways, you would not like them.'

Sarah bites her lip and says nothing. She stares into Monique's eyes, still unflinching.

'Or else…' says Monique, a half-smile on her lips. She leaves the question hanging, so that Sarah is forced to say, 'Or else, what?'

Monique laughs gaily. 'Or else I tell you my own secrets. Stop it, Sarah, stop staring at me like that. It's all right, I won't give you away. I was just teasing. The thing is…' She inserts a pause pregnant with intrigue. 'The thing is, the big thing is – I'm on your side!'

Sarah can't help it; she gasps. 'What— what do you mean?'

'I mean, just that. Exactly that. I, too, am in the Resistance. I'm playing a part, the part of the chic, shallow Parisienne who is open to a lot of fun with whoever is convenient. And so, because I'm known for my shallowness and friendliness, and because my sister is sucking up to them to kingdom come, I get to come here and dine with them and go out with them, and win their trust. And I get them to tell me things, subtly; I get to ease some of their secrets out of them. They call it a honeytrap. My officer friend? He's in the SD, the *Sicherheitsdienst*, the secret police embedded within the Gestapo. The most powerful force in Germany. Even the *Schutzstaffel* hate and fear them.

'But I – I have his ear. Because in the end he is only a man, and I am a woman, and I know the tricks of a woman. Older men tend to fall for women like me, and a clever woman can use that fact to her advantage. In my case, to her *country's* advantage. That's my job, Sarah. Basically, I'm a spy. Not even my sister knows this. So, your secret is safe with me. In fact, now we can work together, you and I. And your Ralf.'

She smiles, and squeezes Sarah's hand, then leans forward and hugs her. And Sarah is so weak with relief, so grateful, so utterly exhausted after the terrible scare of finding Monique reading her letter, that she collapses into her arms and finally lets the tears pour out. Monique strokes her back and comforts her.

'I'm sorry. Sorry I played with you like a cat with a mouse. I know it was terrifying. I shouldn't have done it, but you know me, I'm basically a tease. I couldn't resist. Forgive me, Sarah. Please. I meant no harm.'

Michel has noticed something odd: Sarah crying.

This is so unusual – he's always the one to cry, she to comfort – he gets up from the floor, where he has been playing with his toy car, and runs to the two women. 'Mademoiselle Sarah! Why are you crying? Don't cry!' he says, and tries to wipe her eyes dry with his little hands.

Sarah laughs through her tears and lifts him onto her lap. Now she laughs, and he laughs with her, and her tears are of release. The tilted world, for today, has been set right.

'I feel this is the beginning of an even deeper friendship,' says Monique. 'We are now allies, sisters in the fight for freedom.'

Sarah feels a lift of her spirit; the terror on discovering Monique reading her precious letter has turned into something else. Monique has entrusted her with her own secret, and hers is surely the greater secret, and because of that, somehow, now Sarah has taken a step towards the undercover world of the Resistance. A tiny step, perhaps, but a step nevertheless, and a step closer to Ralf.

Two more weeks pass. Three. February turns to March, and spring approaches tentatively. Monique comes down every weekend now, and they are enjoying the closeness Sarah has always craved. It is good to have a friend at last, a female friend, someone to share her fears and hopes with.

She tells Monique the story of her family, of her sisters, escaped to Switzerland; of her own flight from Colmar with Ralf. She pours out her heart and Monique listens, her eyes, clinging to Sarah's, soft with empathy, never interrupting, never criticising, but truly sympathetic, understanding, asking questions, murmuring words of empathy or shock in all the right places. Sometimes stroking Sarah's hand or wiping away a tear. She tells Monique about Ralf, too; how he saved her from rape, then took her by the hand and brought her to Poitiers and won her heart.

'He sounds like a very special man,' says Monique. 'I don't know of any man who would not have taken advantage, especially after falling in love with you. Any other man would have tried to seduce you. It's so noble!'

'He is, he's really special,' says Sarah. 'But I worry so much on his behalf. It's awful, not knowing what he's doing, where he is!'

In the end it's Sarah who makes the suggestion. 'I'd love you to meet Ralf,' she says, as they sit in the kitchen one evening, chatting over glasses of wine. The Lemoins-Beaulieu house is never short of wine. 'After all, you're both working for the same cause, just in different groups, in different ways.'

Monique shakes her head. 'It's not a good idea,' she says. 'We are in different cells. Each of us has their role to play, and they are very different roles, but both are secret, and secret from each other.'

'Still,' says Sarah, 'you're both so important to me. I have so few friends. Isn't it normal, to want your friends to know each other?'

Monique thinks about this for a while. 'I do understand,' she says. 'After all, you know my friends, don't you? All my shallow party-going friends.'

She chuckles self-deprecatingly. 'Sometimes I get tired of all this role-playing, this false identity I'm forced into. It's so good to meet someone like-minded, so good to have a friend like you. I suppose I'm only human.' She sighs dramatically. 'You know, Sarah, sometimes I, too, get lonely. Lonely behind the façade.

It's been so good for me, opening up to you. It makes me human again, behind the mask.'

'Then you must meet Ralf. He's the most wonderful person in the world, and I just know you'll get on well. I'm so proud of him, and I want you to know him too.'

'That's why I love you so much, Sarah – you're so generous, so full of love, so open, so free from masquerade and charade. I've already learned so much from you. And yes, I'd love to meet your Ralf.'

Chapter Forty-Three

Sarah wants the meeting to be a surprise for Ralf. So when, the following week, he rings to organise a meeting, she does not tell him that there'll be a guest. She and Monique, and Michel, arrive early in the café. Ralf is late, as usual, but by now Sarah is used to the unpredictable nature of his schedule and is not nervous; it's Monique who is a little jumpy. She's still not certain if it's the right thing to do, to intrude on Sarah's and Ralf's special time together. 'I'm sure he'd prefer to be alone with you,' she keeps saying. 'I'd better go and leave you to it.'

'No – no, please stay,' Sarah insists. 'I promise you he won't mind. He's told me many times that he's glad I've made friends and settled in so well. I can't wait to tell him that you're in the Resistance. He'll be delighted!'

'Oh, Sarah, you're a breath of fresh air! That's all I can say. Ralf's a very lucky man.'

'Oh, oh, here he is! He just walked in the door!'

Monique half-turns in her chair. Indeed, Ralf is striding through the café towards them, weaving between the tables; a grin of delight crosses his face as Sarah springs to her feet to welcome him. But as he approaches the table and sees Monique that grin fades. He looks at Sarah, a question in his eyes.

Sarah only laughs. 'Don't look like that, Ralf! It's all right, she's on our side. She knows all about you, all about us. I know it was a secret but she told me her secrets, too. Trust me! Sit down, I'll tell you.'

He does sit down, but his glance at Monique reveals that he's far from trusting Sarah's appeasing words. That look is grim, so grim that Monique stands up.

'Look, Sarah, this isn't right. I told you it wouldn't be right. I'm leaving. I'll leave you two to it.'

But Sarah grabs her wrist and tugs her down. 'Stay, Monique! Please stay! Ralf – you don't understand. You see, Monique, she's an ally! She's in the Resistance too! We can trust her, honestly. I wouldn't have let her come if I'd thought for one moment that it was dangerous. Please!'

'I'm not sure…'

'I'd better go, really. I'm sorry, Ralf. Truly sorry.' Again, Monique attempts to stand up. Again, Sarah pulls her down. Ralf looks from one woman to the other.

'Well, if Sarah says it's all right – if you're sure, Sarah…'

'I am, Ralf; really. Please trust me on this, please don't treat me as a silly child. Not again. Because I'm not.'

'I know you're not, Sarah. It's just that… this is all confidential, you know. Even if she's in the Resistance, you shouldn't be interfering. We shouldn't even all be here together.'

'It's not interference, Ralf. You shouldn't see it like that. We have to know who our enemies are and who our friends are, and I just want you to know who *my* friends are. That's all. Come on, now – try to relax. We're wasting time.'

And so Ralf tries to relax, and so does Monique, but it doesn't go well. Conversation is stilted and shallow, and uncomfortable between the three of them. It's Sarah who finally defines the problem.

'*I'm* the issue, aren't I? You two are both Resistance fighters and I'm not so you can't talk openly when I'm around. *I'm* the fifth wheel on the cart. *I'm* in the way. I've never seen either of you so nervous and it's strange – it makes *me* nervous! So, you know what? I'll leave and you two can talk openly about Resistance things I know nothing about.'

'No, Sarah, that's not what…'

Ralf half-stands as Sarah gets up, tries to hold her hand to pull her back, but she laughs and pulls away from him.

'Ralf, I really want you to know Monique. Really. She's my best friend and she's helped me so much. And, Monique, the same to you. I've never seen you so embarrassed and it's embarrassing to *me* to see you like that. Just be yourself and forget about me for now, and make friends with Ralf. That's all I care about.'

She bends over, kisses his forehead, waves to Monique and walks out of the café.

But only a week later there's an urgent call from Ralf – he needs to meet her, as soon as possible. He even calls the house, an emergency measure. It's absolutely urgent, and absolutely confidential. 'Tell no one,' he says, 'not even Monique. *Especially* not Monique.'

'I couldn't, anyway,' Sarah replies. 'Monique's back in Paris. I didn't even see her again, after the last meeting – did it go well?'

'Sarah, we can't talk about that now. Can you be at the café in an hour?'

She looks up at the hall clock. 'Yes, but I can't stay long. The children will be back from school soon, and—'

'Good. See you there, then.' He rings off.

Puzzled, and a little intrigued, but delighted at seeing Ralf again so soon, she's there five minutes before him, reading to Michel from his favourite book.

Ralf slips into the chair opposite her. He's looking from left to right, and his eyes are wide open. Scared.

'Sarah, I'm in big trouble. I shouldn't even be meeting you like this but you need to know – I'm going underground and we can't meet again for a long time. They're after me – the Gestapo.'

Her heart skips a beat. 'Why? What's happened?'

'It's a mission gone wrong. We tried to kidnap a prominent officer in his Poitiers office. Just to be able to infiltrate his office, steal his records. He's got lists, Sarah, of all the Jews in Poitiers and he's going after them, one by one. Innocent people living their lives, minding their business. It's not just the foreign Jews, now: it's all of them. People like your Madame Hoffmann. But it went wrong, and he was killed. We're on the run; it's me and four others involved. We have to disappear. I wanted to let you know so you won't worry.'

'So I won't worry? Ralf, I'll worry all the more, now! So, you're wanted for murder?'

'That's about it.'

'Ralf! I told you to be careful! I told you—'

'This isn't a time for recriminations, Sarah. I have to go, now. I shouldn't even have come here, it was risky. But I couldn't just disappear without letting you know why. Goodbye, my darling. I'll find you when it's safe again.'

He starts to get up but Sarah pulls him down again.

'Wait, wait – don't go. Tell me what happened with Monique. Did you two make friends after I left?'

He grimaces. 'Hardly. She and I... well, let's just say we aren't compatible. We left soon afterwards and went our separate ways. That was a mistake, Sarah. You shouldn't have interfered.'

'But—'

'I really have to go. Keep safe, my darling – and if anything happens, know that I love you.'

'What do you mean? Wait! Don't go—'

'I'm sorry, I have to. I shouldn't even have come here. It was a last opportunity. I had to—'

He bends over, kisses her on the lips, turns and strides away. 'Wait!' Sarah cries, and gets up to run after him, but she has Michel to deal with, his book and his pushchair, and by the time she makes it to the pavement, Ralf has disappeared. Melted into the crowds.

For the rest of that day, for the whole of that night, she is in anguish; it's as if red-hot coals are burning inside her. She cannot think, she cannot eat, she can hardly breathe, and it's all she can do to focus enough to pretend to the children that all is well, to feed them and give them their German lesson and put them to bed and act as if nothing is wrong when in fact everything is wrong and the world inside her is tumbling into pieces, and she has to pretend it isn't. How can she go on like this? How can she possibly live on, knowing the terrible danger Ralf is in? What if he's captured?

The following morning she's up early: she has to find out more. She turns on the wireless, fetches the newspaper from the entrance door. And yes, it's on the news. On the wireless. In the newspaper. Headlines: *Prominent German Officer Killed by Resistance Fighters.* Nothing about the nature of that German officer, nothing about his work; he's painted a hero, while the culprits are nothing but wicked criminals. There's a photo, rather blurred, of the officer, standing in a group with others. He's named, too: *Oberst* Friedrich Kurtz. Friedrich? Isn't that the name Monique mentioned a few days ago? Could it be— She peers more closely at the photo. Yes, it is, it has to be. It's Monique's friend, the one she was kissing, the one she is courting. Sarah scans the story beneath the headline.

The perpetrators, it says, managed to escape but the police have a good lead and are confident that they will capture them within days. Sarah drops the newspaper onto the table and runs to the pantry, to the sink, and retches over it, but she can't vomit as she hasn't eaten since yesterday and all she can bring up is nasty-tasting bile. She splashes her face with cold water and returns to the kitchen but now Madame Elise is there preparing breakfast for Madame and Monsieur Lemoins so Sarah murmurs a good morning, folds up the newspaper she has left open on the table, slinks back upstairs to her room, where she paces back and forth, unable to think, to do anything; her body, her mind, feel splintered into a thousand pieces. How will she get through the day?

Somehow she does and that evening Monique calls.

'Have you heard the news?' she gasps into the phone, 'Friedrich, my Friedrich, has been killed!'

'Yes, yes, I read it this morning,' says Sarah.

'I can't believe it. That was such a silly thing to do. Those Poitiers *maquisards* – they're such amateurs, to actually kill him! Was your Ralf involved, do you know? Has he contacted you?'

Sarah scrambles to find an answer, or rather, to give an appropriate answer. Best not to give anything away, though. She owes that much to Ralf, however much she trusts Monique.

'I don't know, Monique. I— I haven't heard from him.'

It feels terrible, consciously lying to Monique, her best friend. It's the first lie she's ever told to someone in her trust; the lies she's supposed to uphold, lies to the Nazis, lies about herself and her own identity, lies told to Madame Lemoins, they don't count. This is a different sort of lie, and it feels as if something whole and good within her has cracked. It feels like a betrayal. But it had to be. Telling Monique the truth – that she'd seen Ralf the previous day and he had already told her of his involvement – would have been by far the greater betrayal.

'Well, if you do hear, keep it to yourself. You can tell me, though – maybe I can help. I can hide him, *them*, here in Paris. So, let me know if he tries to make contact, all right?'

'Yes… yes, I will, Monique.'

But she knows she won't. Something doesn't ring true; there's a strange note in Monique's voice. Like a tune that is slightly off-key, indiscernible to anyone but a trained musician. It's there, but she can't put her finger on it, can't quite tune into it. It's just a slight twinge of suspicion, coupled with the knowledge that no, no, she won't. She won't tell Monique a thing more, and never should have told her anything.

The day passes in another twisting, turning clamp of anguish. It's as if she's in a vice squeezing the last breath, the last thought out of her, but at the same time she must function, put on an outward act, smile, talk, play a part, even while everything within her is being slowly strangulated. If the uncertainty regarding her family has been tearing her apart, this is a thousand times worse; it is shredding her. How can she survive another day, another night?

But she does. And the following morning the news is even worse and the agony increases a hundredfold, a thousandfold: *Killer Group Arrested!* scream the headlines, and the following story goes into the details, how the group was discovered in an abandoned house in Poitiers, where they had been squatting; they are even named. There is Ralf's name, his cover name, Karl Vogel, exposed to the world. Sarah can't help it: she cries out as she reads, but luckily, she's alone in the kitchen as Madame Elise has not yet arrived. She manages to finish reading the story. The accused murderers are detained in Poitiers; they will be sent to Paris for immediate trial and, if found guilty, executed.

Sarah sways on her feet as her mind goes blank. A vacant whiteness sweeps through her, an icy-cold pallor that pervades every cell of her body, and her breath stops and she grips the edge of the table so as not to sink to the floor – she has to hold herself together! She cannot collapse, though it is all she wants to do. She must survive this day, the following night, this life! How can she? But she must!

Monique calls again that evening and they speak for a while. Sarah doesn't care, this time, to listen for an off-key note in Monique's voice. It's too late for that. She doesn't care about anything. She has no one else, she cannot pick her friends. At the moment there is only Monique and anyway, it's too late. She cries into the receiver, cries her heart out, and Monique murmurs words of comfort back to her. But what can anyone say, what comfort can anyone bring, at a time like this?

It has been the worst day of her life.

But even the worst is not the peak. The next day, it's there in black and white: *The five killers of* Oberst *Kurtz were yesterday tried and immediately executed.*

This time, Sarah does fall to the ground. This time, Madame Elise is here and finds her there, in a full faint. This time, it's the end.

Sarah blinks, opens her eyes. She's lying on the kitchen floor. 'Child, can you hear me? Can you sit up?' Madame Elise is wiping her face with a cold rag. Her face is benign, caring, concerned. Sarah's head is on a cushion of kitchen towels.

'I— I don't know. Did I faint?'

'Yes – I found you lying here on the floor.'

The icy chill is still there, yet Sarah manages to stutter out some words.

'I— I had some bad news…'

Madame Elise whispers conspiratorially: 'I know. But you can't stay here, child. *Madame* and *Monsieur* will be down at any minute. Can you make it into the morning room? They won't go in there. You must get up. Come, I'll help you.'

Madame Elise helps her to her feet, slings an arm around her upper body, lets Sarah lean against her as she leads her into the little room at the back of the house, used by the family only in the summer months.

She lies Sarah down on the sofa.

'Stay here for a while. I'll be with you as soon as they've gone.'

So, Sarah lies on the couch, waiting, trying to absorb the news. Ralf is dead. Executed. By the Nazis. By the very evil he was trying to fight. Her Ralf, the love of her life; Ralf, the other half of her being. He's dead. Gone. No more. How can it be? How can she live on, with that knowledge? She can't even cry – it's just a hollowness, an emptiness, within her; everything that ever was is lost, gone, disappeared. Life is not worth living. She can't live on, in a world where there is no more Ralf. She can't, she can't… She starts to weep, as silently as possible, because there is movement in the kitchen. Madame and Monsieur Lemoins are there now, but soon there's silence as they all retreat to the dining room for their breakfast; more noises as they leave the house. Footsteps.

Doors opening and closing. Then silence. Then the morning room door opening and there is Madame Elise, and she's smiling and nodding and saying, 'They've gone!' and that's the moment when Sarah breaks down, when she collapses once again into a sobbing, spluttering, choking, gasping heap of misery, into Madame Elise's arms. And that's the moment when Sarah realises: Madame Elise is a mother – one of the chain of marvellous mighty women who have supported and sustained and nourished her all through this odyssey, who have buoyed her up and infected her with love and strength and courage; Madame Elise is another one of them and she, Sarah, never knew it because… because what? It didn't matter. She's here now, she knows it now. She knows. She knows she can melt into Madame Elise's arms, tell all, confess all, release all. Madame Elise has been the silent beating heart of this house all along, unrecognised, invisible, but essential; essential to her, Sarah.

And so it is to her that at last Sarah reveals all, in her that she at last confides.

'I can't live without him,' she says.

'Yes, you can. You must. You cannot give up. It's not what he would have wanted. Think now, what would he have wanted?'

'Me.'

'Yes, dear, apart from you.'

'He— he said the fight was bigger than the two of us. Bigger than our love.'

'Exactly. So, would he have wanted you to just give up, wither away into nothing? Would he have wanted you to die as well?'

'No, of course not!'

'So, I'm asking again, and this time, think carefully: what would he have wanted?'

She does think, now. She sniffs, and wipes her eyes, and thinks carefully, deeply. At last she has an answer.

'He would have wanted me to continue. The fight. For him. For France. For freedom.'

'That's what I think too.'

'But I can't! I'm just a girl! I'm a coward!' she wails.

'No, you're not. You've come this far and you've done well. I've watched you, Sarah, and you've done well!'

'You've watched me?'

'Of course I have. I've watched and admired you. How you handle the children, how you cope. How you are calm and steady and so very mature.'

'*Me*, mature? But— but I'm the opposite!'

'No, Sarah. You don't even know yourself. Yet. But you will. Ralf's death, see it as a challenge.'

'Look how I just collapsed this morning!'

'That's an understandable reaction. But— I hear something, from upstairs.'

It was Michel, screaming.

'Oh *zut*! I'd forgotten. I have to run. I'll come back later, when the children are off to school.'

'Yes, come back. We need to talk some more.'

And talk they do.

'I wanted to warn you,' Madame Elise admits, 'I wanted to warn you about Monique. But I couldn't without admitting that I had myself read some of your letters.'

She blushes shamefacedly. 'I'm sorry, I know it's unforgivable. But in these dangerous times one is forced to do shameful things; one has to know whose side everyone's on. Hiding them under your mattress was a bad idea – did you never think of the person who changes your sheets?'

Now it is Sarah's turn to blush.

'I really didn't think. I didn't notice you,' she admitted. 'And I didn't like you – you were so unfriendly that first day, when I came for my interview!'

Madame Elise shrugs. 'Can you blame me, working in a house of *collaborateurs*, that I am not falling over myself to be sweet and kind to everyone who walks through its doors? But since I can't be nasty to my employers, I tend to be nasty in general, especially to strangers. I apologise. But I soon knew you were different. Those letters…' She shakes her head slowly in disbelief. 'It was so naïve, so dangerous. You should never have written them, never left them there. You must have noticed I was kinder to you later on?'

Sarah blushes.

'I'm sorry. I kind of ignored you then.'

'I understand. I was just the invisible housekeeper. Anyway, I was dying to warn you, to have a word with you. I was really just waiting for the right time. I was horrified to find out that you had introduced Monique to Ralf.'

'And you really think she's the one who betrayed him. Betrayed *them*?'

'Of course. Monique is the most two-faced bitch in the town! She'd betray her own mother. Somehow, she must have had Ralf followed, figured out the kidnapping plan. We'll probably never know exactly what happened.'

Sarah shivered. 'I don't want to know. To think that I— Oh my goodness, does it mean that I was indirectly responsible for his capture? By trusting her, leading her to him?'

'You must not think like that. It's happened and now you cannot afford to stay here a day longer. They'll probably come after you next. Monique knows you're Jewish – it's a miracle they haven't arrested you yet.'

'What should I do? Where can I go?'

'You could try and enter Switzerland, maybe? To join your sisters? Or head for Spain?'

Sarah does not respond. Something is growing within her, stealthily, rising up from her depths; its source is that deep ache of grief that has settled like a stone in her guts, but out of it comes this, this little sprout of – well, what is it, exactly? She cannot put a name to it. It's more, a lot more, than rage. A lot more than outrage. More, even, than her grief. It's something feeding on her grief, something enormous. It is sure and certain and it is curling itself around her being, feeding on her pain and establishing itself in every fibre of her identity. It's almost as if she is becoming a new person and it is happening here, in the kitchen, and now she finds herself rising to her feet, for this thing is real and she can no longer deny it: she knows what she must do.

'Madame Elise, excuse me. I must go upstairs and pack.'

Sarah comes back, holding Michel's hand. She is wearing her outdoor clothes; her canvas bag is over her shoulder, her mountain boots in her hand.

'I have to go,' she tells Madame Elise. 'I have to leave this house. I know what I must do. I've written goodbye letters to the children – I couldn't tell them to their faces, they'd have been too upset.'

'You are not heading for Spain, then?'

'No, I have to finish what Ralf started.'

'I thought so. I'll take care of Michel for today.'

'Thank you, I was going to ask. And I need you to help me – can you hold this boot for me? Hold it upside down.'

She sets Michel down and hands Madame Elise the boot. She removes her little notebook and a pencil from her bag and peers at the sole of the boot.

'It's hard to decipher,' she says. 'But it's still there: a number.'

Madame Elise turns the boot upside down and inspects it herself.

'Yes, a number scratched just below the heel. Shall I read it to you, and you write? It really is hard to make out.'

'Yes, do that.'

So, as Sarah writes, Madame Elise reads the string of numbers out loud. She reads the last number, and says, hesitantly, 'May I ask, what…?'

'It's a phone number,' says Sarah. 'Ralf scratched it there for me. The number of someone called Mathilde – she's in Metz.'

Part Four

Freiburg

Chapter Forty-Four

The tearful heap of misery collapsed on the Beaulieu family kitchen floor: it is no more. This is a new Sarah, a different Sarah. Something else has taken over. Something indefinable yet mighty, sweeping through her, a melange of rage, valour, love; altogether, it sums up to a fearlessness so overpowering all self-concern has flown. It is as if everything Ralf had been has merged into a white-hot flame and entered her body, her heart, and instantly made of her this new person. Madame Elise's words have entered her brain and instantly converted into this: see it as a challenge.

The words struck home. They have ignited this flame, this knowledge that she was none of that, had never been. Had never been that innocent young girl, that naïve little hanger-on, that puddle of tears. *This* has always lain dormant within her, waiting for the words: *stand up! Be your true self! You can!*

She won't look back. This is a new Sarah.

After fleeing Poitiers she'd made her way back to Metz unflinchingly, passing Paris with the spectre of Monique as quickly as she could. Paris, the place where Ralf had been executed and where he must now lie in some unmarked grave, abandoned, forgotten. Up to Metz, where she'd met Mathilde once again. Mathilde had passed her on to the same Free French group that had first accepted Ralf, and now they accepted *her*. It was easy, now, to join the Resistance. She'd thought herself too cowardly, too timid, too immature. That was the old Sarah.

Sarah, it turns out, this new Sarah, is a quick learner, and a fearless one. Immediately absorbed into the Metz Resistance group, quickly trained as a courier, immediately set to work first delivering messages and managing dead-letter boxes, then helping locate and rescue and escort downed airmen, then hauling weapons and grenades and plastic explosives to where they are needed. Since leaving Poitiers she has not cried once. In fact, she has morphed into the most daring, the most underhand, the most reliable courier of all.

She has learned to lie with impunity, to flirt with Gestapo officers about to search her. She can smile coyly and bat her eyelashes and play with a tendril of hair peeping out from her headscarf and say, with just the right combination of bashfulness and come-hitherness, 'Now really, officer, do I look like a spy to you?'

And they beam back at her, uplifted by an instant of feminine charm, and let her pass, along with her basket of apples with a Sten gun at the bottom, and her slips of coded messages stuck into her plaits, and the plastic explosives in the hollowed-out baguettes, and the ammunition in the false lining of her suitcase. Back and forth she travels, from Paris to Metz and back again, to Reims and Rouen and Amiens and even as far south, once, as Orléans. She is their best courier; she has developed a sixth sense, almost, for the trustworthiness of people; she has learned from the encounter with Monique and can now see through façades with unerring accuracy. She can detect lies, but can lie with impunity, so convincingly she herself believes her own lies.

'It is my grandmother, *Monsieur*. I have received word that she is gravely ill and I must visit her in Paris. Both my parents are dead, she is all I have left, and I am taking this packet of *médicaments* to her, given me by a doctor friend. Yes, they are black market *médicaments*, but surely that is forgivable under the circumstances? Surely you can forgive that transgression?'

Or:

'My father has died, *Monsieur*, and I am going to attend his funeral. My heart is broken, he was all I had left in the world.'

She is able to conjure up tears at will, tears that seep from her eyes and run down her cheeks, leaving a snail's trail that she never

wipes away. She can assume a mien of abject misery in the blink
of an eye, or that of a temptress; and she knows exactly which one
will work when and with whom. She should have been an actress,
but no, she is the perfect spy because her acting is always nuanced
and impromptu, always exactly attuned to the recipient of her
subterfuge. She herself is amazed and amused at this emerging
skill, and uses it to her best advantage. The Resistance loves her.
She is one of only a few women, and women are precious to her
colleagues, not only because they are less suspicious considering
the work they do – young men, as ever, are always suspicious,
for why are they not in the army? – but she is good. She is also
desirable. She has many opportunities to form a liaison, many of
her colleagues come knocking at her door, but she repels them
all. She will never love another. Ralf lives on in her heart. It is
his spirit that has fired her, and which has now become hers.

The months spent as a courier for the Resistance have proven her,
tested her, convinced others of her reliability, her skill at being
a spy, an agent, a fearless *maquisard*. And then she is called to a
certain Monsieur Bigot. It is not his real name. Monsieur Bigot is
from the French Intelligence, the *Bureau Central de Renseignements
et d'Action*, the BCRA.

'Mademoiselle Mayer, for some time we have been looking for
someone who speaks native German, preferably a woman. You
have been passed to me by your Resistance cell.' He hesitates, and
Sarah looks at him eagerly, expectantly. She is ready for the next
step, the next mission, the next rung up the ladder of Resistance.
She is ready for anything, for everything.

'Yes?' she prompts, when he says nothing.

'The mission we have in mind for you would be very dangerous.
You are so very young, so inexperienced. But there is no one else. It
must be someone whose German is so perfect she can pass as native.'

Sarah chuckles. 'Then you're looking at her. Officially, I am German – it came about when they marched in and annexed my homeland, my Alsace. My German is native, though obviously, I have an Alsatian accent.'

'Yes, yes, we know that. Your authentic German papers are part of your appeal. And the fact that you are Alsatian: it's perfect, for you will be passing through Colmar. It's your youth and inexperience that gives us second thoughts.'

At the mention of Colmar Sarah's eagerness only increases.

'How am I to gain experience unless you try me?' she says. 'Give me the job, whatever it is.'

'The thing is: it is to enter Germany itself. The job is in Germany. And you would be entirely on your own, there is no one there to help you. You would be on a secret mission where you must rely on your instinct as well as your skill. You would be surrounded by Germans; you will have to mix with them, convince them of your new identity, lie to them, cajole them and, finally, get information out of them.'

Sarah gulps. It's not what she expected. But in her next breath she has caught herself.

'I'll do it, whatever it is.'

'You will basically be walking into the jaws of the tiger.'

She nods. 'I'm ready.'

'It will require a few months of training.'

'When can I start?'

'Immediately.' Monsieur Bigot hesitates. 'There's just one more thing you need to know before you agree.'

'Yes?'

'We can get you into Germany. We will provide you with a travel permit when you pass through – the trains from Colmar to Freiburg carry almost exclusively military personnel now, so you'll need that. But we can't get you back out. You'll have to find a way yourself.'

She gulps. 'Oh… But then, how can I get my information back to you?'

'We have an agent in Basle, a courier system set up from there. You'll have to make contact with him, the rest is organised. So, you do not need to come back. You have the option to stay in Germany until the war ends. And I assure you, the end is in sight. Since the invasion last month the Allies are slowly taking back France. But the Rhine border area east of Alsace remains a headache for us. It is solidly in Nazi hands, and success there is crucial for a final victory. You could help.'

'But… if I want to return before that? I need to get to Colmar.'

There is so much waiting for her in Colmar. She needs to find out what happened to her parents, she is desperate for that news. Having lost Ralf, she must now find the rest of her family.

He shrugs. 'Alsace is still under German annexation. If you want to go after you have completed your mission, well, it is entirely up to you, and you must find your own way. If you want to escape Germany, it's best you make it down to the Swiss border. We know of a farmer down there who has helped people escape. We can give you the address. But it will be up to you to organise your escape. The border is closely guarded by the Germans. It's dangerous, and we cannot help you.'

She considers; does not speak for a while. She is now used to danger; all she has to live for, now, really, is her family. Yet Ralf's death has unleashed a strange new force within her: she must avenge his death, and she must do so by putting aside personal aims and fighting for the freedom of France, as he did. Ralf sacrificed his own happiness – the chance to flee with her – to fight for the Resistance. She must do the same. 'This is bigger than both of us,' he always said. 'Bigger than our need to be together. We must put aside our own little desires and fight for freedom.'

She takes a deep breath. 'I'll do it.'

*

Her training is intense, rigorous. She is taken to a secret training ground somewhere in the north of France.

It's a good thing her memory is so good, because everything she is taught must be kept in her own mind, nothing written down. It is all about German military activity across the border, German military information in general: Wehrmacht and Gestapo uniforms, ranks, equipment, weapons, ammunition. She must study diagrams of insignia, learn to recognise and distinguish the multitude of collar patches in assorted colours; to count and recognise the pips on an officer's epaulettes; to count and recognise the bars and oak leaves on his sleeve. She must learn to recognise the various units: to tell the *Fallschirmjäger* from the *Gebirgsjäger*, to identify the *Waffen SS* and the *Sicherheitsdienst*, to distinguish a soldier from the parachute regiment from a Panzer corps underofficer. It is like studying for an exam at school: but the penalty here could be death.

She must learn to signal in Morse, to code and decode messages; she must choose a poem, which will be the basis of her code. She is stumped for a moment; she has not read much poetry, neither for pleasure nor at school. But then she remembers Psalm 23, 'The Lord is my shepherd', the psalm her mother gave her when she left home, the words of which have occasionally provided such strength and solace. That will be her poem.

Most of all, she must study and memorise maps: maps of the border area along the River Rhine in south Germany, the river that separates the once-French province of Alsace from the German department of Baden. She must commit these maps to her memory so that she can conjure them up at will, not needing paper. In particular, she must learn by heart train routes and schedules, the names of villages, their locations, rivers, bridges and the railway lines connecting these; the most important being the train line between Freiburg and Colmar, via the Neuf-Brisach bridge across the river.

'This is the line that we are interested in,' says her trainer, pointing to a line on the map laid out before them. 'Every day, Germany sends hundreds of troops across that bridge, troops and Panzers. We need to know where and when those trains are loaded. We need to know the source. Once we have the source, it can be destroyed. That must be the main focus of your work: find that source.'

She is coached in her new identity: Hannah Schmidt, a young Alsatian girl whose family was wiped out when their home village was flattened by the Allies. She is looking for relatives in the border region west of Freiburg. An innocent girl, an orphan, looking for a new home.

Her route is explained to her. She is to travel to Strasbourg by train, change trains for Colmar. In Colmar, she is to change again; she will be given her travel permit into Germany, and a new ticket. She must then take the train to Freiburg, over the Rhine.

'Colmar!' she gasps.

'Yes, Colmar. I know it is your home town. But, *Mademoiselle*, you are not to stop there. You are not to interrupt your journey and go off to find your friends and relatives. It's vital that you keep that rule. Colmar is swarming with German military, it's the centre of military activity in the entire region. I know you are anxious for news of your family but you must suppress that anxiety for the time being – there will be opportunities later on to make enquiries, not now. Do you understand?'

She gulps, nods, and swallows the words rising within her: '*But I must! I must go in search of my parents; I must find out what became of them! How can I not go, if I am in Colmar? At the station? How can I not slip away, in search of news?*'

And so she sits now, as instructed, on a bench on platform two in Colmar rail station. Above her head, stuck to the wall, is a poster of Hitler's face. Everywhere, swastika flags and posters. Trains come and go, adorned with more swastikas. Before long, a tall, thin man in a grey suit, carrying a newspaper, comes and sits next to her. He opens the newspaper, reads it. He glances at her, nods: '*Guten tag, Fräulein.* Have you travelled from Lyon today?'

It is the password. She gives the reply: 'Yes, and I am on my way to Strasbourg.'

He nods again, reads a while longer, folds the newspaper, lays it down on the bench next to her, stands up, gives a little bow and walks away.

She picks up the newspaper. In it is an envelope. It will contain her travel permit and her ticket. It's really happening, she is crossing the border into enemy territory. *You are on your own,* Monsieur Bigot had said. And she has never felt so much on her own as now.

Once she is in Germany she might be captured, tortured, killed. They have given her what they call the L-pill. It's a small, rubber-coated cyanide capsule to be hidden somewhere on her body or in her clothing, easily accessible in case of capture. It's an easy way out of an interrogation in case of capture by the Gestapo. The Gestapo are very good at extracting information; their methods of torture can break the most hardened agent. But bite on a capsule and you are put out of your misery: you are dead within seconds, even before the interrogation begins. This way an agent can save the lives of the others who depended on their keeping silent.

It's a quick and painless death, easier than what they will do to you.

But now she is not thinking of the Gestapo, of capture. She is thinking of her parents, her former home, just a few minutes' walk from the station. She has been forbidden to go, but she looks at the clock: the train to Freiburg is much later, after dark. There's so much time.

I need to know! My family, my parents! I cannot do this without knowing! If I might die, I must at least know what happened!

She has to make a decision. It is perhaps the hardest decision she has ever made in her life. She looks longingly at the exit doors: it wouldn't take long to slip away, find out what she needs to know

and return. There is so much time until she catches her next train –
several hours, in fact. She can do it, nobody will ever know. There
is the exit, waiting for her. It won't take long.

But no, she must be a professional. She has been trained: orders
are to be obeyed, rules followed, commands executed exactly as
they were given. It's like in an orchestra: every player must follow
the notes just as they are written. The slightest variation can
destroy the whole performance, and even the soloists must stay
in line, no individual action. She has signed up for the renegade
military of the Free French; she must play according to their rules,
Colmar or not. Anyway, it's true: there are soldiers everywhere, as
Monsieur Bigot warned. She cannot risk it. But still, she wrestles
with herself. How can she sit here, doing nothing, when her old
home is so close?

The temptation is too great. Ten minutes later, she stands up
and walks out the exit door.

She crosses the *Bahnhofsplatz*. It is so different from the station
square of her childhood! Everywhere, the oversized swastika banners
in red, white and black. Nazi flags and posters of Hitler stuck to
the walls. Army vehicles, also adorned with swastikas, parked or
driving through. And soldiers everywhere; more soldiers than
civilians. She straightens her shoulders, lifts her chin and crosses
the square, ignoring the whistles and catcalls.

The square safely navigated, she makes her way through the narrow
cobbled lanes lined with rows of half-timbered houses. Nostalgia
grips her. *She is home! This is Colmar, the cradle of her life!* But it is
not the Colmar she once knew. Nowhere is a friendly face to be
seen. She walks past a woman she once knew, Madame Charron, a
seamstress, and smiles and opens her mouth to greet her, but Madame
Charron does not smile back; she grimaces, and shakes her head, as
if in warning, picks up her pace and walks past without a greeting.

A chill runs through Sarah. Something is wrong. There is a
grimness on the faces of the civilians she passes as with Madame

Charron; those she has known since she was a girl pass by without a word, without a glance. There's something almost sinister in the air.

At last, she reaches *Gerechtigkeitsgasse* and a wave of gladness sweeps through her. *This is home!* But the gladness feels suffocated, ringed in by anxiety, by the knowledge that in only a few moments she will know the truth. Did her parents escape safely? Where are they?

She stands outside her former home. The shop window is broken as before, still boarded up. She presses the button; there is a chime from within, the chime she has always known, but no further sound. She waits, but no one opens it. It's no less than she expected; after all, there was no way her parents could still be here. But still... Perhaps someone lived here, could say... and at that moment a voice screams within her: *God, no! Are you mad, Sarah, to ring this bell? Have you forgotten your training? If anyone lives here, it will be Germans, Nazis! Your parents are not here; they must have escaped and the house requisitioned – by Germans! Get away from here!*

She catapults herself away from the house. A few doors down is the cobbler's shop. She should have gone there right away, because if anyone knows anything, it will be Uncle Yves. She opens the door to a jangle of bells and walks into the narrow shop. It is so familiar: the smell of leather and linseed oil, the cobbler paraphernalia on the shelves, the window with a few odd pairs of shoes, the counter. Behind the counter is a girl with auburn hair, who stands up and smiles.

'Can I help you?' It's the first friendly words she's heard since arriving in Colmar, disregarding the leering calls of the soldiers. But perhaps it's because this girl is a stranger. Uncle Yves must have employed someone to help out front.

'I'd like to see Monsieur Girard,' she says, and gestures to the far end of the corridor, where there's a door opening into Uncle Yves' workshop.

'Go ahead,' says the girl, and sits down again.

Sarah walks forward, opens the door, stands at the threshold. Everything is as before. The workshop itself, the tools, the shelves, the cluttered table – and before it, Uncle Yves, who looks up, sees her and rushes forward to clasp her in his arms.

'Sarah! *Ma petite!* You are back!'

'Yes, Uncle. I'm just passing through so I came to see— to find out…'

Her eyes are clinging to his, asking, begging, longing: *please, please, Uncle, tell me all is well! Tell me they are safe!*

But in his eyes is not the longed-for response. There is no relief, no release, no respite from the awful apprehension that has plagued her for the last year and beyond. Quite the opposite.

In Uncle Yves' eyes she reads the worst. She reads agony and compassion and deep, fathomless sorrow. Her shoulders sag. Without a word spoken she knows the news is the worst.

But it is even worse than the worst.

'They came for them,' he says eventually. 'They came before the month was up. They were dragged onto the streets. They were told they could each take one suitcase but Josef refused to take one, he took his violin instead.'

'That's just like him,' says Sarah. 'Music was his life, more important than clothes. So, they were sent away, to a camp. It's the thing I feared the most.' Her eyes are wet; she must constantly wipe away the tears.

'But— but, my dear, it is worse. Perhaps I should not tell you this – after all, it does not matter now. But— but…'

'But what?'

'Your little sister, Sofie, she began to wail. She screamed, said she was not going anywhere.'

'Oh, no!'

'Your mother tried to calm her, but she would not be calmed. A soldier slapped her, she kicked him. They tried to hold her, but she kicked and screamed. And in the end… they shot her.'

'They shot my sister?' She is paralysed with shock.

Now Uncle Yves is crying, too. 'Right there on the street. You can still see the bloodstains between the cobbles. We tried to clean it up, I and some of the neighbours, but—'

'You were there? You saw it happen?'

He nods. 'Several of us were there; we wanted to help, to stop it happening, but what could we do? Your father, your mother, your other little sister, they were dragged away, screaming. Your father, he was yelling, *Shoot me too, you Nazi pigs! Shoot me too!* But they didn't, of course they didn't. They were loaded into a vehicle and driven away. We don't know where to. One of the German camps, it is said. I tried to get information but there was none. We just don't know, we won't know till after the war.'

Somehow, she finds her way back to the station, past the wolf-whistling soldiers and the swastika banners. She boards the train for Freiburg. The carriage is almost empty – a good thing.

She bites into her knuckles, forcing the waves of grief down, down, down into that locked box where her torment over Ralf is also buried. She cannot give in to it.

She has a job to do. And that dark place within her, that burial ground of deepest agony, it provides her with the momentum for that job. Today the momentum has been fortified a hundredfold.

She is of steel.

So here she is, in Freiburg. She knows the worst. During the train journey she has tried to digest the news: that her beloved youngest sister is dead, her parents' fate unknown. There is nothing to be done. At least she now *knows*. But was it better not to know, and still have hope? Probably not. It is the worst possible outcome… She had so hoped for their escape! Yet still, there remains a spark of hope – that after the war, which will surely end soon, these terrible camps will be emptied and she will be reunited with her parents and her sister Manon. But there have been rumours – rumours that the labour camps are actually death camps. She cannot allow herself to believe it. No. Her parents and sister are alive in a camp somewhere and she will find them after the war. She must cling to that last hope; she cannot let her grief devour her, distract her from her mission. She must move forward, perform the job she is here to do.

But before she can begin her actual work, there is *this* to be done. The worst job of all. This, too, is a deviation from the plan but this time she is not breaking any rules: 'You are on your own,' Monsieur Bigot had told her, 'and you must make your own decisions. Make sure they are good ones.'

It is a shame that she and Ralf never exchanged home addresses for after the war in case of separation; no more than a promise to contact each other through Margaux. Not only a pity but a lapse in judgement, for here she is, in his home town, with no idea where his parents live. But she has clues. His father is an orthopaedic surgeon, that she knows. And works in a hospital, a Catholic hospital, Ralf had said; since he refused to join the Nazi Party, he could no longer work at the Universitäts-Klinik. It is easy to find out that there are two Catholic hospitals in Freiburg, the Loretto and St Joseph's. It's not hard to track down Doctor Sommer at St Joseph's.

The receptionist is a thin, stiff-backed woman with steel-grey hair pulled back into a severe bun. She stares at Sarah with ice-blue eyes that drill into hers, as if to say, *you don't look like a real patient.*

And she is right: Sarah isn't a real patient. She's a harbinger of news, the very worst news a parent can ever receive.

'Doctor Sommer's appointment schedule is full for the next few weeks,' she says sternly. 'I can put you down for November.'

'No, no! I have to see him today – now. It's private. Can you let him know, please – my name is Hannah Schmidt, but he doesn't know me, he won't know—'

'If he doesn't know you, how can it be private? He's extremely busy, you know. If it's private, you can contact him at home.'

'No, no! I can't— It's just... Can you ask him, please. It's urgent. Tell him it's about Ralf.'

'About Ralf?'

She frowns, and her eyes narrow. 'Is that all? Just Ralf?'

'Yes, just Ralf. He'll know. Please... Just talk to him, ask him.'

She is drained, exhausted, dreading the meeting, but it has to be done. Before she can do anything else, she must do this. It's not part of her mission; she is acting out of bounds, and looks nervously behind her just in case Gestapo officers have followed her from the cheap hotel she'd booked into last night. She wishes she'd had a decent change of clothes. She is back where she started: old clothes, a threadbare tweed skirt, a striped cotton blouse, a cardigan and, of course, her trusty bloodstained boots. No more Monique's elegant cast-offs. Once again, she is a new person, a new identity, a new incarnation, a reinvention of herself.

The receptionist replaces the receiver.

'Doctor Sommer says you may enter,' she says grudgingly as a patient exits the room. Sarah nods her acknowledgment, walks to the door with the shiny brass sign, raises her hand to knock... But before she can do so the door swings open and Doctor Sommer is on the threshold, a bear of a man, holding out a hand to her, pulling her in, closing the door behind her. His face: it is unbearable. The misery, the hope, the dread, the anguish written all over it.

'You have news of Ralf – of my son?' he says, and his voice cracks.

'Yes,' says Sarah. That is all she can say, and it is enough. Her face collapses, and for the first time since that breakdown in Poitiers, she dissolves into tears, great big heaving sobs, so that Doctor Sommer, this stranger, grabs hold of her to support her and they stand there, clinging to each other, racked with shuddering wails.

*

Doctor Sommer informs his receptionist that he is going home, to cancel all further appointments and to send home anyone who comes. He and Sarah leave the hospital and walk to the tram station, take a tram that passes the Martin's Gate to the Wiehre, an upmarket area of Freiburg. They walk up *Prinz-Eugen-Strasse*, a wide, leafy street where elegant villas stand back from the road in park-like gardens. He leads her through the gate and up to the front door of one such villa. A chocolate-brown Labrador bounds up, leaps at Doctor Sommer, greets Sarah with a wagging tail, writhing body and smiling face.

'This is Bruno,' says Doctor Sommer. 'Ralf's dog. Ralf loves – *loved* – animals, dogs especially.' He turns the key. They enter a grand carpet-laid hall. A woman bustles out of one of the many doors.

'Franz? You're early… What— oh!'

The woman stops. Her gaze flits from one face to the other, taking in their expressions, reading them, deciphering, first unbelieving. Then, as understanding sinks in, her own face crumples and she flings herself at her husband.

'*Nein, nein, nein, nein, nein!*' she splutters, clinging to him as if to dear life. 'Don't say it, don't!'

Doctor Sommer doesn't say it. He doesn't have to. It doesn't have to be spoken out loud. Sarah, too, is now crying unreservedly. She has let go of the armour that has been holding her upright since that last day in Poitiers, abandoned the façade of steel. She has given in to the grief that has gouged a gaping hole into her being, an abyss, and she has fallen into it. Set against the wall is a cushioned chair and she lets herself sink into it, buries her head in her hands.

Doctor Sommer pulls away from his wife and turns to Sarah, gesturing towards her.

'*Liebling*, this is Hannah. She is – *was* – Ralf's fiancée. She is as devastated as we are and we must treat her as a daughter. She has told me part of the story – she'll tell you now.'

Between her tears Frau Sommer nods and says, '*Ja, ja,* come, let's go into the kitchen. I'll make us some coffee. Excuse me, I'm so… I'm so…'

She breaks down once again, seems about to collapse. Sarah jumps to her feet, forgetting her own grief, and she and Doctor Sommer help Frau Sommer to her feet, help her stumble into the kitchen, sit her down at the corner table. Doctor Sommer moves over to the stove to make the coffee. Frau Sommer is struggling to regain her composure, sniffing, swiping at her eyes with a napkin, looking up at Sarah, apologising, trying to be a good hostess while dealing with the bomb that has exploded in her heart.

The coffee is real coffee, a treat, and the cake is a home-made apple tart, a thing Sarah has not eaten in, it feels like, years. While eating, she tells her story. She admits that Hannah Schmidt is not her real name.

'I can't tell you more,' she says. 'I'm sorry, but it would be dangerous for you, in case— Well, I just can't. But I need you to know that Ralf was the bravest, most upright, most noble man I've ever met.'

She won't tell them, of course, that she hasn't met many young men at all; but of the ones she has met, he was the best, and not just because he loved her.

'We were to marry, after the war,' she says. 'He so wanted to be a doctor, a surgeon, like you, Doctor Sommer,' she adds, looking at the man who would have been her father-in-law. 'It's just – just diabolical. He died fighting for the good of others. He's a hero. You should be proud of him.'

'We have always been proud of Ralf, of all our children,' says Doctor Sommer. 'Ralf had everything in front of him, he was a young man in his prime. So many young men, like him, sent off to be blown apart – what madness is this?'

'Diabolical – that's the right word,' says Frau Sommer. 'It is devilish, what this Hitler is doing. A whole generation of young men sent off to be killed just to realise his insane ambition. He is the devil incarnate.'

'*Grössenwahnsinn*,' agrees Doctor Sommer. 'Megalomania. Sheer madness. We were actually even more proud when they informed us that he had defected. Yes, we were worried, but we knew he had done the right thing. Poor Ralf, he is – *was* – never cut out to be a soldier. Some young men are – they can't wait to run off to their deaths. But not Ralf. He was so excited about following in his brother's footsteps. Max, you know, is in his fifth year of medical studies, but he too was conscripted; he had to do a practical year in a field hospital. In Russia. So, we worry about him as well. Thank goodness Reinhard is too young to be conscripted.'

'But if the war continues a few more years…' says Frau Sommer.

'It won't!' says Sarah, with confidence. 'It will be over within a year, I am certain of that. The Allies have invaded. They are pushing north through France; they have already retaken Paris. The Nazis are being driven back. They are losing in the east as well. The war will be won by the right people, Frau Sommer. Evil is not going to win.'

'You really believe that?'

Frau Sommer's eyes are liquid with hope.

'I know it. Ralf did not die in vain, he died on the winning side. And he was betrayed.'

She tells them a little about Ralf's mission as a *maquisard*, about his last assignment, how it went wrong through betrayal.

Frau Sommer reaches out to take her hand. 'And you came here, just to tell us that?'

She nods. 'But also to do some work of my own. I am helping to bring about the defeat of Germany. I can't tell you more – but I must leave soon.'

'I'll tell you what you should do, Fräulein,' says Doctor Sommer. 'Spread the word. Talk to people, to ordinary Germans. Tell them you come from France, from Alsace. Tell them what you know: that the Germans are facing a devastating defeat. Tell them the Wehrmacht is fleeing from the Allies. Strike fear into their hearts. So many people, unfortunately, still believe Goebbels' lies – they still believe that a great victory will be ours, that God is on our side, that we cannot lose because of that. You must disillusion them.'

'That's exactly what I have in mind.' Sarah smiles through her tears. 'Demoralisation of the enemy is one of our tactics. It is to weaken them mentally. It's one of the secret weapons of war, and I am in the best position to implement it. It's part of my mission.'

Yet they do not let her leave. They want to hear everything about their son, from the very first moment Sarah met him. They want to hear about the journey south, and then Ralf's apparent desertion of her.

'That's how I saw it, at the time: as desertion,' says Sarah. 'But of course that was only my petty *Kleinmädchen* self, the little girl who wanted his protection. Ralf knew better. He knew it was right for me to go forward on my own, to find my own feet, and though I was vexed with him at the time, now I know he was right. He always said it was bigger than us, and it was.'

She pauses, reflecting. The Sommers wait patiently for her to continue, and then she picks up the story again.

'All my life I'd been protected,' she says. 'First by my parents, my mother in particular, then they pushed me out of the warm nest of home – they had to – and still I found protection. There was always some wonderful woman who took me under her wing. They just appeared out of nowhere, these ersatz mothers. But above all, there was Ralf, protecting me, bringing me to safety. And I needed that protection – I was so naïve! I knew nothing about reality. Ralf was wonderful, Frau Sommer, Herr Sommer.' She looks from one to the other and they nod, their faces contorted in the effort not to weep with pride. 'He brought me to safety and then he let me go so I could find my own wings. And I did. I made some mistakes.

Serious ones, as it happened. Trusted people I should not have trusted, overlooked those I should have. And then, Ralf's death, it...'

Now it is her turn to scrunch up her face. The Sommers take one hand each and there they sit, around the table, holding each other's hands, and then Frau Sommer gets up and says, 'I'm going to ring Stefan. You have to meet him.'

Doctor Sommer looks at Sarah. 'Ralf's best friend,' he says. 'Lucky enough to get into university a year before Ralf, so he wasn't conscripted. He'll be a doctor too. He needs to know all this, he might be able to help you.'

All afternoon they gather, and one by one they hear the news. Reinhard, Ralf's younger brother, and Silke, his little sister, back from school. Then Stefan, who calls another friend, Hans. Hans, like Ralf, is a deserter, living in hiding, in the underground: the German Resistance. Sarah learns that it is thriving, but if it was dangerous to be in the French Resistance, the German counterpart is ten times the danger. Hans slinks in and out in the night, but he leaves a contact address for Sarah and they will meet again.

Into the night they talk, Sarah repeating her story again and again, highlighting new aspects of it. A young woman joins them, Stefan's girlfriend, who introduces herself as Ulrike Böhm; she too is in the German Resistance. Officially a medical student, from a town further south of Freiburg, near to Basle.

Sarah frowns, and says, 'You live near Basle, you said?'

'Yes, at least, my parents do. I'm in Freiburg most of the time, though, for my studies. I work in a café near the station. Why?'

'It's just that I have an idea. Would you like to help?'

'Yes, indeed! What can I do?'

'When the time comes, could you deliver a message, if necessary? It would save me going back and forth.'

'Of course! Just tell me when, and how.'

They talk into the night, she and Ulrike. And Stefan, and Hans, as they used to do when Ralf was here. It is comforting, to be with people who knew Ralf. Sometimes they cry, and they comfort one another, and they tell her stories from Ralf's youth. One day, when the war is over, they will retrieve his body and hold a memorial service. When the war is over. Words of hope that link them all together. At the end of it all she feels that she is part of this family, part of his group of friends. That they are behind her. That her mission now is not only to avenge Ralf's death but to make his sacrifice worthwhile, to let them know he did not die in vain, for she is here to continue his work.

Which will start tomorrow.

Later, Frau Sommer takes Sarah to a little room up in the eaves, where she is to spend the night. She sleeps well, for the first time in months, and in the wee hours she is up. Frau Sommer prepares her a breakfast, makes her coffee, worries around her like a mother hen. She accompanies Sarah out the side entrance, towards the garage. A bicycle is leaning against the garage door, Frau Sommer's, which she is lending to Sarah – it will make her work so much easier. Sarah takes hold of the handlebars. Frau Sommer stands beside her, hands behind her back, face distorted in the effort not to cry once again.

'Here, dear, this is for you. It's going to be cold on that bicycle.' She pushes a pair of gloves and a cap into Sarah's hands. 'And some *Proviant*, for your lunch. Just a sandwich.' She drops a small packet, wrapped in waxed paper, into the cycle's basket. 'Are you sure the suitcase is secure?' She tries to wobble the little case held in place on the bike's carrier, but it's held tight, so she nods and squeezes Sarah's hand on the grip.

'Goodbye, my dear. I wish you all the best. Be careful, be safe, and when the war is over, you must visit us again.'

The bicycle almost topples over as Sarah lets go for a moment to fling her arms around Frau Sommer – a spontaneous gesture that takes the older woman off guard, but she immediately responds in kind, abandoning the polite formalities of her standing. She gulps, and repeats, 'Be careful and come back.'

'I will,' Sarah promises.

She wheels the bicycle through the garden gate and into the street, and sails down into town, towards the station. Her mission has begun.

Chapter Forty-Five

Sarah's brief is simple, precise and very specific. Her job is to find out where and when the Wehrmacht troops are loaded into the trains that will take them over the bridge and into France. It is information vital to the Allies' mission to recover Alsace. Monsieur Bigot suspects that there is a central station, a gathering place where these soldiers are collected, sorted, boarded, dispatched: almost invariably, to their deaths, for the trains run in one direction only, returning empty.

'Hitler's orders for Alsace are, "fight to the death",' Monsieur Bigot said. 'But we think death should come first. Why waste their time fighting, when we can bomb them to kingdom come?' He chuckled at that, but Sarah found it impossible to enjoy his macabre humour. Nevertheless, she does not question her mission and has no qualms: she will do it.

The maps, railway tracks and official train schedules are ingrained in her memory, information she can pull up at will. But being here, now, actually in the place of action, she must figure out exactly how she will go about making her discovery. The obvious route is, of course, to start at Freiburg station. This is the beginning of the line to Colmar, though it is unlikely the soldiers will be loaded here, in the middle of a small city. Still, she must ensure that she can, indeed, eliminate Freiburg. There is only one thing for it: to wait, and watch.

She knows from her schedule that the trains arrive in Alsace, after crossing the Neuf-Brisach bridge over the Rhine, at seven in the morning, when it is still dark. The journey from Freiburg to Brisach is just over an hour. That means it must leave Freiburg some time before 6 a.m. Everything else is unsure. As it's a special train for troops, she can't be sure where it stops on the way, or how long these stops last, or if it even stops at all – perhaps it's a through train. All of this is what she must find out.

And so, today, she starts at Freiburg. She pedals the borrowed bicycle down to the station. The curfew has not yet been lifted, but there is an early-morning train to Karlsruhe and if stopped, she'll say she needs to catch that train: she is starting a new job in Karlsruhe.

But she is not stopped, and arrives safely at the station. Already it is bustling, travellers awaiting their trains to elsewhere in Germany. Somehow, Sarah can't imagine any train being loaded with soldiers here, in the midst of this hustle and bustle, but she takes the opportunity to chat with other passengers. She sits on a bench on a platform, next to a middle-aged woman sitting behind a large suitcase. She smiles at the woman. '*Guten Morgen! Kalt heute, ja?* Cold today, isn't it?'

It is, indeed, quite cold, more like December weather than late October. She is thankful for the gloves Frau Sommer gave her, glad for the sheepskin-lined jacket and thick stockings she has been provided with by the French Intelligence.

'You must look dowdy,' they told her. 'German women have no dress sense, no sense of chic. You must look drab and boring, but neat and clean at all times – typically German.'

'*Guten Morgen,*' replies the woman now. 'Yes, it's too cold for the season. I have heard that our poor troops on the Eastern Front are suffering terribly – terribly.' She shakes her head in sadness.

Sarah is quick to grab the opportunity. She speaks softly, gently, comfortingly. She has recognised the shadow of great grief in the woman's eyes.

'Have you lost someone over there?'

The woman's eyes fill with tears.

'My son! My dear, dear son! My husband! And two nephews are still there, the dear boys!'

'I'm so sorry,' says Sarah and is about to continue, to turn the conversation to the local area, when the woman swipes away her tears and her voice becomes hard, brittle.

'It's all because of those *verdammte Juden*! Those damned Jews, those greedy pigs! This war would never have taken place if not for them! I am happy to sacrifice my son and my husband and my nephews to rid the world of that pestilence!'

Sarah's sympathy dissolves into thin air, like the breath of white mist from her lips as she speaks.

'I agree,' she says. 'The Jews are responsible for everything. I was happy, over in Alsace, the day when they were all carried away. Good riddance, I said!'

'You are from Alsace?'

'Indeed!' she says. 'I just came from over from there yesterday. I am looking for relatives of mine, because my family home up near Strasbourg has been flattened. My parents were killed by marauding Americans. All ethnic Germans in Alsace are being murdered. I was lucky to escape – I happened to be in Colmar at the time. Women are being raped. Even little children are being murdered. It's truly terrible. The Americans are thirsty for blood. And the French are worse. I had to flee – it's terrible! Our poor boys, they are being obliterated by the enemy.'

The woman pales, but delivers her own take on the situation. 'No, that can't be true! Did you not listen to Herr Goebbels last night? We are enjoying a great victory in Alsace. We are driving the enemy back, destroying them piecemeal.'

But Sarah shakes her head, lowers her voice, leans in to the woman conspiratorially. 'No, it's not true. He is only trying to placate the nation. I have just come from there. I am looking for my uncle and aunt, the Schmidts, Heinrich and Ute Schmidt. They live somewhere around here. Do you happen to know them?'

The woman's face is now white as a sheet, her brow wrinkled with worry. Ignoring Sarah's question, she says: 'You saw this, with your own eyes? It is said that Herr Goebbels tends to exaggerate the truth—'

'He does more than exaggerate! He tells blatant lies! Don't believe a word that man says – the enemy has completely decimated our armies all over France and now they are reclaiming the precious Alsace! It is terrible! I cannot bear it, that's why I have come back to Germany to seek relatives living here. I have been made homeless, along with many other ethnic Germans in Alsace. I'm wondering if our soldiers in Baden near the border can stand up to them. Do you know where they are stationed? I'm worried we will be overrun.'

The woman shakes her head. 'There are no troops stationed here in Freiburg – perhaps further west, near the border? But you know, they say we cannot possibly lose! Hitler has a *Wunderwaffe* – a miracle weapon, a weapon that he will at the very last minute release and which will ensure our victory!'

Sarah shakes her head. And it is as if in doing so she shakes off layers of politeness, restraint, propriety, good breeding – all of her mother's insistence never to tell a lie. The ninth commandment of the religion of her forefathers, if not that of her agnostic father: *Thou shalt not bear false witness*. A living rage, a red-hot wrath, surges up within her. This woman, along with the hordes of Germans who have placed this man in power – this Adolf Hitler – this ideology that has wrecked a continent, flung thousands, hundreds of thousands, into homelessness, that has caused death and destruction and carnage; that has dispatched young men in the prime of their lives, men like Ralf, young men on both sides, fresh-faced, passionate, undeserving, into the jaws of hell and torn them from life: this woman, along with all of her like-minded countrymen, deserves punishment. They deserve to melt in fear or repercussions. They deserve all that is coming to them, and now she, Sarah, has the power to spread a very subtle weapon among them: the weapon of fear. Just as she and millions all over France, all over the Continent, have trembled in fear, so must this woman. She takes a deep breath to curb the furious thudding of her heart. She must be in charge, she cannot let her rage show. And so, when she speaks, her voice is calm, collected. She waves her hand in dismissal.

'Only propaganda. The thing is: the *Amis* have an even more powerful *Wunderwaffe*. Once released, it can pulverise an entire city in seconds, reduce it to rubble! It won't be long before Freiburg and all its outskirts is nothing but ruins and blood. It's not safe here.'

The woman by now is shaking. She stands up and hurries away, murmuring, 'I have a train to catch.'

While talking to her, Sarah has been keeping a careful watch. From her bench there is a good overview of all the platforms and her suspicion proves true: not only is there no sign of mass boarding of a train by German troops, there are hardly any soldiers to be seen at all.

At 6.15 she gives up. Freiburg is not the place, she will move further west. Consulting her mental railway map and schedule, she notes that the next station south of Freiburg is Brühl; here, there is also a *Güterbahnhof*, a freight station built specifically to divert rail freight cargo from Freiburg's main station. A town has sprung up around the station; she decides to head there now, linger around Brühl for the day and, like today, investigate. Are the soldiers boarded here? Tomorrow will tell.

She rides the bicycle towards Brühl, following the signposts out of the town. At Brühl, she checks into a small hotel near the freight station. She spends the day prowling the town, looking, listening for signs of major military activity in the area; talking to people. Encouraged and amused by her conversation earlier today with the woman at Freiburg's station, she decides that this will be her modus operandi: spread rumours and misinformation and doubt, and in that way undermine civilian confidence. In wartime, the least rumour is likely to spread far and wide, in ever-widening circles, gaining momentum and drama each time it is told. So today she is quite the conservationist. At lunchtime, she chats with the waitress who serves her a bowl of the house speciality, a bowl of bland rabbit stew.

'Yes,' she says, 'it's true. The enemy has advanced right to the western banks of the Rhine. They have destroyed all our forces over there. I myself saw the carnage as my train passed through the French countryside on my way to Freiburg. It was devastating, I tell you! I saw dead bodies, dead German soldiers, just lying there in pools of blood – those poor boys! Their poor mothers! It's said that they have inflatable dinghies and they'll be making the crossing into Germany very soon.'

'Really? But my fiancé – he was brought back from the Eastern Front specifically to fight for Alsace. Herr Hitler said we could easily defend it. Surely God is on our side?'

Sarah makes the sign of the cross. Her trainer has taught her how to do this – it's a good way of reinforcing her supposedly German background.

'Bless him!' she says. 'Bless all of our brave boys fighting for the Reich! Do you know where he is stationed? You need to warn him.'

The girl shakes her head. 'It's all top secret,' she says. 'Just that it's somewhere near the river, he did not say exactly where.'

'I'm sorry for all our boys. God seems to have deserted us,' says Sarah in a mournful voice. 'I, too, believed that we were invincible but what I have seen…' She crosses herself again. '*Jesus, Maria und Josef* – who would have thought it? The enemy is everywhere in France. I'm afraid we are losing.'

'You know, I never trusted that Herr Goebbels. I've always had the feeling he's selling us a pack of lies.'

'Herr Goebbels? Lord have mercy! The man only has to open his mouth and the lies pour out. You shouldn't believe a word he says, or better yet, whatever he says, be sure the opposite is true!'

'I'll tell my fiancé,' says the girl. 'He really believes Herr Goebbels' lies. They all do, they think they are going to win over there. They believe that Germany cannot lose.'

Sarah shakes her head. 'If they go over there it is straight into the jaws of death,' she warns. 'You must tell him that.'

'Thank you for telling me. I'm going to tell him – he has leave this weekend and I'll see him.'

'Tell everyone,' says Sarah. 'It's better to flee this area – it's so dangerous. They'll be invading soon and then God help us! I'm looking for my relatives so I can warn them.'

'Yes, I will,' says the girl. 'I'll tell my family. I suppose we should all move away from the Freiburg area.'

'Yes – everything around Freiburg is easy pickings for the enemy. Do you know, they have inflatable boats so big and strong they can carry tanks? They're going to overrun Germany in a week or two. If I were you, I'd disappear. Go up north, or to Bavaria – anywhere but here. Spread the word! Don't let your loved ones stay here!'

'I will. Thank you so much!'

Sarah wipes her lips with her serviette, pays her bill and leaves the restaurant with a wave to the girl. As she looks back, she sees that the girl is already deep in conversation with a group of diners at another table. She smiles to herself. If Maman could hear her now! Maman taught her never to tell a lie, and she never did, before the war. But now, she is quite willing to lie with impunity – it's part of her mission. 'Spread doubt and discord,' Monsieur Bigot had told her. 'Spread uncertainty among the civilians. Undermine their confidence. The rot will set in, the inner rot that will destroy the enemy from the inside, sap away their strength from within.' Maman would not mind this lie. She would, in fact, cheer her on: it's a lie for victory.

That poor girl. She is innocent of any wrong-doing, no doubt, but she is part of the problem and must be part of the solution. Sarah buries what little guilt she feels about lying to her and walks away.

At Brühl station early the next morning it's almost a repeat of yesterday, though the station is much smaller – only two platforms – and there are hardly any other passengers, the few that there are heading north, to Freiburg, either to visit the city or to catch a connecting train. Sarah sits on that platform and, as on the day before, draws her neighbour – this time a man in a tweed coat and grey hat – into conversation. They nod to each other, exchange remarks on the weather, before she launches into her spiel about the situation in Alsace.

'I wonder if you can help,' she says. 'I've been looking for my relatives who live in Brühl – Herr Heinrich Schmidt and his wife Ute – do you happen to know them? I've asked everyone, but I can't find them.'

The man shakes his head, tells her he knows many Schmidts but not this particular couple. It's a common name.

'I'm desperate to find them,' Sarah says, 'I need to warn them. I came here from Alsace because the Germans destroyed my home and killed my parents. I'm terrified now! I want to warn my relatives; they need to leave too! It's so dangerous. The enemy is poised on the other side of the Rhine, ready to invade. Herr Goebbels won't tell you that, of course. He wants to use the people in this area as a shield, because when the enemy arrives they'll show no mercy. I'm worried we cannot withstand them. I've heard we have thousands of troops stationed here, near the river. Do you know where they are?'

The man shakes his head. 'Thousands of troops? No, not thousands. We see the odd soldier, of course – it's war, after all. But not thousands.'

'They must be here somewhere! I fear for them. I wish I could warn them, somehow. They'll be marching straight into the jaws of death.'

The man frowns. 'That can't be right, surely? Hitler promised we would keep Alsace, no matter what.'

'That won't happen. Alsace is already almost completely vanquished. I've been there, I know. They're keeping the news from the people of Freiburg and the border towns because you are to absorb the first attacks. You are to be sacrificed when the attack comes.'

The man's eyes are by now wide with terror.

'Thank you for telling me,' he says. 'I don't think I'll go into work today. I'm going to get my wife and children, we need to leave right away.'

'That's a good move. Get as far away as you can – and spread the word!'

'I'm going to telephone my place of work as soon as I get home and warn them. It's a big insurance company, they need to know – they all have families, too.'

'Yes, you should do that. It's like when Germany invaded Paris. Do you remember, how all the Parisians fled? Now unfortunately the tables have turned and it's we Germans who have to flee.'

'Indeed. Thank you for telling me, Fräulein!'

He rushes off. Sarah glances up at the station clock: a quarter to six. A local train approaches, stops at the platform and the few remaining passengers get in. On the other platform, a freight train rushes past. The passenger train jolts, creaks, its wheels begin to turn, it drives off. The station is now completely empty. No sign of soldiers pouring in to board a train to Alsace.

Sarah picks up her bicycle, mounts it and heads west again, to the next town down, the next hotel. It's so much colder today. If it starts to snow, the bicycle will be of no use...

The following days proceed much the same as the first two. Every station, early in the morning, a bench, a wait, a conversation. Sarah's stories become ever more frightening, the danger she speaks of ever more imminent, her voice, her own fear, ever more convincing. One woman actually jumps to her feet and runs off to warn her family when Sarah talks of the enemy's '*Wunderwaffe*', the incredible miracle weapon that can pulverise a whole town within seconds. 'It's an American invention,' she explains. 'It's top secret...' But the woman is already on her feet, bustling away.

And so Sarah passes from station to station: Hugstetten, Gottenheim, Wasenweiler, Ihringen. She talks to people, as many as she can, and as well as telling her own tales she tries to extract information about military activity in the area. Are there any barracks nearby? She embellishes her story to make her questions more convincing. She has, she explains, a soldier brother who is supposedly in the area; she needs to pass on to him the news of their parents' deaths. Yes, it's wonderful that our German army is prepared to fight to the last man, but are they really going in? If so, how, and where?

But nobody seems to know anything. Nobody knows of a special train carrying hundreds of soldiers into Alsace every single morning. It's frustrating, and disappointing, and Ihringen is the last town before Breisach, on the eastern Rhine bank.

On the last day, in Ihringen, however, she runs into an older man who shares her lunch table; to her great delight, a railway enthusiast.

'Yes,' he says, 'we can be proud of our troops. They'll fight to the death, to the very last man. I should say, the last boy – they are now very young, unfortunately, but they are so eager to give their lives for the *Vaterland*. We should be proud of our youth!'

'Indeed, they are worthy of our respect – giving their lives for all of us, even though it now seems to be futile... How sad that in spite of their noble sacrifice, we shall lose this war.'

'We won't!' says the gentleman. 'At the last moment Herr Hitler will release his *Wunderwaffe* and save the day. Mark my words.'

Sarah doesn't want to discuss Hitler's *Wunderwaffe*.

'But it's our boys, our brave boys over there, who we must pray for,' she says and crosses herself. 'May God protect them.'

'Don't worry, *gnädiges Fräulein*. God is on our side. Our boys are giving their lives for a cause greater than us all. It's for the glory of Deutschland. *Heil Hitler!*' He gives the Hitler salute, and Sarah nods and joins him by flinging out her right arm.

'I salute them, our boys, whenever I see their train passing by!' says the man. 'I say to myself, there go our heroes, our brave German heroes.'

'They pass by here? In a train?' She hides her eagerness as best she can.

'Indeed. Every morning, at dawn.'

Her heart begins to pound.

'Where do they come from, these soldiers?' she asks casually. 'I mean, where do the trains come from? Where do the soldiers board it – somewhere further north?'

'Yes, yes,' says the man. 'Northeast of Freiburg, near Denzlingen – there's a big barracks there. That's where they are collected. There's a small station there, Degenfeld, built specifically for the barracks. They then take the *Güterumgehungsbahnlinie* straight down to Breisach, non-stop.'

The freight detour line! *Of course!* How foolish of her! And to think she had already seen this train. While waiting at the Brühl station, talking to the man in the hat, it had rushed past and she had assumed it was just a freight train. *That* was the train she was looking for...

A few hours later she is in the village of Degenfeld, south of Gundelfingen. She has come by train, leaving Frau Sommer's bicycle at Freiburg station for the time being. Never in her life has she been so happy to see German soldiers; the slate-grey of their uniforms, some of them with swastika armbands; army vehicles; swastika flags and banners and posters. A wave of relief washes the burden of failure from her mind: she has found what she has been sent to find. Sniffed it out, found its location, and now, all she needs are the details.

The village seems to consist of only a very old station with two platforms that seems to have been called back into service, a larger building next to it which looks just as ancient and has been made into a hotel and restaurant, and a few smaller buildings clustered around the station and hotel; a small grocery, and sad-looking grey homes with shuttered windows. All the buildings, all the lampposts, are festooned with swastika posters and banners. Every window has a swastika stuck to it.

Sarah enters the hotel. There's a lobby, bare except for a desk in a corner. Above it, a huge portrait of Adolf Hitler decorated with a row of swastika flags. The receptionist looks her up and down.

'What are you doing here?' she asks. It's such a direct question, Sarah cringes. She remembers that Germans love directness: no beating around the bush, no polite chit-chat. Just the plain, unadorned truth.

She resurrects the story about her brother.

'I'm from Alsace,' she explains. 'I had to flee when the *Amis* came. It was terrible! My parents were killed. My brother is stationed in a regiment around here. Unfortunately, I don't have the details of it. I must inform him that Mama and Papa are dead – ruthlessly murdered by the enemy. He's only seventeen, he needs to know. We are now alone in the world!'

'Good luck with that – there are thousands of soldiers here,' she is told. And with that the receptionist turns away before Sarah can attack her further with 'information' about the situation in Alsace; the first victim who has turned away in time to avoid her verbal onslaught.

Sarah's room is small and cold and bare: just a single bed with a thin mattress and two threadbare blankets folded at the foot, a bedside table, a wooden chair, a wardrobe. A bathroom is down the corridor, shared by the other rooms on the floor, but it seems she is the only guest. Why would anyone ever come to this godforsaken place, anyway?

She spends the afternoon walking. She walks east of the village, calling up the memorised map, and ends up in a place called

Heuweiler, but there is not a whiff of a soldier or a regiment. She walks back via Gundelfingen. On the way it starts to snow, lightly, covering the ground with a pristine cloak of white. She raises her head to the sky, lets the snow melt on her cheeks. It brings up memories of home, of Colmar, of Alsace, when the family would sometimes go out to the snow-covered countryside and the children would scream with joy as they raced down the hillsides in their sleds. They would build snowmen. Maman and Papa, laughing with them as they raced about the fields, flinging snowballs at each other.

Over. All over, the past obliterated not only by time but the horrors of war, so that memories bring tears not of nostalgic joy but of deep mourning, gouged into her heart and into her being, into the abyss where Ralf too is buried in a cemetery of agony. She cannot bear it; she turns back towards the hotel.

At the village's edge she runs into a group of young soldiers. They greet her enthusiastically. She jolts herself back from wallowing in the sloughs of anguish and puts on a cheerful face.

'*Guten Abend*,' she says, 'what are you boys up to?'

'Looking for beautiful women,' says one of them with a laugh. 'But our vehicle got a flat tyre and we have to walk back to the barracks. And see, we've found one! Luck is on our side. Where are you heading for? What are you doing in this lonely part of the world?'

They introduce themselves. They laugh at their own names, which all begin with H – Horst, Heinrich, Heinz – and Sarah swings into step beside them. Horst and Heinz are both just sixteen, too young, really, to flirt, much less to fight. Heinrich is seventeen. She tells them: 'I'm looking for my brother – he's a soldier, just like you. Perhaps he's in your regiment. Do you know him? His name is Reinhold Schmidt. He must be about your age. Blond? Blue eyes?'

'Lots of boys named Schmidt at our barracks – they come and go every day. No chance we can talk to all of them or learn their names. Are you sure he's there?'

'I'm not sure of anything,' says Sarah. 'I just know he must be stationed somewhere in this area. I was hoping someone might have met him. I need to give him some bad news.'

Her face turns mournful.

'Our parents were killed a few days ago, in our home near Strasbourg. We are now orphans. I need to find Reinhold to tell him not to come home again – we have no home, we have no family! Our home is in enemy hands, our family obliterated!'

She starts to cry. The boys look at each other, embarrassed. Heinz pats her on the shoulder.

'I'm so sorry,' he says, 'about your parents. I wish I could…'

'We'll ask around at the barracks,' promises Horst. 'We'll make a mission of it. Who knows, sometimes miracles happen, and perhaps he's there. We'll look for him, right, boys?'

'Would you do that? For me?'

She has managed to dry her tears and they walk on.

'We promise. We'll start as soon as we get home.'

'Unfortunately, there's not much time. Tomorrow we leave for Alsace. We are going there to fight the enemy.'

'Oh, really?' Normally this would be Sarah's cue to launch into her speech about the horrors lying in wait in Alsace. But she cannot: she cannot lie to these boys. Her conscience is biting, hurtfully. Today, she cannot tell tall tales; she cannot exaggerate, she cannot scare them. They are so confident, so eager, so innocent in their bubble of invulnerability. How can she prick it? They will march to their deaths anyway. Or rather, be railroaded to their doom.

They come to a crossroads. The boys say goodbye. 'We'll look for your brother,' says Heinrich. 'If he's there, we'll find him.'

The words are at the back of her mind: 'Don't bother, he doesn't exist.' But she swallows them. She, too, is a soldier of sorts: sentimentality is not allowed.

'So, your barracks are up this way?'

'Yes – about three kilometres up the road.'

'Good luck!' she calls as they stride off, and she means it. In her heart she knows that no luck awaits them, or rather, only bad luck. It's a pitiful waste of life, but there it is. Ralf's life, too, has gone to waste.

She returns to the hotel; she is hungry and would normally have supper, but, walking through the dining room on her way to the stairs and her room, she finds it full of German officers, many of them bearing the swastika on their arms. They are jovial and raucous, and as she walks through, many of them call out to her:

'Beautiful girl! Join us, have a drink with us! Come on, don't be shy!'

She gives them all a half-smile and passes through, up the stairs to her room. She will go hungry tonight.

Chapter Forty-Six

The following day Sarah stands at the forest edge, concealed by the fir trees, hardly believing her eyes. Before her, a high wire fence. Beyond it, row upon row of barracks. Sombre grey oblong buildings, boringly basic in structure, functional and bleak and forbidding. She knows at once: this is it. This is where the killing machine that is the Wehrmacht collects its human munition, stores it, dispatches it. This is where lives are gathered and sorted and shipped away, living bullets bound for Alsace, to give and receive death. It is a chilling sight. Not a living soul is to be seen. The place is silent, dead, and that makes it all the more sinister.

She scouts around the forest edge, assessing the limits; the wire fencing is at least eight metres high, as if it is a prison camp, as if the soldiers must be contained. The buildings are in five rows of eight, lengthwise. Each one has three rows of fourteen windows along its length and four along its breadth. How many soldiers does each barrack contain? A hundred at least. She calculates, using a modest low count of 100 per building, that it would be 4,000 men altogether. It is beyond belief; no wonder Germany seems to have an unending supply of fighting men! They are brought here and kept, to be sent off by rail into France via Alsace as required.

In the cover of the trees, she walks the length of the perimeter; the front edge of the enclosure contains some activity, which she can observe from the forest. There is a large gate with sentries, a large building that seems to have an administrative function and an empty concreted area in front of the barracks, where a few covered trucks are parked. She guesses that the soldiers will be transported in those trucks to the train station at Degenfeld, loaded onto those endless waggons, dispatched. Dispatched in both senses of the word.

She thinks of the young men she met yesterday. Horst, Heinrich, Heinz; all of them younger than Ralf, boys who have barely completed their formal schooling, bright-eyed boys eager for adventure, confident of victory, innocent of purpose; boys fed on an empty promise of Germany's future glory and eager to fight for it, not knowing the evil at its heart; boys recruited from here and there, most likely the more southern regions of Germany: Baden and Rheinland-Palatinate and Hesse; boys ripped from their families and stuffed into these bleak edifices, a temporary holding habitat, then stuffed into figurative cannons and launched to their inevitable deaths. Because most of them *will* die, she is sure of it. Each has a mother, a father, sitting at home in heart-wrenching ignorance of their son's fate, but knowing in their hearts they'll never see their beloved boy again.

This is a killing factory, a place to give as well as receive death. They are only Germans, she tells herself, part of the Nazi engine of destruction. Why should she care if the boys she met are used and abused in this horrifyingly inescapable process? But she does. She shudders, takes a deep breath, straightens her shoulders.

None of that, she tells herself sternly. *It's pure sentimentality. Pull yourself together, Sarah. Do your job: your job is to report back to your superiors, let them know what you have discovered, find out more.* When, how often, are the soldiers collected? How many at a time? What route do they take? This is the priceless information she's been sent to gather, and gather it she must. Even if, because of that very information, before too long the Allies will send their bombers and flatten this entire area. Only rubble will remain, the lives of Horst, Heinrich and Heinz snuffed out. Their mothers and fathers will weep, like Doctor and Frau Sommer. What of it? It is none of her business. Collateral damage, it's called. Sentimentality, feelings, have no place in war.

She decides to watch for a while. There must be a sign of life, apart from the sentries, sooner or later. They can't all stay indoors for ever. She is hungry and cold. There is an apple in her jacket pocket; she takes it out and eats it. Walking helps banish the cold. Keeping clear of the outside areas, she walks through the forest, between the trees, up and down. Dusk is fast approaching. She'll stay till nightfall, she decides, and then walk back along the road to Degenfeld. If she meets anyone, she'll say she is lost – she'd been looking for a farm belonging to her relatives and taken the wrong road. She'll smile and flirt and play the innocent. Maybe have a conversation, if they are so inclined. Let them know of the utter devastation in Alsace, in the whole of France; the demolition of the German forces. Spread the news that Germany is losing the war. Confuse and demoralise the enemy; spread rumours, sprinkle tiny titbits of doubt. That's how the enemy can be destroyed from within: you build up an edifice of insecurity in their minds, weakening their confidence, their resolve.

As darkness gathers a cold mist descends on the area. Flood-lights flare on, so that the garrison seems covered in a bright blue sheath. Yes, there is movement. She can see men walking within the compound, men in uniform. Probably boys. Sounds; is that music? Singing? Yes, it is. Probably some kind of self-entertainment. She shivers. It's colder than ever, time to go.

She turns her back on the garrison and walks through the forest for a little way before emerging and stepping onto the road, headed for Degenfeld. She has walked for barely fifteen minutes before she hears a slight rumble, growing stronger: the sound of a vehicle approaching from the direction of Degenfeld. She moves from the centre of the road to the edge. There is a bend in the road, a glare of light growing stronger, the rumble, too, louder. She retreats into the cover of the trees to watch. The funnelled glare of a headlight lights up the road and then it is there: a large covered army truck. Then a second, and a third. Eight trucks in all drive slowly past.

They are, no doubt, filled with soldiers, replacements for those who have been sent off most recently.

The trucks rumble past, leaving only blackness. The road is unlit, but there's a half-moon and she can make out the road and walk along it. She comes to a bridge; it is about 50 metres long, crossing a river. She'll check her map when she's back in her room, find out the name of that river. Tomorrow, she'll wait at Degenfeld station. Fill in the last piece of the puzzle…

She has one last mission: to deliver this vital information.

It is still dark when she slinks from her hotel room and makes her way to the station. There has been light snowfall overnight, and it is still snowing gently. The world looks so pristinely clean, the streets all white and pure in the moonlight; it is hard to believe that somewhere out there, the snow is red from the blood of men, men of all nationalities; allies and foes fallen to Hitler's insanity, their blood leaking into the earth. So many lives have been lost already, and she has the knowledge that will help to end yet more lives.

She walks on, finds the station and crouches down in the shadow of an outbuilding to wait. Waiting, too, is a train, shrouded in darkness: a long metal beast crouching before her in the darkness. She shivers in the bitter cold, hugs herself, rubs her arms, wrings her hands enclosed in the gloves Frau Sommer has provided. The seconds tick past. She counts them into minutes. Five. Six… Ten.

In the distance, the rumble of a vehicle, growing louder by the second: they have arrived. She stands up and presses herself against the shed, dark against dark, watching.

Lights; the station springs into life. Voices, shouts, commands. Footsteps. A man walks along the train, opening the carriage doors.

Here they come. Men in uniform, swarming over the platform, boarding the train. She hears laughter; the men – boys, actually – seem in high spirits as they climb into the carriages. At last, action after the dull tedium of the barracks. Lively, strong boys on the cusp of adult life: she can see their shadows through the carriage windows as they take their seats.

You are on a train to your deaths, she whispers soundlessly. *You will probably all be dead by midnight.*

A whistle blows; the engine shudders. There are jolts and jerks, the clanging sound of metal on metal as if the beast is waking up, stretching, yawning. And then it crawls away towards the west, towards Colmar, and death.

She returns to her hotel. Her bed there is calling, though it will no longer be warm. She will make it warm. There is time for a few hours of sleep.

She spends the following morning in her room, making notes of all her information, transforms it all into code, using Psalm 23 as the basis. Central to the information: the location of the Degenfeld barracks. That task completed, she packs her bag and heads out into the street, walks the few steps to the station.

The village is quiet, not a soldier to be seen and hardly a civilian. It's hard to believe that only a few nights ago it was swarming with military men out for a night of rare fun; it is now dead. As they soon will be. She boards a train to Freiburg, her mission almost over. One last thing to do…

The café where Ulrike works is just a block from the station, near the University. Sarah sees her through the window, enters, sits down and waits. The café is full, and Ulrike is the only waitress, rushing from table to table taking orders. Finally, she arrives at Sarah's table. Sarah orders coffee; Ulrike takes the order and goes off, returns with the coffee. Sarah stealthily removes her notes and slips them into the folds of a serviette. She drinks her coffee and leaves.

Ulrike will proceed to her home village near Basle, and then on to Basle, where Monsieur Bigot's contact, and the Free French courier route, is in place. From then on, Sarah's information will make its way to the Free French Intelligence service. It is out of her hands now: Her job is done. She is free. She returns to Degenfeld.

Sarah's spirits are as low as they have ever been. Her mission is complete, now she can go home. But she has no home, no family in Germany or anywhere nearby. Where can she go? What can she do? She is stuck in Germany until the war ends and that could be months. She could return to Freiburg, to the Sommers, but no, she cannot ask them for refuge even though, now, theirs is the nearest thing she has to a home – it would put them in too much danger.

Switzerland, Monsieur Bigot had said. There are border crossings there, with a 50:50 chance of capture by the Germans. Switzerland is where her sisters are; she should really go there, join them in Sion, give them the news of her parents, of Sofie's death. They should band together, wait out the war together and then find out which camp their parents and Manon have been sent to. There is still hope, surely? Yet Switzerland, a country unfamiliar to her, does not call, her sisters do not call. Not yet.

Alsace calls. Her short break there had been too short. She needs to see Uncle Yves again, find out more, wallow in her memories and her sadness. And then another place calls, another home. Margaux, Victoire, Jacques. The château where it all began, the people who helped her in her first agonies of separation. They had given her solace and comfort, they would do so again. She has to get back there. But how? She does not have a return travel permit to Colmar. Perhaps there are ways to get one?

She walks back to the station. The ticket office is closed, the place is deserted. She walks out into the street again, deliberating: there *must* be a way back to Colmar!

She walks to the town hall, a small half-timbered building in the village square. This, too, is practically deserted – but not quite. The door opens directly into a small office, where a young woman sits at a typewriter, furiously typing away. She looks up eagerly as Sarah walks in, as if she has been lonely and is grateful for the break, for the company.

'Can I help you?'

'Yes, I wanted to know how I can get a travel permit to go to Colmar.'

The girl frowns. 'To Colmar? A travel permit? Sorry, no, it is an impossibility.'

'But there must be some way? I have to get there, it's so important! You see…'

She relates the story she has concocted.

'My parents live there. I have received news that my mother is dying. Please! I have to go and visit them – I need to go! Surely there is someone? There must be someone with the authority. Perhaps the Mayor? Can I see him, please? Maybe I can persuade him?'

She is rambling now, but it's only because this time the lie serves a genuine, personal need. She is now desperate to return to the only place she has ever called home. Even if her family is not there, the streets are still the streets of home and, most of all, the last friends she has are all there.

'Please?'

The girl hesitates and then says, 'A week ago I would have said yes. The Mayor is a good man and maybe he would have helped you. But, you see, even he cannot help you now. All trains to Colmar have been cancelled, all civilian trains. Only military can go there now. Have you not heard the news, Fräulein? The enemy have taken over the entire Alsace. The whole province is in the madness of war – people are dying and it is dangerous for civilian Germans to be there. They are all fleeing! So, it is possible to leave Alsace but not to enter it.'

'Surely it's not that bad?'

She knows it isn't that bad. It's she herself who has spread the rumours that the Allies have almost conquered Alsace, that

Germany is losing. Now she must pay the price for her own successful lies…

'It's terrible, Fräulein! Colmar is just one huge bloodbath. I am sorry about your mother, but really, you must accept that you cannot go.'

But she won't accept it. Out of all the words this young lady has said, one sentence jumps out: only military can go. She herself has seen the train puff off this morning, Colmar-bound. Another train will leave tomorrow morning. And the day after that. Somehow, she must get on one of those trains. And she thinks she knows how.

'Thank you, Fräulein. I know you did your best, I accept that I cannot go.'

'I'm sorry about your mother,' says the girl again as Sarah walks out.

That evening, Sarah decides to have a meal in the hotel restaurant. Last night she bought some pastries to eat in her room, avoiding the restaurant again, because as she walked through, the officers sitting at the tables stared at her, grinning. Some even called out to her: *Eat with us, Fräulein! I'll buy you dinner, there's a free chair at our table.*

Tonight, she will gladly accept such an invitation. Tonight, instead of ignoring the calls, she turns and smiles, glances around the room, fixes on one particular table where there's a free chair.

'*Gerne,*' she says tonight, 'Gladly. Thank you.'

'Be our guest,' says one of the officers, grinning giddily. She can tell from the insignia on his collar that he is a colonel, an Oberst: three oak leaves. He is fawningly attentive to her, as are the others, but he is the worst. Or rather, the best – exactly what she had hoped for.

She gives her name as Hannah Schmidt and reels off the same story she gave the girl in the town hall: her mother in Colmar is dying of cancer, and she must get there.

'We are ethnic Germans, and we so hoped that Germany would win the war! And I still hope, you know... There is always hope, isn't there? Even when everything seems lost, we can win. God is on our side! I came to Freiburg to work a year ago and I have not seen my parents since then. I must see my mother before she dies!'

She doles out the lies, improvising as she speaks. They fall so easily from her lips, now – she who had never spoken a single untruth before this war started.

She wipes a tear from her eye. 'But there are no more trains! I can't even get a ticket, much less a travel permit! It's a catastrophe!'

Surreptitiously, she watches the officers. Their faces are earnest with sympathy. The Colonel – Oberst Hagenmeier is his name – places a beefy hand on hers.

'Don't cry, *liebes Fräulein*. I'm sure we can help. Surely Germans must help one another? Is that not true, my colleagues?'

They look a little uncertain, then all nod eagerly.

'There is always place for one more,' says one.

'Especially for a so-charming *Fräulein*,' says another.

'German families must be together, especially during hard times,' says yet another. 'Isn't that what the Führer says? Isn't that his basic principle?'

'*Heil Hitler!*' they cry, and their arms shoot out.

And indeed: the gallant officers of the Wehrmacht to the rescue. Early the next morning Sarah is once again at the station, but this time on the platform, not in hiding, and she has her packed suitcase with her.

She stands at the entrance to the platform, waiting. Around her the soldiers swarm, looking back, some whistling under their breath. More and more swarm past: where are her officer friends?

Oberst Hagenmeier hooks her by the elbow. 'Come, my dear, you will join us in the officers' carriage – you won't be with the riff-raff!'

He escorts her into a carriage at the very back of the train. 'The back is safest,' he explains. 'In case the enemy tries to derail us.'

For the first time Sarah actually grasps the danger of what she is doing. Travelling in a Wehrmacht train, from Germany into France! In the company of – no, as a *guest* of – the enemy! Somewhere in that situation there is a hidden joke, but she can't laugh. She is too weighed down by sorrow, by grief, and it takes every effort for her to play the part of the grateful young German girl delighted to be escorted by all these gallant officers, to share their carriage, to converse gaily with them as if there is no war raging out there; which is the impression one would gather if one were to judge by the good humour of the officers, each one vying for her attention.

But Oberst Hagenmeier has made it quite clear that she is *his* guest, and that perhaps, once in Colmar, if the fighting is not too intense, they can meet again?

'Why not?' says Sarah, and her eyes hint at better things to come. She never knew she was such a good actress, able with only a thought to put a coy sparkle into her eyes. Oberst Hagenmeier replies with a flirtatious dig into her ribs and a teasing chuckle.

The train gives a jerk, and they are off.

Soon they are speeding westwards. Soon they are on the Rhine bridge at Breisach. Soon they are over the bridge, in Alsace. Sarah gives a satisfied sigh of relief. She has done it, she has come home.

Chapter Forty-Seven

The squeal of brakes is deafening, a clattering bang, the crunching crash of metal against metal. The carriage leaps to one side, sways, topples, rights itself again, still swaying. Men cry out, fall against each other, cling to seats and rails, fall to the floor; Sarah finds herself beneath a mass of male bodies. One by one, though, they all disentangle themselves. Someone has taken hold of her hand, her arm; she is being pulled to her feet: it is Oberst Hagenmeier.

'What— What happened?' she stutters.

'We've crashed, derailed – probably an ambush,' he replies. He has lost his visor cap. His face is as pink as gammon. 'Are you hurt? The enemy – we must try to escape – come with me, Fräulein!'

He opens the door and gives her a hand to help her jump from the carriage. In the chaos, someone has managed to break one of the windows which now form the roof of the carriage, now lying on its side in a field. Before them there is total chaos: carriages in a zigzag heap, some overturned, men in uniform pouring from doors and windows, people, shouting, crying out, scrambling out of windows and doors.

'You stay with me!' the Oberst orders Sarah, pushing her behind him, and he barks orders at the ordinary soldiers trying to bring order to the disorder. 'We must flee before the enemy arrives!'

But it is too late. Suddenly they are surrounded. Other soldiers, other uniforms, those of the Free French army; men carrying rifles, aimed at them; more soldiers barking orders, but this time in French.

'Hands up, everyone! *Hände hoch!* Walk over there, into that field! *Vite, vite!* Hurry, you Nazi pigs! *Schnell!*

The Germans are quick to follow orders. Hands raised, they all march towards the field they are directed to. French soldiers are everywhere, pointing rifles at them, screaming insults.

'Nazi *Schwein*! Pigs! Scum!'

One of them notices Sarah, pulls her out from the line.

'Look what we have here, a German whore! Come here, you little slut!'

She is grabbed by the arm, thrown to the ground. A grinning French soldier kicks her in the ribs. Others gather round, grinning, leering.

'Trying to sneak into France to do your whoring, are you?'

Someone pulls her to her feet.

'You'll see exactly what our French women had to suffer at the hands of the Nazis! Take her away, we'll deal with her later.' She is pushed and shoved away from the train wreck. A captive, but not of the Nazis.

Later, Sarah finds herself in a long, low brick building surrounded by Free French soldiers. They are close, *too* close. She has been slapped and kicked multiple times. She has tried to speak, yelled at them in French:

'I am not German, I am French!'

'Then what were you doing in that train, sneaking into Alsace?'

'I'm an agent! I was spying, in Germany, for France!'

Her suitcase is still in the chaos of the train, but her papers are in her pocket.

'Your papers!'

She pulls them out, but without much hope: they are the wrong papers for this situation.

Indeed, the soldier inspecting them snorts and throws them to the ground.

'Hannah Schmidt – a German. Yes, we believe you are a spy, but a German spy being sent into France. Why else would you be on that train?'

'I lied! I wanted to come back. I am from Colmar. I am Jewish! I belong here – I live here. I went to Germany to get information. Believe me, I am French – I am on your side!'

'Why on earth would we believe you, you little German whore?' More kicks, more slaps. Someone rips away her coat.

'Do you know what your German friends did to our women? Do you want a taste of it yourself?'

Kicks, slaps. She tries to kick back, slap back; she fights, but it only enrages them all the more. She is held from the back by one of them while she kicks at the others. Pain, excruciating pain. Pain as she has never known it, beyond her imagination. She howls with the pain.

'Grab her legs, pull off her trousers!'

The men are now not only angry, they are spiteful, mean. They paw her; hands everywhere. She howls, screams, scratches, but to no avail: she is writhing on the floor as they pull at her trousers. But then, someone walks in and they cease. They pull her to her feet and hold her in a vice, but the men straighten up and stop molesting her.

'What's going on here?' barks the newcomer.

'Sir, we have captured a German spy. She was on the train we ambushed.'

She manages to haul her mind away from the pain. 'I am *not* a German spy! I am a *French* spy! I was in Germany on a mission and I can prove it!' she yells in French.

The newcomer looks from her to the men, and then says, 'Let her go.' To her, he says, 'Follow me.'

She bends down and picks up her papers. He leads her down a corridor, to a small room with a desk and a chair. He does not introduce himself.

'So then, tell me. You say you are a French spy? How can you prove it?'

She hands him her papers. 'They are forged,' she says, 'My real name is Sarah Mayer. I am from Colmar, I am Jewish.'

She explains everything, but he only frowns and looks sceptical. 'But you cannot prove any of this. Why should I believe you? Who is your commanding officer?'

'He is in Metz. His name is Monsieur Bigot.'

But even as she says the words her heart sinks, for that is not his real name. She does not know it. She has no idea who is her real commanding officer. As Monsieur Bigot told her back then: *You are on your own. If you are caught, we cannot help you.*

He meant, of course, caught by the Germans, by the Gestapo. Now she has been caught by the French, but he still cannot help her: she is truly alone.

Her interrogator is silent for a while, thinking. Then he says, 'Very well. There is no way to prove what you say, but we will give you a chance. We will send you to Paris – you will be interrogated there by an expert in German espionage.'

She grasps at that escape route. Surely an expert in espionage will decipher the truth? Surely he will be able to contact Monsieur Bigot, help her to be free? She is hopeful.

Not so, though, as she is bundled, handcuffed, into the back seat of a car. Another soldier climbs in, sits next to her. She is hurting all over, her entire body a bruise.

The driver turns to look at her. 'Filthy German spy!' he snarls. 'You know how the Germans treated our Resistance fighters when they were caught? How they were tortured until they told your secrets? Well, the French have taken lessons in interrogation. You will learn the French methods, which are even worse, because we are fired by the flames of revenge. If you do not talk, you will die!'

The car speeds away, towards Paris.

Chapter Forty-Eight

It's an impressive, huge building on Boulevard Mortier. She is led into it by the soldier who sat next to her on the back seat. The driver has disappeared. *Thank goodness*, she thinks. The whole drive down to Paris he bombarded her with threats: of all the terrible things she is about to encounter during interrogation. The French are out for revenge, he said. 'Did you not hear that the Carlingue was worse than the Nazis? You will be lucky to survive.' And so on.

She has tried so hard to be strong. To remember Ralf, his courage, his fearlessness. But it's no good: she's terrified, and ashamed of herself for the sheer panic that is attacking her from deep within. For all the bravery she has managed to muster over the past few months, at heart she is just a simple woman, who loves simple things: family, friends, sweetheart. She wants no more than a simple life with loved ones, she is not made for war. Is anyone? Isn't war an aberration, a complete distortion of what it means to be human? She closes her eyes and grasps tightly the only anchor she has. Words. She says them to herself, again and again: '*Yea, though I walk through the valley of the shadow of death…*'

But here it is. This soldier seems a mite kinder than the driver, though, and so she finally musters the courage to tell him: 'I need to go to the toilet, urgently. Please…?'

He blushes, and leads her to a door with *Toilettes* written on it. 'I'll wait out here,' he says.

She holds out her wrists, still handcuffed.

'Please?' she says again. No other words are necessary.

He unlocks the handcuffs.

'Hurry up,' he says gruffly as she enters the lavatory.

Once she is in the cubicle, her hands free at last, she bends over, removes a boot. Removes a hairpin from her hair, fiddles with the heel of her boot. Prises open a small flap. Digs it out.

The capsule. The cyanide pill. 'Death will be instantaneous,' Monsieur Bigot said back then at her interview.

She places it in her mouth, between gum and cheek. It is safe there. When the time comes, she has only to bite into it.

She knows she cannot withstand torture. Death is preferable. Perhaps – just perhaps – she will meet Ralf. Perhaps she will meet Sofie. Who knows? *'I will fear no evil, for thou art with me.'*

She emerges from the lavatory. Her soldier escort is waiting; he half-smiles as he sees her. He handcuffs her again, and leads her down a corridor, up some stairs, down another corridor. As they go, they pass various people, all of whom stare, intrigued, then look away. She feels naked, exposed, and is tired of it all. The deadly capsule, clamped beside her gum, is now her only anchor. She will follow where Ralf went, into death. What does she have to live for, anyway? Two sisters: they will grieve for her, but in the end they will recover and be fine without her. Everyone has lost love ones and they will accept her death and move on with their lives. Rebecca will surely look after them. And Margaux, and Uncle Yves. They all care; but soon they too will forget. Life goes on.

Yes, the will to live is strong, but also the longing to be free of it all. To sink into the arms of death. Maybe, just maybe, she'll meet Ralf there, if what they say about heaven is true. *'Thy rod and thy staff to comfort me…'*

She is led into an office; it is small and bare, furnished only by a desk with a chair on either side of it. A woman is placing a jug of water and a glass on the desk. She glances at Sarah and grimaces.

'Sit down here and wait. Herr Dahlke will be along in a minute.'

Herr Dahlke. So, it is to be a German interrogator. She's not sure if that is good or bad. She touches the cyanide capsule with her tongue: she's ready.

The woman opens the door to exit the room, but there are voices. '*Merci*, Mademoiselle Vandame,' says a voice.

It is strangely familiar. That V – he'd never mastered it, had he? Because in German the V is pronounced as an F, and he'd learned a written French rather than an oral French, from a German teacher. He'd never got it right. How often she'd made him repeat it – again and again – and besides, that voice! Unmistakable. But no! It can't be, surely…

She swivels around in her chair. Half-stands.

He is closing the door, his back to her.

He turns around. Their eyes lock.

And then – they lurch at each other. His arms are around her, pulling her tight. She cannot reciprocate, for her wrists are in handcuffs still, but she is weeping, weeping as if her heart would break, and then she pushes away from him, spits into her hand. Holds up the capsule to him.

He gasps, then, still holding her, turns back to the door.

'Guard!' he calls. 'You there, bring the key! Unlock her cuffs!'

And then she is really free, and in his arms.

Later, he tells her his story.

'We were put in a train, handcuffed, bound for Paris, for Fresnes prison,' he explains. 'We all knew it was the end, that we would be executed. But… well, we too have bodily needs. I asked to go to the toilet, and one of the guards escorted me there. He told me not to lock the door. But then the train drew to a halt; there was some kind of extraordinary stop. It was night, pitch-dark outside, but there was a faint glow from a road nearby and I could see an embankment sloping down to it, fairly steep. It was risky, I knew. If the train stopped for a long time, well, they'd certainly find me. But it was a risk I had to take. I managed to open the window, climb onto the toilet seat, climb out, jump. I rolled down the embankment.

'That's where he found me: at the roadside, unconscious. A farmer, on his way home. He packed me into his cart and took me home. I woke up later and remembered nothing. They cut open my handcuffs and they fetched a French doctor, a friendly doctor. I regained my memory gradually. It seemed the train had not stopped for long and by the time they discovered I was missing, the farmer had found me and I was gone.

'They put up notices, of course, and tried to find me – apparently I was dangerous. But by that time I was being cared for.'

'Why didn't you call me? Why didn't you…'

'I couldn't – I had had a severe concussion. I did recover, but it left me with a complete blank as far as numbers are concerned. I could not remember your number. Nor Mathilde's. Nor my Resistance colleagues. I could remember names, and places, but not telephone numbers. They were all gone.'

'But you could have come to Poitiers, looked for me there? Asked Régine?'

He shook his head. 'Frankly, I assumed you would have gone immediately to Switzerland, like I told you to. I saw the newspaper article, saying we had all been executed – though they got the number wrong, didn't they? Only four were killed, not five.

'I assumed you thought I was dead. There was nothing I could do about that – I knew I'd find you after the war. Eventually, after several months with the farmer's family, I rejoined the Resistance, but a different group. By that time the Allies had invaded France, Paris was French again and French Intelligence was delighted to find me, trained me in interrogation… and, well, here I am!'

She tells him her story.

'Monique!' He sighs. 'She is the key. I never liked her, always doubted her, but you pushed her on me.'

'I'm sorry, so sorry. I was such a naïve little girl, back then. So hungry for friendship. I swallowed every word of hers.'

'She tried to seduce me, you know, but I refused. I think that made her more angry than ever. Betraying me was also an act of personal revenge.'

Sarah shudders. 'Madame Elise thinks she works for the Carlingue.'

Ralf takes her hand, squeezes it.

'You're lucky to have escaped yourself,' he says. 'You too were in terrible danger.'

Sarah shakes her head. 'No, I think in spite of everything, Monique loves her nieces and nephews, she genuinely loves them. She was glad I was with them, says she's never seen them so happy. She'd want to preserve that. I was small fry – she needed me only to get to you.'

'But you're a Jew. Surely that was something to betray?'

Again, Sarah shakes her head. 'The Beaulieus don't hate Jews per se. They don't have that ingrained horror of us that the Nazis try to spread. For them, it was just expediency – they were courting Germans, so had to avoid Jews. Monique wouldn't have cared much that I'm Jewish.'

She sighs. 'I'm sorry for those children, though. The family will face hard times. They were absolute collaborators and will pay the price.'

'They deserve it. They'll be tried and punished when this is all over.'

'Monsieur Lemoins was actually a good man, I believe. He married the wrong woman and was drawn into their web of Nazi-love. Poor man, poor children.'

'Well, it's behind you. Don't waste your sympathy on him – he must have had a choice at some point. As for Monique: at the very least, her hair will be shaved off; it's what happens to French women who slept with German soldiers. Perhaps she will be tried for her betrayal. But we can forget her. Now it's *our* time. Are you ready for freedom? Do you remember how we always said, "When the war is over"? That time has come, Sarah. It's our time now.'

They walk out of the building hand in hand, onto the streets of Paris. They walk along the Seine. They hold hands. They hug. They dance. They make love.

For Ralf and Sarah, the war is over; they have found each other again. But peace is still far away, for both of them. A myriad obstacles face them both.

Chapter Forty-Nine

Barely a week after Sarah and Ralf's reunion, the barracks outside Degenfeld are bombed to rubble by the Allies. No more trains packed with German soldiers will cross the railway bridge into Germany. But more is to come, and for them both the news is chilling: it turns out that Sarah's scaremongering was not entirely fabrication, for the Royal Air Force attacks Freiburg on 27 November. Over a period of just 25 minutes more than 1,900 tons of bombs are dropped. The newspapers are full of exultation: over 2,000 deaths are estimated in the widespread destruction of the city. Miraculously, though, the magnificent cathedral escapes the attack intact.

But Ralf and Sarah are shocked to the core, and now it is Ralf's turn to be anxious about *his* parents, Sarah's turn to support him. No news is coming out of Freiburg; there is no way of establishing contact.

In December, January and February the Allies attack the area again and again, damaging and destroying several railways and locomotives on the freight line around Freiburg. Sarah's information has been put to good use. But the end of the war is not a given. It turns out that Hitler does indeed have a *Wunderwaffe*. It comes not in the form of an actual weapon, but as a surprise attack on 1 January 1945 on Alsace, named Operation Nordwind. It is the last major German offensive on the Western Front, and because Hitler is now incandescent with rage, because he has nothing more to lose, it is vicious and desperate, the final devastating attack of a raging beast fighting for survival. It turns the idyllic landscape of Alsace into a bloodbath; the snow turns red with the blood of Germans, Frenchmen and Americans. It is carnage. But gradually, slowly, the Allies gain the advantage. Colmar is finally liberated by American and French forces on 2 and 3 February 1945.

On 5 February, the defeated German army destroys the Rhein bridge at Breisach.

Alsace is free, and belongs to France again. The whole country breaks out in celebration, and for Ralf and Sarah there is, finally, news. They travel to Basle and at last Sarah is able to make contact with Ulrike Böhm, Stefan's girlfriend who helped her in her mission. Her news is a stone lifted from Ralf's heart: the Wiehre area of Freiburg is undamaged, his parents' house still stands, they and his siblings have escaped, unharmed. There is still no way of contacting them directly, however, for the postal service is in shambles, and travel into Germany is impossible.

And then, in May, the war is truly over. Hitler has committed suicide. Germany has surrendered. It's the moment they have been waiting for.

Ralf and Sarah leave the rubble of bombed-out central Freiburg and walk up *Prinz-Eugen-Strasse,* hand in hand. Her heart is near to bursting; it is throbbing wildly, madly – not, as during the weary years of war, in fear, but in dizzy excitement. She can hardly bear it. And yet: 'It's all my fault, their grief,' she says. 'If it were not for me, they'd not have known you were supposed to be dead. I brought them the worst news of their lives. I feel so guilty.'

'Don't,' says Ralf. 'Because now you're about to bring them the best news of their lives.'

They do not talk any more, just squeeze each other's hand, look at each other, swing arms. Sometimes she gives a little skip, sometimes she stops and hugs him; all through the inability to contain her joy.

He opens the latch on the gate to number 26. They walk up the garden path. They look at each other, grinning, then he presses the bell. Three times; it was always his signal when he came home from school.

A light goes on within the house; the narrow oblong pane of frosted glass in the heavy oak door lights up. A shadowy figure appears behind the glass; a female shape – Ralf's mother. He and Sarah exchange a smile, a hug. The door opens.

Frau Sommer's cry is the sweetest sound Sarah has ever heard. No music in the world can equal the unmitigated joy of a mother as she flings her arms around her child returned from the dead: alive, and free.

Epilogue

But though the war has ended, life continues as a roller-coaster ride between joy and despair.

Joy, when Sarah travels down to Sion to be reunited with her sisters, Thérèse and Amélie. She finds them thriving, living still with their escort Rebecca, who has found work as a teacher in a primary school, attending school themselves. Rebecca has become a surrogate mother to the girls; they love and respect her. For her they have become the children she always longed for: her daughters.

Despair, when Sarah must tell her sisters that their parents have been sent to a camp in Germany and nobody knows, as yet, where, and what has become of them. The rumours coming out of Germany are dire: every day, more horror tales. Reports of death camps, mass graves of hundreds of unnamed bodies, thousands, hundreds of thousands, maybe even a million or more, deaths: Jews, gypsies, undesirables.

More despair yet when her sisters learn that their youngest, their beloved little Sofie, is definitely dead, shot down by the Gestapo outside her own home.

Joy, when Sarah and Ralf marry in a quiet civil ceremony in Freiburg, in the midst of close friends and family. Sarah, Thérèse and Amélie are welcomed into the Sommer family. Loving arms close around them: 'You will always have a home here,' says Frau Sommer, who has become Tante Gisela to the younger girls, and Mama to Sarah.

In the back garden of the Sommer home, there is celebration. The high point is when Doctor Sommer sets up the sawhorse, places a thick log across it and hands Ralf the two-handled saw. Ralf grins at Sarah: 'Are you ready?'

She looks at the saw and frowns: 'What's this about?'

He laughs. 'It's a German wedding tradition: sawing the log. We have to cut it in half, together. Look, stand here, hold the saw.' He places her on one side of the log.

Sarah understands immediately; she grasps the handle of the saw and Ralf, on the other side of the sawhorse, holds the other handle, and together they saw: back and forth, back and forth, laughing, stopping for breath, sawing again, until, at last, the log cracks in two. Everyone laughs and claps and cheers: they have done it!

Doctor Sommer explains to Sarah: 'The sawing of the log signifies the first obstacle the bride and groom must overcome in a lifetime of inevitable future obstacles. The only way to do so is to work as a team. You've shown that you can do it.'

But Ralf shakes his head. 'Actually, we've already done it, haven't we? We're still together, we've survived the war – I can't think of a greater obstacle than that!'

Grief, when they all return to Colmar and visit their old home. Sofie's blood still stains the cracks between the cobbles. They can never again live in this house. Gladness and sadness mingled at the meeting with their old friends and neighbours: Uncle Yves, the Petits and, of course, family on their mother's side, Leah's mother and sister. Sadness, on learning that Leah's two brothers – their uncles – have been killed, but their wives and children live on; tearful joy at that reunion.

Hope, for the sisters: the tiny hope that somehow their parents and Manon have survived. Sarah resolves to do all she can to discover their fate.

For Sarah, another joyful, tearful reunion: Margaux, Victoire, Jacques, Eric – the Château Gauthier connection. Thérèse and

Amélie have never met them, for they were forced to take a different route, via Basle, once the body of Krämer was found by his regiment and the German presence on the route over the Vosges was increased, making it too dangerous for refugees.

Delight, when Margaux leads Sarah across the cobbled courtyard and flings open the door to a rather dilapidated-looking barn. 'Surprise!' she cries, and Sarah gasps with joy. Her father's tools! They, and all their instruments, hidden away when they fled their home town, are safe. Uncle Yves arranged hiding places for every one of them, even their mother's cello. There will be music again.

And more: for with the return of all the precious, almost irreplaceable tools needed for a violin-making enterprise, she can dream. For Sarah's long-term idea is this: a violin shop in Freiburg. Not just yet, for, as during the war, nobody in Germany has the spirit or the interest or the finances for violins. But music will never die. Music is the source of joy and hope and new life. She will give free lessons to children for the time being, help music return to Freiburg, and one day, perhaps when Ralf has qualified as a doctor, perhaps after she has had her own children, she will be a violin-maker again.

She returns to Freiburg with Ralf, while Thérèse and Amélie proceed with Rebecca to the latter's farm near Winzenheim: there, they will live together, the girls will attend school as soon as possible and Rebecca will bring the farm back to life. Before leaving, Rebecca takes Sarah aside and tells her: 'Sarah, I hope above all else that you find your parents, that they have survived the horrors of camp. Some did, you know, and just maybe… But if not, well, I'd love to adopt the girls, if you agree.'

Sarah has no words. She simply opens her arms and Rebecca falls into them. It is an unmitigated, but silent, *yes, of course.*

Sarah is now fired with a new obsession, a single aim: she must find out what happened to her parents and Manon. She investigates, studies lists of Jews taken to the various camps. Her heart turns cold on finally finding their names: they were received into Auschwitz in July 1944.

Though the news is not unexpected, on reading their names she breaks down in tears at the certainty. Further research discloses that Leah and Manon Mayer were killed by gas a few days after reception into the camp.

Her father's name is not on any list. Not on a list of the dead, not on a list of the living. What happened to Josef Mayer? Could he possibly have survived Auschwitz? But if so, where is he? Once again, her heart swings on a silver thread of hope. Perhaps... just perhaps.

In desperation, she travels to Auschwitz herself, transported by that single thread of hope. Her heart is a single prayer: *let me find him, oh Lord, let me find him! Let me at least know what happened to him!*

But in spite of all her efforts, there is no news. She returns home in despair.

It is only a year later that a newspaper headline grabs her attention: *The Musicians of Auschwitz.* She reads on. Indeed, there was actually an orchestra at Auschwitz! It was formed in 1940 by seven musicians, who had their instruments sent to them, and over the years the orchestra grew, not only tolerated but encouraged by the camp authorities.

Sarah's heart begins to thump wildly. She remembers what Uncle Yves said: that Josef took his violin with him as his only piece of luggage. She flings herself into a new line of research. What happened to those musicians? Perhaps they are on a separate list somewhere? Maybe they survived? But if so, if by some tiny chance they, or at least Josef, survived, why have they, why has *he*, not resurfaced?

She travels back to Auschwitz, talks to people who would know, digs in archives. At one point she finds a blurred photograph of the camp orchestra, taken, it seems, in late 1944. She studies the faces of the musicians. There, on the front row, is a man who could very well be her father... Only then does she read the caption below the photo: these Jewish musicians were deported to Bergen-Belsen in November 1944.

And it is in a list of the Bergen-Belsen dead that Sarah finally finds her father's name. Her odyssey of truth-finding is over. The last seedling of hope has wilted, and died. She joins her sisters in Alsace, and in Colmar, she organises a Jewish memorial service for her parents and youngest sisters. But the roller coaster of life, having reached its lowest trough, swings up again. There is a new light in Sarah's eyes as she says a tearful goodbye to Thérèse and Amélie.

'Life goes on,' she tells them. 'Today we cry, but tomorrow we dry our tears and we will smile again.'

She takes both of their hands and places them on her abdomen. 'There's life in here,' she tells them. 'New life: a baby! We must all move on. Play your violins, make music, find love, live life to the full. The war and all its horrors are over. This time next year you will have a little nephew or niece, and Ralf and I will have a son or daughter.'

And the joy rising up within her, the gladness evoked by that spark of new life, is enough to absorb all the grief, all the misery, all the darkness that has weighed her down. Her sisters cry out in utter delight: arms rise up, six arms falling around three sets of shoulders, pulling each other close as they lurch together and fall into the longest embrace any of them has ever known, weeping, laughing, rejoicing. Together.

A Letter from Sharon

Dear Reader,

Thank you for reading *The Violin Maker's Daughter*; I do hope you enjoyed the story, were absorbed in it, and carried along on Sarah's adventure! If you'd like to hear when my next book is out, please sign up to my mailing list:

www.bookouture.com/sharon-maas

For me as a writer it's always a great thrill to know that there are readers out there – *you!* – whom I don't know, will never know personally, yet are connected to me by these words, the story they form. Somehow, we are connected…

If you did enjoy the book, why not help it find more readers? You can do this by recommending it to your friends and family, or through social media, or by writing a review. And perhaps we can meet again in another book – why not?

Some of the secondary characters in *The Violin Maker's Daughter* appear in another book of mine, *The Soldier's Girl*, also set in Alsace. This is a region in France which I've visited many times and which I think is a wonderful setting, as it has a rich culture and turbulent history. Modern Alsace is of course war- and turbulence-free. I hope my books inspire you to visit one day! The countryside is spectacular, the villages charming, and the wine is the best in France – though of course I'm biased!

Thanks again,
Sharon Maas

Historical Notes

This story is fiction, but the background is very real. The annexation of Alsace and Lorraine by Nazi Germany took place in 1940, and as described in this book, caused immense tragedy and upheaval among the citizens of the two regions. Most tragically, all Jews were evacuated, most of them being sent to the South of France.

All the characters are also fictional, but Sarah Mayer's story is inspired by a true heroine of World War II, Marthe Cohn, née Hoffnung, a Jewish girl whose large family were forced to flee Metz at the start of the war. They moved to Poitiers, where her mother, Régine Hoffnung, helped many other fugitive Jews: hid them, homed them, and helped them to move on to safety. The fictional character of Régine Hoffmann is based on this outstanding woman. Marthe's fiancé, Jacques, joined the Resistance but was arrested and executed, a terrible tragedy which gave her the strength to herself join in the struggle against the Nazis. Like my character Sarah, she was sent into Germany to gather information for French Intelligence. Her true story is riveting, and you can read it in her biography, *Behind Enemy Lines*.

There is (and was) no village of Degenfeld north of Freiburg, no Degenfeld Barracks, no military trains from there into Colmar, as described in this novel. Freiburg was, however, indeed bombed during the autumn of 1944 as well as other targets in the region. Colmar was indeed the last French town to be liberated in the war; Hitler's Operation Northwind was indeed the last major German offensive of World War II on the Western Front. It was a complete failure, but the loss of life on both sides was immense.

Acknowledgements

Immense thanks to the team at Bookouture who helped bring this book out into the world, especially to my wonderful editor, Lydia Vassar-Smith. Lydia has been with me for several books, and it is her constant faith in me, her genuine love for the stories that I somehow manage to squeeze out (always a miracle for me!) and her sure hand, sharp eye and unwavering support that help bring these stories to life. It is the editor's polishing touch that brings a book to its peak form, so thank you, Lydia! It goes without saying that the rest of the Bookouture team also worked to the best of their ability, so thanks to Kim Nash, Noelle Holten, Alexandra Holmes, Leodora Darlington, Jacqui Lewis and Jane Donovan.

What would I do without friends, especially writing friends? Writing is by definition solitary work, so it's been great to have 'sisters in crime' with whom I can discuss the highs and the lows, who understand the writing journey because they are themselves on it. So, immense thanks to Renita D'Silva, Debbie Rix and June Considine (aka Laura Elliott) for lending an ear when I needed it.

Thanks too to the enthusiastic bloggers and reviewers who have until now been of immense support for my past books – hopefully, you'll love this book just as much! Thanks to my writer friends in specific Facebook groups such as the Bookouture Lounge, the Savvy Authors' Snug, World War II Authors, the Irish Chapter of the Historical Novel Society, especially Dianne Ascroft, as well as Marion Kummerow, Genevieve Montcombroux and Rachel Zaouche, treasure-houses of World War II knowledge. Especial thanks to Genevieve Montcombroux for reading a draft of this novel and correcting me on several details specific to wartime France. Thanks to the posters on the 'researchers and experts' area of Absolutewrite Water Cooler for your somewhat grisly tips on shots to the head! Thanks also to James Beatley, Dublin violin-maker, for his fascinating information on this little-known skill.

Thanks to the Irish connection: Tony, Noreen and Danny and the rest of the clan who facilitated my move to the border area and helped to make me comfortable in my new homeland, giving me a stable background for my writing.

Last, but not least, thanks to my children, Miro and Saskia, for their patience and early-morning cups of tea delivered silently during that crucial daily 'do not disturb' writing session.